Prop
The Prince

JENNIFER LEWIS

Published in Great Britain 2015
by Mills & Boon, an imprint of Harlequin (UK) Limited,
Eton House, 18-24 Paradise Road, Richmond, Surrey, TW9 1SR

PROPOSITIONED BY THE PRINCE © 2015 Harlequin Books S. A.

The Prince's Pregnant Bride, *At His Majesty's Convenience* and *Claiming His Royal Heir* were first published in Great Britain by Harlequin (UK) Limited.

The Prince's Pregnant Bride © 2011 Jennifer Lewis
At His Majesty's Convenience © 2011 Jennifer Lewis
Claiming His Royal Heir © 2011 Jennifer Lewis

ISBN: 978-0-263-25242-2

05-1215

Harlequin (UK) Limited's policy is to use papers that are natural, renewable and recyclable products and made from wood grown in sustainable forests. The logging and manufacturing processes conform to the legal environmental regulations of the country of origin.

Printed and bound in Spain
by CPI, Barcelona

THE PRINCE'S
PREGNANT BRIDE

BY
JENNIFER LEWIS

Jennifer Lewis has been dreaming up stories for as long as she can remember and is thrilled to be able to share them with readers. She has lived on both sides of the Atlantic and worked in media and the arts before she grew bold enough to put pen to paper. Happily settled in England with her family, she would love to hear from readers at jen@jenlewis.com. Visit her website at www. jenlewis.com.

For Sue, my fun and generous friend and neighbour,
who helps make living here such a pleasure.

One

"**W**hat do you mean I *have* to marry her?" AJ Rahia tried to keep his voice down. Waiters passed out champagne, and the polite hum of conversation buzzed in his ears. The woman in question stood only a few yards away, in the well-dressed crowd of mourners at the wake.

His mother took his hand between her two soft ones. "It's your duty. If the king dies, one of his brothers must marry the royal widow."

The carved walls of the old palace seemed to close in on him. "That's ridiculous. It's the twenty-first century. And I'm sure she doesn't want to marry me any more than I want to marry her." He resisted the urge to turn and glance at the petite young widow he hadn't even seen since her wedding five years earlier.

His mother tilted her head and spoke softly. "She's as sweet as she is beautiful."

"Mom!"

"And I have no other sons."

AJ stiffened. Something had happened during his own birth that left his mom unable to have more children. Just another burden of guilt that settled uncomfortably back on his shoulders each time he returned to Rahiri.

He'd just arrived for his brother's funeral—or whatever you called it when there was no body—and already his ticket back to L.A. was burning a hole in his pocket.

"I'm sure she'll want to mourn for at least a year before she thinks about marrying again." He rested his hand on his mom's shoulder. She was so tiny. Or he was so huge. He resisted a powerful urge to hug this very demanding but fiercely loving woman. "Then you'll find the perfect husband for her."

"You can't *choose* a king." His mother looked up, her eyes imploring. "A king is born."

"And I wasn't born to be king. Most people are convinced I was born to direct big-budget action movies, which is why they give me so much money for it."

His mom waved her hand, dismissive. "Child's play and you know it." She took his hand and squeezed it between her palms. "Come home. You belong here, and we need you."

He ignored the tightening in his chest. "To rule the country? I don't think so. How about Cousin Ainu? He's always trying to run everything. He'd be thrilled."

His mom narrowed her eyes, which caused her mascaraed lashes to clump together. "The Rahia family has ruled Rahiri for as long as anyone can remember. That chain of tradition cannot be broken."

"Change can be good." He didn't sound as convincing

as he'd hoped. "Out with the old, in with the..." He stopped in horror as his mom's usually sharp black eyes filled with tears. "I'm sorry, that was insensitive of me. I didn't mean that Vanu's death was...was..."

A good thing?

Though it had been his first thought when he'd heard the news.

On the other hand, if he was suddenly expected to fill his brother's narrow designer shoes, it was a very bad thing.

"I know, sweetheart. You can't help speaking your thoughts. You were always like that, wild, free-spirited—"

"And totally unsuitable to be a monarch."

He wasn't quite such a wild child as his reputation suggested, but the image could work in his favor now.

"Come talk to Lani." His mom's lipsticked smile did nothing to mask the steely determination in her eyes. AJ glanced around. Hopefully none of the gathered mourners had any idea of her intentions. Especially his brother's widow.

She pulled him across the room with a pincer grip on his hand, pink nails digging into his flesh. "Lani, dear, you remember AJ? Vanu's younger brother."

Panic flashed in the young woman's eyes. "Y-yes," she stammered. "Yes, of course I do. Pleased to meet you again." A forced smile quivered on her lips.

She knew.

And was horrified.

AJ extended his hand and shook hers. Her fingers trembled against his palm. Small and slight, she was wrapped in a traditional blue mourning dress, partially covered by her long, loose hair. He'd remembered her unusual eyes—gold-brown, like polished tortoise-shell—but not the haunted look in them.

"I'm so sorry for your loss." He glanced away from her face, which was polite in Rahiian tradition. And good advice in any case because Lani Rahia was an extraordinary beauty.

Clear, fine features mingled her Rahiian and American heritage. Her skin glowed like the proverbial milk and honey. Her thick, lustrous hair looked brown in ordinary light, but if touched by sunshine it shone brilliantly as pure, twenty-four carat gold.

He could see why his brother—or was it his mother who had truly chosen her?—had picked Lani as queen despite her humble background.

But he had no intention of being her king.

Lani pulled her hand back fast and wiped it on her dress before she could stop herself. That handshake was supposed to preface intimacies that made her stomach turn.

She was expected to marry this man simply because he was her husband's younger brother.

At least he had the good grace not to stare her in the eyes the way most Americans thought normal. He wasn't American, of course, but she felt too fragile to meet anyone's gaze for long. He'd lived in L.A. the entire time she'd been at the palace.

Taller than his brother, she noticed. And broader, too. In the glimpse she'd caught of his face he looked kind.

But she knew only too well that appearances could be deceptive.

"Vanu's disappearance must have been a terrible shock." The deep voice hung in the air, since it took a moment for Lani to emerge from her frenzied thoughts to realize he'd spoken.

"Oh, yes. Terrible. He went out late one night—to think, he said—and he never came back."

She'd lain in bed, shaking with terror, waiting for him to return and "finish the job." He'd said he would, with that cruel hiss in his voice and a cold gleam in his eyes. The hours had ticked by as she awaited her doom.

Then the sun rose, and the birds started to sing.

"It must be so hard not knowing what happened." She heard compassion in AJ's voice. What kind of name was AJ? She didn't even know his real Rahiian name. No one ever called him by it.

"We still don't know what happened." Lani's mother-in-law dabbed at her eyes with a handkerchief. "But after ninety days—" She pressed a muffled sob into the linen. "A successor must be chosen."

Lani stiffened. According to Rahiian tradition, the successor would take her as his wife. Presumably the tradition existed to provide protection for the children of royal widows and avoid jostling for succession between children and siblings of the late king. But she didn't have any children.

"Ninety days…that's still at least a month away. Who would normally succeed, if the king had no siblings?" AJ asked his mother.

She dabbed at her eyes. "Impossible. The king always has siblings. The ability to bear many children is a Rahiian blessing." She coughed a sob into her handkerchief.

Lani glanced at AJ, whose brow furrowed with distress. "Mom, don't upset yourself. Please. We'll get it all figured out. Don't you worry."

He slid his big arm around his mother's back and rubbed her shoulder. Lani felt a flush of warmth at the kind gesture.

"Thank you, sweetheart." His mother smiled at AJ. "Why don't you take Lani out on the veranda for a rest? I'm sure she's exhausted after the funeral and having to talk with all these people."

The big man glanced at Lani. She swallowed. She'd rather be here in this frying pan of semi-strangers than alone, in private, with her...future husband.

Surely they wouldn't make her go through with it?

"Would you like to, er..." He extended his arm, inviting her to take it.

Lani fought the urge to recoil and reached her fingers up to his. His forearm was thickly muscled, not hard and wiry like her husband's—her late husband's. Her skin tingled with awareness—or was it terror?—as she slid her arm into his.

He cleared his throat. "Please excuse us." He nodded to her mother.

"Of course." His mother's smile broadened as she no doubt saw her plans moving one step closer to completion.

Lani tried to maintain a neutral expression as they walked slowly across the room together. Did all these people expect her to marry this man? Were they eagerly looking for signs of fresh commitment when her husband was barely cold in his grave?

Technically he wasn't in a grave at all, since they'd never found a body. Or his boat.

"Sorry about my mother," AJ murmured as they stepped out into a cool, empty hallway. His voice echoed slightly off the white stone floor. AJ pulled back his arm, and hers fell to her side. A small blue parrot stared at them from his perch in the latticework.

"She's just doing what she thinks is best." She glanced at him, trying to gauge his feelings.

"Do you think it's for the best?" He frowned, and peered at her. His eyes were a warm dark brown, like polished teak.

"I don't know." Her voice came out a choked whisper. "I'm inexperienced in these matters." And not about to defy a thousand years of royal tradition in the face of a Rahiian prince. If he was anything like his brother, he'd let her know his disapproval in the harshest terms possible.

"You're a grown woman. Do you think it's natural to marry a total stranger?"

His question embarrassed her. "I only met Vanu three times before I married him."

"Let me guess, my mom fixed up the whole thing." He raised a straight black brow.

Lani nodded. Her long hair felt hot on the back of her neck and she wished she could run to her room for a good cry.

And not over the death—or supposed death—of her husband. For herself, and the no-win situation she faced: another unhappy royal marriage, or disgrace and dishonor for refusing it. Tears pricked her eyes and she raised a hand to cover them.

"Please don't cry." AJ's gruff plea rang off the wood-beamed ceiling. "Come on, let's go sit on the veranda. Some fresh air will do us both good."

His words were supposed to be funny, since the hall they walked along was open to the gardens, like nearly every room in the sprawling palace. Carved wood cast shade and the high roof kept out tropical rain, but birds and pretty lizards darted freely amongst the ornate columns.

Yet the air itself seemed oppressive, thick with expectation.

AJ Rahia was tall, well over six feet, and her head barely reached his shoulders. Her small steps, bound by the long wrap of her skirt, made her scurry to keep up with his bold strides. He noticed, and stopped to wait for her.

He wore a dark suit, American-style, and must have been hot in the tropical humidity. "Would you like a cool drink?" She lowered her eyes, not wanting him to hear any hint of suggestion beyond mere politeness.

"No, thanks. Listen, it's not personal. I'm sure you're a very nice girl. I've just got a life in the States. I direct movies—"

"I know," she rushed. "Your mother is very proud. She watches the whole *Dragon Chaser* series at least once a month."

He stopped dead. "You're kidding."

"Not at all. She installed a complete home theater system in the old feasting chamber last year for better stereo sound."

AJ's eyes widened. "She's never said a word."

"She's a big fan." Lani couldn't help the tiny smile that sneaked across her mouth. He looked so totally astonished. "She loves the lead actor, too. She thinks he's cute."

"Devi Anderson? Cute!" AJ burst out into a loud guffaw. "I swear, nothing could surprise me more. Well..." His brows lowered. "Except that I'm expected to marry you."

Lani swallowed. She lifted her hair off her neck and rearranged it down her back, her eyes glued to the floor.

Should she apologize for being a burden? It was hardly her fault.

And he might take it the wrong way.

He didn't look anything like his brother, but that didn't mean he didn't share the same twisted soul. That he wouldn't lash out when she least expected it.

"Sorry, I shouldn't keep bringing it up." He frowned and turned away. "It's just so…ridiculous. And I have a big investor meeting on Tuesday I must get back for."

A tiny flame of hope lit in Lani's chest. He really didn't plan to stay and marry her. He obviously didn't want to. She should be offended, but instead she felt relief.

Even if she didn't believe in true love any more, she'd had enough of marriage for one lifetime.

They'd reached the veranda, where big armchairs nestled under palm fronds with a view over the forested Haialia valley. They sat in two chairs separated by a carved-wood table.

"What do you think happened to Vanu?" AJ turned to look at her.

She shrank from his inquisitive gaze. "One of the boats went missing from the palace dock. A small yacht he used to sail sometimes. Some say he might have taken it out. There was a storm that night." She swallowed. Images of Vanu disappearing into the dark sea crowded her brain.

"If there was a storm the boat could have broken free by itself. They do that quite often. The palace dock isn't well protected." AJ wove his long fingers together and looked out over the valley.

"I know, but the island isn't that big and everyone's been searching for him for weeks. He must have left."

She bit her lip. "And he didn't take a plane. They're all accounted for."

"Why did he go out in a storm?" AJ's eyes rested on her cheek.

Which heated. No one could know the truth. Her marriage was over now and there was no reason for anyone to know that it had been…hell on earth.

She owed that much to her mother-in-law, who'd done everything to welcome her as a daughter and who worshipped and loved her eldest son.

"I think he was restless. Couldn't sleep." She fixed her eyes on the horizon, where rainforest haze hung just above the treetops. "He often walked in the gardens late at night. He didn't sleep much."

"Yeah. He was like that as a boy, too. It sometimes seemed like he never slept."

An odd tone in AJ's voice made her glance at him. His brow was furrowed in a frown. He must miss Vanu, the older brother he'd never see again.

AJ's face was undeniably handsome, with broad, well-cut cheekbones and a slightly cleft chin. His mouth was wide and friendly. So different from his brother's pinched, bony countenance.

She'd married Vanu because she had to. That's what everyone said. What simple village girl—the daughter of a laundress, no less—would turn down a chance to be queen?

She didn't have a good answer at the time.

"How's my mom taking it?" AJ's frown deepened.

"Very hard." Lani twisted her fingers together. "She cries a lot, and that's not like her."

"It's a terrible thing to lose a child." AJ rubbed a hand over his mouth. "At least she has you. I know she adores you."

Lani pushed a smile to her lips. "She's been so kind to me. Everyone has."

Well, except Vanu.

"So if I take off back to L.A., I imagine you'll rule as queen."

Lani sat bolt upright. "Me? I can't. I'm not royal."

"You may not have been born royal, but you're already queen, in case you hadn't noticed." Humor danced in his dark eyes.

"Technically speaking, but not really. I'm just a village girl."

"I thought you were born in New Jersey." He raised a brow.

"My parents divorced when I was seven, and my mom moved back to Rahiri." People tried to make more than they should of her foreign birth and the fact that she was half-American. It gave her unusual features and coloring, nothing more.

"You seem more educated than the average village girl." His penetrating gaze made her belly tighten.

"We have good schools here. Your father saw to that when he was king. Many of our teachers received scholarships to study abroad, and brought their knowledge back to Rahiri."

"But your father's a professor, isn't he?" AJ leaned closer, until his masculine scent tickled her nostrils.

What was he trying to prove?

"Of geology. He encouraged me in my studies, and I was going to read history at the university, but I left my studies when I became queen."

Vanu hadn't liked to see her with her head in a book. He said such a pretty head should be completely empty.

"You should start again. Why not?" He shrugged.

"I never had the patience for school. I'm at my best running around on a set."

"You're happy in L.A.?"

"Ecstatically so. I can honestly say I don't miss Rahiri one bit."

"Your mom misses you."

"I know. That's why she comes up with so many excuses for shopping trips to Rodeo Drive." He grinned. "I enjoy her visits and I think she single-handedly keeps the U.S. economy afloat."

"Is this your first visit to Rahiri since the wedding?"

"Yes. Maybe I should feel bad, but I'm busy and I don't fit in here." He pushed a hand through his thick black hair and leaned back in the woven armchair. The heavy muscling of his body was visible even inside his dark suit.

She was still surprised that he hadn't visited once. And they expected him to become king?

Not very likely. Which meant she was off the hook as his wife.

She blew out a long, slow, silent breath. The sooner he left, the better.

"It is beautiful here, though." He stared out at the mist-shrouded horizon, a crevice of gold and blue sky nestled between rainforest-covered hills. A toucan flew up into a nearby baobab tree, its bright beak held aloft. "I'd forgotten how beautiful it is."

His mom's quest to convince him to stay continued unrelentingly over the following days and nights.

"Here, sweetheart, have some coconut stars." Her favorite treat hovered under AJ's nose on their tooled silver platter.

"No, thanks, Mom, really." After three days of funerary feasting, he wasn't sure he'd ever be able to eat again. "Did I tell you my plane leaves at 6:00 a.m. tomorrow?"

"What?" Her eyes widened with horror. "You can't. You've barely had time to get to know Lani."

He glanced around, making sure the woman in question was nowhere nearby. "I've spent hours and hours with her. She's sweet."

"And she'll be a good queen, with you as her king." His mom folded her arms. Her gold bangles clinked together.

"Not possible."

"Not only is it possible, it is inevitable." Steel shimmered in his mom's voice and gleamed in her eyes. "Although it took a tragedy to bring you together, you and Lani are destined to be together."

"I'm destined to begin post-production on *Hellcat Four: The Aftermath* in three weeks' time. And after that, if the funding comes together, I'll be making *Dragon Chaser* part five."

His mom waved her hand, jangling her bracelets. "Part four, part five. What will it matter if there are so many already? There is only one Rahiri, and you are our ruler."

"People are counting on me. There's a lot at stake."

"My sentiments exactly." She leaned in, giving him a whiff of her familiar honeysuckle perfume. "We're all counting on you. I am counting on you."

AJ's back tightened. No one here had counted on him for anything before. He wasn't the heir, the chosen one. Now suddenly everything had changed, but he was still the same person inside.

His mom grabbed his arm. "Here comes Lani. Don't tell her you're leaving. You're not leaving."

AJ jerked his arm back. "I'm leaving. But I'll be nice to Lani before I go."

He smiled at the stunning young widow as she walked into the room, her embroidered pale-gold dress gleaming in the candlelight. Gold earrings glittered in her lobes and a ruby hovered at her throat. Decked out for sacrifice.

His stomach turned that she was so willing to go along with his mother's foolish plot. Did she have no spine? Did she want no say in the choice of her future husband?

"Hey, Lani."

"Hello, AJ." Her head dipped slightly, deferential, which annoyed him all the more. He liked women with some spunk, some fire.

"Come with me." He threaded his arm though hers and led her from the room. Away from his mother's anxious ears.

He ignored a flicker of heat from the touch of his skin against hers. He could not possibly be attracted to this shrinking violet barely out of another man's arms.

They walked through a high doorway and out into a palace courtyard ringed with potted palms. "You're too nice, you know."

"I...I..." Her hesitation irked him further.

"Can't you say anything for yourself, can't you speak your mind?" His growl startled her.

She glanced up, honey-colored eyes wide. Was she afraid of him?

"I'm sorry." She bit her full, pink lip. A flash of heat to his groin sent a surge of fury through AJ. Just because she had a pretty face did not mean she'd make a good wife. Maybe she deserved to be married off to some stranger.

A silky lock of gold-hued hair fell forward as she hung her head.

He had no interest in how that hair would feel under his palms, or trailing over his chest as she crouched over him, maybe panting slightly, golden eyes wide with desire.

Because that would never happen.

He scowled and turned away. "I'm flying out tomorrow. You're on your own, sister."

"What?" Her voice rang across the room, high and breathless.

He spun around to face her. "You heard me. I'm done playing my part in this charade. You and I have nothing whatsoever in common, and I have no intention of sacrificing both our lives on the altar of Rahiian tradition. I'm going back to my real life."

She blinked, speechless. Hardly a surprise. She didn't have much to say for herself at the best of times. But her cheeks reddened. "You dislike me."

Her words sent a fist of guilt to AJ's gut. She hadn't actually done anything wrong, after all. She'd been trying so hard to be a sweet Rahiian maiden.

Shame he couldn't stand sweet Rahiian maidens.

Her ruby shone bloodred at her throat. Set in an ornate gold setting, the royal jewel had probably been worn by many sacrificial lambs before her. He pitied and despised these women, so ready to give their whole lives to the service of a man. For a country that didn't care if they lived or died.

He stared down at her—she barely came up to his shoulder—and cocked his head. "You're too...nice."

"I'm not nice at all. Really." The words rushed out. Was she so afraid of failing in her royal duty? "I mean, I try to be, but…"

Words failed her once again. The pink flush of her cheeks gave the inappropriate impression that she was aroused. Her lips, parted in protest, looked full and ripe, ready for kissing. The look in her eyes, glossy with terror, could easily be mistaken for a gaze shimmering with need. Desire crept over him like the tropical heat, uncoiling in his belly, unfurling along with his fury over this crazy situation.

For once he wanted this girl to give him an honest reaction. He was letting her down. Screwing her over. Just once he wanted to hear her words ring harsh in the air, sense her anger pulse on the night breeze, or maybe even feel that small hand slap him hard across the face.

Then maybe he wouldn't feel so guilty.

Surely she had a dark side. Everyone did.

He took a step forward, pulled her into his arms and crushed his mouth over hers.

For a second Lani froze, and he half braced for her reaction.

Then her arms stretched around his back and her slim body molded to his. Her mouth softened, opened to welcome his kiss. Her fingers dug into the muscles of his back and drew him closer, until her breasts crushed against his chest.

Surprise and sharp lust flashed through AJ. Lani was kissing him back—hard. Her breath came in unsteady gasps. Heat pulsed between them, urging their heart-beats into a fevered dance. A tiny moan quivered in

Lani's throat as he thickened against her, his desire provoking a fierce arousal.

This was *not* the response he'd expected.

TWO

He pulled away first. Lani's hand flew to her lips, left
suddenly cold and bare. She didn't want to open her
eyes but she forced herself. AJ's dark gaze fixed on
hers, wide with—shock.

What just happened?

He'd initiated the kiss, his action deliberate, forceful
even. But she couldn't shake the impression that he
hadn't wanted to kiss her.

Her lips still stung and tingled with stray pulses of
energy. Her nipples pressed against the crisp fabric of
her dress, above her pounding heart. The hand now
pressed against her mouth—hot with her own unsteady
breaths—had just a moment ago been fisted into his
shirt, clutching at his thick muscles.

Shame flushed through her in a hot wave. He must
have kissed her out of a sense of responsibility, to prove

he could step into the role everyone expected of him, whether he liked it or not.

And she'd responded in a way that was anything but dutiful.

Was she going mad? She gulped. Her body felt hot, thick with unfamiliar sensation. She couldn't bring herself to glance at AJ again. He hadn't moved an inch since he'd pushed her away.

He'd had to push her away, to stop her clinging closer and tighter, pressing his body to hers with a fierce grip. At her own husband's funeral.

Or whatever you called a funeral without a body.

She must be mad. There was no other explanation. Should she apologize? Anger flashed inside her. He'd taken the kiss—stolen it—so anything it led to was his fault.

Still, no one would have expected her to respond with…desperation.

He'd thought she was too nice. Now he knew she was anything but.

Her face heated and she glanced up. AJ shoved a hand through his thick, black hair. His lips parted, but he didn't speak.

I'm sorry. The words hovered on her tongue for a single instant—automatic, a learned response—before she swallowed them, bitter and tasteless. She didn't owe him an apology. She didn't owe her late husband one, either, for that matter. These powerful men took what they wanted, without a thought for those they took them from. Which is why she didn't want to marry again—especially not another Rahia.

Her treacherous thoughts pounded in her brain like a headache. If he knew what she was thinking he'd…

Lani gathered her skirt and rushed for the door.

* * *

AJ stared after Lani as her gold dress disappeared through the carved archway. He hadn't said anything to stop her, since he couldn't think of what to say. He had no idea what to even think. If his mom knew they'd shared such a steamy kiss, she'd probably be over the moon. Or would she be scandalized that it had happened before the funeral feasts were even finished?

He blew out a hard blast of air. He'd expected her to squeal and slap him. To defend her virtue and hurl angry words in his face. To hate him.

Which was his intention. Then she wouldn't want him to do his duty and marry her. He'd be off the hook.

Instead she'd seemed to…enjoy the kiss.

He shook his head, trying to shake loose a sensible thought. Maybe she'd faked it. As a royal wife—especially his brother's wife—she must have had plenty of practice faking pleasure when she didn't feel it.

Still…

The way her fingers had clawed at his back. How her mouth had opened to welcome his, her sweet breath hot on his tongue. He'd even heard a tiny moan, like the cry of a bird, newly uncaged, escape her throat before he came to his senses and pulled back.

His stiff suit barely hid the reaction she'd provoked in his body. His blood seemed ten degrees hotter and his fingertips prickled with stray urges. Probably the urge to rip off that expensive gold dress and sink into the soft flesh beneath.

He hurled a curse. How could he think such a thing about his brother's wife? He hadn't wanted to come back here, and this was a perfect example of why. He lived

a nice, sensible life in L.A. —well, by L.A. standards—
where things like this just didn't happen.

Still…he'd dated more than his fair share of women
and he'd never been kissed like that before. Curiosity
mingled with the lust thickening in his blood. There was
clearly a lot more to Lani Rahia than he'd expected.

That night, AJ sat three seats away from Lani at an
official state banquet observing his brother's passing.
Dressed in mourning blue, with an elaborate gold
necklace that probably weighed more than she did, she
looked every bit the royal widow.

Ears pricked, he listened for her voice. She barely
spoke, though, only offering polite morsels of conversation when necessary. When he glanced her way,
her lips were pressed together, as if trying to keep
something in—or perhaps, after this afternoon, to keep
something out.

He attempted to hold up his end of the conversation
with an elderly member of the royal guard who shame-
lessly checked international cricket scores on his phone
in between courses. By the time dessert was served, AJ
had resolved to corner Lani and ask her what happened
this afternoon.

His plan was thwarted when Lani vanished halfway
through the fish course. There was some commotion,
and a footman went to help her to her room.

He turned to his mother, seated diagonally across
the table. "What's going on? Where's Lani gone?"

She patted her lips with a napkin. "Not feeling well.
Poor Lani's taken Vanu's death so badly. She's been in
and out of bed since he disappeared." She reached over
and patted his arm. "I'm glad you care. She's a sweet
girl."

AJ cleared his throat. "I'm sure she is."

"Perhaps you could go look in on her after dinner." A thoughtful smile crossed her lips. "Just to see if she's comfortable."

"I'll do that." Had grief caused her unexpected response earlier? He shuddered with revulsion at the sudden idea that she'd mistake him for his dead brother. Did her disappearance from dinner have anything to do with their unexpectedly passionate kiss?

Either way, he wanted to know more.

Lani slammed her bedroom door closed and leaned against it. Alone. It wasn't easy to get even one minute by yourself in a royal palace. Nausea rose inside her like a wave, and she planted her feet on the floor to ride it out. Was it guilt that drove this sickness to surge and torment her day and night?

Or something else?

She listened for footsteps. No sound except the evening song of insects in the gardens outside. Now was the perfect time. Everyone in the palace was either eating at the banquet, or waiting on the diners. Even her mother-in-law, who hovered over her day and night, wouldn't leave her guests until the meal was done.

Lani crept across the room and switched on the light in the adjoining bathroom. It gleamed with the rich gold-veined marble and the solid-gold taps Vanu had installed. He'd loved to luxuriate in the bath while she massaged the knotted sinews of his arms and back. It was still hard to believe he'd never glare at her from across the room and hurl an unreasonable demand again.

Guilt snaked through her. She shouldn't think

such thoughts about the dead. It was bad luck, if nothing else.

She crept into the small private changing room where she kept her personal items. Buried among the tampons she knew no one would disturb was a prize she'd gone to great lengths to obtain.

She held her breath as she fished inside the box and felt for the packet. Her fingers stung with fear as they rested on its plastic cover. She glanced over her shoulder before she pulled it out, then she ripped open the packet and reached for the printed instructions inside.

Another wave of nausea blurred her eyes and made her clutch at the nearby wall, fingernails scraping on the hard, carved stone. Then she drew a deep breath. Better get it over with.

Hold stick in stream of urine. Place on level surface for thirty seconds. Plus sign indicates a positive result. Minus sign indicates a negative result, she read from the package.

Stomach clenched and hands shaking, she followed the instructions, then paced the large bathroom while she waited for the results. How odd that she'd wanted a child so much when they first married. Dreamed of holding her son or daughter in her arms and lavishing him or her with kisses and smiles.

Then when Vanu had revealed himself to be heartless, soulless, she'd prayed to remain empty so no child would have to grow up with a father like him.

It was easy; Vanu rarely touched her. If anything, he seemed repulsed by her body, by her very femininity. They hadn't been intimate for at least two years until that last night, when she'd told him exactly what she thought of him, and he'd taken her by force.

Tears sprang to her eyes and she swiped at them

with the back of her hand. The pink stick must have revealed its answer by now, but she didn't dare look. If the result was negative, then she'd done her duty as a royal wife and could maybe even slide back into the realm of ordinary people. If not, she could be the mother of a future king, a duty that would bind her for the rest of her life.

At first it hadn't occurred to her that she could be pregnant. Vanu had taken to berating her for her infertility and inability to produce an heir. He took pleasure in taunting her with this, even when conception was technically impossible because they never had sex. She'd almost started to believe his lies.

When he went missing she suffered bouts of sickness. At first she'd assumed them to be guilt-related. If she hadn't confronted him, he wouldn't have stalked off into the night. She'd told no one she was responsible for his disappearance.

As the weeks went on, her illness had been accompanied by other disturbing symptoms—moodiness, sensitive nipples and a slight thickening at her waist. No one else had noticed, but she could no longer pass these things off as "guilt" and she knew for sure they weren't from grief, as others might have suspected.

She grabbed the stick and pulled it close, willing herself to be strong. A tiny pink cross filled the circle on the handle.

She was pregnant—with Vanu's child.

She sank against the wall, breath coming in shallow gasps. What now?

A loud knock on the door made her jump. She shoved the stick into a pile of towels and rubbed the tear tracks from her eyes. "Who is it?"

"AJ." His gruff voice penetrated the heavy wood.

"I'm, er, unwell."

"I know. That's why I came."

"Thanks, but I'll be fine."

"Let me in. Please. Just for a moment."

Lani hesitated. AJ might be a hard-partying Hollywood director, but he was also next in line to the Rahiian throne. She couldn't ignore him.

She glanced in the mirror and attempted to compose the stricken face that greeted her. She slapped her cheeks to bring back some color, tucked a strand of loose hair behind her ear then hurried to the door.

AJ tapped his foot on the polished stone tile outside the door. Lani probably didn't want visitors if she wasn't feeling well, especially him. Bad enough that he was supposedly her unwilling future husband, but the events of earlier made the situation even more awkward. If she'd slapped his face and told him to get lost, everything would be going smoothly, but now...

Still, he needed to see her or he'd never sleep tonight.

The door creaked open, revealing a tiny sliver of Lani's famously beautiful face.

"Have you been crying?" The question burst from his lips. She shook her head, lips pressed together. "You're allowed to, you know. You are recently widowed."

"I know." Already fresh tears sprang up behind her dark lashes. "Sorry, it's just been such a busy week with all the ceremonies."

"You must be exhausted." Though that didn't explain the kiss. "I came to apologize for kissing you out of the blue like that." He straightened his shoulders. Funny, he hadn't come here to apologize, but the sight of her lovely face stained with tears had an uncomfortable effect on him. Even now, she was breathtaking, her long, golden brown hair streaming behind her shoulders and her lips soft and pink.

He cursed his physical reaction. Was this any way to behave with a grieving widow, even if you were supposed to marry her?

"I appreciate the apology." She almost whispered it. "I know that technically you have nothing to apologize for, since I'm supposed to marry you, but it took me by surprise."

"Took me by surprise, too." A smile tried to spread across his lips but he fought it back. "I wasn't expecting such an enthusiastic response."

Her cheeks flushed. "I don't know what happened. I've been through a lot lately. Too many emotions…" She trailed off, dropping her lashes to cover her eyes.

"And there I was taking it personally." He reached out and touched her arm, which wasn't easy since the door was barely open a foot. "Listen, no hard feelings. I meant what I said about leaving, so you don't have to worry about me trying to jump into Vanu's bed. I think I actually wanted to get you angry at me. I regret that."

"No hard feelings."

"You really are a sweet Rahiian maiden."

"Sometimes I wonder." She glanced up at him, and for a second he thought he saw a twinkle of mischief in her eye. Desire snapped through him and he fought a sudden urge to lean in and kiss her again.

"Are you sick?" He struggled to remember the reason he'd supposedly come here. Maybe he'd unwittingly hoped for another intoxicating kiss.

"Not really." An odd expression flashed across her

features—panic, almost. She glanced over his shoulder, as if expecting something frightening in the corridor. "I'll be fine. I should get some sleep." She grasped the door with her fingers, ready to close it.

"Would you like something from the kitchens?" He wasn't ready to leave yet.

She shook her head. "I'm not hungry. I ate most of the meal."

"A glass of wine, or something to help you unwind?"

Her eyes widened. "No, thanks."

"Do you want to talk? I know it's rough sometimes being a member of the royal family. You have to be on your best behavior all the time and can't let your hair down." He glanced at her impressive tresses. "And you have a lot of hair."

For a second she looked like she might smile—or even invite him in—then she glanced over his shoulder again.

This time he turned around to see if there really was anything to look at. Nothing but stars winking through the carved openings in the corridor wall.

"There's no one here. We're alone, though I'm not sure how much comfort that is to you." He smiled, trying to be reassuring. He had a weird feeling that she did want to say something.

Her lips twitched in an agonizingly sensual motion, and she blinked rapidly. "It was nice of you to come check on me. I'll be fine." Her tears had dried and her eyes shone again. Sad, but beautiful. "It's been a long day." She tilted her head slightly and looked at him though her lashes. "And I apologize for my role in the kiss. I don't know what came over me."

"No apology needed. And whatever came over

you, it was rather lovely." He flashed a smile, then an odd feeling swept through him. Another powerful urge to kiss her. Her skin looked so soft, shining in the lamplight, and he could smell her soft scent in the narrow space of the doorway. Her dark gaze seemed to call to him: Help me.

His lips met hers, hard and fast, but this time she pulled back and slammed the door. The wood bumped his forehead and sent him staggering back into the corridor, lips still buzzing from that lightning fast but incredibly powerful touch.

"Idiot." He said the word aloud and smacked his head. What was he thinking? Still, did she have to slam the door like that?

He glanced around, relieved the corridor was still empty. What was it about this woman that made him act so crazy?

Lani ran back into the bathroom, where she closed and locked the door. It had been the one safe place where she could hide from Vanu—discounting the many hours they spent safely in public spaces—where she could lock the door and shut out his cruelty.

How odd—how awful—to now be hiding from his brother.

Or was she?

Her belly tingled with stray sensation—awareness of the swift touch of his fingers as he leaned in to kiss her. His lips had brushed hers for a split second, but seemed to have branded her with fire. If she hadn't slammed the door so fast she'd have rushed into his arms.

Which meant that yes, she was hiding from him.

And she was hiding from her mother-in-law. She'd

have to tell her about the pregnancy immediately, before it became any more obvious.

Just now she'd fought a strange, almost insane urge to tell AJ everything when he asked her if she wanted to talk. What wouldn't she give to be able to confide in someone? To seek comfort in a pair of strong arms that wanted to soothe and comfort her rather than to hurt her.

Lani shivered. She'd been through so much in the past few years. Even though Vanu had rarely touched her, his tongue could bite hard as a lash. His brother was so different. Famous as a playboy, AJ seemed laid-back and warm, easy going and nonjudgmental. What would it be like to have a relationship with someone who genuinely liked people?

Not that she'd ever find out. Of course he wouldn't stay. He had a life—a big, famous life—to get back to. Rahiri was a little speck of forested land in the middle of the wide Pacific to him. It wasn't his home anymore.

For a split second she envied him his freedom. It must take some confidence to walk away from the royal family he'd been born into.

For the last few weeks she'd entertained thoughts of having a normal life, maybe even going back to New Jersey to visit her father and her two stepsisters who were now in high school. It would be fun to just, say, go to a mall and giggle over some shoes.

A long sigh slid from her mouth. After tonight's news, that would never happen.

She reached down and pulled the stick out of its hiding place amongst the fresh towels. Yes, the little pink cross was still there, sealing her fate as the mother of the newest member of the royal Rahiian dynasty.

* * *

The next morning, after an almost completely sleepless night, Lani approached her mother-in-law at breakfast and asked if they could meet privately.

"Lani, you look terrible!" Priia Rahia took her daughter-in-law's face in her hands. "We all loved Vanu, but you must take care of yourself. Eat some eggs, and some papaya." She loaded the ripe fruit onto Lani's plate. "And of course I'll talk to you." She gave a bright smile.

Much as Lani loved her mother-in-law, she could often hear the wheels turning behind Priia's composed expression. She probably imagined this would be a private chat about her future relationship with AJ—a million miles away from her intended purpose.

Maybe something in her expression made Priia realize the situation was serious. "Come with me right now. Bring your breakfast and eat in my study."

The older woman hooked her arm through Lani's and guided her out past the stone-faced waiters. "Bring fresh tea," she called behind her.

Marching down the hallway, her mother-in-law looked crisp and efficient as always, her black hair short and glossy, her traditional dress perfectly arranged over her neat, plump body. She projected an aura of calm and warmth that Lani had appreciated so much over the last few years, though that had been shaken by Vanu's disappearance and presumed death.

Lani was shivering slightly by the time they reached the shell-pink sanctuary on the east side of the house. Morning sun streamed through the windows, illuminating her mother-in-law's collection of bird statues and the traditional embroideries she made into cushions and wall hangings.

"Take a seat." Priia pointed to a plush pink armchair. "Be sure to eat. You've looked pale lately. Are you feeling better?"

She swallowed. "A little." She looked down at her plate; the contents looked inedible. "I'm not really sick." Her heart started to pound. "I've just been feeling ill because..."

Priia tilted her head, expectant. Her lips pursed into a familiar smile. "What, dear?"

"I'm pregnant." The words fell out on a sigh.

Priia's eyes snapped open. "Did I hear you right? You're expecting?"

Lani nodded, unable to push words past the lump in her throat. "I think so." No need to mention that she'd taken a test. She had all the usual symptoms, anyway. "At first I thought it was stress over Vanu's disappearance, but now I'm pretty sure it's..." She glanced down at her stomach, which appeared flat beneath the green and blue pattern of her dress.

"A baby." Priia clapped her hands together and a broad smile lit her face. "How marvelous!"

"Yes," whispered Lani.

"A ray of light in our darkest hour." Priia sprang to her feet and strode across the room. "A miracle."

It didn't really feel that way to Lani, which only added to her crippling burden of guilt. She should be happy. A baby was always a reason to celebrate in Rahiri.

Unless it was the child of your unloved and evil late husband.

"We must celebrate. We'll plan a big party. What a marvelous way to move forward after the sad days of the funeral." Priia was almost dancing around the room.

"A baby! Our Vanu's child will carry on his legacy here in the palace."

Lani bit her lip. That's what she was worried about. Which wasn't fair. The innocent child might be nothing like Vanu at all. Everyone else in the royal family was warm and kind, including the father-in-law who'd died before she came.

"Oh, sweet little baby clothes. I must start embroidering right away." Priia patted Lani's cheek affectionately. "I wonder if he will have your lovely golden coloring. Or it could be a she." She frowned. "Of course we won't know for—" She grasped Lani's arms. "How far along are you?"

"I'm not really sure." She didn't want to pinpoint the night Vanu disappeared, though that was certainly the date of conception. "A few weeks, at least. I'm just starting to show."

"Oh, do let me look at you." Priia snatched Lani's untouched plate from her lap and tugged her to her feet. She patted the rumpled fabric over her belly. "I can't feel much yet, but I took a while to show with my boys. We Rahias don't have large babies, but they grow up to be big strong men." Her beaming grin was almost infectious.

Almost. Lani struggled to look at least slightly happy about the circumstance, but instead her lip wanted to tremble.

"You're worried, aren't you? Scared." Priia took Lani in her soft arms. Her expensive scent enveloped her for a moment. "I know it's not easy having a baby when you're a widow. The child reminds you of the man you've lost."

Lani looked down. Her words were painfully true.

"But look on it as a wonderful chance to let him live again through his child."

Please, no! Lani blinked rapidly, trying to keep her emotions in check.

Priia pressed a finger to her lips. "Though this does rather complicate things with AJ. It's not easy for a man to raise another man's child, even if it is his brother's."

"I don't think AJ wants to marry me." Lani said the words quickly.

"Don't take it personally. He's just gotten off track with this Hollywood business. He'll realize that his duty lies with us in Rahiri." Her mother-in-law's face grew serious. "Oh, my goodness."

"What?" Lani's chest grew tight at the look of alarm in Priia's dark eyes.

"According to our laws of succession, the baby is next in line to the throne." She stared at Lani, her face growing pale.

Thoughts clicked into place. "So AJ doesn't inherit the throne."

"Not if Vanu has a child." Priia bustled across the room and stared out the window toward the forest. Then she spun around. "Oh, I do so want AJ back home with us. He was so unsettled as a child, always jealous of Vanu and in a rush to get away. I'm sure things would be different now that he's grown and matured. Now that my husband and oldest son are gone, it would warm my heart to have my youngest son here with us. And I do believe he'd be a very good husband to you."

Lani remained silent. A stray memory of his lips on hers assaulted her and caused color to rise to her cheeks. She had no idea what kind of husband AJ would be, and she'd rather not find out—kiss or no kiss. Vanu was enough husband for one lifetime.

Priia's expression hardened. "Don't say anything. Don't mention the baby."

"To AJ?"

"To anyone." She gripped Lani's wrists. "Let no one find out until you're safely married to AJ. Then they can think it's his."

Revulsion at the proposed deception coiled in Lani's already queasy gut. "But I'm weeks along, almost two months."

Priia loosened her grip and rubbed Lani's arm—which didn't feel all that soothing over the goose bumps that had formed there. "You can say it's premature. We really do have small babies. Even big, strapping AJ was barely six pounds at birth. No one will ever find out."

"You wouldn't even tell AJ?"

"Why? Better to let him think the baby is his." She tilted her head and looked right into Lani's eyes. "Sometimes men are happier if we keep some secrets from them. It's part of our work as women to keep the world running smoothly."

Lani could feel a cold sweat breaking out on her back. "I don't like deception. And what if AJ doesn't want to marry me?"

Priia's lips formed a tight smile. "He will."

Three

AJ's plane left for L.A. at six o'clock the following morning. He was not on it.

"Thank you, sweetheart." His mom's expression alternated between tears and smiles. "You don't know how much it means to me to have you here. I couldn't survive the loss of one son if I didn't have another."

AJ didn't really follow her logic—or like it one bit—but he nodded. Apparently he had no resistance to female pleading and weeping. Hopefully in a few days his mom would calm down and he could make his escape.

"Have some papaya, sweetheart." She pushed a platter laden with the shiny golden fruit toward him.

His stomach recoiled. "I'm not hungry." The bright sunlight flooding the breakfast room contrasted strongly with his mood. Lani picked at her own breakfast on the other side of the big, polished table. He kept his eyes firmly off her. She had a very unsettling effect on him, and he didn't need any more crazy things happening. Getting a door slammed in his kisser was quite enough.

His mom clapped her hands together, bracelets jangling. "We're going to plan a party."

Lani's head shot up. He sneaked a glance at her, and saw her eyes wide with alarm.

"Isn't this an odd time for a party?" AJ leaned back in his chair. "Especially after all the funeral events. Lani's probably exhausted."

Lani didn't meet his gaze, just stared at her teacup.

"I think it's important to show people that this is not an end for the Rahias, it's a new beginning." His mom's crisp smile had firmly replaced her tears.

A sense of foreboding hummed in AJ's gut. He strongly suspected that he played a key role in that "new beginning." "I really can't stay long, Mom. I have script meetings for my new movie."

"You could do them via teleconferencing. We have it set up in the throne room."

"It's not the same." He didn't want to go anywhere near the blasted throne room. There really was a throne in there—an impossibly ancient piece of volcanic rock carved with mysterious markings—and he had a nasty feeling he'd end up on top of it if he wasn't careful.

"Of course it is. And Lani and I can be your assistants, can't we dear?" She shone her megawatt smile on Lani.

Who gulped, visibly. "Oh yes. I do enjoy your films." Her voice was as flat as her expression.

"What do you like better, the violence or the sex?"

"There isn't really that much of either." She tilted her elegant head and her long mane of brown hair swung in front of one shoulder. "What makes your movies so good is that you use suspense and anticipation to keep the audience on their toes. Teenage boys probably think they saw all that stuff when they leave the theater, but really you kept their hearts pounding by making them think it was going to happen, or had just happened. It's very clever."

AJ's mouth hung open for a second. "You really have watched them."

"That's why we installed the theater, dear." His mother patted her lips with a napkin.

Lani's eyes sparkled. She was clearly delighted to defy his expectations. Her bright gaze sent a shimmer of—something straight to his core.

Great. Just what he needed.

"We're your biggest fans." His mother patted his hand. "And we'll have the party this Saturday."

"How can you plan it so quickly?"

She smiled. "Easy, dear. No one turns down an invitation to the palace, and we have the most talented and creative staff in the Pacific."

"There is that." AJ winked at her. "You really are something, Mom. If a party will make you feel better, you go ahead and have one."

"You will be there."

"I'll be there." He didn't hide the sigh of resignation in his voice. How could you argue with your own grieving mother? "Just don't ask me to make any speeches."

"Why don't you two go pick some flowers? We'll use them to decorate the ballroom."

AJ raised an eyebrow. A flower-picking expedition? Clearly his mom had not given up on the idea of getting them together. "I'm sure the flowers are happier in the ground."

"Nonsense. They bloom better if you pluck them from time to time. Don't they, Lani?"

Lani smiled. "Some of them do. I'll go get the shears and some jugs for them." She didn't look at AJ.

His mom's lips curved into a smile. "Take good care of Lani, won't you? Don't let her strain herself."

AJ glanced at Lani, who once again was looking away. No doubt she was quite capable of deciding just how much strain she could handle. His mom probably had visions of him carrying her up hills or lifting her delicately over puddles. Hopefully Lani wouldn't expect him to, as he had no intention of going within five feet of her. She was dangerous.

They set off into the gardens, AJ carrying two metal jugs. Lani tucked a pair of shears into the pocket of her dress. It had rained overnight—as it usually did—and the leaves glistened with raindrops. A swallow darted around them as they headed toward the orchid forest down a narrow path of carved stones. Lani had removed her sandals and walked barefoot, Rahiian style. AJ kept his Skechers on, though he regretted it as they became increasingly sodden. "I'd forgotten how wet it is here."

"That's why they call it the rainforest." Lani shot him a cheeky look. The unusual golden color of her eyes struck him and he snatched his gaze away.

"Soggy, is what I call it. Now, L.A. has my kind of climate. A nice dry desert."

"With a decorative haze of smog." Lani marched straight ahead, her pretty toes splayed on the mossy stones.

"Exactly. Who needs to see all those mountains anyway? Hey, there's a flower." A delicate bloom peeked its head around the trunk of a tree.

"Lovely." Lani stopped and walked up to it. "But it's rather a rare orchid that only blooms every four years. I think we should leave it to enjoy its moment of glory here in this beautiful place. I'm not sure it would be happy in the ballroom."

AJ snorted. "I'm not sure anyone's ever happy in that ballroom, but they darn sure pretend to be. Why is Mom so good at getting what she wants?"

"She puts a lot of energy into everything she does. And she's a very loving person."

"Yes, she loves it when things go her way."

"She's always treated me like a daughter."

"You are her daughter. In law, at least."

"My mom runs a laundry and my dad is American. I'm hardly Rahiian aristocracy. She could have treated me quite differently."

AJ shrugged. "So? Snobbery is not really a Rahiian thing. You're probably more aware of it because of your years in America. Was it odd moving here from New Jersey? It must have been quite the lifestyle change."

She laughed. "I missed my bike. And my friend Kathy. I loved the beaches and all the colorful birds." She tucked a strand of hair behind her ears. "And of course I missed my dad."

"They got divorced?"

"Yup. My mom never really became Americanized. She refused to learn to drive, and she hated being out in crowded shops, so she tended to buy everything at the corner store."

"If corner stores in New Jersey are anything like the ones in L.A., she was getting ripped off."

"I'm sure. She didn't like American clothes and

wouldn't cut her hair. At first my dad thought all those things were cute, but after a few years he got tired of her traditional attitudes and began pushing her to adapt."

"But she didn't."

"She couldn't. She's very shy. She probably only married him in the first place because she was too timid to say no." Lani bent down to smell a pretty white lily at the base of a tree.

"Or he swept her off her feet."

"Probably some of that, too." She walked ahead, veering from the path into a little tunnel through the undergrowth. "But after eight years he called it quits and packed her off back home."

AJ ducked to avoid wet leaves brushing his hair. "Did Vanu sweep you off your feet?"

She flinched slightly, just a slight tic of her shoulders.

"It must be painful to think about him."

"It's okay. It wasn't really like that. Vanu saw me in the marketplace one day. He liked the look of me, and your mom found out who I was and invited me to the palace. It was all very formal. The marriage proposal was delivered to our house—behind the laundry, of course—by his footman."

"Not very romantic." AJ watched her slender form, clad in its delicate floral pattern, stepping daintily through the forest.

"Not at all. I didn't even know him at that point. We'd had about five minutes of conversation."

"So why did you agree to marry him?"

She shrugged. "Everyone said I had to. There really wasn't any question of not marrying him. My mom would never have forgiven me, for one thing, so I'd have spent the rest of my life in the laundry with her glaring at me." She made a face.

"I see what you mean. Well, rest assured this time. Even my mom can't force you and I to get married."

She froze, then kept walking. For a second she wrapped her arms around herself like she was cold—impossible since it was already at least eighty-five degrees, even in the lush shade.

"Have I offended you?" He snatched a leaf from a nearby shrub, then wondered why he'd done it. He pressed the plump, succulent leaf between his fingers.

"Not at all. I admire your independent attitude."

"You could always develop one yourself, you know." He was tempted to reach out and prod her in the ribs, but pulled his hand back at the last second. Even the thought of touching her made his fingertips prickle with awareness.

She was silent for a moment. "No. I couldn't let your mother down. She's been too good to me. She's lonely, you know, since your father died. She misses him very much. And now, losing Vanu…" She rubbed her arm, as if soothing goose bumps.

"She's lucky to have you, Lani."

"She's expecting us to find some flowers. We'd better get to work." Her wry glance made heat flash in his core. Didn't mean anything really. She was stunning—anyone would be attracted to her. Seductive, almond-shaped eyes fringed with dark lashes, her perfect small nose, her finely cut, sensual mouth…then all that sleek, golden brown hair falling about her slim shoulders. If she weren't his sister-in-law he'd want to put her in a movie.

"I guess we'd better find some it's okay to cut. You lead the way."

He followed her across a wide lawn surrounded by yellow hibiscus in full bloom, then down a little hill toward the nearby beach. He could smell the ocean in the air, crisp and salty and slightly fishy.

"These are my favorites." She pointed to white petunias, scattered like confetti at their feet where the jungle faded into the beach.

AJ glanced at the Rahiian ocean for the first time in years. Bright turquoise, it stretched forever, the horizon punctuated only by the nearby island of Naluua—an emerald dot fringed with white, floating in the clear blue bowl of sea and sky. "Damn."

Lani glanced up. "What?"

"I forgot the power of the sea."

Humor sparkled in her golden eyes. "They say the ocean in California is stunning."

"Not like this." He kicked off his shoes and strode out onto the fine white sand. The silky texture wrapped around his toes like a familiar embrace. "And ours is always warm." The beach wasn't wide. He reached the water in less than twenty strides, then stood while a small wave swept in sea foam to cover his toes. "Ahhh, now that feels good."

Lani laughed. A sweet, high, golden sound. It echoed and thrilled somewhere deep in his chest. He glanced at her, and basked in the warmth of her smile. It felt good to see her look happy, even if only for a moment. "Come on in." He extended his hand.

He regretted the gesture instantly. Touching her was definitely a bad idea. His skin tingled and the hairs on his arm stood on end even at the prospect.

It was likely she felt the same way, as she walked gingerly across the sand and dipped her toes into the water a good ten feet away. She sighed as the water swept around her delicate ankles. "I haven't done this in a long time. You take the water for granted when you live here."

"I guess you have to be gone a while to appreciate it." The sun warmed his face while the water lapped over his toes and his heels sank deeper into the soft sand. "Vanu and I used to spend hours down here, hunting for different shells and insects. It certainly is a good place for a kid to grow up."

Lani's smile vanished. AJ frowned. He shouldn't have mentioned Vanu. She obviously missed him. Maybe her Vanu was very different from the one he remembered? Brothers often had adversarial relationships.

He tried to ignore the recoil in his gut as he thought of her in Vanu's arms. Which was insane, since she was Vanu's wife. And how could he feel jealous over a woman he didn't have or even want?

The wind whipped Lani's hair to one side, revealing her striking profile. Okay, maybe he did want her. But not in any way that was appropriate under the circumstances. She wasn't some bubbly production assistant looking for a spot on the casting couch, or a cheeky starlet hoping for a bit part as well as some action.

Maybe that was part of the appeal. At least with Lani he knew she had absolutely no interest in scoring a part in one of his movies. Lately he'd found himself suspecting even the most seemingly sensible women of having ulterior motives for dating him. That's just how it was in L.A. Everyone seemed to have an agenda.

Then again, maybe Lani had an agenda, too, but he hadn't sniffed it out yet.

* * *

Lani snuck a sideways look at AJ. Proud head tilted to the horizon, he looked every bit like one of the ancient Rahiian carvings of The Old Ones. Which was funny, because until now, she'd have described him as a classic Hollywood bad boy. With his slicked-back dark hair, mischievous grin and wide, highly kissable mouth, he must have women chasing him through Beverly Hills. But now, in the strong light of the sun reflected off the ocean, she could see nothing but the classic planes of his face and the powerful body of an ancient warrior-god.

She blew out a breath. Was this really a useful line of thought?

Perhaps it was, since Priia was counting on her to convince AJ to marry her. She might as well find him attractive in that case. Guilt rippled over her like the seawater at her feet. She was supposed to trick him into marrying her so she could pass off her baby as his. Could she even live with herself if she did that?

She remembered his comment about this being a good place for a kid to grow up. She tried to imagine Vanu as a child, but couldn't. The innocence and curiosity of childhood seemed totally at odds with Vanu's harsh cynicism.

"Why did you leave Rahiri?" The question was blunt, but she wanted to know.

AJ looked out at the horizon, frowning. "Too small for me."

"You wanted to live somewhere with more going on?" She dug her toes into the sand. If he did somehow get suckered into marrying her, he'd be bored within a week.

"Yes. And where I could figure out what I really

wanted to do. Here my whole life was mapped out already—brother to the future king. I wanted more."

"And you found it." His life in L.A. must be exciting, fun. Rahiri was pleasant, but it was a peaceful place. No doubt he found it dull.

"I did." He turned to her, his expression oddly determined. "I went to college, discovered film and the rest is history." A wry grin lifted one corner of his mouth. "Okay, not exactly history, but cult film history, anyway. I enjoy my life."

How could his mom expect him to give up the life he loved and move back here, where once again his life would be mapped out for him? Cold fear mingled with the guilt trickling through her. She didn't want to be a party to spoiling AJ's life.

"Was it hard to leave?"

"Not at all." He turned a frank expression to her. "Vanu was the future king, and I was just the younger brother. I was a bit of a hell-raiser in my teens, too. I think everyone heaved a sigh of relief when I got on that plane to L.A."

"I know your mom missed you."

"And I missed her, but that doesn't mean it would have been better for me to stay here. Aren't we supposed to be finding flowers for her?"

"Yes." Lani glanced back at the green growth at the edge of the beach. "We're not doing a very good job. Honestly, I hate picking flowers. They look so much prettier and happier attached to their roots."

"Then we won't pick any. Let me guess, you think I'd be happier back here attached to my roots." Lani froze. He asked the question casually, looking up the beach and even walking away from her. He wasn't putting her on the spot.

Should she say the things her mother-in-law would want? That he'd be happy and content in the bosom of his family and helping the people of Rahiri?

She couldn't. "I don't know. If you love the life you have, it seems a shame to give it up."

The soft lapping of the ocean softened the silence between them. He slowed and she caught up with him. Tension stiffened his broad shoulders, pulling them tight against his collarless pale cotton shirt.

She watched him closely. "Do you feel a sense of duty to Rahiri?"

That question was fair enough. The son of a king was born to a life of duty, even a younger son. It did no harm to remind him of that.

He turned to face her, brows lowered. "I didn't, before. I was glad to leave all that to Vanu. There wasn't room for two of us here. Now that he's gone…" He turned to stare along the beach, where it rounded the corner of the cove and disappeared behind a clump of palm trees. "I don't know. Maybe I do feel a few stirrings of something. It's a shame you and Vanu didn't have a child, then there'd be another heir and I'd be off the hook."

Lani swallowed. She was glad he wasn't looking at her, as her face involuntarily tightened. If she told him about the baby… She fought to stop her hand rising to her stomach.

The baby. Again, guilt cascaded through her. She'd hardly given a thought to the new life growing inside her. Terror and misgivings far outweighed any joy she should feel as a new mother.

She'd wanted a baby so badly, but that was before she understood how complicated, difficult and painful life could be, even when on the surface everything was smooth and appeared normal. Vanu had awakened her to a sinister undercurrent that could spoil even the happiest of circumstances.

Although he was gone, she could still feel its dark tides tugging at her, enveloping her in this mess of subterfuge and obligation that threatened to trap AJ into an unwanted marriage.

She did feel a sense of duty, though. There was no denying the obligation—the love—she felt for her mother-in-law. If only there was a solution that would make everyone happy.

A thought occurred to her. "The country needs an heir." Her voice was low, soft, almost lost in the sound of the ocean and the rustling of leaves. "You could come back and rule...without marrying me."

AJ turned to her. At first he was frowning, then his brow softened and he looked like he might smile. "I could take that personally."

"I just want you to know that the two things don't have to be linked."

"According to tradition, they do."

"Traditions can be updated. It's the twenty-first century." And perhaps the laws of succession could be adjusted to make AJ and his heirs successors, instead of her unborn baby.

She was grasping at straws and she knew it.

AJ glanced down at her hand, which had come to rest on her belly. She pulled it away like it burned. He looked at her curiously for a second, then turned and walked back up the beach, still carrying the two empty brass jugs. "Ninety days until the successor must be chosen." His words carried on the breeze. "I haven't counted but we can't be too far off."

Lani's stomach clenched. "It's been fifty-two days

so far. Your mom is keeping count on an abacus." This also meant she was fifty-two days into her pregnancy— soon she'd really start to show.

AJ shoved a hand through his hair. "I don't know why, but I never thought I'd be in this position." He turned to face her, squinting against the bright sun. "I'd left Rahiri behind, a collection of memories and familiar faces that I'd visit from time to time but never actually return to." He blew out hard. "I don't fit here anymore."

Lani swallowed. "You have your own life. I understand that." Though she was certain his mother and the island elders wouldn't sympathize too readily. He was in a tough spot. At least she had the good luck of having absolutely no choice whatsoever. Her fate was tied to the royal dynasty, no matter what. "Only you can decide what to do."

"How can I simply decide to marry my brother's wife?" He finally put the two jugs—still empty—down in the sand and strode toward her. He picked up her hands and held them. "How can I take a woman I've barely met, and pledge my life to her?" He looked down at her hands, tiny in his. Already heat snapped between them in the warm morning air. AJ stiffened, perhaps also feeling the unsettling power. "I don't know you."

"Does anyone ever really know anyone else?" The cryptic reply rose to her lips. Her body shivered slightly. The proximity to his powerful chest seemed to stir something inside her.

"Perhaps not. We're all works in progress, after all. Maybe lives can be cast, like a film, and then we take up our roles and see what we can make of them." His dark eyes fixed on hers in a penetrating stare. "Do you think so, Lani?"

There was an edge to his voice that tightened the tension snapping through her. "Some would say you were cast in the role of royal son the day you were born." That answer would be approved by her mother-in-law.

She wanted so badly not to say the wrong thing, to ruin everything for the family and for Rahiri. If it was her fate to marry a strange man who didn't want her, then so be it. She could put up with almost anything after her years with Vanu. At least AJ seemed warm and kind.

And he was very handsome. Sun shone on the stern planes of his face as he looked down at her, confusion roiling in his narrowed eyes. His hands still held hers, tight, and heat was building between their entwined fingertips.

Lani tried to root herself firmly in the soft sand, to stay grounded no matter what might happen. Would he try to kiss her again? This time she must accept the kiss. That's what everyone would want. Her lips pulsed in anticipation and heat bloomed deep in her belly.

AJ's mouth, however, was set in a hard line, his brow furrowed. He dropped her hands and pulled back, then wiped his palms on his khaki pants. Lani's arms fell to her sides, fingertips prickling at their sudden abandonment.

Relief trickled through her, along with the ever-present guilt and a thickening fear of what the future held for all of them.

"You know what? I think we should pick some flowers for the party," AJ said gruffly. "At least we can manage not to disappoint my mom on that score."

"Of course." She tried to sound crisp and sensible. "I know a grove where we can fill both jugs without damaging the growing plants. Follow me." She marched past him up the sand, then wondered if it was appropriate to command a royal son—a future king, perhaps—to follow her. Life was so confusing once you became entangled with centuries of tradition and expectation. A foolish girl, she'd had no idea what she was getting into. What she was getting her future children into.

She heard AJ's steady footfalls behind her. He was too confident, too at home with himself to get upset by following a woman. What a refreshing change from Vanu, who would have spent the whole day needling her with the error of her ways. And AJ's solid presence behind her was reassuring. Since Vanu disappeared she'd become afraid of being alone out here in the jungle. What if he suddenly reappeared, crueler than ever, to take his revenge on her for being happy that he'd vanished?

What would AJ think about that? That she was happy his brother was dead. Yet another secret she had to carry with her to the grave. The burden made her heavy on her feet.

Her hand had strayed to her belly again and she jerked it away. "Not much farther." If only she could tell him about the baby. If he knew all the facts, they could really talk, and come to some decisions together. But it was her duty—her royal obligation—to remain silent.

They reached a shady grove where lush white lilies clustered around the trunks of trees. "We can cut these. They only bloom for a few days, and they reproduce like crazy." She pulled the small shears from her pocket and cut a clump of stems. The full, pale blooms looked suddenly bereft, severed from their roots. She shoved them quickly into AJ's offered jug.

"Lucky flowers to live such a carefree existence. And now they get to attend one of Mom's royal balls." His warm grin evaporated some of the gloom that had settled over her. "At least the party will keep her busy for a few days so she won't be too sad."

"She does love organizing things." Lani smiled. "And she's never happier than when surrounded by a thousand of her closest friends."

"And I guess you and I can plaster smiles on our faces for an evening. Though you can imagine what they'll all be thinking."

Lani bit her lip. "Yes. I think I can."

"They'll be whispering—so, is that film-director son going to marry the widow?" He spoke in a funny, Rahiian busybody voice that made Lani laugh, despite the ball of dread that had settled firmly at the bottom of her stomach.

"They will. Most likely they'll assume it, since you're still here."

"We could walk around scowling at each other, just to make things exciting and keep them guessing." He shot her a wry smile.

Lani managed to smile back. They had every reason to keep guessing. She certainly was. Would AJ agree to marry her? Would he believe her "premature baby" was really his? Or would he take off back to L.A., leaving her to raise her child by herself?

Or was there another outcome, perhaps harsher than she could even imagine, that had not yet presented itself?

Four

Violin music hummed over the murmur of a thousand conversations as the ballroom filled to capacity with Priia's invited guests. Sweat prickled inside AJ's stiff collar. He wore a starched black tunic and matching pants, a funerary version of Rahiian party attire. The sleek getup would look downright hip on the streets of Beverley Hills, but the traditional garb made him itch as if he'd stepped into someone else's skin.

"Arun!" He startled at the sound of his given name—no one ever used it—and glanced up to see a white-haired man approaching. AJ immediately recognized his father's oldest friend. Despite his stiffened gait and wrinkled visage, the old man's eyes twinkled as brightly as ever as he gripped AJ in a fierce embrace. "It's so good to see you back home again. Your return brings both tears and smiles to all our eyes."

AJ swallowed. "It's good to be back." The lie scorched his tongue and he took a quick swig of punch. "How are you these days, sir?"

"Sir? Sir!" The tanned face creased into a million lines. "What way is that for our new king to address one of his subjects. You should call me Niuu like all these other overdressed fools."

Our new king.

AJ fought the urge to come right out and say "I'm not staying," but he didn't want to ruin his mom's party. "I'll try. Old habits are hard to break. I feel a bit like a kid again, surrounded by all my parents' old friends."

"You are a kid, my boy, at least compared to me, and that's what Rahiri needs. Fresh energy to take us into the future. You will keep making films, won't you? My wife and I do enjoy the *Dragon Chaser* series."

"Films, yes, I imagine so." It was the ruling Rahiri part he didn't intend on. "I'm surprised people here watch my films."

"We're so proud of you, Arun, making a name for yourself and for our island in Hollywood."

AJ fought a smile. He certainly didn't think of himself as representing Rahiri with his work. Maybe that is how people here saw it, though. He'd never given the matter much thought.

The old man grasped his upper arm. "Do keep funding the schools, won't you? They're our future. So much young talent on this island. And our healthcare system is second to none. Your father put all that in place, and it will take a strong guiding hand to keep the rudder steady as you lead us into the future." The gnarled fingers tightened around his biceps. "You're strong, all right. Built like one of the ancient ones! Quite unlike your brother, Vanu." The man's expression grew clouded. "We're all sorry for his loss, of course, but ready to move into the future under your capable leadership."

"I appreciate your faith in me." AJ searched his brain for things to say that didn't disappoint but didn't actually commit him to anything. Or make his growing guilt any more agonizing.

"Naturally I have faith in you. You're your father's son. He raised you to be a man and take responsibility for those in need." He clapped his other hand on AJ's bicep, holding him in a kind of armlock. "We need you, Arun, and we're proud to have you as our new king."

AJ opened his mouth but no words came out. He glanced over the old man's shoulder and caught sight of Lani on the other side of the room. Standing dead still amidst the swirling crowds, she looked pale and lost. "Please excuse me."

He hurried through the crowd, managing nods and waves to faces he hadn't seen in years. Lani didn't even see him approach. Her eyes were fixed high on a carved column, her expression vacant, as if trying to forget where she was.

"Lani, you okay?"

She jumped and blinked. "Of course." Her wide eyes gave her a startled expression.

"You look like a three-toed sloth who's accidentally fallen out of her tree onto a multilane highway."

"Funny, since that exactly how I feel." A tiny smile tugged at the edges of her lovely mouth—then disappeared.

"Too many people wanting something from you? I

know how that is." What did Lani want? If he asked, he knew she'd give him the party line from his mom rather than a straight answer. She'd say she wanted to marry him, whether she did or not. And why would she? They'd barely met and weren't at all suited to each other. He was a hard-partying film director and she was a quiet village girl—albeit a royal one. "You don't look well."

"I'm fine." The words flew from her lips and she lifted her shoulders, like she was trying to convince herself as well as him. "Just a little tired. I haven't been sleeping well lately."

Probably still grieving for Vanu. Again he felt that unfamiliar prick of jealousy. Which was ridiculous. How could he begrudge his brother anything now that he was dead? This whole crazy situation was messing with his mind.

"Maybe you should go somewhere and sit down." He offered his arm, bracing himself against the powerful effect she had on him.

She didn't move. Her dark lashes lowered, then she looked up at him with those haunting golden eyes. "I'm fine, really. I'll make more of an effort from now on. Your mom needs me to. And we'll be stuck sitting down for hours once the speeches start."

"The speeches. That's one part of Rahiian culture I really haven't missed. Has anyone broken a new record for longest speech ever?"

"I think it's still at five hours." She smiled. "At least it's very relaxing for the listeners. And you know you'll have to make a speech."

He grimaced. He would, too. What on earth would he say? Usually he was good at speaking off the cuff, but the stakes were a little higher here than at an investors' meeting. "You're lucky being a girl, so you're off the hook. If I do become king I'm going to change that right away so all the ladies get to make speeches, too."

Lani's eyes widened, but they sparkled with humor. "Your mom would love that. She'd go on all night."

"Wouldn't she?" He laughed. They both knew he was joking about becoming king.

Wasn't he?

Lani watched AJ melt back into the well-dressed throng amidst smiles and exclamations. He stood almost a full head above most people in the room, and moved like a king among them with his broad shoulders and easy, confident manner. Everyone in the region was happy to see him back. Pleased that the Rahiian succession would be a smooth and effortless affair following time-honored methods.

People kept a respectful distance from her. As a widow in mourning, she was not expected to eat and dance and chatter along with the guests.

But they all expected her to marry AJ. They just had no idea he didn't want to.

She wasn't sure whether to feel relieved or alarmed. He seemed to have every intention of going back to L.A. He'd said nothing to suggest otherwise and he hadn't asked her opinion, either. If he had, of course she'd have said she wanted to marry him. What else could she say?

Her fingers had stung with anticipation just now when he reached out to give her his arm. All the tiny hairs on her arm had stood on end, craving his touch.

Now she wondered if she'd done the wrong thing in refusing.

The whole situation was so confusing and disturbing. She was expected to entice him to marry her—immediately—but she didn't want to trap him into a lifetime deception she'd be forced to maintain.

And she didn't want to be married to a man—another man—who didn't love her.

"Sweetheart, come sit down next to me. They're starting the speeches." Priia glowed with good cheer, as she always did at her festive gatherings. She bloomed and shone with the energy of other people. Naturally gregarious and effortlessly charming, she was born to be a queen. Lani envied her tireless energy and outgoing personality.

She led Lani to a cushioned chair at the high table. "Sit down." She patted the cushions. "And have some coconut stars. You need to keep your strength up."

"Thanks, you're too good to me." Lani took one of the coconut treats, then wondered what to do with it. Her stomach, hidden beneath the thick sash of her gold-embroidered dress, certainly wasn't in any condition to handle food.

"Nonsense, dear. You're the light of my old age." She leaned in, conspiratorial, eyes shining. "And soon you'll bring a new bright light to life among us."

Lani blanched and tried not to glance around. What if someone overheard and guessed what she meant?

A dignified-looking elderly man wrapped in the distinctive clothing of a nearby island walked out into the center of the floor, where the speeches took place. At first Lani sat stiffly in her seat, wondering if her fate would be pronounced or speculated upon. Instead he launched into a semi-poetic history of the region, laden with myth and superstition, and she soon let her mind drift.

Another speaker followed, then another, chanting as much as speaking, celebrating the community of the islands and the long-held peace that united them in this beautiful place. Lulled by the warm atmosphere, Lani relaxed into her cushions and even managed to nibble on her coconut star.

She sat up abruptly when the master of ceremonies called AJ—or rather Arun Jahir—to the floor. She glanced over at him, and watched him rise, face expressionless, and walk out into the center of the room. His crisp black garb emphasized the strength and dignity of his movements. Head held high and back straight, he moved like a monarch, even if he didn't want to be one.

A little flash of pride surprised Lani. She liked AJ and sympathized with the awkward situation he was in. She still didn't really understand why he'd kissed her— twice—but under the circumstances it was excusable, even if her initial response wasn't. He obviously wanted to do the right thing, but like her, he wasn't sure what that was, and he wisely knew that the wrong choice would have lasting, painful consequences.

Lani shifted in her chair, remembering the tiny consequence she carried inside her. Her fear and anxiety about the situation she found herself in now warred with stray sparks of excitement and eager anticipation of her baby's arrival. How could she not look forward to holding that tiny, warm body and feeling the grip of a plump hand on her finger?

AJ studied the crowd in silence for a few moments.

When he began to speak, his voice was deeper than she remembered. Like the others, he spoke of the long history of the royal line, the legend of how their people had first arrived on long boats from a far-off land, how they'd fought and made peace.

Lani watched, heart pounding. How did AJ manage to sound so perfectly like one of the wise men of the region? You'd never guess he'd been gone for more than a decade. He seemed to carry the cadence and rhythm of the ancient stories in his blood—his royal blood—and why wouldn't he, descended as he was from a long line of kings?

The fierce nut of pride inside her grew and she found herself pressing hot palms together in her lap. Any woman should be proud to have a man like AJ as her husband, even if he wasn't royal. She could feel a hum of excitement, almost like a wave of heat, rising in the room. Everyone could feel it. She glanced around and saw eyes glowing, cheeks brightening, as AJ carried them all on a tide of emotion. His words echoed like drumbeats around the room, their meaning less important than the man who spoke them and the spell he wove with his powerful voice.

He paused, looked up at the high-beamed ceiling, then started to walk. At first Lani thought he was simply returning to his seat. Disappointment that his performance was over warred with relief that no permanent commitments had been made or broken.

But then he stopped. He turned to his mother—seated only about two feet from Lani—and bowed deeply. Feeling something about to happen, Lani stiffened.

"I am proud—" AJ's voice boomed through the

packed ballroom "—to take up the staff of tradition, and assume the role of king as my father and brother have done before me."

Lani gasped. Everything dimmed a bit and she grasped the arm of her chair to keep a grip on reality.

"And I am pleased to take Lani Rahia as my wife, according to royal custom." His eyes fixed on hers as the last breath fled her lungs. Unable to govern her features into anything but terror-stricken panic, she sat frozen as every eye in the room turned to her.

The faces blurred and she found herself gasping for breath. She felt Priia's soft hand on her arm. "I'm so happy, my daughter." Priia's tear-filled voice penetrated her foggy consciousness. "What a great day this is for Rahiri and for all of us."

Lani tried to say something, but her mouth wouldn't move. How could AJ do this without even consulting her?

Because he was the king, and she was no one. A royal widow, rather like a recently vacated crown, free for the taking and passing on.

Anger prickled through her, battling with the fear. The New Jersey upbringing and the freedoms she'd learned to take for granted challenged the quiet acceptance she'd tried so hard to school in herself.

And AJ had no idea she was pregnant. She felt angry that he hadn't even asked her opinion about the marriage. How would he feel if he knew she carried his brother's child?

If she went along with Priia's plan, he'd never find out. He might suspect something, might wonder at the "premature" baby in such perfect health. He might notice features or traits that fitted his brother better than himself—but he'd never know for sure.

This was one small but deadly advantage women had always had over men. They didn't really know if they were the father of a child. Only the woman held that secret.

"Lani, are you okay?" Priia's voice penetrated the thick fog of her thoughts. "Have some water." She felt a glass pressed to her lips, and she struggled to swallow the cool fluid.

"I...I think so" was all she could manage. She brushed a droplet from her lips, glad that at least she'd managed not to cry. Alarm snapped through her as she saw AJ, climbing the stairs on the dais, moving toward her.

"Stand up, dear," whispered her mother-in-law. She rose shakily to her feet, patting her dress and hoping its creases didn't show any hint of a belly. Every eye in the room felt like a laser searchlight ready to reveal all her fears and misgivings—or were they hopes and dreams?

Majestic in his carriage and bearing, AJ stood in front of her and took her hand. Her fingers trembled in his and heat flushed over her. "Will you take me as your husband?"

Their eyes met—locked onto each other—as he asked the question. It wasn't traditional to ask. He'd done that out of consideration for her.

Or had he? Since she could hardly say no, here amidst the gathered throng of royal admirers.

"I will." Her voice sounded so quiet, so meek, even in the deadly hush of the ballroom. She wondered if AJ would smile, but he didn't. His face, like hers, seemed frozen into a kind of noble mask. Two people acting out roles history had determined for them, and in which emotion and personal opinion played no role.

A cheer rose from the crowd, echoing off the high ceiling and bouncing around the room. Glasses lifted and people began to stamp their feet on the floor, a customary display of enthusiasm.

"Both of you, walk around the room." Priia's urgent whisper penetrated her consciousness.

AJ's arm slipped inside Lani's and drew her down the three stairs to the ballroom floor. The skin of her arm felt hot and feverish against the dark fabric of his jacket. She tried to keep her steps steady, and school her face into an expression of quiet happiness.

AJ's arm felt rigid, tense. He marched with slow dignity, not his usual relaxed gait. No doubt becoming king would turn him into a different person—it already was. Would he become a hard, cold man like Vanu once the wedding vows were sealed?

Cold terror crept through her, tightening her muscles. The stamping feet and calling voices created a blanket of sound that seemed to suck the air from the room and leave her gasping. So much expectation, so many hopes and dreams, and the nation's future hidden in the darkness of her own belly. The pressure weighed on her like a thundercloud and she felt her head becoming light. "I think I'm going to faint," she managed, head tilted toward AJ's powerful jaw.

Her rasped whisper was lost in the roar of the crowd. AJ marched on, oblivious, his face set in a grim smile. Perhaps he'd forgotten she was even there?

The faces started to swirl together, a hot mix of colors with flashes of blackness. Her ankles wobbled and the floor seemed to tilt. She dug her nails into his arm, looking for purchase, and he glanced down.

"I—I don't feel well," she stammered, blinking.

Alarm filled his eyes. "We'll go outside for some air. There's a door over here." He led her past some tables of excited guests, to a side door. Before he left, he turned and bowed. "Please stay and enjoy yourselves."

Seeing that he and Lani were about to leave the room together, the crowd went wild. Perhaps they assumed some kind of romantic action was about to take place. A wave of nausea rose in Lani's throat at the thought that she'd soon be all alone with AJ.

Her future husband.

Outside the door, the cool night air hit her face like a welcome slap. She sucked in a breath and pulled her arm from AJ's, then wondered if she was even allowed to do that.

The lamplight cast AJ's face into shadow, and for a second he looked menacing, unreadable. She didn't know this man but was expected to spend her life with him and sleep in his bed, whether she wanted to or not.

Panic flashed through her and spurred her feet into action. The corridor blurred as she found herself running headlong toward the garden. She didn't know why she was running, only that she had to move—to act on the fierce instinct to flee that reverberated through her whole body.

"Lani, where are you going?" AJ's voice rang after her, and sped her steps. She heard his heels on the stone, marching at first, then jogging along behind her.

Where am I going? The question echoed around her mind as she ran, sandals slapping on the smooth tiles.

There's nowhere to go. The corridor led down to the manicured part of the garden, with a fishpond and perches for the wild birds that ornamented the trees. But its fringes descended into the thick, dense jungle that cloaked the island in its tight embrace. There was no escape.

The stone tiles gave way to grass, cool and damp in the evening dew. She ran a few steps, then felt a strong arm catch her around the waist, almost knocking the breath from her lungs. The baby! If he knew about it he'd never have grabbed her there. But he couldn't know.

She wriggled, instinctively trying to free herself, but his grip was too strong. He wrapped his other arm around her, holding her from behind. "Lani, stop running. We need to talk." Her nerve endings snapped with the desire to run on, but she knew it was hopeless. "I know you're scared but we're in this together."

His deep voice reverberated in her ear, oddly soothing. But she didn't want to say anything. What else could she say but *I'm pregnant.* Yet she'd sworn to keep the baby a secret.

"I didn't intend to spring the whole thing on you. It took me by surprise as well." He turned her in his arms until she stood facing him, no longer pressed against him, but with a couple of inches of warm air between them.

She tried to ignore the strange sensations in her breasts and belly, the odd pulses of desire that only worsened the strange situation. "I thought you were going back to L.A."

That's what she'd hoped for, though she hadn't dared

admit it to herself until just now—when the possibility was gone.

He frowned, features angular in the cool moonlight. "I did, too." He drew in a long breath. "But tonight, surrounded by all those people, the air thick with our island's past and heavy with its future, I knew my place is here. I couldn't shirk my responsibility and still live with myself."

Lani nodded. Again that little kernel of pride throbbed inside her. AJ truly was a man of honor. "Rahiri is lucky to have you," she managed. The words sounded hollow, empty. Shame he wasn't so lucky to have her, a woman who intended to keep a huge thing secret from him for the rest of her life. If she told him, though, he wouldn't be king. She'd break Priia's already suffering heart and put the entire burden of the monarchy's future on herself and her unborn baby. And she'd still be expected to marry again.

AJ's frown deepened. "I'll do my best to be a good husband to you."

He softened his grasp on her arms. He'd been literally holding her in place—preventing her from running off again—and perhaps he realized the grip was at odds with his soothing words.

Lani wobbled slightly on her feet. "I'll do my best to be a good wife." Her words hung in the still night air, the lie echoing off tree trunks and winding itself around them like a vine.

How could she be a good wife if she deceived him about the paternity of the child he'd raise?

Lani's golden eyes shone with anxiety—and why wouldn't they? AJ's chest tightened. This poor girl had no say in her own fate. Of course she could refuse him, but she was far too polite and kind for that. He could have offered to take the crown but refused to marry Lani, but for some reason he knew marrying her was the right thing to do.

Maybe it was that first kiss?

In the kiss all pretense had fallen away. All the tension had evaporated and there was nothing left but… passion. Could that happen again now that they were pledged to each other for life?

Lani's chin tilted high as she met his gaze. She looked so earnest, determined to meet her fate bravely. Everything seemed so awkward.

His synapses tingled as he contemplated kissing her. Perhaps that would cut through all the layers of ceremony and nerves and anticipation and jump-start the connection he'd felt between them that first night. "I have an idea."

Dark lashes lowered, she looked coyly away, like a young girl who'd never been kissed. But he knew better. Somewhere beneath that demure surface lurked a smoldering cauldron of passion that he ached to taste again.

"What?" she murmured, daring to glance up.

He replied by lowering his face to hers. He did it slowly, to give her a chance to react and respond in her own time. At first she flinched slightly, as if to dodge him, then she seemed to steel herself and tilted her lips to his.

Their lips met like opposing magnets coming together, pulled by an unseen force. A shock wave of desire crashed through AJ as Lani's mouth opened to greet his. Her body softened and he wrapped his arms around her, hugging her close. Heat gathered between them and his skin hummed with awareness of her body. His fingers itched to tug at the embroidered fabric of her dress and pull it away to reveal smooth, golden skin.

Her mouth tasted like warm honey, delicious and inviting. He deepened the kiss, trailing his fingers down her spine. Lani kissed him back, tongue reaching for his, her arms wrapped around his waist and her slim body straining against him.

But something was different.

Her actions lacked the sense of raw abandon he remembered from their first kiss. No breathless moans pierced the night air. Her fingertips pressed into the muscles of his back, but with a forced quality, not the fevered intensity he remembered.

He pulled away slowly. Lani's eyes opened, and he noted their look of curious alarm. Did she wonder if she'd put on a good enough show of passion?

AJ fought the urge to frown. It didn't help that they were out here in the dark garden, while all the guests still drank and talked inside. "Let's go somewhere more comfortable." Then they could talk in private and get more used to their new situation.

"Okay." She blinked. Quiet and accommodating as usual. Would he ever know what went on in her mind, behind that polite smile?

He took her arm and they walked down the corridor. "We won't be missed at the party. They'll have more fun talking about us if we're not there." He shot her a smile.

"Yes." Her arm felt rigid in his.

AJ led her through the lamplit passages of the private

quarters of the palace and into his private sitting room. It adjoined the bedroom; no one would come to disturb them here. The guests would stay until dawn, then stumble drunkenly to their chauffeured cars.

Priia had redecorated the room in his absence, in a simple, masculine style that he rather liked. No doubt now he'd be expected to move into the royal bedchamber, but there was no way he'd spend the night in a room where Lani had once slept with Vanu.

He gestured to a low chaise covered in soft leather. Lani perched stiffly on the edge of it.

"Would you like some wine?" He gestured to the stocked bar in one corner.

"No, thanks. I'm fine." Her rushed response surprised him. He moved to the cabinet and poured a glass for himself. He sat next to Lani on the sofa, each of them upright, formal, painfully separate. Even his favorite vintage tasted slightly bitter on his tongue.

What had he got himself into?

He set his glass down. "You don't have to marry me, you know."

Lani's gaze snapped to meet his. "But of course I want to." The gleam of panic in her eyes warred with her reassuring words.

"I know my mom has probably put a lot of pressure on you, and now I've piled on some more by publicly declaring I'd marry you, but I don't intend to force you into anything. If you want to call it off, just say the word."

He braced himself for her response. Her rejection.

The events of tonight had lit a fire inside him—a fire of warm ancient traditions and comforting rituals, and he'd committed to keeping that fire alive. The prospect of spending his life with the beautiful Lani had suddenly seemed to be one of the sweeter benefits of taking up the role his country expected of him.

Even now, her golden gaze sent a charge of electricity snaking through him, and his fingertips ached to roam over her soft skin.

But not if she didn't want him. He had more than enough women after him back in L.A. There was no reason on earth good enough to force a woman into bed with him if she didn't want to be there.

"I don't want to call it off." Lani's words came out in a staccato rhythm. "I want to get married as soon as possible." She wiped her palms on the shimmering fabric of her evening dress.

AJ cocked his head. "Then why do you look so damned unhappy about it?"

"I am happy, really." She reached out to him and wrapped her arms stiffly around him. The goose bumps on her arms rasped his skin.

"You have a funny way of showing it." Still, the hopeful gesture warmed his heart. He turned and put his arm around her. Only to find that she was shivering, her whole body tense and rigid.

He raised a thumb to her cheek and stroked it. "You need to relax."

"I know. I'm just…excited."

Panicked, more like. Maybe she was afraid he'd want to make love to her tonight? "We don't have to rush into anything."

"Oh, but we should. Everyone is expecting it." Something flashed in her eyes, panic, or calculation, he couldn't tell which. Curiosity unfurled in him like a flame.

He tilted his head and held her gaze. "You think they expect us to sleep together?"

"Probably, yes." She nodded.

He lifted a brow. Heat flared in his groin. "Do you think we should?"

Her cheek heated under his thumb. "Yes, I do." Her voice was low, breathy.

AJ blinked. He'd not expected that answer. In fact he'd had no intention of doing more than kiss her for now. But maybe she wanted to get such a big milestone out of the way? Or to make sure he was a considerate lover before she committed the rest of her life to him? There were many possible explanations, under the bizarre circumstances.

And since he was a healthy male, any one of them would do. He rose from the sofa, and took her hand. "Then I guess we'd better go into the bedroom."

Five

Lani followed AJ, her hand in his. She could do this. It was best for Rahiri, and for the family. AJ would be king, his mom would be happy, and her child would be free to grow to adulthood before taking on the responsibilities and pressures of the monarchy.

AJ turned to her on the threshold and took both her hands in his. "Are you sure?"

She hesitated. He was truly a thoughtful man, one who deserved a better woman than she. But if Priia's plan was to succeed she must...do the deed with him at the earliest opportunity.

Do the deed. Even the phrase suggested a crime, but she couldn't really call it "making love" under circumstances like this.

Making love. She'd never done that with Vanu, either. No love had existed between them, though she'd certainly tried hard to find some in the first few months— before she'd realized Vanu had no love lurking anywhere inside him.

AJ stroked her cheek again, which made her shiver slightly. A warm shiver of pleasure. His touch was gentle, encouraging, his big hands sensitive. Lani lifted her own fingers and gingerly caressed his shirtfront. Thick muscle rose to greet her fingertips through the crisp, black surface.

He had a sensational body. She'd seen him swimming in the lagoon one morning while she was on her way to breakfast. Her heart had almost stopped beating at the sight of his broad shoulders gleaming in the morning sun while water licked over his sturdy, bronzed physique.

Desire rose inside her, trickling up from her core. She could do this. And enjoy it.

AJ's hands reached for the sash at her waist and pulled carefully at the elaborate knot. She helped him get it undone and the thick strip of silk fell to the floor at her feet. He stroked her back, then put his hands on either side of her waist, caressing her through her dress.

Her breath caught. What if he felt her belly and noticed it was no longer flat? It wasn't very round, but in the last couple of days there was a noticeable bump.

Guilt forked through her and she plucked at the buttons of his shirt. Better to get on with things and get him so wrapped up in the act that he didn't notice anything strange about her body.

And he thought she was so *nice*.

Her heart hammered wildly as she pulled his black tunic away from his skin, revealing his smooth, strong chest. Her nipples tightened, straining against her bra, and her insides seemed to twist into a knot. Was this excitement okay for the baby? She knew sex was supposed to be fine during pregnancy, but somehow it seemed wrong to feel pleasure under the circumstances.

AJ's dark eyes met hers as she glanced up at his face. He smiled. "I think I might be the luckiest man alive."

Lani swallowed. No, the luckiest man alive would have a wife who was honest and open, not one who needed to have sex with him as soon as possible so it would look like her child was his.

She dropped her gaze to the button on his pants, and worked at it. Her fingers sprang away as if stung when she noticed the thick, hard arousal hiding beneath the zipper.

AJ laughed. "As you can see, I'm quite attracted to you."

She managed to smile. "And I to you." An understatement. Her insides pulsed with arousal and somewhere deep inside her ached in a way she'd never felt before.

AJ unfastened her dress—a single hook held the whole thing together—and pulled it carefully away from her skin.

The warm night air caressed her, but as she stood there, naked before him, an ache of longing opened inside her. A deep, cold loneliness that craved something—sex, love, companionship—all the things that had never come together in her life before.

Now this kind and handsome man offered her all those things and more.

Tears sprang to her eyes and a sob tore from her throat.

"What's the matter?" AJ moved his hands from her waist to her shoulders, where he held her steady. He frowned, no doubt getting irritated by her hot-and-cold behavior. "Is being my wife such an awful fate?"

Another sob shook her from head to toe. "I can't do this." Tears fell from her cheeks and dripped onto her bare breasts.

"Then you won't. We'll get dressed. I'm not going to push you into anything."

Lani froze. "But we have to." The shrill sound of her own voice startled her.

AJ frowned and shoved a hand through his hair. "Why?"

"Because I'm already pregnant."

Her words rang in the air like the clash of a ceremonial gong. AJ frowned, trying to process the information. "You're carrying Vanu's baby." His gaze dropped to her stomach, then her hands flew to cover it.

She nodded, eyes filled with tears.

A horrible, cold sensation settled over AJ. Just when he'd finally committed himself to this new life, when he'd chosen to marry Lani, and was looking forward to sharing his life with her…his brother's long, strong and deadly arm reached out to him from beyond the grave.

"Why didn't you say anything before?"

Lani shuddered. "I didn't know until a few days ago. Then I took a test, and…" She looked down, apparently unable to meet his gaze.

AJ stared at her. He couldn't understand the secrecy. His mom was so anxious for them to marry, to keep the family together in the traditional way. Maybe they'd decided he'd be less likely to marry her if he knew she was carrying Vanu's baby.

"So you thought you'd marry me and pretend the child is mine?"

"I didn't want to…" She swallowed. Lani looked like she wanted to say more, but couldn't.

"But my mom put you up to it."

She nodded. "She said it would be better because then you would be the next in line to the throne, and not the baby."

AJ spun away and blew out a curse. "I can't believe you women cooked this up. I've never been hungry for the throne. I'd have been quite happy to leave and let your child rule Rahiri."

"I think that's what your mom was afraid of. She wants you here."

He knew. Her obvious happiness at having him back home had been a source of guilt and torment to him—until he'd decided to stay.

"What about you?" He peered at her through narrowed eyes. "You don't need to marry me. Either way your child will inherit the throne."

"My child's not even born yet."

"Your child's not even showing yet." AJ's eyes raked over her belly. "And at this point I'm not even sure whether to believe you now. Get dressed."

The command startled her into action and she picked her dress up off the floor and pulled it back on. AJ buttoned his pants and turned away. If she really was pregnant and wanted to pretend it was his, no wonder she'd been so anxious to have sex right away. Desire had nothing to do with it.

Revulsion and anger flashed through him. She'd seemed so sweet and innocent—now he knew she was anything but. Lovely Lani had schemed to lure him into a lifetime of deception.

He'd never wanted to come back here. His gut instincts had told him to leave as soon as possible. If anything the instinct had become even stronger after his explosive kiss with Lani. He should have known her pretty facade hid a dangerous and deceptive core. What kind of woman would kiss another man when her husband was barely gone?

He peered at her, hating her beauty and the mix of fear and alarm in her wide, golden eyes.

He turned from her and strode across the room. He should never have promised to stay. It went against everything he wanted from his own life. He loved his film career and his group of friends in L.A. He had no interest in getting married and settling down into some routine existence.

But the ancient ceremonial drumbeats had stirred something lying dormant in his blood. They'd kicked his heart into a primal rhythm and drawn him back into the mysterious and powerful pull these islands exerted over anyone who'd lived here. The magic of the lush jungle and the bright, clear ocean formed a paradise of beauty that could entice any man, much like a stunning woman.

Seductive—and dangerous, in that you never knew what hit you until it was too late. Until you were trapped, bound by tradition and the expectations of people you didn't even know.

Well, no more. He'd weakened for a moment and taken up the mantle they all wanted to thrust on him, but he could throw it off just as easily.

He turned to Lani, who stood just to the side of the wide bed, already rumpled by their almost-lovemaking.

She'd said she was so happy, that she wanted to climb in that bed with him.

All lies.

"You disgust me."

She flinched slightly, as if his words stung her. "I'm sorry."

"More lies. You're not sorry, or you wouldn't have done it."

"I did tell you the truth."

"I'm sure you have your own motives for that choice, too." Perhaps the prospect of bedding a man she didn't love—or even like—had proved too much for even her hardened sensibilities? "No doubt you've decided that marriage to your husband's brother is too much to stomach—tradition be damned."

She blinked. "I'm willing to marry you."

AJ let out a growl. "Willing? How kind of you to be so generous with your life. With your body. Allow me to throw your sacrifice back at you. Please leave." He gestured to the door, hand shaking with fury. Her wide-eyed desire of only a few minutes ago was so obviously fake, and it disgusted him that she'd tried to trap him into sex with her when she viewed the entire arrangement as a chore.

But she didn't move.

"Leave." His command echoed off the walls, and no doubt out into the night since the windows were open.

Lani seemed to shrink a little. She gathered her dress about her. "The guests are probably still here."

"Then what are you worried about? That they'll see you in a state of undress and assume you've been in my bed? I thought that was what you wanted." He narrowed his eyes. "Or was that only when you intended to trick them into thinking your baby was mine. It doesn't look so good if you sleep with me when you're pregnant with my brother's baby, does it?"

She shook her head. "I didn't want any of this." Tears welled in her eyes.

"Me, either, but you at least chose your role by marrying my brother. I got shoved into this dog-and-pony show from the moment I was born. It took me years to work my way out of it and I almost made the biggest mistake of my life letting you and my mom suck me back into it with trickery and deception. With a face like that I'd imagine you're used to getting your own way."

Her tear-filled gaze only fueled the indignation pricking his muscles. "I told you to go."

If she didn't get out of here, he might get suckered in by some sob story she'd cook up. She still clutched her dress awkwardly about her. He grabbed her sash off the floor and thrust it at her, his fingers instinctively flinching back from hers as she took it. Her touch was deadly and her wanted her out of sight and mind before anything else could happen.

Less than an hour ago he'd promised to stay and take his place as king here. Filled with ancestral pride and hope for the future, he'd enjoyed the sense of comradeship and even destiny as people welcomed him home.

Under false pretenses. There was already a new king or queen waiting to take the throne, hidden beneath the rumpled folds of Lani's dress.

She struggled with the sash, wrapping its length about her still-slim waist. He wondered if there really was a baby. Perhaps this was her last-ditch effort to send him running? He didn't know what to believe anymore. Confusion and anger warred inside him. He was used to being the director, setting up the action, telling people what to do. If something didn't work out he could fix it in post-production—ruthlessly cutting and even reshooting if needed.

There were no retakes in real life.

Her sash now retied, Lani slipped on her sandals. Her fingers shook—and that stirred a trace of pity in his heart.

He crushed it quickly and moved to open the door. From down the corridor he could hear voices, the sound of feet on the stone. Revelers leaving the party. What kind of scandal would it cause for Lani to run past them, eyes filled with tears?

Surely they'd expect no less from a grieving widow forced into marriage with a man she barely knew. Nothing about this situation was pretty.

Lani hesitated in the doorway, plucking nervously at her silk dress.

"Can't face them?" His voice was cold. "Maybe you could just tell them the truth, like you did with me."

She hadn't said a word for some time and her silence was starting to rub him raw. Who was she to stand there looking so innocent and hard-done-by? Suddenly he was the bad guy, the one who threatened to ruin everyone's careful plans.

Lani's lips quivered before she finally spoke. "Your mom wants to keep it a secret."

"Do you do everything she tells you?"

Her silence answered his question.

Irritation flashed over him. "She needs to learn that you can't manipulate people like puppets." Maybe that's where Vanu got it from. He'd certainly pulled the strings in their world from behind the scenes. It was time for someone to snap the strings right off. He grabbed her arm, hating the way his skin heated when he touched her. "Come on, let's get this charade over with."

Lani pulled her arm back. Not wanting to get into a wrestling match, he let it go. "It was such a happy evening for your mother."

AJ frowned. He could still hear the hypnotic drumbeats somewhere in the distance. People were dancing and laughing and enjoying the vision of the future they'd all conjured together such a short time earlier.

"Your mom's been so sad lately. Can't we let her enjoy her party?" She didn't meet his gaze.

"Let the happy charade continue and ignore reality for another day?" His muscles tightened. "Why not? But I don't think that should extend to keeping you in my room all night." He shot her a harsh look. "It's a little too crowded in here with you and your baby."

Not to mention your dead husband. He didn't say that, though. He wasn't totally insensitive.

"Would you mind escorting me along the corridor?" She said it softly, still not lifting her eyes to his. Very Rahiian and traditional. "Everyone will know something's wrong if they see me by myself."

He was tempted to say no. Everything was wrong; it was better people should find out. This whole pretense sickened him. And he hated the way Lani's soft voice tugged at his sympathies and made him want to save her from humiliation.

How could she be so infuriating and still so beautiful at the same time? Her skin glowed in the soft light from the wall sconces, and her hair shimmered like gold thread. "Sure," he growled.

He did not touch her this time. No need to feel heat

flash over his skin where there should be revulsion. He marched down the corridor with Lani hurrying along beside him in her long dress. Lani's room was on the other side of the palace, past the area where the party was still taking place. Laughter and music spilled into the hallway as they marched on. Groups stood chatting in the hallway outside the ballroom, smiling as they approached.

AJ's insides contracted. All these people now saw them as the happy couple with a bright future ahead of them.

If they only knew.

"So serious, Arun." An older man he recognized as one of his father's ministers smiled at him. "Already the weight of responsibility is carving lines into your face."

He attempted to soften what must be quite a scowl. "I'm just escorting Lani back to her room. She's tired." He didn't have to make up stories.

"I'm sure she is." He didn't wiggle his eyebrows but the implication was there. AJ saw a slight flush rise to Lani's cheeks.

She should be embarrassed. That's exactly what she'd wanted. Now everyone thought they'd sealed their pact with wild lovemaking. He cursed the desire that still coursed through his body at the sight of her. All his instincts had told him to stay far, far away from Lani and everything she represented.

They'd been right.

"Your mother is so happy, Arun. What joy you're bringing to all our people." The former minister's wife patted his forearm. "And I've never seen a lovelier couple."

The last remark was addressed to Lani, who replied, "You're sweet, but I really must get some rest."

Her smile made her look so innocent and adorable. They had no idea why she needed rest.

AJ's tension eased slightly as they moved away from the excited guests and down the dimly lit corridor away from the ballroom. He had no intention of returning this way and facing innuendo about exactly what he and Lani had been up to. He'd rather traverse the pitch-dark garden.

Lani now walked ahead of him, shoulders tight under the fall of hair cascading to her waist.

Just a half hour ago he'd run his fingers though that silken mass and imagined them as partners—husband and wife. That idea had evaporated like the dawn mist, and now she again seemed like a semi-hostile stranger.

When she reached her room, Lani turned and fixed wide, worried eyes on him. "Thank you for helping me run the gauntlet."

"I don't know why I did." He cocked his head. "Obviously I'm a soft touch."

"You're not. You're a man of honor and that's evident in everything you've said and done so far." Her voice was steady and she leveled a clear gaze at him. "You should be king and it's a terrible shame if I've somehow ruined that."

Her words stopped his negative thoughts in their tracks. No one cared what Lani really wanted. She was expected to do whatever it took to ease the succession and make life easy for other people. None of this was her idea. What did she have to gain from sleeping with him, let alone marrying him? She'd probably rather be curled up with a good book and some saltines.

"Why did you agree to go along with my mom's plot to trick me into marrying you even though you're already pregnant with the heir?"

"She didn't know I was pregnant when you first came. I didn't, either. I found out that first night, when I was ill and left dinner early."

Things started to fall into place.

He frowned when he realized that first passionate kiss had come before she knew about the baby. "So the wheels driving us into marriage were already rolling and you figured it was too late to stop them?"

"Your mom was so excited about you staying. And I liked the idea of my child being able to enjoy being a kid, without the pressure of already being a monarch. On some level the idea made sense, until…"

"Until you tried to get naked with me. Then there was nothing to hide behind."

"I'm not cut out for deception." She met his gaze with a hard stare of her own. Then it softened. "And you don't deserve that. You're a good man."

Her ridiculously long hair fell about her shoulders. Her oddly shaped traditional dress didn't hold together well without the sash. Those big eyes still brimmed with tears that glittered in her thick lashes. He fought a powerful urge to take her in his arms and comfort her.

Was he angry with her or at the unfortunate effect she had on him? She was just trying to do what everyone wanted of her. Tradition had shoved her between a rock and a hard place and he couldn't help wondering which one he was. "I am glad you told me."

"I couldn't have lived with myself if I didn't." She held her neat chin high.

"Why would you put up with marrying a stranger in the first place?"

She looked away for a moment. "For Rahiri." She looked back at him, expression serious. "And for your mom. You can see how happy everyone is to have you back."

He shoved a hand through his hair and let out a bitter laugh. "So you have every reason to marry me except... me."

Her cheeks darkened. "I'd have been proud to have you as my husband."

AJ shook his head. "Proud. I'm not sure that's entirely the sentiment I'd hope for in my wife, but it's an interesting one."

Lani swallowed, obviously embarrassed by her unsatisfactory response. "I am attracted to you." Her shy whisper made a chuckle rise in his throat, and sent a jolt of lust to his groin.

"I'm grateful for that, at least." He cocked his head. "I wouldn't want to marry a woman who finds me repugnant." He crossed his arms, trying to not be seduced by the rather dazed expression on her too-beautiful face. "So you were prepared to put up with me for the sake of Rahiri."

She shrugged, and for the first time a sparkle of humor lit her eyes. "I figured I could handle it."

"Your willingness to do your patriotic duty is impressive." He couldn't stop a smile hovering at the corners of his mouth. Then he remembered she'd intended to pretend her child was his. Her traditional dress concealed her shape. "How far along are you?"

Her face tightened. "Almost two months."

"You conceived right before Vanu disappeared?"

She nodded. "That's why I didn't know I was pregnant. When I felt ill, or tired, I just thought it was stress."

"Vanu never knew about the baby."

"No." She held his gaze a little too boldly, as if she expected him to read something into that.

He wasn't sure what to think. They'd been married for nearly five years, so why did she only become pregnant now? It was odd, unsettling. Too…convenient, somehow. "No one would have ever known it wasn't my baby if you hadn't told me."

"I would have known." Something glittered in her eyes. Determination, perhaps, or some of that steely strength hidden under her pretty exterior. Desire rose again inside him, a simmering flash of heat that warred with his anger at the deception.

"I appreciate your honesty." He hesitated, thoughts weaving themselves in his brain even as warmth rose through his body. When he'd stated his intent to become king, he'd meant it. Tradition and honor now pumped through his heart along with his red blood cells. Suddenly it had seemed as if his whole life had led up to this night, when he assumed the responsibilities of leadership. He'd marshaled casts of hundreds, managed budgets and planned for contingencies. He knew how to deal with crises and manage difficult people and situations. The result, so far, had been about ninety minutes of entertainment for anyone who cared to watch, but as king of Rahiri he'd have the power to shape lives through investment in education and infrastructure.

Lani wasn't the only reason he'd decided to stay. And now she wouldn't be the reason he'd leave. "Maybe your little revelation doesn't have to ruin everything."

She blinked. "No?"

"Don't play the innocent, now." He laughed. "You know what I mean. We could still get married."

Her cheeks reddened. "Even now that you know?"

"It's a baby." He shrugged. He could raise a child. What did it matter if it was his biological child or not? He'd never given much thought to family life, but the prospect held some appeal.

And he couldn't deny that Lani held considerable appeal, too. Brave as well as beautiful, she'd risked everything to tell him the truth. Surely he could take a risk on a woman like that if it meant fulfilling the role everyone seemed so desperate for him to take on.

"I'm excited about having a baby." Her face brightened. "I've been longing for one for years. It's like a dream come true…" Her lips faltered. "Just at the wrong time."

He wanted to ask why it had taken so long to conceive, but he held his tongue. Instead he said, "I'm not afraid of raising my brother's baby."

A dark shard of worry sliced into his mind. What if Vanu's baby was like Vanu? He fought off the nasty thought.

AJ flexed the muscles in his back. They suddenly felt tight, maybe under the weight of so many expectations. "So the child would never know?"

"Things could get complicated because of royal succession."

"I suppose we could tell him when he came of age, but I can see how it makes more sense to keep it quiet. When we decide it's time for him to become king, I can quietly step aside."

"Yes, then there's no real need for him or anyone else to know."

"And he won't be traumatized by finding out as an

adult. It does make more sense." AJ rubbed his temples, which throbbed slightly. In one evening he'd decided to change his whole life and embrace a new one—now suddenly he'd taken on fatherhood, too. A curse fell from his lips.

"What?" Lani looked alarmed.

"I'm suddenly on the brink of being a father, and I never even got to enjoy your naked body. That seems a real shame."

Lani blushed. "Sorry I ruined everything."

"You did the right thing. There'll be plenty of time to catch up later—with no tears, I hope." He paused and studied her face. "If we do get married, that is."

Doubt still swirled in his mind and heart. Everything had happened so quickly, and with such deadly finality. Each decision he made seemed a matter of life and death.

"I'm not going to pressure you into anything." Lani spoke softly, gazing off to one side. "I never wanted to. It's your decision, and now you have all the facts."

AJ took in a deep breath and straightened his shoulders. "I committed myself to Rahiri tonight, and to you, and I stand by my decision." Conviction filled his heart. "Your courage in choosing to tell the truth gives me every reason to trust you as my wife."

Lani blinked, obviously embarrassed by his words. Her cheeks still shone like roses.

"But you really are far too beautiful for your own good." He managed a snarl as he said it.

Lani shrugged and shot him a wry smile. "That's what my aunt Freda used to say. She said girls like me end up in trouble."

"And you did." She looked startled, eyes suddenly wider. "By joining the Rahiian royal family, I mean.

Life in the palace isn't all eating bonbons and being fanned by faithful servants."

"No, there are the big parties, the long banquets. It's exhausting." A smile brightened her eyes for the first time since her revelation.

"Lucky thing we're both young and strong enough to handle it." AJ found his hands once again itching to reach out to her. "Maybe we can make a go of this marriage thing. Heck, we might even enjoy it."

Her eyes shone in the dim light of the bedroom. AJ picked up one of the hands dangling at her side, and pressed its softness between his palms. "The more I get to know you, the more I like you."

She bit her lip. "And I like you, too. That's why I couldn't lie to you."

He frowned. "The big question is whether we can lie to everyone else."

"For some reason that doesn't bother me." Lani's smooth brow furrowed slightly. "It's no one else's business where our child comes from. It's between you and me that the truth is important."

AJ stared at her. "You know, that makes perfect sense. If we're married, it's *our* child. Vanu's gone and he's not coming back, so he's not being cheated out of anything. We'll raise the baby as ours, with all the love and affection we'd shower on any child we have."

Lani's hand stiffened. She bit her lip, then peered into his eyes. "I just had a thought. What if we do have more children and you find yourself wanting the oldest child that really is yours to inherit the throne instead? Things could get complicated."

AJ stared at her for a moment, trying to understand her dilemma, then he laughed. "I'm not an Egyptian pharoah with a desire to dominate the world. I will certainly not start interfering in matters of succession other than by bowing out for the next person to take over."

Lani's smile returned. "I had to ask, but I believe you. You don't seem like that type."

Though Vanu would have been. The unpleasant thought pierced the warm mist of happiness that had drifted back into the room.

AJ picked up Lani's hand and kissed it, trying to dispel the image of Vanu that hovered suddenly in his consciousness. Would his cruel older brother haunt him for the rest of his days as he raised his child?

Lani's hands, so soft and scented like lilies, filled his senses. She sighed as he pressed his lips to them.

No. Vanu could not cast darkness over his life from beyond the grave. He was dead and gone, in the past, and AJ would let him stay there. He and Lani would make a bright future for themselves and their child.

He lowered her hands and looked into her eyes. Mysteries glistened in their golden depths. He didn't know where this marriage would lead them, but the adventure invited him to climb aboard. He kissed her softly, his lips just brushing hers.

Lani tilted her chin, pressing her mouth to his as her lashes lowered. AJ wound his arms around her slim back, holding her close. Tension fled his muscles as he let himself sink into her softness. She sighed and writhed gently against him, her passion natural and soft, not like earlier when she'd seemed—desperate.

He let his fingers roam lower, to cup her firm backside and caress her long, elegant thighs. Fantasies of having those thighs wrapped around him heated his blood. Lani's fingers dived into his hair and slid under his collar, making his skin hum with arousal. He could feel her nipples tighten under her dress, and he knew she was aroused, too.

His fingers prickled with the desire to peel off her silk gown and bare her golden skin, but a powerful instinct deep in his gut told him to wait. He pulled back a few inches and smoothed her dress. Her belly quivered slightly beneath his touch.

Lani was recently widowed, pregnant and obviously alarmed and confused by the strange dilemma she'd found herself in. This evening's events were enough to give anyone whiplash, and he didn't want to rush headlong into steamy sex— Well, he did, but that would only make the situation even more explosive and unpredictable.

He needed to be strong for both of them. "I'll sleep here in your bed tonight." She blinked at him, those golden eyes still wary. "But we won't make love."

Her cheeks flushed. Relief or disappointment? It didn't matter. Or maybe it was the word *love*—so strange and inappropriate under the forced circumstances that pushed them together.

When he made love to Lani for the first time it would be right. He had the rest of his life to enjoy his bride, and for tonight he'd put her needs before his own.

"You sleep on this side." He pulled back the covers. She climbed in, still in her dress. "And I'll sleep on the other."

Six

Lani managed a few hours of fitful sleep. It was hard to relax when your life kept changing so drastically from minute to minute, let alone next to a man who stirred your senses and scrambled your thoughts. AJ had gone to the gym early, as usual, and she showered and changed in her own room, with growing anxiety. Her mother-in-law had no idea she'd told AJ about the baby, or that the revelation had almost sent him packing and she didn't relish telling her.

At the breakfast table, Priia beamed, half-hidden behind a stack of newspapers from around the region. "Front-page story in every one!"

Lani glanced at the *Aipu Clarion*. The story directly beneath the announcement of Rahiri's new king declared that a newborn goat on a neighboring island had shown evidence of magic powers. "Are we on the front of the *New York Times?*"

Priia waved her hand dismissively, which caused her gold bracelets to jangle. "They probably haven't even woken up yet. Besides, those big papers prefer bad news to happy news like ours." She leaned in, eyes wide. "How are you feeling?"

"Fine." Lani spooned some pineapple onto her plate.

"Not too exhausted after last night?" She winked her mascara-encrusted lashes.

Lani gulped and lowered her voice to a whisper. "I told AJ about the baby."

"What?" Priia's shriek pierced the air. She spun around and looked relieved that no servants were nearby. She grasped Lani's hand. "Why?"

"It was too big a thing to lie to my future husband about." She sat close to Priia. "He was shocked at first, but glad that I'd told him."

Manicured fingernails dug into her skin. "He's still willing to go ahead with the marriage?"

Lani nodded. "He seemed okay with it after we talked."

Priia let out a huge sigh and released her grip on Lani's wrist. "Thank heavens! Oh, my goodness. You were brave. Or crazy, I'm not sure which." She fluffed her hair. "Of course, I'm not surprised that he was still willing to do the right thing."

Tension cramped Lani's muscles. Everything was so complicated. "He's agreed to keep the baby's parentage quiet so that he can become king."

"Perfect." Priia rose to her feet. "Better than I could have hoped for. You truly are a gift, my dear." She kissed Lani's cheeks and swept from the room.

Lani was eating a piece of melon when AJ walked in, a guarded expression on his face. "I'm not sure if I had a night of violent and colorful dreams or if I made a lot of very bold promises last night."

"The evidence is in the papers." She pointed to the stack. "If it's on the covers of *The Napau Inquirer*, then it must be true." The cover photo of them both, snapped right after his announcement, showed the look of surprise and terror on her face. Hopefully people would take it for delight.

AJ raised a brow, then frowned. "*King AJ*. It doesn't really roll off the tongue, does it?"

She laughed. "I don't know why not. Half the names in Rahiri are barely pronounceable. And as king, you get to make the rules, anyway."

"There's a comforting thought."

A waiter whisked in with AJ's favorite breakfast— two slices of French toast with crispy bacon—and another stack of papers.

AJ grabbed a magazine off the top. "Made *The Hollywood Reporter*. 'Dragon Chaser Helmer Catches a Crown.' Makes it sound a bit like a Frisbee, doesn't it?" he said as he sank into a chair. "Oddly enough, the crown's sitting pretty easy on my head this morning." He tilted his head and peered at her with those seductive dark eyes. "That may have to do with the lovely lady that comes along with it."

She felt her face heat as a smile crept across her face. At least they hadn't actually made love last night. That would have definitely been too much too soon. Her attraction to him was alarming under the circumstances.

AJ's phone rang. "Ugh, not again. I've been besieged by phone calls since before dawn. Mostly from people who work with me. They're all afraid they'll be out of a job."

He took the call, reassuring someone that he had every intention of completing his next movie, but he couldn't talk details right now.

Lani poured him some tea and waited until he put the phone away. "Tell them they'll just have to move to Rahiri."

"Yeah. Maybe I'll open a studio here, get all those bigwig execs to fly to me rather than the other way around."

"Your mom's always trying to pump the tourism industry here."

"What tourism industry?"

"True, but maybe this is Rahiri's big chance to finally land on the world map. Direct flights from London and Paris, five-star hotels, celebrity guests." She winked.

"Don't get her started, I beg you." AJ leaned back in his chair. "One thing at a time. The possibilities do seem pretty limitless right now, though, don't they?"

Media swarmed the palace, first the local TV stations and then the entertainment shows from L.A. and beyond, all intrigued by the Hollywood playboy about to become king.

At first Priia tried to fob them off with bright announcements of her own and warnings that the happy couple were "busy," but by the afternoon, it was obvious that a press conference was in order and they scheduled it for the following morning. Priia suggested Lani wear a pretty, pale-yellow dress with shimmering embroidery. She attempted to deck AJ out in a colorful ceremonial tunic, but he managed to mollify her by wearing an Armani suit.

"What a stunning couple!" she exclaimed. "Of

course they all want pictures, and they must have them."

"I'll bet they're also looking for some dirt to dish," murmured AJ. Lani had tried to ignore the same dark thought. Happy news didn't sell nearly as well as disaster.

"Just hold your chin high and remember the proud history of our island." Priia stroked her tall son's cheek.

"Thanks for the advice, Mom." AJ shot Lani a mischievous glance. Lani had noticed that AJ usually gave his mom lip service, then did whatever he wanted.

"And Lani, if they ask you too much, tell them you're still mourning. Don't let them upset you."

Lani gulped. Hopefully AJ would do most of the talking.

Priia's main assistant put her head around the door. "They're waiting for you on the veranda. I served them tea and coconut stars just as you suggested."

"Wonderful." Priia clapped her hands. "Then they'll all be in a good mood. Come on, my dears. Let's give them a glimpse of Rahiri's gorgeous new royal family."

They stepped out on the veranda, and Lani froze when she saw how many people had gathered. At least fifty, many of them with cameras pressed to their faces. Voices began chattering, reporters reeling off live commentary, as she and AJ took their seats under some very hot, rapidly erected lights.

Microphones thrust toward them. "AJ, how does it feel to marry your brother's wife?"

Lani blanched. AJ leaned back in his chair, confident and relaxed. "I don't know. We're not married yet."

"You're leaving a lot of broken-hearted women

behind in L.A.," quipped one rather flamboyant reporter. "Do you feel you're ready to settle down?"

"Absolutely."

"I can see why," declared a bold female reporter. "Your fiancée is stunning." She pointed her mike right at Lani. "How do you feel about taking a new husband when you've barely had a chance to mourn the first one?"

Lani cleared her throat. "It's traditional."

"But surely, in the twenty-first century, some traditions seem a little barbaric."

AJ grasped her hand firmly. "No one is forcing Lani and me into this marriage. We're both pleased to hold our family together in the way chosen by our ancestors."

"Give us a kiss, then!" coaxed an older male reporter with a British accent.

Lani shrank into her chair. Could they really expect them to put on a show for the cameras?

"Please don't offend my bride's royal dignity." AJ managed a tone that was both formal and jesting. "And give us a chance to get the relationship off the ground at our own speed."

"There must be pressure on you to produce an heir to the throne, since your brother didn't."

Lani gulped. It was hard to resist pointing out there was one on the way already.

"None whatsoever. We're young and strong and will be here for a long time to come." His cheery retort soothed her.

"Lani, is it disturbing to you that Vanu's body has never been found?" A young female reporter thrust a microphone at her.

She stiffened. "I've accepted the fact that it may

never be found. We all searched long and hard for his boat, but found no sign of it. The ocean is deep and keeps many secrets."

She could never let *anyone* know the deadly secret that she was relieved Vanu was gone.

Reporters clustered around the palace all day, hoping to snap a candid shot of the couple. AJ's celebrity status had turned the story into a hot property, and the internet buzzed with speculation and innuendo about the arranged marriage. Once pictures of Lani hit the media, revealing that she was not only royal but also strikingly beautiful, interest only grew.

Lani peeped out behind the closed wooden shutters. "Do you think we'll ever be able to go outside again without being photographed?"

"They'll lose interest eventually." AJ spoke while thumbing a message on his BlackBerry. "Something more dramatic will happen."

"What are you going to do about the movie you're supposed to edit in a couple of weeks?" There were so many things they still hadn't talked about. Did AJ think he could continue his Hollywood career and rule Rahiri at the same time?

"The editor can start work without me. He has the script and storyboard with my notes, and of course we can videoconference. As things progress we'll make new plans. I signed up for the job and I don't shirk a commitment."

"Which is why you're still here." She looked up, suddenly shy. AJ appeared so strong, invincible, even. But how much of this whole experience had he not thought through yet? He was obviously trying hard to do the right thing. But what if he wasn't ready to give up the thrills and excitement of his life in L.A.?

She couldn't help thinking about those "broken-hearted" beauties he'd left behind. Who was he texting? Already a little thread of jealousy twisted inside her. She rose to her feet and paced along the wall of shuttered windows.

AJ looked up. "I'm restless, too. Let's go out for a walk."

"With the entire press corps following us?"

He rose to his feet, tall and handsome in a white shirt and loose linen pants. "We'll ditch 'em." He winked at her. "Follow me."

He took her hand and led her along the corridors toward the east wing. "Aren't we heading right for them?"

"Yes, but they won't see us." He opened a door that she'd always assumed was some kind of closet, and stepped into the darkness. Her hand tingled in his as she stepped in after him. "Look out, there are some stairs." She followed him down, her heart pounding louder as they went farther down the strange staircase.

"Is there a light?" she whispered, wondering when the staircase would end.

"I don't think so." He squeezed her hand. "But we're nearly there."

"Where?"

AJ chuckled. "Nowhere."

The stairs ended, and stone clapped against the bottoms of her sandals. "What is this place?" Tiny points of light overhead—like cracks in the ceiling—illuminated a large room. The temperature was cool, a good twenty degrees lower than the midday warmth of the palace.

"Your guess is as good as mine. No one's used it in years. Vanu and I used to sneak out of the palace this way."

Cold fear trickled through her and she glanced over her shoulder. She could easily picture Vanu haunting a dim, subterranean space like this.

If he was even dead. The reporter's question from earlier nagged at her brain. Yes, it did unsettle her that they hadn't found a body. How could it not? Sometimes it seemed he was everywhere, his cold, wheedling voice in her head, criticizing everything she did.

She squeezed AJ's strong, warm hand. "Where does it bring you out?"

"You won't believe me if I tell you." Their shoes clicked along over the stone tiles as they headed farther and farther from the palace. The room narrowed again into a passageway, and Lani was alarmed by a roaring sound that grew louder as they walked.

She glanced up at AJ and saw his amused grin in the scant light from above. The thin strands of light became fainter until the corridor was almost pitch-black and the roar overhead boomed like the New York City subway. If AJ wasn't boldly leading the way, she'd have turned and run back to the palace long ago. They rounded a corner and a shaft of golden light broke through the chink between two doors. AJ pushed the doors open and led them out into blinding sun.

As her eyes adjusted, Lani realized the roar of sound was the crashing of a waterfall. They now stood directly behind the flow of water as it cascaded down the hillside.

Lani stared at the wall of water. Tiny droplets splashed her face and arms. "It's beautiful." She had to shout to make herself heard. "I've only ever seen it from above."

"Let's go somewhere quieter," murmured AJ in her ear. His hot breath on her skin made her shiver. Still holding her hand, he led her along a ledge of rock only a foot wide, then down a vine-covered hillside. The quiet rustle of the forest gradually replaced the rush of water over rock.

"Now I can breathe." AJ stretched and turned his face to the sun, which shone down through the trees. "I don't like living in a fishbowl."

"I'd think you'd be used to it, living in L.A."

"There you expect it when you're out and about, but they don't follow me home. I'm not that interesting." He grinned.

"You're apparently interesting enough to justify big travel budgets for all those journalists."

"It's not every day a B-movie director becomes king." He lifted his hand and stroked her cheek. The soft touch of his thumb made her shiver with pleasure. "And marries his brother's wife."

She tensed at his words. "And they don't even know about the baby. That would be quite a story."

"One more reason to keep it our secret. Everyone should be allowed some secrets." His fingers trailed down her back and his face hovered close. The scent of his skin, masculine and seductive, filled her senses. His lips met hers slowly, a soft collision, then they melted together.

Heat flooded through her as the kiss deepened. Her hands fisted in the soft cotton of AJ's shirt. She probably shouldn't be feeling desire, given the strange circumstances, but it pounded through her like a drum. Maybe all the years of pent-up longing, all the rejections and slights and hurts of her first marriage, had left her with a deep hunger.

She pressed herself against AJ, feeling her body mold to his hard chest. He groaned and his hands roamed down to cup her backside. He grew hard against her as arousal leaped between them like electric current.

"I am very attracted to you," she whispered when their lips pulled apart.

AJ laughed. "I can tell." He pressed another kiss to her moist lips. "And I like it when you're really hot for me, not just trying to push me into bed to carry out a complicated plan."

Lani blushed. "I'm so sorry."

"Don't be. This is making up for it." Her nipple thickened under his palm. "Come a bit farther into the jungle. If things haven't changed too much, there's a peaceful spot I remember."

He led her through a semi-tangle of vines and spiky palms until they reached a huge fig tree. Its enormous violin-shaped leaves shaded out the hot sun; underneath them grew a lush carpet of soft moss dotted with tiny white flowers. AJ gestured for her to sit down.

She lowered herself onto the cushioned surface and AJ joined her. "What a perfect place." Gnarled branches curved over them like protective arms.

"I used to sneak off and come here. I'd sit up in the tree, tucked away behind the leaves. No one ever found my hiding place." He nibbled her earlobe softly. Lani almost jumped at the sensation of his hot breath on her ear. "But I think I've found a hot spot on you."

She giggled. Then gasped when he did it again. Little flashes of sensation darted through her body. "How did you do that?"

"You mean this?" He trailed the tip of his tongue

along her neck, just below her ear. She shuddered at the sudden surge of heat deep in her belly.

"That, too," she breathed. "What's going on?"

A grin spread across AJ's sensual mouth. "It's called arousal." His brow furrowed. "This is new to you?"

"Completely." She'd never known anything like the pulsing heat that pounded in unexpected parts of her. He must be surprised that a married woman would be so…ignorant. "It wasn't like that before. It was very… official." She swallowed. What an odd way to describe her own sex life. Still, better than the truth—that it was virtually nonexistent and that "perfunctory" might be a better description. Vanu had never spent a single second touching her body just for pleasure.

Her train of thought went off the rails as AJ's hot mouth tracked down her neck. She writhed against him, enjoying the strange feelings that trickled right to her toes. He'd unbuttoned the back of her dress and now slid his hands inside it. When his fingertips touched her belly, her muscles contracted, making her buck against him.

"You're very sensitive." His deep chuckle rumbled against her skin. "Very responsive." Still behind her, he pushed her dress over her shoulders and it fell to her hips. He plucked at the thick embroidered sash that wrapped around her waist as part of the ceremonial dress for the press shoot—and served to hide her pregnancy. The silken folds pulled away and her dress fell about her thighs.

"How thoughtful of you to bring a blanket," murmured AJ. He spread the pretty blue and yellow cloth on the soft moss in front of them. "Our national dress does have its benefits. And here I was thinking it outdated and silly."

Lani laughed. "I guess the ancestors knew more than we realize." She lay on the silky fabric, stretching herself out in the dappled shade of the tree. Oddly, she didn't feel at all self-conscious, or even particularly naked. There was something accepting and easy about AJ that made her feel comfortable with him.

If she could be considered "comfortable" with so many different sensations and emotions pulsing and leaping through her body.

AJ's fingertips trailed along the inside of her thigh, stirring little rivulets of excitement beneath her skin. She let out a ragged sigh, which AJ met with a mischievous grin.

Suddenly she wanted to feel his body with her fingers. She unbuttoned his shirt and slid her hand inside. His skin was hot, the muscle hard and unyielding. She dragged her fingernails gently over his chest, down toward his waist. AJ flinched, his eyes half-closed, as she drew near the button on his pants. A smile crept across her mouth as she saw the evidence of his arousal pressing against his zipper. She let her fingers wander lower until her knuckles brushed his erection.

Judging from his languorous smile, AJ enjoyed her attentions. Encouraged by his sultry stare, she unbuttoned and unzipped his pants. They stripped off his clothes and underwear together, until they both lay naked on the embroidered blanket of Lani's colorful sash.

Shimmering droplets of sunlight snuck through the canopy to paint warm patterns on their skin. The peculiar fragrance of the jungle—thick, rich and almost honeyed—mingled with AJ's raw, masculine scent to create an intoxicating cocktail of arousal.

His thickly muscled body was a feast for the eyes. Lani eased herself closer to him until their chests bumped gently, then she let her fingers caress the rough skin of his thighs and the flat expanse of his belly. A mix of excitement, exhilaration and embarrassment stung her fingertips every time she drew near his erection. When at last she plucked up the courage to touch him, and to enjoy the feel of all that rigid passion in her hand, she almost cried out with relief.

Her fingertips vibrated with excitement as she let them explore the long, hard shape, and she drew in a long breath. She'd never actually touched that body part before. Vanu would never have given her the chance to play with him.

AJ leaned in and whispered, "I'm not even inside you yet and you're already breathless."

"Look who's talking," she teased. He jumped and jerked under her touch, muscles flexing as she caressed his skin. Desire rolled between them like a jungle mist, licking their skin and heating their blood.

On the one hand, Lani craved the feeling of him inside her. On the other, she loved the anticipation, the tension of the wait. She stroked his inner thigh with her forefinger and enjoyed the ragged groan that slipped from his chest. "You're killing me."

"But softly," she whispered, breathing her words into the hot skin of his neck before nibbling his ear the way he'd done with hers. His tortured response only heightened her pleasure. His skin tasted salty and delicious, and she let her tongue explore the chiseled line of his jaw, then probe between his lips.

Their kiss grew deep as they pressed their bodies together. AJ's hardness jutted into Lani's side and for a second she felt a twinge of apprehension. He was so...

big. So unlike Vanu. What if she couldn't handle him? What if it hurt?

"What is going through your mind?"

She cracked open her eyes to find AJ's fixed on her. An expression of amusement brightened his face.

"Uh, nothing."

"That's what I'd hoped for, but expressions keep fluttering across your face like a flock of birds."

"I guess I'm just nervous." She bit her lip. "I'm not… experienced. I don't want to let you down."

"Let me down?" AJ laughed. "About the only way you could do that is by standing up and getting dressed. Now stop worrying." He feigned a stern frown. "In fact, I'm going to do my best to wipe all thoughts from your mind."

In an instant his mouth was between her legs. Lani gasped with shock as he sucked—quite hard— and caused her body to jerk as a sweet, sharp thrill ricocheted through her. He flicked his tongue back and forth over her sensitive spot, which made her muscles convulse and twitch in a way that was downright alarming. She writhed on the soft fabric of her sash, grasping first at the silky fabric and the ground beneath, then at AJ's head and shoulders as he drove her further and further into a mysterious world of intense sensation and shocking pleasure.

She cried out as a fierce ripple of sensation jolted her. Waves of heat rolled through her, emerging from her mouth as moans. She realized her fingers were fisted in his thick hair, and she pulled them loose, then groped for him as another alarming tidal wave surged through her.

AJ's hands roamed over her, stroking her waist and breasts as he rose up to meet her. Her eyes opened to see his dark gaze blazing just over hers. "Much better." His wicked grin only stirred the fevered passion pounding through her.

"Enter me, please." She craved him inside her, ached for him.

He chuckled. "You make yourself sound like Aladdin's cave." His words rasped hotly at her neck as he lowered himself over her. "I can't wait to come in, but I don't know the magic word."

Quivering with excitement, Lani lifted herself to meet him. "Please."

"That's an easy one to remember." He layered hot kisses on her face and neck. "Please may I come in?"

"Yes, yes," Lani gasped, almost shouting at the way he tortured her. She tilted her hips to him, begging with her body. She could feel his heartbeat through his skin, strong and insistent, like her own. His musky, male scent only added to her torment. She could tell he was every bit as aroused as she. Was he going to torture her forever?

He entered her very, very slowly. First with his fingers, probing her slick depths. When he decided she was ready—and oh, was she ready—he probed her with the tip of his member. A tiny cry fled her lips as anticipation got the better of her.

She pushed her fingers into his back, unconsciously urging him on. Warmth and pleasure filled her as he slid inside her and his chest lowered over hers. His throaty moan filled her ear as he started to move. She arched against him, taking him deeper, welcoming him into her body and into her life.

I love you. She got an urge to say it, but something held her back.

It was too soon for love; the circumstances were

too strange and pressured. She didn't want to seem too demanding, as if she expected him to love her back.

And maybe it was just sheer madness, the delicious thrills cascading through her as AJ moved inside her.

AJ pulled her upright until they were in a sitting position, legs interlaced, facing each other, with him still buried deep. A perfect position for kissing.

AJ licked her lips, and she returned the gesture, tasting his smile, then enjoying the slight roughness of his cheeks. She could feel him inside her, slight movements, subtle throbs, letting her feel his arousal and the deep connection between them.

When kissing—and barely moving—threatened to drive her completely over the edge, AJ lay back until she was sitting on top of him. Alarm flashed through her. She was supposed to be in control, and she had no idea what to do.

"Anything," he murmured, as if in answer to her question. "Whatever feels good."

She trailed her finger along the middle of his chest, eyes half-open to enjoy the view. She wriggled a little, and felt him move inside her. A smile spread across her face and his at the same time. "This definitely feels good."

Eyes closed again, she gently rocked back and forth, amazed at the new points of pleasure this position awakened. She found herself moving faster and higher, experimenting with rhythms to take herself right to the next peak, and then pulling back. Beneath her, AJ groaned, his hands stroking her skin, teasing her.

"Let go," AJ urged her.

Could she? Something inside her kept holding her back. She'd never experienced this kind of arousal before. She could tell she was close to the brink of something big, and it scared her.

"It'll feel good, I promise." AJ's soft voice penetrated her thoughts.

Living at the palace she'd grown used to being "on duty" all the time. Always polite and prepared and ready for anything—even the worst Vanu could dish out. "Letting go" was no longer in her vocabulary. She had been too busy shoring herself up.

A bird chirped overhead and a warm breeze caressed her skin. She'd almost forgotten they were deep in the jungle. Apparently she'd let go quite a lot already!

She quickened the pace, and AJ encouraged her with his roving hands. Hot spots of excitement seemed to become even more sensitive and the tension inside her built and grew until she felt white-hot all over.

Something in her brain told her to slow down, but her body urged her to keep going—and she obeyed, moving with more and more urgency until suddenly everything seemed to explode into a million pieces, showering stars down over them where they lay on the jungle floor.

She collapsed onto the solid expanse of AJ's chest. His breathing labored, he wrapped his arms around her and held her in his soft embrace while the shower of stars gradually drifted down and settled around them, leaving her tingling and warm in all sorts of unexpected places.

"See what I mean?" AJ said after a while.

She nodded, not quite able to form words. She'd never imagined that sex could be like that. Her previous experiences had been so stilted, so fraught with tension, that she honestly hadn't enjoyed them at all—though she'd certainly pretended to. Vanu had made no such pretense.

With AJ everything was completely, utterly and gloriously different. At least she thought it was. "Did you enjoy it, too?" Her voice sounded a little shaky.

AJ's chest rumbled with laughter. "What do you think?" His dark eyes glittered with humor.

"I don't seem to be able to think at all right now."

"Good."

AJ loved the feel of her in his arms. Completely relaxed, Lani sprawled over him like he was a giant mattress. It was intriguing that such a fiery vixen lived beneath that placid exterior. Well, he might have guessed, after the way she practically kissed his face off that first time.

"What are you laughing about?" Her voice tinkled in his ear. She sounded happy, which filled him with joy.

"At how my life is filled with surprises. In a good way." He stroked her hair.

Who'd have ever imagined him planning to settle back in Rahiri? In truth, Vanu had been the reason he'd left. The future king, Vanu had been cherished and encouraged and adored. Intelligent and charming when he wanted to be, he'd wrapped his parents around his long and surprisingly strong fingers.

AJ could remember the cruel grip of those fingers all too well, though often as not Vanu used words with more brutal force. He employed his considerable genius in coming up with ways to make AJ look guilty of something, meaning that AJ was nearly always in trouble, even when he did manage to keep a lid on his admittedly rambunctious nature.

But now Vanu was gone. And with the happy result that he'd left a lovely wife in dire need of a new husband. Vanu must have turned on the charm with Lani. She had probably never gotten a glimpse of his dark side. Why spoil her memories? He decided to keep his to himself.

"Only seven months until our baby arrives." He spoke softly, stroking Lani's cheek.

She started slightly. "It seems so soon."

"Tell me about it." He was still trying to wrap his mind around the idea of being a father. He'd decided that the baby would be his in every way. Well, every way that mattered, and that's how he intended to approach the situation. "Do you have a nickname for him or her already? One of my producers used to call hers Jellybean while she was pregnant."

Lani laughed. "I don't. I guess I should come up with something." She gazed skyward for a minute, her golden eyes thoughtful. "Puaiti."

"Little flower. But what if it's a boy?"

"Why can't a boy be a flower, too?" She raised a slim brow.

"Good point. Why should girls get all the nice-smelling pretty stuff? How's little Puaiti feeling?"

Lani closed her eyes for a minute and rested her fingers on her stomach, as if listening. "I'm not hearing any complaints."

"Do you feel any kicking yet?"

"No. I don't think that happens for a few more weeks. I don't really feel different at all. Well, except when I feel ill." She paused and looked right at him. "You know something? Ever since I told you about the baby, I haven't felt ill at all."

"Maybe Puaiti realized she'd have to make you sick or you wouldn't realize she was there."

"Quite possible. And she'd have been right." She frowned. "But why are you calling Puaiti a she? She could be a he."

He shrugged. "We'll just have to use both."

"Would you like to find out the gender before the birth?"

AJ stroked Lani's cheek. "I don't know that I would. I'm getting used to being surprised, and I find I like it. Do you have a preference for a girl or boy?"

Lani shook her head. A sweet smile played about her lips. "Either will be wonderful. I've wanted a child for so long, and your mom is going to love having a grandchild to spoil."

A crashing sound in the undergrowth nearby made them sit up. "What was that?" AJ peered through the leaves. He'd been gone a long time, but he didn't remember any forest animals big enough to make that much sound.

"I don't know." Lani grabbed her dress. "We'd better get dressed."

AJ tugged his shirt and pants on, then helped rewind Lani's rather wrinkled sash around her still-slim waist. He continued to hear a rustling sound in the distance.

"Was that a voice?" whispered Lani, eyes wide with alarm.

AJ strained his ears. It was hard to distinguish sounds above the low hum of the jungle, all the insects and birds and the rustling leaves. Then again, he did hear a voice. "It's a man. Speaking English." Why would someone be way out here? "Maybe the journalists have started wandering about looking for scandal."

"If they find us they might well have it." Lani smoothed her dress with anxious fingers. "We're not married yet."

"We'd better head back to the passageway." He took Lani's hand and led her back up toward the waterfall. He didn't want her being harassed by some bozo out for a picture and quick buck.

They set off up a steep hill. At the top, he heard the voice again, and turned to peer through the trees. It was impossible to see anyone through the dense leaf canopy, but then he heard quite clearly: "They say he went out late at night on a boat."

AJ froze. The were talking about Vanu. Could they be looking for the body?

Lani didn't seem to have heard. She was distracted, adjusting her sandal.

"But what if he didn't get on a boat? What if he came out here and got lost?"

An icy finger of dread slid down AJ's back. He didn't want Lani to get wind of their idle speculation. "Are you okay?"

"Great." She smiled brightly. He led her farther up the hill until the roar of water cloaked out all other sounds. Still, an odd sense of unease nagged at him. Suddenly all these curious strangers were trudging through their jungles and making footprints on the beaches. What if they did find something?

And what if it was something none of them expected at all?

Seven

"Thank heavens you're back!" Priia stood up from the plush armchair surrounded by her embroidery tools. Servants had whisked AJ and Lani to her study as soon as they'd been spotted back in the palace hallways. The servants slipped out, closing the door behind them.

AJ's heart thumped. Something was wrong but no one would tell him what. "What's going on?"

"We just got a phone call that a reporter found Vanu's boat."

Lani froze. "Where is it?"

Priia dabbed at her eyes with an already moist handkerchief. "On the tiny atoll to the northwest. The one they call Egg Island."

AJ shoved a hand through his hair. "Did they find Vanu?"

His mom shook her head. "So far there's been no sign of him."

AJ shot a glance at Lani. Her hands were trembling and one of them flew to her mouth.

"So he could be alive." AJ managed to force out the words.

"Yes. It's possible." Priia sniffed. "The atoll is small but very densely wooded. There's plenty of food there for someone to survive."

Dread crawled over AJ like a poisonous spider. Could Vanu be hidden somewhere in the forest?

Lani had begun to weep. Probably with joy that her once-dead husband might still be alive. AJ sucked in a ragged breath as a bitter taste filled his mouth. "We need to send out a search party."

"They're getting ready to leave. The fire department and the lifeboat service are all involved. And of course the journalists." She pressed her handkerchief to her face. "It seems too much to hope for, but maybe he's about to come back to us."

Lani approached Priia and put her arms around her. AJ's heart swelled at her generous gesture. Caring and thoughtful as well as lovely, Lani was far too good to be wasted on Vanu. Anger roiled in his chest along with savage jealously. Could Vanu return from the grave and snatch Lani from his arms?

Yes. That was exactly the kind of party trick Vanu would take great pleasure in.

"Didn't they search Egg Island when he disappeared?" He couldn't understand how Vanu's boat could appear like a horrible vision after all this time.

Priia looked up. "It's a dense forest, with many natural caves. The boat had drifted into a cavern that's hidden at high tide." She let out a sob. "It will be hard to find him if he's still alive, but we must keep positive."

A knock on the door startled them all. "Come in," said Priia, shakily.

The head footman entered, head slightly bowed. "The reporters, they're anxious for a statement."

"Oh, goodness." Priia waved her handkerchief. "AJ, could you go tell them something?"

"Like what? We don't know any more than they do. Less, probably."

The head footman seemed to shrink a bit, and stared at the floor. "They want to know how this affects the wedding plans."

Lani let out a little gasp, then hid her face.

The dark reality of the situation settled over AJ like an executioner's hood. "It's off. Lani can't consider remarrying while her husband might be alive." His words came out cold and hard.

And what about the baby he'd grown to think of as his? Vanu would claim the child as well. It was his, after all, just like Lani.

AJ suppressed a curse. Only a brief while ago he and Lani had lain, wrapped in each other, surrounded by the warm embrace of the jungle, looking forward to a joyous future together with their new family.

Now he saw that future evaporating like a jungle mist.

"Did they find any signs that he survived?" AJ questioned the footman.

"They found footprints leading up out of the cave. So it seems he did walk away from it."

Lani whimpered and tears rolled down her cheeks. AJ tried to suppress the ugly surge of anger that rose in him at the sight. She was obviously distressed and hopeful that Vanu was still alive.

Yes, it hurt. Especially since he'd felt a deep connection with her during their lovemaking. Of course that was probably his body talking rather than his brain. "I'll go join the search party. Just stay away from the press until we know more." He turned and marched from the room, unable to even look at Lani.

AJ cursed himself for being drawn into this nightmare. How had he gone from wanting to leave at the earliest opportunity to hating the fact that he'd *have* to leave?

He returned late at night, sticky and tired from combing through the jungle. It probably hadn't done his soul much good that he was hoping against hope that they'd find a body, not a live Vanu with an ugly smirk on his face. As it turned out, they'd found nothing at all and the search was scheduled to resume the following morning.

No one spoke much at dinner, and Priia retired early, begging a headache.

Lani seemed very tense, avoiding his gaze. No doubt she felt guilty that she'd made love to another man while her husband might still be alive.

"It's not your fault," he murmured. "You had no idea he might still be out there."

"I know." She didn't meet his gaze. "No one could have known."

"The fire chief thinks he's alive." He studied her face. A muscle spasmed in her cheek. "They found traces of a fire in another natural cave. Looks like someone stayed there."

"That's wonderful." Lani's voice sounded oddly hollow. "It would be such a miracle for him to survive for so long by himself."

"He never was the rugged, outdoors type." AJ frowned.

It was hard to imagine Vanu picking a berry to feed himself, let alone lighting a fire. He'd required a large staff just to get dressed in the morning. "But I suppose anything is possible. People can act differently in a life-or-death situation."

"Yes." Lani sat ramrod straight. Unapproachable. Not that he'd even think of trying to touch her now. How odd, when he'd enjoyed touching almost every inch of her luscious body only hours earlier.

His life seemed to be spinning like a weather vane in the wind lately. He'd had calls from L.A. this afternoon asking if—due to the shift in circumstance—he'd be back to oversee the edits for *Hellcat*. He'd replied honestly: that he had no idea.

The dim light in the dining room picked out the gold threaded through Lani's lustrous hair. Soon, perhaps Vanu would be running his bony fingers through it again. AJ fought a wave of revulsion. "How are you feeling? I'm sure the stress must be hard on you when you're pregnant."

"I'm okay." She shot him a wary glance with those wide, honey-colored eyes.

He cursed the surge of lust that jolted through him. "Must be a little odd to be dangling between two men like this." His words sounded cruel, and maybe that's what he intended. Pain tightened his muscles and hardened his heart.

Lani shuddered and a small sob escaped her mouth. "It's terrible."

AJ's hands itched to reach out and touch hers. But that would only deepen his torment. "No one will ever know what happened between us today. It'll be yet another secret we'll keep forever."

Lani nodded. Tears glittered in her eyes. "Yes. I won't tell anyone. Especially Vanu."

AJ's flesh crawled at the thought of her talking to Vanu again, sharing intimacies. In such a short time he'd developed powerful feelings for Lani. He'd never felt anything like them before in all his years of adventures with the fairer sex.

And the child. His initial revulsion at the deception had quickly transformed into a firm conviction that he could raise this child and love it as his own. He'd been prepared to lie and pretend and carry out a charade to everyone else's fantasy of the perfect royal family come true.

He glanced up and saw Lani's delicate profile turned to look out the window. Just yesterday his bold and tender new feelings had been convenient rather than crazy. Now they were disastrous. He had to comfort and support the woman he craved as she hoped and prayed for the safe return of her husband.

Pain crashed over him in an untidy wave. He staggered to his feet and sucked in a breath of moist night air.

He'd spent his childhood in his brother's shadow, and now it stretched out from the grave to cast him into darkness once again.

Lani didn't love him. Didn't have any feelings for him other than a sense of duty and some rather unexpected lust. He'd been fool enough to mistake that for far more.

He'd never let himself make that mistake again.

Lani paced back and forth in her room all morning. The crews were out for the second day, combing through the jungle on the uninhabited atoll.

She hated the way they described it as "searching for Vanu," as if they'd find him there, perhaps lazing on a sandy beach, waiting for them to take him home. No one said anything as grim as "hoping to recover a body." Priia wouldn't hear any of that. As far as she was concerned, he was alive and well and on his way home.

And Lani knew she was probably cursed to eternal damnation for hoping otherwise.

How could she wish someone dead? Only a truly evil person would have a thought like that. Obviously she wasn't the "nice" girl AJ had originally mistaken her for. She'd certainly jumped on him with reckless abandon, and she couldn't even blame it on "duty" anymore. She'd made no effort to hide her lusty enjoyment of AJ's body.

She blew out hard. Everything had been so perfect for those few brief hours. Now she was back, snared in the web of pretense and pain that had been her marriage to Vanu. Pretending to be happy—or at least content—while inside she was longing for freedom.

A knock on the door startled her.

"Dinner is ready." The shy girl servant darted in and out like a lizard. No one would look her in the eye since Vanu's boat was found. They'd all been so thrilled about the plans for the wedding and AJ's return to Rahiri, and now they were supposed to be overjoyed about Vanu's possible survival.

No one knew what to think or how to behave. Least of all Lani. AJ was giving her the cold shoulder, too. She understood that he was in an awkward situation, but it was upsetting to suddenly feel as if she couldn't talk to him.

She wandered along the hallway slowly, not looking

forward to the meal. Terrified of any further news of Vanu's miraculous survival.

When she arrived in the dining room, she saw Priia sitting in her usual chair, sobbing, while AJ wrapped his arms around her.

All the servants hung their heads and ducked their gazes as she passed.

"They found his body." AJ looked up and mouthed the words softly, then tugged his gaze away immediately.

Relief welled inside her like a flood. "Oh, no," she managed, trying to sound upset. Her hands started shaking and her heart pounded. She wanted to jump up and down or shout because she'd been so afraid of being Vanu's plaything again. Happy tears sprang to her eyes and she let them roll down her cheeks.

She resisted a sharp urge to ask for details to make his death real, but managed to restrain herself. What did it matter how he died, as long as he was really gone for good.

AJ looked up at her tears, then glanced away. Priia's sobbing was merciless, inconsolable, as it had been in those first days and nights after Vanu disappeared.

"I'm so sorry, Mama," whispered Lani. She stroked Priia's hand. "It was too much of a miracle to hope for." Her own tears splashed into her mother-in-law's lap and mingled with Priia's, despite their very different motivations.

"At least we'll have his child," rasped Priia. Lani's eyes widened. Apparently in her grief she was forgetting that no one knew about the pregnancy. She glanced around. The servants had tactfully left the room. Still...

AJ's brow was lowered and his expression dark. He wouldn't meet her gaze.

"The child will give us something to live for," continued Priia, through her sobs. "It does seem cruel that we have to go through mourning him again. I was finally coming to terms with his loss, and now…" Her shoulders shook.

Lani squeezed her hand. "We'll just have to go on as best we can."

"I've got some phone calls to make." AJ's voice was gruff. Lani looked up, startled, as he strode from the room. She wanted to run after him, to ask him for details about Vanu's death—perhaps to reassure herself that this time he really was dead.

She also wanted reassurance that everything was still okay between them.

Her stomach contracted and a wave of nausea rose through her. Her first in several days. She had a grim feeling that everything had changed between her and AJ. That Vanu's unexpected reappearance, even in death, had somehow ruined everything.

AJ stormed along the palace corridor, blood pounding in his brain. How had he ever thought this could work? Had he really believed he could step into Vanu's shoes—precious Vanu, the beloved eldest son who could do no wrong—and take over?

Ridiculous. He must have been totally addled by lust. It was hard to blame himself because, after all, Lani was undeniably one of the most beautiful women on earth. He'd let desire interfere with his common sense and even convinced himself that she had feelings for him.

But of course she hadn't fallen madly in love with

him right after her husband's death. She was still in shock, especially with the pregnancy messing up her hormones. He'd come on way too strong and she'd reacted as she felt she was supposed to. Just trying to be a "nice Rahiian maiden," when all along she was carrying a torch for Vanu.

He shoved into his room. The room he'd spent his childhood in and been glad to leave. Which seemed ungrateful, since not many people would complain about spacious chambers in a royal palace. But they'd felt like a prison to him once, and now the decorative carvings started to look like bars again. He'd almost—almost—been trapped into living someone else's life.

He picked up the phone and pushed the third button on his speed dial. His producer, Jerry. When Jerry answered he didn't mince words. "I'll be back tomorrow. Sooner if I can get a flight."

"But I thought your brother turned up dead."

"He did."

"Sorry, I didn't mean to say that so crudely. I'm sorry for your loss."

"I know. It's okay." Being honest that you were glad someone was dead was one of the last taboos left.

"Doesn't that mean that you need to take over?"

"You can't take over from a living god, and I'm not going to walk in his shadow the rest of my life. I've got a good life in L.A. and I'm coming back to it."

"Isn't there some tradition that you have to marry your brother's wife?" Jerry's tone didn't hide his curiosity—the same kind of prurient interest that had sent the media chasing down to Rahiri to ogle them.

"There was, but I'm breaking with it. Why should she be forced into marrying someone she doesn't care about?" Not to mention giving her late husband's baby to him to raise. His chest tightened.

"That is a bit heavy. Still, you two looked good together on *Entertainment Tonight*."

"Jerry, you and I know better than anyone how easy it is to create an illusion with a camera."

"Too true. Well, if you're ready, we'll soon be right back at it. Give me a call when you hit town and we'll hash through some details."

"Perfect."

AJ put down the phone, a mixture of conviction and regret mingling in his heart. What a vivid fantasy it had been, for a few brief days. King AJ and his lovely family, ruling the island paradise he'd finally come home to.

Way too sappy to put in a movie, so why would he think it could happen in real life?

He jerked open the closet door and grabbed an armful of clothes off the rack. Shoved them right into his suitcase. He didn't need servants to fold and fluff everything for him. He'd gotten along just fine without them for over a decade and he was damned if he'd turn into a spoiled fop like Vanu.

He went into the bathroom and swiped his toiletries off the marble shelf and into a plastic bag. A scan of the room confirmed that he'd removed all traces of his brief presence.

Now to confront Lani.

His chest ached. He'd so much rather have slipped away without seeing her again. Experience had proved he didn't have much self-control around her. Getting to know her hadn't helped, either. Did he really have to find out that she was warm and thoughtful as well as gorgeous? It would have been better if he'd left right after the funeral.

He would have preferred as well not to know how responsive and exciting she was during sex. If that's how she performed with a man she was being forced to marry while still mourning her husband, imagine what she'd be like if she was really in love?

Don't. There was no point in thinking about what-ifs. He was not going to participate in this arranged marriage charade any longer.

He zipped up his suitcase and pulled out the handle. Soon he'd be marching along the corridors at LAX, a free man again.

Finding Lani wasn't easy. He walked all over the palace, asking everyone he met for almost an hour, tension building in his muscles, before he finally tracked her down on a stone bench by a reflecting pool in the garden.

She glanced up, startled, as he approached.

"Don't worry. I'm not staying." He almost growled the words, then regretted his hostile tone. This whole mess wasn't really her fault. She'd been bullied into it, the same way he had.

He glanced at the round pool, where reflected leaves danced across its shimmering surface, hiding its depths from view. "You'll be a good queen until the baby comes of age. The elders are wise and thoughtful and really don't need any help to run the country, though I'm sure they'll welcome new ideas about education and—"

"You're not really leaving." Her eyes widened.

"I really am. Booked on tonight's flight. Back on the course I should have stuck with from day one." Before he'd become intrigued, then utterly seduced, by her.

Her face totally still, she stared at him, apparently lost for words. And why should she have to come up with words? They were all tired of saying things they didn't mean. She that she was thrilled to be marrying a total stranger, he that he was so sad his rotten older brother was dead. Enough with the pretense.

"It'll be hard on Mom. That's the one part I really regret."

Lani blinked. He saw her shoulders stiffen. "Yes. But why are you leaving? Is it because of me?" Her lips tightened.

"It's not because of you." He shoved a hand through his hair. He owed her his honesty after all they'd been through over the last few days. "If anything, you're the reason I almost made the wrong decision to stay. You're a good person, Lani, as well as a very beautiful one. But you're my brother's wife, not mine. I can't step into his life and walk in his footsteps. I have my own life that I made for myself, and that's where I need to be."

"Everyone wants you to stay." Her voice was oddly hollow.

AJ straightened his back. "Everyone? I doubt it. I don't think people pay much more attention to who's in the palace than to who's on *Instant Millionaire* every Wednesday. I'm going to make an announcement to the media so there won't be any guessing and suspense."

"Have you told Priia yet?" Lani twisted her hands into her skirt.

AJ's stomach clenched. "I'm going to tell her now, and I know it won't be easy."

"She'll be devastated."

"I know, but it can't be helped." Better than entering into a marriage with a woman who hadn't chosen him, and who'd never stop being his brother's wife.

Lani looked down at her lap, avoiding his glance. Maybe she resented the fact that he'd decided to put emotion before duty. After all, she'd demonstrated her readiness to sacrifice everything for the good of Rahiri.

He wasn't made of such stern stuff.

And he really did want her to be happy. "I hope the rest of your pregnancy goes smoothly." His voice softened. "And that the birth is uneventful. You'll be able to tell everyone that it's Vanu's baby now. No more living a lie."

Lani swallowed. "Yes. I suppose that's good." Her voice sounded flat. "Things did get awfully complicated."

"Which should have been the first clue we were heading in the wrong direction." His fingers itched to touch her, just one last time. To feel her soft skin beneath his palm and inhale her delicate floral scent.

But he resisted. "Goodbye, Lani."

"Goodbye, AJ." She looked up at last, wide eyes brimming with tears. "Good luck to you. I hope everything works out the way you want it to."

He frowned. "Thanks. And for you and the baby, too. I'm sure I'll be in touch after things settle down a bit."

She nodded, lips pressed together. She hadn't risen from the bench. Just sat there like a lovely statue, fingers twisted into the silk of her dress.

He spun on his heel and marched away before he could do anything stupid.

Lani slumped on the bench as he walked away. She didn't even have the urge to run after him. It seemed normal, natural, that she should be left here alone and loveless while he went back to his life in L.A. Isn't that just what she'd expected, after all?

He'd been swept along on the tide of excitement that they'd mistaken for destiny—all the pomp of the funeral and Priia's festive gathering—and he'd gotten temporarily sidetracked into thinking he'd like to return to Rahiri.

Vanu's unwitting intervention had woken him up.

Trust Vanu to ruin everything.

The reappearance of his boat and the resulting hitch in their plans had given AJ time to realize he didn't want the life Priia had plotted out for him—or her.

It hurt—really hurt.

She pressed her fingers gently into her belly and tried to ignore the hollow space that seemed to be opening up inside her. At least she had the baby to look forward to, and AJ was right, the elders could rule the country without any help from the palace. They'd certainly been doing it while Vanu was king, as he'd taken zero interest in the country's affairs. Rahiri would be fine.

But would she?

It didn't seem fair to taste happiness like that, then have it rudely snatched away.

At first she'd been wary of AJ, and hoped he'd leave. But now that she'd gotten to know him, she wanted desperately for him to stay. He'd looked genuinely excited about raising the baby with her. She'd been so sure that—at last—everything was going to work out for the best. That she'd finally get to be happy.

But that had been too much to hope for.

A few weeks ago she'd have been pleased to be left quietly alone. She hadn't known about the baby then, but she'd at least been relieved to be rid of Vanu. Now she craved the family she'd always wanted as a child.

A mother and father together, as hers had been when she was little, before their marriage broke up and she and her mother came back to Rahiri.

She let out a deep sigh, picked up a small stone and tossed it into the pool. A splash radiated out into huge ripples that filled the round surface and lapped against the walls. AJ's arrival had changed everything, even her dreams.

She no longer wanted to be left quietly alone, merely to live out her days without having to endure cruel treatment from a man she despised. Now she wanted so much more: affection, conversation, humor and, of course, the dangerous and delicious passion that AJ had awakened in her.

But AJ didn't want to share it with her. He'd chosen to return to his life in L.A. and the freedom that came with it. He wouldn't be tied down by responsibilities to a nation, or a woman.

Sadness soaked through her. Probably right now AJ was telling the reporters who never left the palace of his plans to abandon Rahiri—and her. In a short while she'd be paraded in front of them to embrace her new, solitary role as queen, and to announce the pregnancy.

And she'd do it all alone. Not physically alone, with her doting mother-in-law and the palace staff all around her, but in the ways that were important, the empty, hungry places in her heart, she'd be alone.

"We must stop him!" Priia's voice rang out into the garden from the nearby sitting room. "I told him he can't go. It's impossible!"

"We can't stop him," Lani mouthed back in barely a whisper.

Her mother-in-law ran out into the garden and

grabbed her arms. "AJ's heading for the airport." Her long nails cut into Lani's skin. "He can't leave us. We need him."

"I know we want him here." Lani rose and spoke softly. "But he needs to leave and we have to let him."

Priia's eyes were still wide with shock. "I could call the airport and tell them to ground the plane."

Lani shook her head. "You can't keep him here by force. It has to be his choice."

"But he chose to stay. He announced to all of us at the banquet that he…" The first tear rolled from Priia's dark eyes.

You pressured him into it, Lani wanted to say. But she held her tongue. No need to pour salt on Priia's already sore wounds. But this was exactly why it was a bad idea to go after him now. Trying to force the issue hadn't helped at all. He was still leaving, and they were right back where they started.

Which wasn't such a bad place after all.

She drew in a steadying breath. "We'll be fine. The baby will be our next king or queen."

Priia looked up. "The baby, yes! Oh, sweetheart." She drew in a steadying breath. "And now I suppose we can tell people it's Vanu's child."

Lani looked down. "Yes, there's no reason not to."

Her mother-in-law dabbed at her eyes with one of her embroidered handkerchiefs. "It is a blessing having his baby to remember him by. And you can rule in the meantime. It's been a long time since Rahiri had a queen, because usually our people have so many boys ready to…"

Her voice trailed off, then she cleared her throat. "You're right, of course, my dear. We must meet every challenge life throws at us with our heads held high.

Thank the heavens for bringing you into our lives, sweet Lani. I don't know what I'd do without you."

They hugged and Lani did indeed feel a tiny bit reassured. She'd gotten along just fine without AJ around before, and she'd be a-okay without him again.

At least she hoped so.

Eight

AJ had hoped that media coverage of Rahiri would cease now there was no longer a Hollywood director involved. Apparently, though, he was not the main attraction. He'd been back in L.A. two months and stories continued daily on the splashy entertainment shows and in the celebrity press, and blogs buzzed with the latest tidbits and speculations from the palace.

He'd underestimated the hold Lani's beauty would have on the popular imagination. People couldn't seem to get enough of her stunning face, which could not take a bad photo. Her slightly exotic features and unique coloring entranced and intrigued people and made them want to know more about her and her fabulous royal existence.

Which didn't help, because AJ couldn't stop thinking about her, either.

He strode across his foyer and grabbed the newest

pile of mail off the hall table. He'd arranged for his clipping service to send him everything related to the palace, not because he felt personally involved, but so he'd at least know what was going on if someone asked.

He flipped through a thick file of fresh clippings, forcing himself not to linger on any pictures. There was one in particular they seemed to latch on to, a half profile shot that perfectly captured the adorable tilt of her nose and the sparkle in her golden eyes.

He knew what they'd cut out of the photo—him. She'd been gazing at him with that bright look on her face. Now he was the villain of the piece, the one who had let her down to pursue his big-deal career and go back to chasing designer miniskirts in L.A.

They were half-right, really.

But his dropping out of the picture had only seemed to intensify their interest in Lani and her predicament: the lovely princess, so recently widowed and now jilted by her presumed fiancé. Her pregnancy had hit the media like a neutron bomb. Poor lonely Lani, left to raise a child with no one to care for her.

Of course he knew better. She had a staff of nearly fifty and a mother-in-law who rarely gave her a moment's peace.

One story told of the hordes of men who'd submitted details and photos in the hope that she'd choose one of them to be her husband. He was pretty confident the applications were being shredded on arrival at the palace, but he couldn't help feeling a sting of envy.

Which was ridiculous, because eventually Lani would marry someone else.

He turned and strode back into the kitchen. His home used to seem so calm and uncluttered. Lately it just looked bleak. All the black and white furnishings looked garish and pretentious after the soft natural hues and hand-carved woods of the palace.

At least he was busy. Editing sessions on *Hellcat* stretched late into the night and he was already deep in pre-production on the next *Dragon Chaser* movie.

That meant he wouldn't have time to read all the blogs and websites his Google Alerts were picking up about Lani's upcoming coronation. Already he knew exactly what kind of dress she'd be wearing, and the ancient hammered-gold jewelry she'd put on and how her palms would be painted with berry juice and her skin brushed with golden pollen. He didn't know this because he'd grown up in the palace. He'd learned it all on *E!* along with everyone else.

An enterprising retailer in Beverly Hills had come out with a line of Rahiian dresses, woven from the rich silk of the island but cut to reveal a bit more gym-toned leg than the originals.

Twice he'd seen Lani paraded before the cameras with a tight smile on her lips. He could imagine his mom behind the scenes, urging her out there and telling her to put on her best face. But he could see past it. Her mouth might be forced into a cheerful grin, but the light in her eyes had dimmed noticeably.

Or did he imagine that? Maybe he just wanted her to be pale and pining since he'd gone. He'd already told them he wouldn't be there for the coronation. Let them sing Vanu's praises and exclaim over how AJ would never have made a good king, with his Hollywood decadence and fickle attitudes.

He didn't want to see Lani, either. Not so soon. He couldn't guarantee his immunity to her vibrant smile. Just a whiff of her scent might send him into a tailspin.

The taste of her was still too fresh on his lips, the pain of leaving her too raw in his heart.

It was for the best though. He wasn't Vanu and sure as heck didn't want to play second fiddle to his brother's memory for the rest of his life. Much better to move on and strike out for new frontiers.

Speaking of which, an old flame of his had left a message on his machine. A Danish beauty who'd had a small part in one of his early movies was back in town for a couple of weeks and wanted to get together. Probably just what he needed to pry his mind off Lani.

He reached for the phone and listened to the bubbly message again. Why not take her to the premiere of the new Spielberg movie that Friday? She was good company. Loved to dance, too. They could have some dinner, then go out to that new club everyone kept raving about.

But something kept his fingers from dialing her number.

He found himself wandering back into the kitchen, where the stack of clippings lay sprawled on the stone counter, that now-famous picture on the top. Lani's wide eyes, sparkling with what anyone might mistake for happiness, seemed to look right at him, just as they had when the picture was taken.

AJ drew in a deep breath. He'd get over her. Eventually. But until then it wasn't really fair to take out another girl. He'd only be looking at her and wishing he was with Lani.

Better to wait until time took the edge off a bit. Until he started to forget the soft touch of her fingers on his skin, and the sweet song of her laugh.

Of course, it would help if he could stop thinking about her for five solid minutes.

Lani lay awake in her bedroom, staring at the dark ceiling. Counting imaginary sheep didn't help. Counting live lizards didn't help, either. Even the baby seemed restless and unsettled. It was hard to sleep when something was eating at you.

She'd promised herself that she'd never tell anyone the truth about Vanu. That she'd keep up the pretense of a happy marriage and allow her mother-in-law to remember her eldest son as a paragon of virtue.

But something AJ had said made her think it was her silence on the subject that had driven him away. That he thought of her as Vanu's wife, and that he couldn't step into his brother's life and walk in his footsteps.

She hadn't really made the connection at the time, but lately the thought pestered her night and day: Would he feel differently if he knew that she hated Vanu and was secretly glad he was gone?

Such a blunt declaration would definitely bare the darkness in her soul, even if Vanu had put it there. AJ might despise her for her disloyalty, and if Priia ever found out—which she might, since AJ was not one to mince words—she'd be shocked and deeply hurt, as much by Lani's betrayal of Vanu as by the idea that her son was not the sweet boy she chose to remember.

Then there was the baby. Vanu's child. If she told people that Vanu was harsh and cold and unloving, would her child learn this about his or her own father?

Still…if she never told anyone, these thoughts might torment her and keep her awake at night for the rest of her life.

AJ had been gone for nearly a month—twenty-three days, to be precise—and she still ached for him. She hadn't seen or heard anything of him in all that time, except the secondhand report that he would not be coming to the coronation. But she could remember the feel of his body against hers as if he'd just left the room. Alone at night, she imagined his hot breath on her skin and heard his voice soft in her ear.

If she phoned him, she really could hear his voice in her ear. She could air her thoughts and get the truth about Vanu off her chest. Yes, she'd have to live with the consequences of that decision, but could that be any worse that sitting in this prickly nest of lies and half truths?

She sat up and eased her feet down onto the cool tile floor. Pressed her hand to her belly for a moment for strength, even though she wasn't sure whether her sudden plan would be good or bad for her baby.

She crept across the dark room and found her phone where it lay on top of the dresser. She rarely used it, since she usually went to see her friends and her mom in person for a chat, like most people in Rahiri.

But L.A. was too far away for a drop-in visit.

She picked up the phone with a steady hand. It was after 2:00 a.m., so past midnight in L.A. Not a great time for a call.

Her heart pumped faster. She should really put the phone down and go back to bed.

Instead she opened the top drawer and pulled out a folded piece of paper. She didn't have AJ's address and phone number in L.A.—why would she?—but she'd found them in the old leather-bound address book Priia kept on her study desk. She wasn't sure at the time why she wanted them, just that she did. She'd already mapped AJ's address on the computer and peeped at the "bird's-eye view" of his sleek apartment building, like a spy on a covert mission.

She murmured his phone number like a mantra, knowing that at any time she could invoke him—live and in person—with a few pressed buttons. She knew from watching him that AJ answered nearly every call he got, which was a lot, so she was fairly sure he'd pick up at any time of the day or night.

And after midnight he'd be home alone.

At least she hoped he would. Fear flashed through her. What if he'd forgotten her already and was lost in the arms of a lascivious starlet?

She inhaled a deep breath and pressed the cool phone to her mouth for a moment. Didn't matter. She wasn't calling to beg him to come back, or tell him she loved him and couldn't live without him. Her only goal was to tell him the truth about Vanu, just because it felt right.

And to hear his voice one last time.

Her trembling fingertips had trouble hitting the right buttons on the tiny phone and she misdialed twice before she finally got the number right.

It rang. Why had she decided to call so late at night? It was rude. He'd probably be annoyed. Her thumb hovered over the disconnect button while her breath caught in her lungs.

Then he answered. "Hello." The sound of his voice sent a shock wave of emotion through her. She didn't know what to say.

"Hello, AJ."

"Lani." He sounded shocked. He could probably tell from the number that the call was from Rahiri, but he obviously didn't know it was her. They'd never talked on the phone before.

"Yes, it's me." Her head swam with such a tangle of thoughts that her mind went completely blank. "How are you?"

"Getting along. Keeping busy. How are you?"

Lani paced her bedroom. This wasn't how it was supposed to go. Phony pleasantries exchanged like strangers. "I'm fine." She wanted to say so much more, to shout it. To pour out her feelings and tell him how much she missed him.

"And the baby?"

"Good. At least I think so. I have a doctor's appointment tomorrow, but I've been feeling pretty good." Except for the nausea, but that probably was stress this time. "I'm sorry to call so late."

"Is Mom okay?" His voice filled with concern. He must be wondering exactly why she would call in the middle of the night.

"Yes. She's really busy with the coronation plans. She misses you, of course." She then regretted saying that, like she was trying to prod him to guilt. She really should get to the point before she lost her nerve and kept the truth to herself forever. "I called to tell you something."

"Oh?" He sounded reserved. What did he think she would say? That she loved him and wanted him to come back? Her face heated. If only her thoughts would stop running away with her.

"It's that…" she hesitated. How did you tell someone that you hated their brother? "Vanu and me… We didn't…we weren't…" Words hovered just out of reach. AJ was totally silent at the other end. "I didn't love him."

AJ said nothing. She could imagine him frowning. Thinking.

"I didn't like him." Emboldened by his silence, she went on. "He was cold to me, cruel, even." She swallowed, and walked back across the dark bedroom. "I hated him."

The harsh words fell from her lips easily, then hung in the air like a judgment. Cold dread trickled through her. She couldn't take the truth back now.

"What did you say?" AJ's voice was low, almost a whisper.

Lani froze. Was he horrified by her blunt confession? Disgusted by her lack of compassion for his dead brother? "I'm sorry. Maybe I shouldn't have said it. I know he's your brother and even if he wasn't I shouldn't speak ill of the dead. Now you know what I'm really like. See? I'm not nice at all like you thought and I have evil thoughts inside my head and—"

"I hated him, too." AJ's words rang bold and clear through the phone.

"What?" She spun around, startled.

"I hated him. *Hated* him. What did he do to you?" Sudden concern tightened his voice. "Did he hurt you?"

"Not physically, at least not that much. But he was cruel. He'd taunt me and belittle me, then be all smiles if there was anyone around."

"I don't believe it." AJ sounded incredulous.

Her shoulders stiffened. "It's true."

He laughed. "I don't mean that I don't believe *you*. I believe you completely, because that's exactly what he used to do to me."

"You never said anything."

"Nor did you."

"I didn't want to offend you."

"Same here." He let out a loud guffaw. "I can't believe we were dancing carefully around Vanu's memory when neither of us could stand him."

"Your mom has no idea he was like that." Lani drew in a deep breath. "I didn't want her to find out, either."

"I used to tell her, back when I was a kid, and she never believed me, anyway. He was always her sweet little princeling. He really knew how to turn it on when he wanted to."

"I know. It was like living with two completely different people. The public Vanu and the private one." Relief rolled through Lani, warm and soothing. "I tried to make him happy, but after a while I realized it was hurting me that made him happy." She stiffened when she remembered their last encounter, the one that had left her pregnant. Why shouldn't AJ know about that, too? She didn't want him to think she'd lain willingly in Vanu's arms after all he'd done to her over the years.

"I didn't want to conceive a child with him." She hesitated for a moment, wondering how he'd take what she was about to say. "He forced himself on me, said he was my husband and could do whatever he wanted. That it was his right."

She knew it wasn't about love, or even pleasure, for Vanu. It was about inflicting pain, abusing his power.

"He raped you." AJ's voice was hoarse. "If he was still alive I'd kill him. He was a sociopath. I didn't realize that until long after I'd gone, of course, and had time to get some distance. He's given me great inspiration for my movie villains over the years. I always thought it was lucky he didn't have any real interest in ruling the country, or he might have turned into a dictator."

"I think he was too lazy for that." Lani laughed, a weird, high-pitched sound, more a release of tension than anything else. "And he really didn't like people. I suspect he found it a lot of work pretending to be normal."

"So why did you cry when you learned he was dead?"

"Relief. I was dreading the awful possibility that he'd come back and make me miserable again. All those mornings of waking up to his angry face and hearing him criticize everything I did."

AJ let out a long sigh. "How come you didn't tell anyone Vanu was a sadistic bastard? Were you going to stay married to him forever if he hadn't died?"

Lani blew out. "I was trying to be brave. I didn't want to hurt your mom and let down the royal family by causing a scandal. My mom always made a big deal about how a woman should never air her dirty laundry. She never spoke about her own marriage and divorce." She shoved a hand through her hair. "I knew I was taking on a big responsibility when I married the future king. I guess I figured I'd have to live with my mistake."

There was a silence. "Just like you would have lived with your duty to marry me, if I hadn't left."

Lani didn't know what to say. It was true. As she'd gotten to know AJ, she'd realized the duty would have been a pleasure. She didn't want to push her luck by saying that, though. She'd called to tell him how she felt about Vanu, not to put pressure on him to do anything about it.

"Why did you decide to tell me now?" AJ's voice had an odd sound to it.

Lani swallowed. "I don't know exactly. I just wanted to tell you the truth."

"The truth. That's been an elusive little... Don't go anywhere."

"What do you mean?"

"Don't leave the palace."

"Why not?" She glanced over her shoulder. She felt under siege all the time lately, with press everywhere and people taking photos of her whenever she even looked out the window.

"So I know where to find you." His voice had a ring of command to it.

Why did he want to find her? Did he plan to come and scold her for keeping the truth hidden all this time? She'd only been trying to protect the family name.

The truth had been her enemy since she'd come to this palace. She'd danced around it, skirted it and fluffed over it so many times since she'd had the misfortune to marry Vanu. And there was one powerful truth she still kept locked tight in her heart.

She'd never told AJ that she loved him.

"Joe, you still got that jet out at Burbank?" AJ marched across the room, picking up items of clothing and tossing them into his bag.

"Do you know what time it is?" His friend's gruff voice assaulted him down the phone. He and Joe had shared a house when AJ was in film school—two kids with too much money and no sense of direction. They'd seen each other through more than a few scrapes since. Joe was now a successful film agent with a passion for cars and planes.

"Late, yeah. I can wait until dawn to leave, though." Every moment away from Lani was agonizing right now, but no need to torment other people with his desperation.

"Dawn? What the heck are you talking about? Where do you need to go in such a rush?"

"Home. Rahiri."

"I thought you'd decided once and for all that L.A. was your home." Joe's voice softened a bit.

"It's complicated. Anyway, I need to get to Rahiri as soon as humanly possible."

He heard a long sigh. "Let me guess, that gorgeous almost-wife of yours is involved somehow."

"Lani. Yes, I need to see her." And touch her, and hold her and kiss her—if she'd let him.

Joe chuckled. "I think everyone in America wants to see her, given the amount of media coverage she's getting. I doubt most of them had even heard of Rahiri until the two of you became such media darlings."

"Why am I friends with you?"

"Because I have a plane, apparently. And yes, I'll take you, but not until first light."

"I love you, Joe."

"And I'm not the only one you love, from the sound of things. See you on the tarmac." Joe hung up the phone.

AJ drew in a deep steadying breath. In only a few hours he'd see Lani again. Hearing her voice had undone all his hard work of trying to move on. Not that he'd been at all successful. He couldn't even stand to talk to her anymore. The distance between them was too agonizing and he had to see her right away. He didn't want to exchange one more word with her until they were face-to-face. Too easy for misunderstandings and complications to arise.

It was still dark when he arrived at the airport, but he wasn't surprised to see the lights on inside his friend's beloved plane. Joe was outside checking out some piece of machinery and he laughed when he saw AJ. "I knew you'd be here at least an hour early."

AJ shrugged.

"Lucky thing I came out here right when I hung up the phone—and she's ready to go."

"I really do love you." AJ grinned and heaved his bag inside the tiny cockpit.

By the time dawn came they were already out over the ocean, and the tentative rays of sun illuminated the featureless plain of dark water. They stopped to refuel and grab a late breakfast in Hawaii. Another seven hours or so of empty ocean and they'd be there.

His heart rate increased as they passed the first of the green, sand-fringed islands that dotted the route to Rahiri like giant stepping stones.

Would Lani resent him for ruining all their careful plans and leaving her in the lurch?

Of course she would. She'd borne the brunt of all the insatiable media curiosity that stood his hair on end—while dealing with pregnancy and the organizational and emotional drama of preparing to become Rahiri's official monarch.

But she'd called him. At a time when no one else would know and—as far as he could tell—with no hidden agenda other than to air the ugly truth she'd kept hidden all along.

She hadn't asked him to come back, but right now nothing could stop him.

"Is this a round-trip excursion or are you staying

for good this time?" Joe's voice jolted him from his thoughts.

"It all depends."

"On Lani the lovely."

"You got it." He wouldn't force himself on her. He'd always resolved not to do that. Rahiian or not, every woman deserved to choose her own husband.

"Speaking from personal experience, I've learned that women will let you make a mistake once, but they don't look too kindly on you screwing up the same way a second time. What made you change your mind about her?"

AJ hesitated. He'd probably mentioned his older brother to Joe in passing a few times, but had never revealed the full extent of his malice. In general he preferred to leave Vanu buried in the past. But was that perpetuating the fraud that had driven him and Lani apart? Still, he didn't want to say anything without asking Lani. If she wanted the ugly details of her first marriage kept secret, he'd oblige.

"Maybe I just came to my senses."

"Don't lose 'em again, okay? This is a long flight to make at a moment's notice." Joe turned and shoved him.

"I'm living and learning every day, bro. This time I plan to get it right."

"I did warn you that marriage isn't for the faint of heart?" Joe had been married three times and, by his account, paid untold amounts of alimony to his three former beloveds.

"Many a time. You're probably at least fifty percent responsible for scaring me off marriage until now. That and the fact that the divorce rate in L.A. is around seventy percent."

"What's the divorce rate like in Rahiri?"

"I have no idea. Haven't lived there in a decade. Lani's mom was divorced, though I suppose that took place in the States."

"You just make sure it doesn't happen to you."

"I'd have to be married first." A possibility that had blossomed in his mind again. Sure, it would be easier if it weren't for the whole royalty angle, but the prospect of making Lani his wife made his chest swell with excitement.

The sun was climbing across the sky by the time Rahiri came into view, its familiar teardrop-shaped outline beckoning him like an old friend. "Skip the airport and head straight for the palace. There's a long paved drive with palm trees on each side. You can land right there."

"And get a royal summons? I'd rather go to the airport."

"Too far away. It's almost an hour's drive from the palace."

"I thought that was so their royal majesties don't have to be troubled by the drone of engines."

"It is, but I'm sure they'll survive."

"Your mom was really pissed off last time." They'd done it once before, years ago, when AJ returned for a family party with a group of friends.

"I can handle her. I already called and told her we were coming in. Didn't want to get shot at on approach now that everyone's so paranoid these days. She wasn't happy about it, but she'll survive." AJ scanned the ground through the small side window. Already he could make out the multilayered rooftops of the palace and the lush grounds. Lani was down there somewhere. How would she react when she saw him?

Joe guided the plane expertly into a straight line with the drive, which was mercifully free of vehicles and pedestrians. "Here goes nothing."

As they roared to the ground and taxied down the drive, AJ's pulse went into overdrive. As soon as the plane stopped, people came running out of the palace. He jumped from the plane, scanning the faces.

"AJ!" His mother's scream rose above the din of voices. "Didn't I tell you never to land on the drive? It's dangerous—there could be a pothole, or a fallen tree branch."

"Palm trees don't have branches, Mom." He gave her a hug. "Where's Lani?"

"She's being measured for her coronation gown. They're doing it in the ballroom because of the good light in there. Hey, where are you going?"

AJ had already slipped her grasp and strode into the palace, heading for the ballroom. Staff members stared at him, and hushed whispers buzzed amongst the polite greetings.

He had no idea how Lani would respond to his sudden arrival, but at this point he really didn't care, he just ached to see her. The palace corridors seemed endless as he marched along them, past the secret passageway he'd sneaked into with Lani, past all the other doorways and hallways where they'd exchanged glances—and more.

"Did you return to claim the throne?" A black-clad reporter, brandishing a tiny video camera, leaped out of a doorway to his left.

"How did you get in?" AJ lunged toward him, responding instinctively to the invasion of privacy.

"Couldn't stand to see your brother's wife claim

the throne?" A female reporter darted up behind him, holding up a camera phone.

AJ grappled with the first man, getting him in an armlock. "Guards! There's an intruder."

People rushed around them, servants hurried along the corridors and reporters poured in through the unsecured and glassless windows that ringed the palace and linked it to the gardens outside.

AJ grappled with a smelly man in a plaid shirt and yelled to the servants to make sure none of the scum got anywhere near Lani. Reporters who'd been hanging around the palace bored out of their skulls for weeks surged in after the others, shutters whirring and microphones thrust in his face.

"Are you back for good?"

"Is *Dragon Chaser Five* going to start shooting?"

"Did you fly the plane yourself?"

"Is the baby really yours?"

"Did you miss Lani?"

This last question made him look up, and his eyes met the beady blue ones of a blond reporter he vaguely recognized.

"I did miss Lani."

The scrum of reporters suddenly hushed.

"Did you come back for her?"

"I came back to see her." He didn't want to claim more than that. He wasn't sure if Lani even would see him, after he'd promised to marry her—in front of the whole world—then welshed on the deal.

"Do you want to marry her?"

"I think that's a bit premature. I…" Something caught his eye behind the reporter's head and he looked into the long hall leading to the interior of the palace.

Lani. Flanked by two guards, standing only a few feet away. Her face was blank, expressionless.

Blood rushed to AJ's muscles and he pushed through the crush of reporters. He'd imagined her so many times, soft honey eyes, long silky hair hiding her slim figure, her hesitant walk and sweet laugh and his vision seemed conjured to life in front of him.

But as he approached her, Lani seemed to shrink from him. She glanced at the reporters behind him— why were they still there? Couldn't the guards throw them out?

"Let's go somewhere we can talk."

She nodded.

He turned to the guards. "Make sure they don't follow us." He reached out to take Lani's arm, then noticed how stiffly she held her body and pulled it back. What did she think of his sudden appearance?

Nine

Lani marched as fast as she could beside AJ. Her thoughts ran in all directions. Why was he here, and so suddenly? Hope mingled with terror and anticipation as they drew farther away from the crowd of crazy reporters and into the quiet recesses of the palace.

"In here." AJ opened a door into the darkened throne room. She stepped past him, agonizingly conscious of his big, broad physique and the energy that always crackled in the air between them.

None of the hundred sconces or the incongruously high-tech video conferencing equipment was turned on, and the only light came through a small skylight in the ceiling. The massive "throne"—a squarish chunk of black basalt etched with symbols so ancient that no one could actually read them—hulked in the middle of the room.

AJ closed the door quietly behind them. The shaft

of light from overhead threw his strong features into high relief, including the frown etched in his brow. "I had to come right away, to apologize."

"For what?" He had much to apologize for, but she didn't want to jump to any conclusions.

That, and she didn't know what else to say.

"I feel like such an ass. Why couldn't I see it?" AJ turned and paced across the room, disappearing into the semi-darkness. "Why didn't I realize that Vanu had made your life hell, too?"

"I kept it secret." Her voice was almost a whisper in the vast chamber. "Until I couldn't keep it secret any longer."

"Before your middle-of-the-night phone call, I didn't even realize what I'd done." He strode back across the darkened room. "That I'd let my own fears and insecurities get the better of me. I didn't want to live a life being second-best, the backup, the understudy after the tragic loss of my glorious brother who was loved and missed by all."

His eyes gleamed in the half light, and he let out a snort of disbelief. "But that brother never existed at all—except in my own mind, as my tormentor. The man who died was a small and petty individual who lived for his own amusement. That man can't keep me from Rahiri—or from you."

He drew her into his arms, and she rested her head against his broad chest, feeling protected and comforted for the first time since Vanu's boat was found. Desire flared inside her like a spark under an encouraging breath.

"I missed your smile." AJ brushed his thumb over her mouth—her smile appeared magically beneath his touch.

Lani leaned into him. "I missed your laugh." The palace had seemed so empty, so dull and lifeless despite all the staff bustling to and fro.

"I missed laughing. I haven't done much lately." He stroked her back, and his fingers stirred up rivers of sensation. She'd tried so hard to forget the feelings he aroused in her, and she couldn't keep them from flooding back.

"Me, either."

His lips hovered just over hers, close enough so she could feel their heat. Excitement buzzed in the air and made her skin tingle. Was it real? Could AJ really be back? Was everything going to be okay?

It seemed too much to hope for. Still, he was here, with his arms wrapped around her. Something she'd dreamed of in spite of herself the whole time he was gone.

"I missed your kisses," she whispered.

"I missed yours." He swiped a kiss close to her lips, but not quite on them. Her lips stung at the sudden and unexpected denial. "But maybe I don't deserve to have any more."

"You may not, but I do." She narrowed her eyes at him.

"So true." He lowered his lips gently over hers, slid his tongue provocatively between her lips and gave her a kiss that made her toes curl.

Her nipples tightened against his chest and she ran her hands over the ridged muscle of his back, enjoying his strength. It made her feel safe, though it shouldn't really, he hadn't made her any promises.

She'd learned not to count on anything for sure except the sweetness of the present moment. "I'm glad you came back," she whispered. Even if he didn't stay, she'd always have this moment to remember, when she felt safe and whole and loved, for a while.

AJ nuzzled her ear. "I missed you like crazy. I tried to put you out of my mind and to distract myself with the films and parties and all those things I used to enjoy, but I found I didn't want any of it any more. Not without you."

Her heart contracted painfully. "I missed you, too." She'd ached for him, night and day. "But you'd left me, and there was nothing I could do about it."

"Except phone me." He stroked her cheek.

"I was scared to tell the truth. I wasn't sure if you'd be angry, or think I was nuts."

"I am, and I do. I don't think you should have put up with any of that nonsense from Vanu." He lifted her chin until their eyes met. His gaze was filled with concern. "You should have told him he was a jerk and dumped him."

Lani swallowed. Left in her heart was the one truth she'd never told anyone. "I did."

"What?"

She pushed back, separating herself from AJ inch by inch. "I told him, that night, after he…forced himself on me…that he could kill me if he wanted but that I wouldn't stay married to him for another day. I told him I hated him." The memory of her own voice, shrill and serious in the night, made her shiver.

AJ stared at her. "And that's why he left. Why he went out on the boat."

"And why he died." Her words, spoken softly, rang like a tolling bell off the stone walls. "How did he die? No one's ever told me. Trying to spare my feelings or something."

He rubbed a hand over his mouth and looked away.

"Anyone's guess, really. There wasn't much left. Just the skeleton. A lot of animals and birds on that island."

She let the ghastly image sink in.

"It was definitely him, though. They checked the teeth against his dental records. He won't be back again."

She didn't know what to say or do. How could she be pleased to hear such grim news?

AJ reached for her hand. "It's not your fault he's dead."

She clenched her fist inside his grasp. "I wanted him dead." The words flew from her mouth. "It's ugly but it's the truth and I can't change that."

"It's his fault that you felt like that, and I could kill him again myself for putting that sadness and guilt into your heart. You need to let go of it."

"I want to. Maybe that's why I had to tell you the truth. I had to tell someone."

"Were you worried I wouldn't believe you?"

"A little." She hesitated and watched his expression. "And I was a little afraid that you wouldn't care."

"Because I ran out on you?"

She nodded.

"But now you know that I did that because of my own past with Vanu. I gave up telling people about it a long time ago. I wanted to leave him in my past." He reached toward her and stroked her shoulder. "I think we should both do that."

Lani swallowed. "We can't."

"Why not?"

"Because I'm still carrying his baby."

AJ's eyes dropped to her belly, which was still barely more than flat. "It's hard to believe there's a whole person in there, getting ready for life."

Lani swallowed. Did he now intend to be a father to that tiny person, or simply an uncle? She didn't dare ask.

He frowned, thoughtful. "Your baby won't be raised by Vanu. All of his or her genes come from my mother and father, just like mine, and from you. There's no reason why Vanu should cast a shadow over the child's life. We'll raise it with affection and love."

"And if he or she does have any problems or issues, we won't pretend they don't exist. We'll do our best to help. I've had enough of trying to pretend things are perfect when they aren't. I've spent way too much time trying to be nice and make everything go smoothly, and all my efforts nearly ruined everything. Trying to make everything perfect by glossing over the truth is at the root of all of our problems."

"You're right." He tilted his head. "And I've spent my adult life creating and maintaining elaborate fantasies for the screen. I guess my childhood prepared me really well for that."

Lani filled her lungs with air. "From now on we'll face problems head-on, and talk to each other honestly about them."

"That's a promise." AJ stared at her, his expression unreadable. "I love you, Lani."

She froze. The words entered her brain, but it didn't know what to make of them. What did love even mean? She'd tried to love Vanu, and failed miserably. She had strong feelings for AJ, but she'd told herself time and time again since he left that they were most definitely not love.

It wasn't until he'd gone and left her alone again that she'd realized she loved him.

He reached for her hand and she let him take it. He must have noticed it was trembling slightly.

She didn't know what to say. She wanted to say, "I love you, too," but it seemed too much, too soon, when she didn't even know what his intentions were.

And despite all her exhortations to get real, she was afraid to ask.

Words failing her, she stepped forward and kissed him hard on the mouth. Too much emotion. She couldn't process all the strange feelings roiling in her mind and body.

AJ's arms around her waist sent heat flooding to her core. She clutched him closer, winding her fingers into the fabric of his shirt, then plucking and tugging at it until she pulled it loose from his pants.

Their kisses grew more frantic as she struggled with his buttons and clawed the fabric away from his chest. She yanked at his belt buckle, hating that she had to pull back even a few inches to get her hands on it. She just wanted to bury herself in AJ's large body, to lose herself in him and revel in the sheer fact that he was right here, right now.

Her nipples stung and tingled with intense arousal as they brushed against his bare chest through the thin fabric of her dress. AJ's hands roamed over her as she kissed his face and his neck and pushed his shirt off over his muscled arms and back.

His eyes gleamed with passion as he undid the fastening on her dress and let it fall to the floor.

Impatient with his stiff jeans, Lani pushed and shoved at them until they fell past his powerful thighs and he stepped out of them and stood, clothed only in the pale light drifting through the skylight above.

Lani shivered in anticipation at the sight of his

arousal. AJ pulled her to him, his chest heaving. He lowered his mouth over hers and took her in a kiss that sucked the breath from her lungs. Lani kissed him back with all the emotion she'd locked away deep inside her after he left. All the pain and hurt mingled with affection and passion and exploded over them both, locking them together in a powerful embrace that shut out the world.

Lani felt AJ lifting her off the floor, carrying her in his strong arms. She didn't open her eyes, just let him take her wherever he wanted. It felt good to stop planning and worrying and scheming and simply go with him.

He set her down in a sitting position on a smooth, stone surface that contrasted intriguingly with the hot, yielding strength of his body. The sensation made her wriggle against him, as he stood in front of her, his erection level with her very aroused sex.

"Now," she pleaded, gripping him gently with her fingers. She needed to feel him inside her. She wanted him to fill the gap he'd left when he went away.

AJ entered her slowly, pulling her to the edge of the stone and wrapping her legs around his waist. She groaned as he sank deep inside her and a sensation of relief and joy filled her from the inside out. She pressed her body against his and hugged him tight as he moved slowly inside her.

I love him.

The words filled her brain as the notion filled her heart. Again. Was that enough? It should be. Love— and whatever those other sensations were called—filled her to overflowing and made her gasp as AJ moved over her.

He kissed her gently, then firmer, and lifted her up

so she was in his arms, still moving with him. She felt light as a feather, supported by his powerful frame. Her arms and legs still wrapped around him, AJ eased himself into position on the stone surface so she was sitting on top of him, her feet resting on the throne.

AJ sucked her neck and she arched her back, taking him deeper still. She found she was able to move over him easily, keeping a tight hold around his neck and back, and moving up and down with her feet. Moving faster, and then slower, she let emotions and sensations cascade over her.

Pure pleasure trickled through her body and she wanted to enjoy it to the fullest. She'd known so little pleasure in the last few years that it was like a precious jewel she wanted to hold and admire for as long as she could.

Judging from the sounds he was making—earthy groans and whispered endearments—AJ was enjoying it, too. His hands moved tirelessly over her skin, stroking and supporting at the same time.

She kissed him, thrusting her tongue into his mouth in time with her movements. The sensation was cheeky and delicious. With AJ she could take risks and do silly, fun things without worrying about being judged or scolded.

She peppered kisses all over his face and ran her hands through his thick, silky hair, drinking in the masculine scent of his warm, sweaty skin. She loved the rough feel of his cheek against hers, the firm pressure of his fingers on her skin.

Although her climax hovered so close she could almost feel the convulsions, she delayed it. She slowed the pace, pulled back just as she was about to burst. Part of her wanted to forge ahead and taste the sweetness of their joint explosion, but the rest of her wanted to prolong this blissful experience as long as she could.

She still didn't know why AJ had come back, or for how long. He'd said he loved her, but she knew love wasn't always enough. Right now that didn't matter. What she shared with AJ was already so much more wonderful than anything she'd experienced in her years of marriage, and if it was all she got, she could live with that.

She kissed him, drinking in his scent and tasting the sweetness of his kiss as if this was the last time she'd touch him. Savored each precious millisecond of his hands on her skin and his hard belly pressed to her soft one. She moved so slowly, as if she could alter the passage of time and prolong the present moment infinitely.

"You're torturing me." AJ's whispered words tickled her ear.

"Maybe you deserve it." She trailed a light fingernail along his spine.

"I do." He nipped at her ear. "But you could encourage me to be a bad boy more often with this kind of punishment."

Lani pressed her breasts into his chest, enjoying the sting of pleasure in her nipples. "Maybe I will. It seems I enjoy inflicting torment." She shifted her weight slightly, and felt him move inside her.

"I should have known there was more to you than meets the eye."

She opened her eyes and met his dark gaze. "I warned you when we first met."

"You did." He narrowed his eyes and raked them down her body, causing her skin to tingle. "Maybe that's what intrigued me. Then the way you kissed me…"

"You could tell I had a dark side."

"Or a delicious side. Either one worked for me." AJ licked her mouth and she shuddered in response.

She pressed her mouth to his ear. "Do you think it's possible we bring out the worst in each other?"

"Absolutely." He lifted her chin with his thumb so he was looking into her eyes again. "Why else would we be making love on our nation's ancient throne?"

Lani gasped and looked down. "Oh, no."

"Oh, yes. What did you think we were sitting on?"

"I don't know." She frowned. "I didn't think."

AJ's mischievous chuckle rocked them both. "I never would have imagined it could be so...comfortable. I can't help wondering if anyone's done this before."

Lani let a wry smile lift her mouth. "We really don't know that much about the customs and culture of the Old Ones. Maybe this is exactly what they did on it."

"Very wise of them, in my opinion. Perhaps we could revive the custom."

"Apparently we already have."

AJ shifted his weight and moved deeper inside her. Lani arched her back and shuddered, again dancing just microseconds from release. Could this really be a new beginning? If AJ stayed and became king, almost anything was possible, for Rahiri as well as for her.

Are you staying?

The words hovered just behind her lips, but she swallowed them back, afraid to spoil everything. He'd come back, and that was enough.

She leaned into him and started to move again, letting the delicious sensations pulse through her until she started to lose control. This time she didn't stop, but pushed them both over the edge of pleasure into the strange, dark, powerful, empty space beyond, where thoughts and feelings collapsed and their bodies became one.

When she finally opened her eyes again, they were both lying back on the polished basalt. She'd never realized how big the great stone was. Side by side, holding hands, they lay under the skylight, the surface oddly soft beneath their totally relaxed limbs.

Lani turned to look at AJ. "What if we've just broken an ancient taboo?"

AJ's mouth swept into a naughty grin. "I'd say ancient taboos are pretty much made to be broken."

A volley of sharp knocks on the carved wooden door jerked her into a sitting position. "Someone's coming."

AJ didn't move. "Not surprising. We did kind of disappear on them."

She jumped off the stone and scrambled back into her dress. "Come on! We don't want them to know what we were doing."

"Why not? It's not a crime."

"It might be if the throne is involved."

"If I become king I can grant us absolution." He eased his pants over his powerful thighs. "Same if you become queen. Though we'd have to decide if we deserve the pardon."

Lani ran fingers through her tangled hair. Now he was just messing with her mind. Unless he didn't entirely know what was on his own mind—which was more than likely. Everything had happened so fast. It was less than twenty-four hours ago that she'd phoned him with her revelation.

More banging on the door made her jump.

"Don't worry, it's locked." AJ winked at her.

She pulled her sandals on. "What shall we say we were doing in here?"

"Hmm." AJ buttoned up his shirt very slowly. "Maybe we could tell them that we couldn't decide who should take the throne, so we both decided to try it out and see how it felt."

"You're terrible!"

"Trust me, I know that. It's the truth, though, isn't it?"

"We haven't discussed who should take the throne." She peered at him.

"Do you want to be queen?" He stopped buttoning and stared at her.

Only if you're king. "Not really. I've been rather railroaded into it."

"Well, that's how it happens, isn't it?" He smiled and went back to buttoning. "In some societies people are stabbing each other in the back trying to seize the throne. In others, we're all keen to dodge the crown that's being thrust upon us." He tucked in his shirt, then stared straight ahead. "I admit I've felt bad about that, too."

"You regretted giving up the crown."

"The crown I could care less about. It's Rahiri I regretted losing. This is a great little nation and it could be even better. Sure, the elders have the people's best interests in their hearts, but they don't have the energy and vision of a younger person who's lived in another culture and been exposed to new ideas."

"I'd been thinking about that. We need more female doctors, and why can't the elders be women, too?"

"You are prepared to take on the role of queen." AJ looked at her, a hint of surprise in his eyes.

Had she said the wrong thing? Would he think she

didn't want him there because she'd been ready to rule the nation? She shrugged. "I had to prepare. I didn't really have a choice."

He frowned. "You're the one person who's never really had a choice in any of this. What do you want, Lani?"

You.

Why couldn't she say it? It was just one word, but it ducked and hid behind her tongue. What was she so afraid of? That she'd scare him away?

"You don't like giving away anything about yourself." He cocked his head and surveyed her through narrowed eyes. "You figure your secrets are safer if you keep them locked away inside."

"I told you the truth about my marriage to Vanu."

"That was a good start, but I want to know about you. What you think, and what you really want."

Another thunderous knock on the door was accompanied by a shout. "Is anyone in there? We're going to break the door down."

"Oh, no." Lani scuttled behind the stone.

"Don't break it down." AJ's voice boomed off the high walls. "I'm in here with Lani and we're both fine."

Are we? The warm glow of lust had dimmed, leaving Lani anxious and apprehensive. All this talking seemed to be tying them up in knots. She'd never been good with words. She certainly couldn't talk easily about herself.

"You didn't answer my question, Lani." AJ ignored the commotion outside, looking only at her. "What do you want?"

What if she told him she wanted him to stay, and he did but was unhappy? Would it be her fault?

"Stop hiding your thoughts from me." AJ stepped toward her. "You're just complicating everything further."

"I want you to stay and become king." She pushed the words out with great effort. Relief mingled with terror formed a fog in her brain.

AJ's expression didn't soften. "That's about me. What about *you?*"

I want to be your wife.

No. There was absolutely no way on this ocean-covered earth she could say that. It would amount to asking him to marry her. She'd never do that.

"Why can't you say it?" AJ put his hand on her shoulder. His dark gaze seemed to pierce her skin, making her even more uncomfortable.

"Because I don't know what I want. I only know I don't want you to go." The words burst from her on a sob. "Maybe I really am too shallow, or too silly for you. You expect me to have all these grand thoughts about my destiny and lots of big dreams or something." She shoved a tear aside. "But I don't. Maybe I am just a simple village girl. I only want to raise my baby and be happy."

AJ stared at her. Tears ran down her cheeks and she didn't try to stop them. That really was the truth about her and if he hoped for more he was doomed to disappointment.

Maybe that's what she'd been trying to hide all along. "I'm not educated or even particularly intelligent." Lord knows Vanu had made a point of that often enough. "I just do my best to help the people around me and try to do the right thing. And sometimes the right thing doesn't feel right at all…" A violent sob racked her body.

"Don't put yourself down, Lani. You're brave and strong—look at all you've endured—and I firmly believe you're capable of anything. Whatever you do, don't let Vanu's opinion of you shape your view of yourself. I'd be nowhere if I'd done that."

"And you're an award-winning director." Another tear dripped off her chin. "That's a big accomplishment." No wonder he didn't want to abandon the career he'd worked so hard to build.

"Being a director is a lot like being a king, really." He thumbed a tear off her cheek. "You have to keep a lot of different people happy while guiding them all in the direction of your vision. I'm beginning to realize that my film career has been the perfect preparation for the job I'm truly intended to do."

"Wouldn't you miss Hollywood and all the excitement of the industry?"

"Not the way I missed you and Rahiri while I was back there." His soft voice tugged at something deep inside her. There was something different in his eyes now, too. A reflective look she didn't remember seeing before.

"I truly think I was meant to live there for a while, and I did enjoy myself—almost as much as the media claimed—but now it's my time to come home."

The last word hung in the air and reverberated off the stone floor.

Then the powerful moment was interrupted by more fevered banging on the door. "AJ Rahia, come here right now!"

"Your mom." Lani couldn't help laughing. "She's probably run out of spin for the reporters."

"Is that any way to talk to the king?" AJ raised a brow. Humor twinkled in his eyes.

Lani drew in a breath. "Are you really going to stay and become king?"

"Only if you'll be my queen." He took her hands in his and held her gaze while he dropped to one knee. "Lani, will you marry me?"

Ten

AJ held his breath while two more fat crystal tears slid down Lani's cheeks.

"I missed you so much, AJ. I almost couldn't stand it when you left. I wanted to be mad at you for abandoning me, but I couldn't. You're the most caring and tender man I've ever met and…" She drew in a shaky breath. "I love you."

His heart squeezed. She hadn't answered his question, though. Did she still worry that he felt forced into marrying her?

"I love you, too, Lani. And I want to marry you because I'd like to be your husband, not because a nation expects it of me. Your beauty seduced me from the first moment I met you, but your generous and giving spirit stole my heart. I want to spend the rest of my life with you."

AJ reached into his pocket and pulled out a wad of

tissue paper. It wasn't easy unwrapping it while keeping a tight hold on her with one hand. He was still half-afraid she'd run off, or just evaporate into the humid air. His good fortune at winning her back seemed too sweet to be real.

At last he managed to free the sparkly gem he'd had to twist arms to obtain in the middle of the night.

Lani gasped when she saw it. "Oh, my goodness, that's beautiful."

"It had better be. It's from L.A.'s finest jeweler."

"You had this planned?"

He hesitated. Did he want her to think he'd been planning this proposal since the day he left and spent days agonizing over ring designs?

No. The truth was what brought them together and what would hold them together into the future.

"Only since 2:00 a.m. I had to drag my friend Niall out of bed. He's a jewelry designer and I knew he'd have something fabulous enough to be fit for a queen." The enormous cushion-cut rock had made even AJ's jaded eyes pop. "Shall we see if it fits?"

Lani nodded, eyes wide. He held her hand gently and pushed the delicate gold band onto her ring finger. The ring slid on easily, then the heavy gem tilted to one side. "It's a bit big."

"We'll get it fixed. It's beautiful and I love it." Her eyes glistened with tears again. "And yes, I will marry you."

AJ picked her up and twirled her around. He must have had the biggest grin in the world on his face.

"AJ, sweetheart—" The voice was not Lani's but his mom's, coming from the other side of the door.

"Do you think she's been listening at the door?" he whispered.

Lani smiled. "Probably. I forgot she was there."

"Me, too. I forget about everything when you're around." He gave her a squeeze. "You think we should let her in on the good news?"

Lani tensed a little in his arms.

"Or are you not quite ready to face the mayhem again?"

She shrugged. "We'll have to sooner or later. Might as well get it over with." She rubbed at her cheeks, and he smoothed away any last telltale signs of her tears. He took her hand and they marched toward the door, which locked from the inside with a massive iron bolt. He pulled the bolt, then caught Lani's hand again as he opened the door and light flooded into the dim chamber.

As expected, a large crowd had gathered outside, flanking his mom, who had those bright spots of color high on her cheeks that let him know she was really agitated.

"Hi, Mom."

"What were you doing in there?" His mom glanced at Lani, who blushed.

"That's between me and Lani and the throne." He cocked his head and gave Lani a sly wink.

Her flush deepened.

He felt strangely calm. "I've come back for good, and Lani has kindly agreed to marry me."

His mom's mouth fell open and she gasped. Then she grasped Lani in her arms and hugged her. "What wonderful news!"

Photographic flashes half blinded him.

"Who's going to rule Rahiri?" A British accent.

AJ held Lani close. "Both of us. We'll rule together until our child comes of age."

"But isn't the baby your brother Vanu's?" An American woman shoved a microphone under his nose.

"Vanu's gone." He glanced at Lani. "I'll raise the child as a father and love him or her as my own until they're old enough to rule."

"Will you keep making films?" a young man shouted from near the back.

"I will. I already have some ideas for films set in Rahiri."

He looked at Lani, whose eyes widened. Then she smiled. "It would be a shame for AJ to waste his creative talents. And there's a wealth of talent on this island that will enjoy working on the films."

AJ put his arm around her. "Rahiri's changed a lot since I was a boy. We have better schools and hospitals. We have cell phones and satellite TV. But the important things have stayed the same. People care about each other and about the land and water they live on. We have customs and culture totally unique to Rahiri that we celebrate and enjoy just as our ancestors did. Lani and I look forward to continuing the legacies of both progress and tradition that my father set in motion."

Cameras flashed and AJ smiled. Already he felt rather relaxed in the new role. Different aspects of their lives seemed to be slotting into place in a neat yet interesting pattern, much like the colorful woven fabrics of Lani's dresses, or the ornate teak carvings on the veranda around them.

They answered more questions together, Lani growing more confident and talkative, her beauty radiant as the noon sunshine.

Finally AJ decided it was time for some peace and quiet. "Now I must ask you to all leave the palace. The family needs some privacy."

* * *

Lani's nose tickled a bit as Priia dusted the traditional pollen on her cheeks with a fat makeup brush.

"It makes you glow so nicely! We should all wear it every day." Her mother-in-law beamed.

"I'm not sure the bees would appreciate that, but it does feel soft." Just like her silk dress, an intricate weave of delicate colors and real gold thread. She'd worn a similar dress for her wedding to Vanu, but this time everything felt different, maybe because it wasn't all strange and alarming like the first time. She knew everyone at the palace and it was already her home. The ceremony marked the happy change of welcoming AJ into her life.

The population of Rahiri swelled to almost double its usual numbers for the joint wedding and coronation. She rarely watched TV but now she made a special effort to avoid it. It was too bizarre to see herself cast in the "rags to riches to happiness" drama they all turned her life into. At least they were right about the last part.

"Where's AJ?" All the fussing made her restless.

"He's getting ready as well, sweetheart. You won't see him again until the ceremony. It's bad luck."

Lani sighed. A hug from AJ would really calm her nerves right now. She wasn't anxious about the marriage itself, or even becoming an official monarch, just ready to get all the official drama out of the way. Although the king usually did the speaking during the ceremony, AJ had suggested that she should say the words, too, to symbolize their equality as monarchs. Of course he was right and it was for the best, but what if she froze and forgot her words in front of all those people?

The sound of her phone made her jump. It took her

a while to find it on the dressing table amongst all the lotions and potions. Even her own hand—nails and fingertips decorated with red berry juice—startled her as she reached for it. "Hello?"

"How's my beautiful bride?" AJ's low voice, relaxed as always, made warmth flood her tense muscles.

"Nervous but okay. How's my handsome husband-to-be?"

"I'll be better when we're alone tonight." His suggestive tone made desire and anticipation trickle through her. Which was funny, really, since they'd slept together every night since he came back. "And the crowns are off our heads again."

"I know just how you feel." What a relief to have a partner she could really talk to. "I feel like we're participating in a costume party of some kind, not a real coronation."

AJ chuckled. "It is a costume party, complete with crowns woven from rare orchids and real gold. All we really have to do is smile and look regal. You've had more practice than I have."

"I wasn't very good at it. I've always felt like a milkmaid who'd stumbled into the palace and been mistaken for a princess."

"Easy to see how that could happen, with your looks."

Lani laughed. "How do you always manage to make me smile?"

"Because you love me, so you laugh, even at my worst jokes."

"I guess that must be it." She sighed. Her chest felt so full. "I do love you. I never thought I'd know real love, especially after I realized I wouldn't find it in my first marriage. What a surprise."

"There's really nothing better than a surprise when you least expect it—at least that was always my chief theory as a director."

"I'm not sure the citizens of Rahiri will feel the same way." She lifted a brow, then realized he couldn't see it over the phone. "They might prefer easy predictability."

"Then we'll try not to declare too many wars or set off too many loud explosions. Your gentle spirit will be a moderating influence on me."

"Maybe it will." She smiled. It was so easy and fun to tease AJ. "Though some might say my spirit is less gentle now it has you encouraging it into mischief."

"Mmm. I'm thinking about last night." AJ's throaty voice stirred heat deep inside her.

"We really should have saved our energy for today." Lani glanced at her glamorously made-up and gold-pollen-dusted visage in the mirror.

"Then we'd be more nervous. Much better to burn off some adrenaline first." AJ's voice slid into her ear, soft and seductive. "And even fresh pollen can't compete with the natural glow of a sexually satisfied woman."

"You're sending my thoughts in the wrong directions." Her pupils were dilating and her cheeks flushing an embarrassed pink. "Perhaps we need to turn our discussion to Rahiri's gross national product."

He laughed. "And how much it's growing due to the sale of souvenirs and tchotchkes associated with our nuptials. Speaking of which, it's almost time to head for the throne room. Try not to think about what we got up to in there when there weren't any crowds around."

Lani sucked in a breath. Would she be able to keep her mind focused on the age-old ceremony when she knew what they'd done on the surface of that ancient stone? "See you there, if I don't pass out from nerves on my way."

"You'll do just fine, your majesty."

Lani smiled as she ended the call. With AJ at her side, anything was possible.

Epilogue

Three years later

"It's lucky we have a home theater," Lani exclaimed, after AJ's umpteenth attempt to catch little Puaiti and return her to one of the velvet armchairs. Within seconds she'd popped up again like a jack-in-the-box and was running around the darkened room.

The credits for *Dragon Chaser 6: The Unveiling* were already scrolling on the screen.

"Yes, she doesn't seem to find the series too riveting," said AJ. He reached out to tickle her as she ran past. "But I suppose she's a bit outside our ideal demographic."

"She'd have a fit if you tried to leave her out." Priia chucked Puaiti's chin as she darted past her seat. "Always has to be at the center of the action, just like her dad."

She looked fondly at AJ. They all knew that in Priia's mind, AJ, not Vanu, who was rarely mentioned, was Puaiti's father.

Apparently Puaiti took after AJ in every way except gender, including a passion for movies, though now, at age three, the Disney princesses were her favorites. She sported a yellow Sleeping Beauty gown as she leapt onto AJ's lap and begged for more popcorn.

Her baby sister, Maya, slept in Lani's arms. She could sleep through almost anything, which was lucky with Puaiti around.

"Ray did a great job. I don't think I could have done better." He gave Puaiti a piece of popcorn and watched carefully while she ate it. Lani had explained that popcorn was a choking hazard and AJ, attentive father that he was, took the warning seriously.

"I think you might have made the chase scene on the bridge a touch more dramatic." Lani stroked Maya's silky golden hair. "I suspect you might have added an aerial component involving the suspension cables."

AJ stared at her, humor glittering in his eyes. "How did you know that's exactly what I was thinking?"

"Well, I have seen your films a few times." She glanced at Priia. "Along with your greatest fan."

Priia dusted popcorn salt off her hands. "My AJ would have made the film very exciting, but he's more valuable here in Rahiri."

"Don't you miss your shopping trips to Rodeo Drive, Mom?" AJ leaned toward her. "You don't have any good excuse to fly all the way to L.A. to shop anymore."

"Sweetheart, thanks to you and your tourism initiatives, I don't need to. There's going to be a Chanel and a Fendi opening right here in the new visitors' village." She leaned toward Lani and lifted a penciled brow. "Possibly a Ferragamo, too, but that's not definite yet."

Lani smiled. "I'm looking forward to the new JoJo Maman Bébé. Maya told me she'd like some designer diapers." She winked at AJ. They both enjoyed teasing Priia about her passion for luxury labels. No one could argue that the visitors now streaming to the island brought funds to build schools, hospitals and other services that would have been unimaginable a generation ago.

"Smart girl." Priia held out her arms. "Why don't you give her to me and go enjoy the sunset. I know our littlest princess has been keeping you busy around the clock all week. Puaiti and I will read Maya a story, won't we, Puaiti?"

The toddler pulled a book from her stash near the video controls. "She loves Winnie the Pooh!"

AJ slipped his hand into hers and the familiar thrill danced up her arm. They walked out onto the veranda as Priia recited the opening lines of *The House at Pooh Corner,* for probably the seventieth time.

The sun was setting over the valley below and she could just make out the roar of the waterfall under the animated hum of the evening chorus. The soft copper light animated AJ's handsome features. She could swear he'd become even more gorgeous—as well as more dignified—since he'd assumed the role of king. The commentators on *Celebrity Watch* had recently made the same observation, much to AJ's amusement.

"Are you sleepy?" AJ stroked her cheek.

"Not in the least." Her body hummed with fresh energy and she wrapped her arms around her husband's waist. A shiver of anticipation made her lips tingle for a split second before they kissed. "Maybe we should sneak off to the throne room and lock the door so no one could disturb us?"

AJ's dark eyes smoldered with familiar passion. "I like the way you think."

* * * * *

AT HIS MAJESTY'S
CONVENIENCE

BY
JENNIFER LEWIS

For Lulu, a gracious lady and a powerful communicator who's encouraged me to slow down and see the big picture.

Acknowledgements:

More thanks to the lovely people who read this book while I was writing it, Anne, Cynthia, Jerri, Leeanne, my agent Andrea and my editor Charles.

One

He won't ever forgive you.

Andi Blake watched her boss from the far end of the grand dining room. Dressed in a black dinner jacket, dark hair slicked back, he looked calm, composed and strikingly handsome as usual, while he scanned the printed guest list she'd placed on the sideboard.

Then again, maybe he wouldn't care at all. Nothing rattled Jake Mondragon, which was why he'd transitioned easily from life as a successful Manhattan investor to his new role as king of the mountainous nation of Ruthenia.

Would her departure cause even a single furrow in his majestic brow? Her heart squeezed. Probably not.

Her sweating palms closed around the increasingly crumpled envelope containing her letter of resignation. The letter made it official, not just an idle threat or even a joke.

Do it now, before you lose your nerve.

Her breath caught in her throat. It didn't seem possible to just walk up to him and say, "Jake, I'm leaving." But if she didn't she'd soon be making arrangements for his wedding.

She'd put up with a lot of things in the three years since she'd moved from their lofty office in Manhattan to this rambling Ruthenian palace, but she could not stand to see him marry another woman.

You deserve to have a life. Claim it.

She squared her shoulders and set out across the room, past the long table elegantly set for fifty of his closest friends.

Jake glanced up. Her blood heated—as always—when his dark eyes fixed on hers. "Andi, could you put me next to Maxi Rivenshnell instead of Alia Kronstadt? I sat next to Alia last night at the Hollernsterns and I don't want Maxi to feel neglected."

Andi froze. How could it have become her job to cultivate his romances with these women? Ruthenia's powerful families were jostling and shoving for the chance to see their daughter crowned queen, and no one cared if little Andi from Pittsburgh got trampled in the stampede.

Least of all Jake.

"Why don't I just put you between them?" She tried to keep her tone even. Right now she wanted to throw her carefully typed letter at him. "That way you can kiss up to both of them at once."

Jake glanced up with a raised brow. She never spoke to him like this, so no wonder he looked surprised.

She straightened her shoulders and thrust the letter out at him. "My resignation. I'll be leaving as soon as the party's over."

Jake's gaze didn't waver. "Is this some kind of joke?"

Andi flinched. She'd known he wouldn't believe her.

"I'm totally serious. I'll do my job tonight. I'd never leave you in the lurch in the middle of an event, but I'm leaving first thing tomorrow." She couldn't believe how calm she sounded. "I apologize for not giving two weeks' notice, but I've worked day and night for the last three years in a strange country without even a week's vacation so I hope you can excuse it. The Independence Day celebrations are well under way and everything's been delegated. I'm sure you won't miss me at all." She squeezed the last words out right as she ran out of gumption.

"Not miss you? The Independence Day celebrations are the biggest event in the history of Ruthenia—well, since the 1502 civil war, at least. We can't possibly manage without you, even for a day."

Andi swallowed. He didn't care about her at all, just about the big day coming up. Wasn't it always like this? He was all business, all the time. After six years working together he barely knew anything about her. Which wasn't fair, since she knew almost everything about him. She'd eaten, slept and breathed Jake Mondragon for the past six years and in the process fallen utterly and totally in love with him.

Shame he didn't even notice she was female.

He peered down at her, concern in his brown eyes. "I told you to take some vacation. Didn't I suggest you go back home for a few weeks last summer?"

Home? Where was home anymore? She'd given up her apartment in Manhattan when she moved here. Her parents both worked long hours and had moved to a different suburb since she left high school, so if she went to see them she'd just end up hanging around their house—probably pining for Jake.

Well, no more. She was going to find a new home and start over. She had an interview for a promising job as an event planner scheduled for next week in Manhattan, and that was a perfect next step to going out on her own.

"I don't want to be a personal assistant for the rest of my life and I'm turning twenty-seven soon so it's time to kick-start my career."

"We can change your title. How about…" His dark eyes narrowed. She couldn't help a slight quickening in her pulse. "Chief executive officer."

"Very funny. Except that I'd still be doing all the same things."

"No one else could do them as well as you."

"I'm sure you'll manage." The palace had a staff of nearly thirty including daytime employees. She was hardly leaving him in the lurch. And she couldn't possibly stand to be here for Independence Day next week. The press had made a big deal of how important it was for him to choose a bride; the future of the monarchy depended on it. He'd jokingly given their third Independence Day as his deadline when he'd assumed the crown three years ago.

Now everyone expected him to act on it. Being a man of his word, Andi knew he would. Maxi, Alia, Carina, there were plenty to choose from, and she couldn't bear to see him with any of them.

Jake put down the guest list, but made no move to take her letter of resignation. "I know you've been working hard. Life in a royal palace is a bit of a twenty-four-hour party, but you do get to set your own hours and you've never been shy about asking for good compensation."

"I'm very well paid and I know it." She did pride herself on asking for raises regularly. She knew Jake respected that, which was probably half the reason she'd done it. As a result she had a nice little nest egg put aside to fund her new start. "But it's time for me to move on."

Why was she even so crazy about him? He'd never shown the slightest glimmer of interest in her.

Her dander rose still higher as Jake glanced at his watch. "The guests will be here any minute and I need to return a call from New York. We'll talk later and figure something out." He reached out and clapped her on the arm, as if she was an old baseball buddy. "We'll make you happy."

He turned and left the room, leaving her holding her letter of resignation between trembling fingers.

Once the door had closed behind him, she let out a growl of frustration. Of course he thought he could talk her down and turn everything around. Isn't that exactly what he was known for? And he even imagined he could make her "happy."

That kind of arrogance should be unforgivable.

Except that his endless confidence and can-do attitude were possibly what she admired and adored most in him.

The only way he could make her happy was to sweep her off her feet into a passionate embrace and tell her he loved her and wanted to marry her.

Except that kings didn't marry secretaries from Pittsburgh. Even kings of funny little countries like Ruthenia.

"The vol-au-vents are done, cook's wondering where to send them."

Andi started at the sound of the events assistant coming through another doorway behind her.

"Why don't you have someone bring them up for the first guests? And the celery stalks with the cheese filling." She tucked the letter behind her back.

Livia nodded, her red curls bobbing about the collar of her white shirt, like it was just another evening.

Which of course it was, except that it was Andi's last evening here.

"So did they ask you in for an interview?" Livia leaned in with a conspiratorial whisper.

"I cannot confirm or deny anything of that nature."

"How are you going to manage an interview in New York when you're imprisoned in a Ruthenian palace?"

Andi tapped the side of her nose. She hadn't told anyone she was leaving. That would feel too much like a betrayal of Jake. Let them just wake up to find her gone.

Livia put her hands on her hips. "Hey, you can't just take off back to New York without me. I told you about that job."

"You didn't say you wanted it."

"I said I thought it sounded fantastic."

"Then you should apply." She wanted to get away. This conversation was not productive and she didn't trust Livia to keep her secrets.

Livia narrowed her eyes. "Maybe I will."

Andi forced a smile. "Save a vol-au-vent for me, won't you?"

Livia raised a brow and disappeared back through the door.

Who would be in charge of choosing the menus and how the food should be served? The cook, probably, though she had quite a temper when she felt pressured. Perhaps Livia? She wasn't the most organized person in the palace and she'd been skipped over for promotion a few times. Probably why she wanted to leave.

Either way, it wasn't her problem and Jake would soon find someone to replace her. Her heart clenched at the thought, but she drew in a steadying breath and marched out into the hallway toward the foyer. She could hear the hum of voices as the first guests took off their luxurious coats and handed them to the footmen to reveal slinky evening gowns and glittering jewels.

Andi smoothed the front of her black slacks. It wasn't appropriate for a member of staff to get decked out like a guest.

All eyes turned to the grand staircase as Jake descended to greet the ladies with a kiss on each cheek. Andi tried to ignore the jealousy flaring in her chest. How ridiculous. One of these girls was going to marry him and she had no business being bothered in any way.

"Could you fetch me a tissue?" asked Maxi Rivenshnell. The willowy brunette cast her question in Andi's direction, without actually bothering to meet her gaze.

"Of course." She reached into her pocket and withdrew a folded tissue from the packet she kept on her. Maxi snatched it from her fingers and tucked it into the top of her long satin gloves without a word of thanks.

She didn't exist for these people. She was simply there to serve them, like the large staff serving each of their aristocratic households.

A waiter appeared with a tray of champagne glasses and she helped to distribute them amongst the guests, then ushered people into the green drawing room where a fire blazed in a stone fireplace carved with the family crest.

Jake strolled and chatted with ease as the room filled with well-dressed Ruthenians. Several of them had only recently returned after decades of exile in places like London, Monaco and Rome, ready to enjoy Ruthenia's promised renaissance after decades of failed socialism.

So far the promise was coming true. The rich were getting richer, and—thanks to Jake's innovative business ideas—everyone else was, as well. Even the staunch anti-monarchists who'd opposed his arrival with protests in the streets now had to admit that Jake Mondragon knew what he was doing.

He'd uncovered markets for their esoteric agricultural

products, and encouraged multinational firms to take advantage of Ruthenia's strategic location in central Europe and its vastly underemployed workforce. The country's GDP had risen nearly 400% in just three years, making eyeballs pop all across the globe.

Andi stiffened as Jake's bold laugh carried through the air. She'd miss that sound. Was she really leaving? A sudden flash of panic almost made her reconsider.

Then she followed the laugh to its source and her heart seized as she saw Jake with his arm around yet another Ruthenian damsel—Carina Teitelhaus—whose blond hair hung in a silky sheet almost to her waist.

Andi tugged her gaze away and busied herself with picking up a dropped napkin. She would not miss seeing him draped over other women one bit. He joked that he was just trying to butter up their powerful parents and get them to invest in the country, but right now that seemed like one more example of how people were pawns to him rather than living beings with feelings.

He'd marry one of them just because it was part of his job. And she couldn't bear to see that.

She needed to leave tonight, before he could use his well-practiced tongue to... Thoughts of his tongue sent an involuntary shiver through her.

Which was exactly why she needed to get out of here. And she wasn't going to give him a chance to talk her out of it.

Jake pushed his dessert plate forward. He'd had all the sticky sweetness he could stand for one night. With Maxi on one side and Alia on the other, each vying to tug his attention from the other, he felt exhausted. Andi knew he liked to have at least one decent conversationalist seated next to him, yet she'd followed through on her threat to stick him between two of the most troublesome vixens in Ruthenia.

Speaking of which, where was Andi?

He glanced around the dining room. The flickering light from the candles along the table and walls created deep shadows, but he didn't see her. Usually she hovered close by in case he needed something.

He summoned one of the servers. "Ulrike, have you seen Andi?"

The quiet girl shook her head. "Would you like me to find her, sir?"

"No, thanks, I'll find her myself." At least he would as soon as he could extricate himself from yet another eight-course meal. He couldn't risk offending either of his bejeweled dinner companions with an early departure since their darling daddies were the richest and most powerful men in the region. Once things were settled, he wouldn't have to worry so much about currying their favor, but while the economy was growing and changing and finding its feet in the world, he needed their flowing capital to oil its wheels.

He could see how men in former eras had found it practical to marry more than one woman. They were both pretty—Maxi a sultry brunette with impressive cleavage and Alia a graceful blonde with a velvet voice—but to be completely honest he didn't want to marry either of them.

Carina Teitelhaus shot him a loaded glance from across the table. Her father owned a large factory complex with a lot of potential for expansion. And she didn't hesitate to remind him of that.

Ruthenia's noblewomen were becoming increasingly aggressive in pursuing the role of queen. Lately he felt as if he were juggling a bevy of flaming torches and the work of keeping them all in the air was wearing on his nerves.

He'd committed to choosing a bride before Independence Day next week. At the time he'd made that statement the deadline had seemed impossibly far off and none of them were sure Ruthenia itself would even still be in existence.

Now it was right upon them, along with the necessity of choosing his wife or breaking his promise. Everyone in the room was painfully aware of each glance, every smile or laugh he dispensed in any direction. The dining table was a battlefield, with salvos firing over the silver.

Usually he could count on Andi to soothe any ruffled feathers with careful seating placements and subtly co-ordinated private trysts. Tonight, though, contrary to her promise, she'd left him in the lurch.

"Do excuse me, ladies." He rose to his feet, avoiding all mascara-laden glances, and strode for the door.

Andi's absence worried him. What if she really did leave? She was the anchor that kept the palace floating peacefully in the choppy seas of a changing Ruthenia. He could give her any task and just assume it was done, without a word of prompting. Her tact and thoughtfulness were exemplary, and her organizational skills were unmatched. He couldn't imagine life without her.

After a short walk over the recently installed plum-colored carpets of the west hallway, he glanced into her ever-tidy office—and found it dark and empty. He frowned. She was often there in the evenings, which coincided with business hours in the U.S. and could be a busy time.

Her laptop was on the desk, as usual. That was a good sign.

Jake headed up the west staircase to the second floor, where most of the bedrooms were located. Andi had a large "family" bedroom rather than one of the pokey servants' quarters on the third floor. She was family, dammit. And that meant she couldn't pick up and leave whenever she felt like it.

A nasty feeling gripped his gut as he approached her closed door. He knocked on the polished wood and listened for movement on the other side.

Nothing.

He tried the handle and to his surprise the door swung open. Curiosity tickling his nerves, he stepped inside and switched on the light. Andi's large room was neat and free of clutter—much like her desk. It looked like a hotel room, with no personal touches added to the rather extravagant palace décor. The sight of two black suitcases—open and packed—stopped him in his tracks.

She really was leaving.

Adrenaline surged through him. At least she hadn't gone yet, or the bags would be gone, too. The room smelled faintly of that subtle scent she sometimes wore, almost as if she was in the room with him.

He glanced around. Could she be hiding from him?

He strode across the room and tugged open the doors of the massive armoire. His breath stopped for a second and he half expected to see her crouched inside.

Which of course she wasn't. Her clothes were gone, though, leaving only empty hangers on the rod.

Anger warred with deep disappointment that she intended to abandon him like this. Did their six years together mean nothing to her?

She couldn't leave without her suitcases. Perhaps he should take them somewhere she couldn't find them. His room, for example.

Unfamiliar guilt pricked him. He didn't even like the idea of her knowing he'd entered her room uninvited, let alone taken her possessions hostage. Andi was a stickler for honesty and had kept him aboveboard more times than he cared to remember. Taking her bags just felt wrong.

She'd said she'd leave as soon as the party was over. A woman of her word, she'd be sure to wait until the last guest was gone. As long as he found her before then, everything would be fine. He switched off the light and left the room as he'd found it.

He scanned the east hall as he headed for the stairs, a sense of foreboding growing inside him. The packed bags were an ominous sign, but he couldn't really believe she'd abandon Ruthenia—and him.

"Jake, darling, we were wondering what happened to you," Maxi called to him from the bottom of the stairs. "Colonel Von Deiter has volunteered to play piano while we dance." She stretched out her long arm, as if inviting him to share the first dance with her.

Since coming to Ruthenia he sometimes felt he'd stepped into a schnitzel-flavored Jane Austen story, where people waltzed around ballrooms and gossiped behind fans. He was happier in a business meeting than on a dance floor, and right now he'd much rather be dictating a letter to Andi than twirling Maxi over the parquet.

"Have you seen Andi, my assistant?"

"The little girl who wears her hair in a bun?"

Jake frowned. He wasn't sure exactly how old Andi was—mid-twenties, maybe?—but it seemed a bit rude for someone of twenty-two to call her a little girl. "She's about five foot seven," he said, with an arched brow. "And yes, she always wears her hair in a bun."

Come to think of it, he'd literally never seen her hair down, which was pretty odd after six years. A sudden violent urge to see Andi with her hair unleashed swept through him. "I've looked all over the palace for her, but she's vanished into thin air."

Maxi shrugged. "Do come dance, darling."

His friend Fritz appeared behind her. "Come on, Jake. Can't let the ladies down. Just a twirl or two. I'm sure Andi has better things to do than wait on you hand and foot."

"She doesn't wait on me hand and foot. She's a valued executive."

Fritz laughed. "Is that why she's always hovering around taking care of your every need?"

Jake stiffened. He never took Andi for granted. He knew just how dependent on her he was. Did she feel that he didn't care?

Frowning, he descended the stairs and took Maxi's offered hand. He was the host, after all. Two waltzes and a polka later he managed to slip out into the hallway.

"Any idea where Andi is?" he asked the first person he saw, who happened to be the night butler.

He shrugged in typical Ruthenian style. "Haven't seen her in hours. Maybe she went to bed?"

Unlikely. Andi never left a party until the last guest had rolled down the drive. But then she'd never quit before, either. He was halfway up the stairs before he realized he was heading for her bedroom again.

Jake stared at her closed door. Was she in there? And if not, were her bags still there?

He knocked, but heard no movement from inside. After checking that the corridor was deserted, he knelt and peered through the keyhole. It was empty—no key on the inside—which suggested she was out. On the other hand, the pitch darkness on the other side meant he couldn't see a thing.

He slipped in—didn't she know better than to leave her door unlocked?—and switched on the light. The suitcases were still there. Closer inspection revealed that one of them had been partially unpacked, as if an item was removed. Still, there were no clues as to Andi's whereabouts.

Frustration pricked his muscles. How could she just disappear like this?

At the foot of the stairs, Fritz accosted him, martini in hand. "When are you going to choose your bride, Jake? We're all getting impatient."

Jake growled. "Why is everyone so mad for me to get married?"

"Because there are precious few kings left in the world and you're up for grabs. The rest of us are waiting to see who's left. None of the girls dare even kiss us anymore, let alone do anything more rakish, in case they're making themselves ineligible for a coronet. They're all fighting for the chance to be called Your Majesty."

"Then they're all nuts. If anyone calls *me* 'Your Majesty,' I'll fire 'em."

Fritz shoved him. "All bluster. And don't deny you have some of the loveliest women in the world to choose from."

"I wish the loveliest women in the world would take off for the night. I'm ready to turn in." Or rather, ready to find and corner Andi.

Fritz cocked his head. "Party pooper. All right. I'll round up the troops and march 'em out for you."

"You're a pal."

Jake watched the last chauffeured Mercedes disappear down the long driveway from the east patio. He needed some air to clear his head before tackling Andi—and watching from here ensured that she couldn't leave without him seeing her.

Could he really stand to marry Maxi or Alia or any of these empty-headed, too-rich, spoiled brats? He'd been surrounded by their kind of women all his life, even in New York. Just the circle he'd been born into. You'd think a king would have more choices than the average Joe, but that was apparently not the case.

Something moving in the darkness caught his eye. He squinted, trying to make out what was crossing the lawn. An animal? Ruthenia had quite large deer that he was supposed to enjoy hunting.

But this creature was lighter, more upright, and moved with a kind of mystical grace. He stepped forward, peering into the gloom of a typical moonlit but cloudy night. The figure whirled and twirled on the lawn, pale fabric flowing around it.

A ghost? His back stiffened. The palace was nearly three hundred years old and built over a far more ancient structure. Tales of sieges and beheadings and people imprisoned in the dungeons rattled around the old stone walls.

Long, pale arms extended sideways as the figure twirled again. A female ghost.

Curiosity goaded him across the patio and down the stone stairs onto the lawn. He walked silently across the damp grass, eyes fixed on the strange apparition. As he drew closer he heard singing—soft and sweet—almost lost in the low breeze and the rustling of the trees.

Entranced, he moved nearer, enjoying the figure's graceful movements and the silver magic of her voice.

He stopped dead when he realized she was singing in English.

"Andi?"

Despite the hair streaming over her shoulders and the long, diaphanous dress, he recognized his assistant of six years, arms raised to the moon, swaying and singing in the night.

He strode forward faster. "Are you okay?"

She stopped and stared at him and the singing ceased. Her eyes shone bright in the darkness.

"What are you doing out here?" He walked right up to her, partly to prove to himself that she was real and not a figment of his imagination. His chest swelled with relief. At least now he'd found her and they could have that talk he'd been rehearsing in his head all night.

"Why don't we go inside?" He reached out for her hand, almost expecting his own to pass through it. She still looked so spectral, smiling in the cloud-veiled moonlight.

But the hand that seized his felt warm. Awareness snapped through him as her fingers closed around his. Her hair was longer than he'd imagined. Almost to the peaks of her nipples, which jutted out from the soft dress. He swallowed. He'd never noticed what…luxurious breasts Andi had. They were usually hidden under tailored suits and crisp blouses.

He struggled to get back on task. "We need to talk."

Andi's grip tightened on his, but she didn't move. Her face looked different. Transfixed, somehow. Her eyes sparkling and her lips glossy and parted. Was she drunk?

"You must be cold." On instinct he reached out to touch her upper arm, which was bare in the floaty evening gown she wore. As he drew closer, her free arm suddenly wrapped around his waist with force.

Jake stilled as she lifted her face to his. She smelled of that same soft scent she always wore, not a trace of alcohol, just flowers and sweetness. He groped for words, but failed to find any as her lips rose toward his.

Next thing he knew he was kissing her full—and hard—on the mouth.

TWO

Jake let his arms wind around her waist. The movement was as instinctive as breathing. Their mouths melted together and her soft body pressed against his. Desire flared inside him, hot and unexpected, as the kiss deepened. His fingers ached to explore the lush curves she'd kept hidden for so long.

But this was Andi—his faithful and long-suffering assistant, not some bejeweled floozy who just wanted to lock lips with a monarch.

He pulled back from the kiss with great difficulty, unwinding himself from the surprisingly powerful grip of her slim arms. A momentary frown flashed across her lovely face—why had he never noticed she was so pretty?—then vanished again as a smile filled her soft eyes and broadened her mouth.

She lifted a hand and stroked his cheek. "You're beautiful."

Shocked, Jake struggled for a response. "*You're* beautiful. I'm handsome." He lifted a brow, as if to assure himself they were both kidding.

She giggled—in a most un-Andi-like way—and tossed her head, which sent her hair tumbling over her shoulders in a shimmering cascade. She twirled again, and the soft dress draped her form, allowing him a tantalizing view of her figure. He'd certainly never seen her in this dress before. Floor-length and daringly see-through, it was far dressier and more festive than her usual attire.

"Happiness is glorious joy," she sang, as she turned to face him again.

"Huh?" Jake frowned.

"Mysterious moonlight and wonderful wishes." Another silver peal of laughter left her lips—which looked quite different than he remembered, bare of their usual apricot lipstick and kissed to ruby fullness.

Unless she'd suddenly turned to poetry—very bad poetry at that—she must be intoxicated. He didn't smell anything on her breath, though. And didn't she always insist she was allergic to alcohol? He couldn't remember ever seeing her with a real drink.

Drugs?

He peered at her eyes. Yes, her pupils were dilated. Still, Andi experimenting with illegal substances? It seemed impossible.

"Did you take something?"

"Steal? I'd never steal from you. You're my true love." She gazed at him as she spoke the words, eyes clear and blue as a summer sky.

Jake groped for words. "I meant, did you take any pills?"

You're my true love? She was obviously tripping on something. He'd better get her inside before she tried to fly from the parapets or walk on the water in the moat. "Let's go inside."

He wrapped his arm around her, and she squeezed against him and giggled again. This was not the Andi he knew. Perhaps the stress of threatening to leave had encouraged her to take some kind of tranquilizer. He had no idea how those things worked, but couldn't come up with any other explanation for her odd behavior.

"You smell good." She pressed her face against him, almost tripping him.

Jake's eyes widened, but he managed to keep walking. Her body bumping against his was not helping his own sanity. Now she'd slid an arm around his waist and her fingers fondled him as they walked. His blood was heating in a most uncomfortable way.

Maybe he could bring both of them back down to earth.

"It was cold of you to seat me between Maxi and Alia."

"Who?" She marched gaily along over the lawn, still clinging to him. No reaction to the names.

"Maxi and Alia. Both of them fighting over me was a bit much to take on top of the cook's roulade."

"Pretty names. We haven't met. You must introduce me sometime." She pulled her arm from his waist and took off skipping across the damp lawn.

Jake paused and stared for a moment, then strode after her.

Since he didn't particularly want any of the other staff to see Andi in this compromising state, Jake hustled her into his private chambers and locked the door. That was the accepted signal that he was off duty for the night and not to be disturbed.

Andi made herself quite at home, curling up on one

of the sofas, with a languid arm draping along the back. "Happiness is as happiness does," she said dreamily.

Jake resisted the urge to pour himself a whisky. "Listen, what you said about leaving. I saw your bags—"

"Leave? I would never leave you, my love." Her face rested in a peaceful smile.

Jake swallowed. "So you're staying."

"Of course. Forever and ever and ever." Her eyes sparkled.

"Ah. That's settled then." He moved to the liquor cabinet, deciding to have that whisky after all. "I am relieved. The thought of managing without you was quite frightening."

Andi had risen from the sofa and was now waltzing around the room by herself, singing, "Someday my prince will come." She twirled, sweeping her pale evening dress about her like smoke. "Some day I'll love someone." Her radiant smile was almost infectious.

Almost. Jake took a swig of his drink. Did she really think they were having some kind of relationship outside their well-established professional one? As much as the idea appealed right this second, he knew it would really mess things up once she snapped out of whatever chemical induced trance she was in.

He'd better remind her of that. "We've worked together a long time."

She stopped twirling for a moment, and frowned. "I don't think I do work."

"You're a lady of leisure?"

She glanced down at her evening gown. "Yes." She frowned; then her expression brightened. "I must be. Otherwise why would I be dressed like this?"

Had she temporarily forgotten that she was his assistant? "Why are you dressed like that?" She'd certainly never worn anything so festive before.

"It's pretty, isn't it?" She looked up at him. "Do you like it?"

"Very much." He allowed his eyes to soak up the vision of it draped over her gorgeous body. Desire licked through him in tiny, tormenting flames.

Andi reached out and tugged at his shirt. Even that made his synapses flash and his groin tighten.

"Why don't you come sit with me." She stroked the sofa cushion next to her.

"I'm not sure that's a good idea." His voice came out gruff.

"Why not?"

"It's late. We should get to bed." The image of her in his bed flooded his brain, especially as it was right there in the next room. But caution tightened his muscles.

"Oh, don't be silly—" She frowned. "How odd." She glanced up at him. "I can't think of your name right now."

Jake was about to tell her, but something made him stop. "You don't know my name?"

She looked up for a few moments, as if searching her brain. "No, I don't seem to know it."

Panic tightened his chest. "What's your name?"

She looked toward the ceiling, scrunched up her brow and clenched her fists. When she finally looked back at him, her expression had changed from glee to confusion. "I'm not sure."

"I think we should call for a doctor." He pulled his phone out.

"A doctor? What for? I feel fine."

He hesitated. "Let me look at you. Did you bump your head?"

She shrugged. "I don't think so."

He put his phone back in his pocket and touched her temples with his thumbs. Her eyes sparkled as she looked up at him and her scent was a torment. He worked his fingers gently back into her hair—which was soft and luxurious to touch. "Hey, I feel a lump."

"Ouch!"

"You have a bruise." He touched it gently. A big goose egg. That explained a whole lot. "We're definitely calling the doctor. You could have a concussion." He dialed the number. "Listen, sorry it's so late, Gustav, but Andi's taken a fall and bumped her head. She's not talking too much sense and I think you should look at her."

Gustav replied that he'd be there in the ten minutes it took to drive from the town, and to keep her awake until he got there.

After letting the staff know to expect Gustav, Jake sat down on the sofa opposite her. It made sense to find out just how much of her memory had vanished. "How old are you?" Odd that he didn't know that.

"Over twenty-one." She laughed. Then frowned. "Other than that, I'm not too sure. How old do I look?"

Jake smiled. "I'd be a damned fool if I answered a question like that from a woman." He decided he'd be better off following the lawyer's strategy of only asking questions he knew the answer to. It was pretty embarrassing that he really didn't know how old she was. "How long have you lived here?"

She stared at him, mouth slightly open, then looked away. "Why are you asking me these silly questions? I've lived here a long time. With you."

Her gaze—innocent yet needy—ate into him. She stroked the sofa arm with her fingers and his skin tingled in response. She seemed to have lost her memory, and, in its absence, assumed they were a couple.

Jake sucked in a long breath. They'd never had any kind of flirtation, even a playful one. She always seemed so businesslike and uninterested in such trivial matters. He'd never really looked at her that way, either. Much simpler to keep business and pleasure separate, especially when a really good assistant was so hard to find and keep.

Right now he was seeing a different aspect of Andi— alarming, and intriguing.

She rose and walked a few steps to his sofa, then sank down next to him. Her warm thigh settled against his, causing his skin to sizzle even through their layers of clothing. He stiffened. Was it fair to offer a man this kind of temptation?

At least it was keeping her awake.

Her fingers reached up to his black bow tie and tugged at one end. The knot came apart and the silk ribbons fell to his starched shirtfront.

"Much better." She giggled again, then pulled the tie out from his collar and undid the top button of his shirt. Jake watched, barely breathing, trying to suppress the heaving tide of arousal surging inside him.

After all, it would be rude to push her away, wouldn't it? Especially in her delicate and mysterious condition.

When her fingers roamed into his hair, causing his groin to ache uncomfortably, he had to take action. He stood up rapidly. "The doctor will be here any minute. Can I get you a glass of water?"

"I'm not thirsty." Her hurt look sent a pang to his heart.

"Still, it's good to keep hydrated." He busied himself with filling a glass at the bar, and took care not to accidentally brush her fingertips as he handed it to her. Her cheeks and lips were flushed with pink, which made her look aroused and appealing at the same time.

She took the glass and sipped cautiously. Then looked up at him with a slight frown. "I do feel odd."

Jake let out a sigh of relief. This seemed more like the real Andi than the one spouting loopy epithets. "You'll probably feel better in the morning, but it can't hurt to have the doctor take a look."

Alarm filled him as tears welled in her eyes. "It's just so strange not being able to remember anything. How could I not even know my own name?" A fat tear rolled down her soft cheek.

Disturbing that he now knew how soft her cheek was.

"Your name is Andi Blake."

"Andi." She said it softly. Then frowned again. "Is that short for something?"

Jake froze. Was it? He had no idea. He didn't remember ever calling her anything else, but it had been six long years since he'd seen her résumé and frankly he couldn't remember the details. "Nope. Just Andi. It's a pretty name."

He regretted the lame comment, something you might say to a six-year-old. But then he didn't have experience in dealing with amnesiacs, so maybe it wasn't all that inappropriate.

"Oh." She seemed to mull that over. She wiped her eyes. "At least I know my own name now." Then she bit her lip. "Though it doesn't sound at all familiar." Tears glistened in her eyes. "What if my memory doesn't come back?"

"Don't worry about that, I'm sure—" A knock on the door announced the arrival of the doctor, and Jake released a sigh of relief. "Please send him in."

Andi's tearful trembling subsided as the doctor checked her over, peering into her eyes with a light, checking her pulse and breathing, and taking her temperature.

As the local doctor, he'd been to the palace before and knew Andi. She showed no sign of recognizing or remembering him. His questions revealed that while she remembered general concepts, like how to tie a knot, she recalled nothing about her own life.

"Andi, would you excuse us a moment?" The doctor ushered Jake out into the hallway. "Is she exhibiting mood changes?"

"Big time. She's not like herself at all. She seemed happy—silly even—when I first found her. Just now she was crying. I think the reality of what's going on is setting in."

"Sounds like a pretty textbook case of temporary memory loss, if there is such a thing." The older man snapped his briefcase closed. "Lots of emotion. Mood swings. Loss of long-term memory. I've never seen it before, myself, but in most cases the memory eventually starts to come back."

"When? How long will she be like this?"

The doctor gave a Ruthenian shrug. "Could be days, could be weeks. There's a slim possibility she won't ever recall everything. She's certainly had a good bump to her head, but no signs of concussion or other injury. Do you have any idea what happened?"

Jake shook his head. "I found her out dancing on the lawn. I didn't see anything happen at all."

"Make sure she gets plenty of sleep, and encourage her with questions to bring back her memory." The doctor hoisted his bag onto his shoulder. "Call me anytime, of course."

"Thanks." Jake frowned. "Can we keep this amnesia thing between us? I think Andi would be embarrassed if people knew what was going on. She's a very private person."

The doctor's brow furrowed even more than usual. "Of course." *Your Highness.* The unspoken words hovered in the air. Jake sensed slight disapproval at his request for secrecy, but he knew the physician would honor it. "Please keep me posted on her progress."

Jake went back into his suite and locked the door. Andi was sitting on the sofa and her mood seemed to have brightened. Her tears were gone, and a smile hovered in her eyes as she looked up at him. "Will I live?"

"Without a doubt. It's late. How about some sleep?"

"I'm not at all sleepy." She draped herself over the sofa, eyes heavy-lidded with desire. "I'd rather play."

Jake's eyes widened. Could this really be the same Andi he'd worked with all these years? It was shocking to imagine that this flirtatious person had been lurking inside her the whole time. Unless it was just a mood swing caused by her condition.

She rose from the sofa and swept toward him, then threw her arms around his waist. "I do love you."

Gulp. Jake patted her cautiously on the back. This could last for days. Or weeks. Or longer.

His skin tingled as her lips pressed against his cheek. "I'm so glad we're together." Her soft breath heated his skin as she breathed the words in his ear.

And this was the woman who'd announced, only a few hours before, that she was leaving for good, that night.

At least that was off the agenda for now.

His phone rang and he tensed. What now? "Excuse me." He extricated himself from her embrace and pulled it from his pocket.

A glance at the number revealed the caller was Maxi. She'd formed a new habit of calling him at bizarre times like the crack of dawn or during his morning workout. This call in the wee hours was a new and even more unappealing attempt to monopolize his time.

Still, maybe there was some kind of emergency.

"Hi, Maxi."

"Jake, are you still awake?" Her breathy voice grated on his nerves.

"I am now." He glanced at Andi, who was twirling around the room doing the dance of the seven veils, or something. "What do you want?"

"So impatient. I just wanted to chat. About you and me."

He shoved a hand through his hair. Maxi was definitely not The One. In fact she could be voted Least Likely to be Queen of Ruthenia, since she was firmly in his "keep your enemies closer" circle. He'd been drawing her in and inviting her confidence on purpose. Not because he loved her, or was even attracted to her. He'd found evidence that her family was involved in weapons dealing and possibly worse, but he didn't have enough proof to do anything about it yet.

None of the other girls dealt in arms or drugs, as far as he knew, but they were all empty-headed and silly. Right now he was more attracted to his own assistant than to any of Ruthenia's pampered beauties.

An idea crept into his brain.

Since Andi seemed to assume they were a couple, why not make it a reality? He had to marry someone. He could announce to the press tomorrow that his chosen bride was his own assistant.

A chill of sangfroid crept over him. Could he really arrange his own marriage so easily? Andi was agreeable, intelligent and practical, perfectly suited to life in the spotlight. She'd worked just outside it for years and knew the whole routine of palace life perfectly. Apart from her presumably humble origins—he really didn't know anything about her origins, but since he'd never met her parents at a ball, he was guessing—she'd be the ideal royal wife.

They'd known each other for years and he could simply

announce that they'd been involved for a long time but kept their relationship secret.

The announcement would send the long-fingernailed wolves away from his door for good. He and Andi could marry, produce an heir and a spare or two, and live a long, productive life in the service of the citizens of Ruthenia— wasn't that what was really important?

Andi had wandered into the bedroom and a quick glance revealed that she now lay sprawled on his bed.

Heat surged through him like a shot of brandy.

Her dress draped over her, displaying her inviting curves like an ice-cream sundae with whipped cream on top. Her gaze beckoned him, along with her finger. His muscles itched to join her on the bed and enjoy discovering more of Andi's wickedly intriguing sensual side.

"Maxi, I have to go. Have a good night."

"I can think of a way to have a much better night."

Jake's flesh crawled. "Sleep knits up the raveled sleeve of care."

"Is that Moby?"

"Shakespeare. Goodnight, Maxi."

"When are you going to choose your wife?" Jake flinched at the blunt question, and the shrill voice that asked it. "Daddy wants to know. He's not sure whether to contribute funds for the new hydroelectric project."

Jake stiffened. This is what it all boiled down to. Money and power. Well, he didn't want to build Ruthenia with ill-gotten gains from the black market, and he'd rather share his life with a hardworking woman than one who thought she could buy her way into a monarchy. "I've already chosen my wife."

"What do you mean?" she gasped.

He moved across the room, away from the bedroom where Andi now sprawled enticingly on the bed. She was humming again, and wouldn't hear him. "I intend to marry Andi Blake, my longtime assistant."

"You're joking."

"Not in the slightest. She and I have had a close relationship for six years. We intend to enjoy each other's company for many more."

Already his pronouncement had an official ring to it. Marriage to Andi was a perfectly natural and practical course of action. He was confident Andi would agree, especially since she seemed to have romantic feelings toward him.

"People are going to be very, very…" She paused, apparently struggling for words.

"Happy for us. Yes. Of course you'll be invited to the wedding." He couldn't help a tiny smile sneaking across his mouth. Maxi had clearly intended to be the featured host of the event.

"Invited to the wedding?" Her growl made him pull the phone away from his ear. "You're impossible!"

The dial tone made a satisfying noise. And now he wouldn't have to even make an announcement. Maxi would do all the legwork for him.

All he had to do was tell Andi.

Three

Morning sunlight streamed through the gap between heavy brocade curtains. Hot and uncomfortable, Andi looked down to find herself wearing a long evening dress under the covers. Weirdest thing, she had no idea why.

She sat bolt upright. Where was she?

His room. She remembered the soft touch of his lips on her cheek. Her skin heated at the memory. "Good night, Andi," he'd said. So she was Andi.

Andi.

Who was Andi? She racked her brain, but the racks were empty. She couldn't even remember the name of the handsome man who'd put her to bed, though she knew they were close.

How could her whole reality just slip away? Her heart pounded and she climbed out of bed. Her chiffon-y dress was horribly wrinkled and had made an uncomfortable nightgown, leaving lines printed on her skin.

She moved to the window and pulled one of the heavy drapes aside. The view that greeted her was familiar—rolling green hills dotted with grazing sheep, rising to fir-covered mountains. The village in the middle distance, with its steep clay-tiled roofs and high church steeple.

Looking down she saw the long rectangular fishpond in the walled courtyard. She didn't recall seeing it from this angle before.

But then she didn't recall much.

Andi what? She pressed a hand to her forehead. Blake, he'd said. How could even her own last name sound alien and unfamiliar?

She walked to the door and cautiously pulled it open. She caught her breath at the sight of him, standing in front of the mirror, buttoning his collar. Thick black-brown hair swept back from the most handsome face she'd ever seen. Warm, dark eyes reflected in the glass. Mouth set in a serious but good-humored line. Heat flooded her body and she stood rooted to the spot.

He turned. "Morning, Andi. How are you feeling?"

His expression looked rather guarded.

"Okay. I think. I…I can't seem to remember much." Had she slept with him last night? Her fully dressed state seemed to suggest not. Her body was sending all kinds of strange signals, though—pulsing and throbbing and tingling in mysterious places—so she couldn't tell.

"What can you remember?" He didn't look surprised at her announcement. Did he know what was going on?

"Why can't I remember?"

He took a few steps toward her and put his hand on her arm. Arousal flashed through her at his touch. "You bumped your head. The doctor says you're not concussed."

"How long have I been like this?" Fear twisted in her stomach.

"Just since last night. The doc said your memory will come back soon. A few weeks at most."

"Oh." Andi frowned, feeling ridiculously vulnerable, standing there in her wrinkled dress with no idea of who or where she was. Except that she was very—very—attracted to this man. "What should I do in the meantime?"

"Don't worry about a thing. I'll take care of you." He stroked her cheek. The reassuring touch of his fingers made her breath catch and sent tingles of arousal cascading through her.

She frowned. How should she put a question like this? "Are we...intimate?"

His gaze flickered slightly, making her stomach tighten. Had she said the wrong thing? She felt sure there must be something between them. She remembered kissing him last night, and the memory of the kiss made her head grow light.

"Yes, Andi. We're going to be married." He looked down at her hands, gathering them in his.

"Oh." She managed a smile. "What a relief that I have you to take care of me until my memory comes back." If it did come back. "It's embarrassing to ask, but how long have we been together?"

"Oh, years." He met her gaze again.

"It seems impossible, but I don't remember your name."

"Jake." He looked slightly flustered, and why wouldn't he? "Jake Mondragon."

"Jake Mondragon." She smiled dreamily, allowing herself to relax in his sturdy presence. And his face was kind, despite the proud, sculpted features. Totally gorgeous, too. She was very lucky. "So I'm going to be Andi Mondragon."

Jake's eyes widened. "Uh, yes. Yes, you are."

Why did he seem surprised by the idea? It was hardly an odd one if they'd been together for years. "Or was I going to keep my original surname?" Curiosity pricked her.

He smiled. "I don't think we'd discussed whether you would change it or not."

"Oh." Funny they hadn't talked about that. After all, what would the children be called? "How long have we been engaged?"

He lifted his chin slightly. "Just since yesterday. We haven't even told anyone yet."

Yesterday? Her eyes widened. "How odd that I would lose my memory on the same day. I can't even remember the proposal."

She watched his Adam's apple move as he swallowed. He must be upset that she couldn't even remember such a momentous and important moment. "I'm sure it will come back eventually."

An odd sensation started forming in the pit of her stomach. Something felt...off. How could she have forgotten her own fiancé? It was disorienting to know less about her own life than someone else did. "I think I should lay low for a few days. I don't really want to see anyone until I know who I am."

Jake grimaced. "I'm afraid that's going to be hard. The media will probably want an interview."

"About my memory?"

"About our engagement."

"Why would we tell the media?"

Jake hesitated for a moment. "Since I'm the king of this country, everything I do is news."

Andi's mouth fell open. "You're the king?" She was pretty sure she wasn't some kind of royal princess or aristocrat. She certainly didn't feel like one. But maybe that explained the long evening gown. She glanced down at its crumpled folds. "How did we meet?"

Jake's lids lowered slightly. "You're my longtime assistant. We just decided to marry."

She blinked. That explained all the sizzling and tingling in her body—she'd been intimate with this man for a long time. How bizarre that she had to hear about her own life from someone else. From the man she'd apparently dated for years and planned to marry.

Then again, if she'd been seeing this man for years, why did his mere presence send shivers of arousal tingling over her skin and zapping through her insides?

A deep breath didn't help clear the odd mix of confusion and emptiness in her brain. She hoped her memory would return before she did anything to embarrass him. "I guess I should get changed. I feel silly asking this, but where are my clothes?"

Jake froze for a moment, brow furrowed. "You wait here. I'll bring some for you."

"It's okay, I don't want to put you to any trouble. If you'll just tell me where they are." She hated feeling so helpless.

"It's no trouble at all. Just relax on the sofa for a bit. I'll be right back."

She shrugged. "I suppose you probably know what I like to wear better than I do. Still, I could come with you. I need to figure out where everything is."

"Better that you get dressed first. I'll be right back."

He left the room abruptly, leaving Andi uneasy. Why was he so anxious for her to stay here? Like he didn't want anyone to see her. Maybe he didn't want people to know about her loss of memory.

She glanced around the room, already feeling alone and worried without him. Did he have to leave? As the king, you'd think he'd just call for a servant to bring her clothes.

Or did things not work that way anymore? When your memory had taken flight it was hard to distinguish between fairy tales and ordinary life.

She lay back on the sofa and tried to relax. She was engaged to a handsome and caring man that she was fiercely attracted to. Maybe her real life was a fairy tale?

Jake strode along the corridor, hoping he wouldn't run into anyone—which was an unfamiliar feeling for him. Usually he prided himself on being up-front and open, but right now he didn't want anyone to know Andi had been about to leave.

That felt…personal.

He was confident she'd keep it to herself until she'd squared things with him. She'd proved over the years that she was the soul of discretion and confided in no one.

Her job was her life. At least it had been until she decided she'd had enough of it. Hurt flared inside him that she could even consider abandoning him and Ruthenia, especially now he'd realized she was the ideal wife for him. This odd memory loss would give him a chance to turn things around and keep her here for good.

He reached her door and slipped into the room with a sense of relief. Her packed suitcases still sat on the floor next to the bed. He closed the door and began to unpack, hanging the clothes back in the closet and placing some items in the large dresser. He intended to make it look as if she'd never thought of leaving.

Some things startled him. A lacy pink nightgown. A pair of black stockings and garters. When had she had occasion to wear these? He didn't think she had been on a single date since they'd moved to Ruthenia.

Guilt speared him at the thought. She was so busy working she had no life at all outside of her job. Why had he assumed that would be enough for her?

He placed her toiletries back in the bathroom. Handling her shampoo bottle and deodorant felt oddly intimate, like he was peeking into her private life. She had a lot of different lipsticks and he tried to arrange them upright on the bathroom shelf, though really he had no idea how she kept them.

She looked a lot prettier without all that lipstick on. Maybe he should just ditch them and she'd be none the wiser?

No. These were her possessions and that would be wrong.

He arranged her eyeliner pencils and powders and bottles of makeup on the shelf, too. Did all women have so much of this stuff? She had a ridiculous assortment of hair products, too—gels and sprays and mousses—which was funny since her hair was almost always tied back in a bun.

It took a full twenty minutes to get her bags unpacked and rearranged in some sort of convincing order. He shoved the bags under the bed and stood back to admire his handiwork.

Too perfect. He pulled a pair of panty hose from a drawer and draped them over the bed. Better.

He was about to leave when he remembered he was supposed to bring her back something to wear. Hmm. Mischief tickled his insides. What would he like to see her in? Not one of those stiff, bright suits she always wore.

He pulled a pair of jeans from one of the drawers. He'd never seen her in those, so why not? A blue long-sleeved T-shirt seemed to match, and he pulled some rather fetching black lace underwear—tags still attached—from the drawer.

He removed the tags. Why not let her think she wore stuff like this every day?

He rolled the items in a soft blue-and-gray sweater and set off down the corridor again, glancing left and right, glad that the palace was still quiet at this hour.

Andi's uncharacteristically anxious face greeted him as he returned to his rooms. She seemed quite different from last night, when she was spouting garbled poetry and dancing around the room. Now she sat curled up on the sofa, clutching her knees.

"How are you feeling?" Her rigid posture made him want to soothe and relax her.

"Nervous. It's odd not knowing anything about myself or my life. More than odd. Scary."

Jake tried to ignore the trickle of guilt that slid down his spine. He had no intention of telling her the truth about her plans to leave. And come to think of it, he hadn't seen any tickets or itineraries in her room. Maybe her plans weren't all that firm, anyway. "Don't worry. It'll all come back eventually. In the meantime, we'll just carry on as usual. Does that sound okay?"

She nodded.

"I brought some clothes." He set them down on the sofa beside him.

She unrolled the sweater and her eyes widened briefly at the sight of the lacy bra and panties. "Thanks."

She glanced up at him, and then at the pile of clothes again.

He resisted a powerful urge to see her slip into that sexy underwear. "You can change in the bedroom if you want some privacy. There are fresh towels in the bathroom if you'd like to take a shower."

Andi closed the bedroom door behind her. If Jake was her fiancé, why did the thought of changing in front of him make her want to blush crimson? She'd probably done it numerous times in the past. This whole situation was so weird. Her own fiancé felt—not like a stranger, but not like an intimate companion, either.

Must be pretty uncomfortable for Jake, too, though he didn't seem too flustered. Maybe he was just the sort to take things in stride. He had a reassuring air of composure, which was probably a good thing in a king.

Andi slipped out of her crumpled evening gown and climbed into a luxurious marble shower that could accommodate about six people. Unlike the scenery outside the window, and even the dressing room/sitting area, which felt at least somewhat familiar, everything in the bathroom suite seemed totally strange, like she'd literally never been there before. Maybe the memory was selective like that in its recall.

The warm water soothed and caressed her and she dried off feeling fresher.

She managed to arrange her hair into some semblance of order using a black comb, and applied some rather masculine-scented deodorant. They obviously didn't share this bathroom as there were no girly items in here at all. Unease pricked her skin again. No real reason for it though. Probably plenty of engaged couples slept in separate rooms. And one would expect extra attention to propriety in a royal household.

The black underwear he'd brought made her want to blush again. Why? It was her own, so why did it feel too racy for her? The bra fit perfectly, and the panties, while very low-cut, were comfortable, too. She was glad to quickly cover them with the practical jeans and blue T-shirt. No socks or shoes? Well, she could go retrieve those herself. She tied the soft sweater around her shoulders and stepped outside.

Jake's mouth broadened into a smile at the sight of her. "You look great." His dark eyes shone with approval.

She shrugged. Something about the ensemble felt funny. Too casual, maybe. It didn't seem right to wear jeans in a royal palace.

"You didn't bring any shoes." She pointed to her bare feet.

"Maybe I wanted to admire your pretty toes."

Heat flared inside her as his gaze slid down her legs to the toes in question. She giggled, feeling suddenly lighthearted. "My toes would still like to find some shoes to hide in. Why wasn't I wearing any last night? I looked in the bedroom and the dressing room, but I didn't see any."

"I don't know." Jake's expression turned more serious. "You were twirling barefoot on the lawn when I found you."

Andi's skin prickled with unease again. "So we decided to get engaged, and then I lost my memory?"

Jake nodded. His guarded expression didn't offer much reassurance.

He took a step toward her. "Don't worry, we'll get through this together." He slid his arms around her waist. Heat rippled in her belly. His scent stirred emotions and sensations and she softened into his embrace. She wondered if he was going to say he loved her, but he simply kissed her softly on the mouth.

Pleasure crept over her. "I guess I'm lucky it happened right here, and that I'm not wandering around some strange place with no idea who I am like those stories you see on the news."

"It is fortunate, isn't it?" He kissed her again. This time both their eyes slid closed and the kiss deepened. Colors swirled and sparkled behind Andi's eyelids and sensation crashed through her, quickening her pulse and making her breath come in unsteady gasps. Her fingers itched to touch the skin under his starched shirt.

She stepped back, blinking, once they managed to pull apart. Were their kisses always this intense?

Jake smiled, relaxed and calm. Apparently this was all par for the course. Andi patted her hair, wishing she could feel half as composed as he looked. Terror snapped through her at the prospect of facing strangers and trying to pretend everything was normal. "Can we keep our engagement a secret for now?"

Jake's eyes widened for a second. "Why?"

"Just so I don't have to answer a lot of questions when I don't even know who I am."

He frowned. "I'm afraid it's too late. I told someone on the phone last night."

"Who?" Not that she'd even know the name.

"Maxi Rivenshnell. She's a…friend of the family."

Andi paused. The name had a nasty ring to it. Maybe it was the way he pronounced it, like something that tasted bad. "Maybe she won't tell anyone."

"I suspect she'll tell everyone." He turned and strode across the room. Shoved a hand through his dark hair. Then he turned and approached her. "But nothing's going to stop me buying you a ring today, and you're going to choose it. First, let me summon your shoes."

Jake parked his Mercedes in his usual reserved spot in the town's main square. No need for chauffeurs and armed escorts in tiny Ruthenia. He rushed around the car to help Andi out, but she was already on her feet and closing the door by the time he got there.

She'd devoured her breakfast of fruit and pastries in the privacy of his suite. At least he knew what she liked to eat. Despite obvious confusion over little things like how to find her way around, she seemed healthy and relatively calm, which was a huge relief.

Of course her reluctance to announce their engagement was a slight hitch in his plans to unload his unwanted admirers, but word would get out soon enough. Ruthenia had more than its share of gossiping busybodies, and for once they'd be working in his favor.

He took her arm and guided her across the main square. Morning sunlight illuminated the old stone facades of the shops and glinted off the slate tiles of the church steeple. Pigeons gathered near the fountain, where a little girl tossed bread crumbs at them and two dogs barked a happy greeting as their owners stopped for a chat.

"The local town," murmured Andi.

"Does it look familiar?"

"A little. Like I've seen it in a dream rather than in real life. It's so pretty."

"It is lovely. You and I saw it together for the first time three years ago."

She paused. "You didn't grow up here?"

"No, I grew up in the States, like you. I didn't come here until the socialist government collapsed in a heap of corruption scandals and people started agitating for the return of the royal family. At first I thought they were nuts, then I realized I could probably help put the country back on its feet." He looked at her, her clear blue eyes wide, soaking in everything he said. "I couldn't have done it without you."

His chest tightened as he spoke the words. All true. Andi's quiet confidence and brisk efficiency made almost anything possible. The prospect of carrying on without her by his side was unthinkable.

"Was I good at being your assistant?" Her serious gaze touched him. "I don't remember anything about my job."

"Exemplary. You've been far more than my assistant. My right-hand woman is a better description."

She looked pleased. "I guess that's a good thing, since we're getting married."

"Absolutely." Jake swallowed. How would she react when her memory returned and she realized they were never romantically involved? He drew in a breath. She wasn't in love with him. Still, she was sensible enough to see that marriage between them would be in the best interests of Ruthenia.

And that kiss had been surprisingly spicy. In fact, he couldn't remember experiencing anything like it in his fairly substantial kissing experience.

Maybe it was the element of the forbidden. He'd never considered kissing his assistant and it still felt...wrong. Probably because it was wrong of him to let her think they'd been a couple. But once a ring was on her finger, they really would be engaged and everything would be on the up and up.

At least until her memory came back.

"The jeweler is down this street." He led her along a narrow cobbled alley barely wide enough for a cart. The kind of street he'd have to fold in his wing mirrors to drive down without scraping the ancient walls on either side. Thick handblown glass squares glazed the bowed window of the shop, giving a distorted view of the luxurious trinkets inside.

Despite its old-world ambience—or maybe because of it—this jeweler was one of the finest in Europe and had recently regained its international reputation as part of Jake's Rediscover Ruthenia campaign. He'd bought quite a few pieces here—gifts for foreign diplomats and wealthy Ruthenian acquaintances. Why had it never occurred to him to buy something lovely for Andi?

He opened the heavy wood door and ushered her in, unable to resist brushing her waist with his fingers as he coaxed her through. The formally attired proprietor rushed forward to greet them. "Welcome, sir." Jake was grateful the man remembered his aversion to pompous titles. "How can we assist you today? A custom commission, perhaps?"

Jake hesitated. Andi might well like a ring designed to her exact specifications—but he needed a ring on her finger right now to make an honest man of him. He certainly didn't want her memory coming back before the setting was tooled. "I suspect you have something lovely in the shop already."

He took Andi's hand in his. It was warm, and he squeezed it to calm her nerves. "We're looking for an engagement ring."

The elderly jeweler's eyes opened wide. His gaze slid to Andi, then back again. He seemed unsure what to make of the situation. Perhaps he'd been following the local gossip columns and was already designing one with Maxi or Alia in mind. "Should I be offering you my congratulations?"

"Most certainly." Jake slid his arm around Andi.

"Wonderful." The jeweler bowed his head slightly in Andi's direction. "My best wishes for you both. And in time for Independence Day, too." A smile creased his wrinkled face. "The whole nation will be overjoyed. I do think a custom creation would be most appropriate. Perhaps with the family crest?"

"Why don't we take a look at what you have in stock?" He tightened his arm around Andi's waist, then loosened it, suddenly aware of how intent he was to hold on to her. Not that she was resisting. She leaned into him, perhaps seeking reassurance he was happy to provide.

A large tray of sparkling rings appeared from a deep wooden cabinet. Jake glanced at Andi and saw her eyes widen.

"See if anything appeals to you." He spoke softly,

suddenly feeling the intimacy of the moment. The first step in their journey through life as a married couple. The rings were nearly all diamonds, some single and some triple, with a large stone flanked by two smaller stones. A few more had clusters of diamonds and there was a large sapphire and a square cut ruby.

Andi drew in a long breath, then reached for a small single diamond in a carved platinum band. She held it for a moment, then extended her fingers to try it on. "Wow, this feels weird. Like you should be doing it, or something." She glanced shyly at him.

Jake swallowed. He took the ring from her—the diamond was too small, anyway—and gingerly slid it onto her slender finger. His skin tingled as he touched hers and a flutter of something stirred in his chest. The ring fit well and looked pretty on her hand.

"What do you think?" She turned her hand, and the stone sparkled in the light.

"Nice." He didn't want to criticize, if that was her choice.

The jeweler frowned. "It's a fine ring, but for the royal family, perhaps something a bit more…extravagant?" He lifted a dramatic large stone flanked by several smaller stones. The kind of ring that would make people's eyes pop. Jake had to admit it was more appropriate under the circumstances.

Andi allowed the older man to slide her choice off her finger and push the big sparkler onto it. His face creased into a satisfied smile as it slid perfectly into place. "Lovely. Much more suitable for a royal bride, if you don't mind my saying."

She tilted her hand to the side and studied the ring. Despite the large size of the stones it also looked elegant on her graceful hands. Jake wondered how he'd never noticed what pretty hands she had. He'd been watching them type his letters and organize his files for years.

"It's a bit over the top.…" She paused, still staring at it. "But it is pretty." She looked up at Jake. "What do you think?"

"Very nice." He intended to buy her many more trinkets and baubles to enjoy. It was worth it to see the sunny smile on her face, and they were supporting the local economy. "Let's buy it and go get a hot chocolate to celebrate."

She hesitated for a moment more, studying the ring on her finger. When she looked up, confusion darkened the summer-blue of her eyes. She seemed like she wanted to say something, but hesitated in front of the jeweler. The shop owner tactfully excused himself and disappeared through a low door into a back room.

"I guess he trusts us alone with the merchandise." Jake grinned. "There must be a million dollars worth of rocks on this tray."

"I'd imagine a crown inspires a certain amount of trust." She looked up at him, eyes sparkling. "I'm still getting used to the idea that you're a king."

"Me, too. I'm not sure I'll ever be completely used to it, but at least it's starting to feel like a suit that fits. How does the ring feel?"

Andi studied the ring again. "It is lovely, but it's just so… big."

"He's right, though. It makes sense to go dramatic. Do you want people muttering that I'm a cheapskate?" He raised a brow.

Andi chuckled. "I guess you have a good point." Then she frowned. "Are people going to be shocked that you're marrying your assistant?" She bit her lip for a moment. "I mean…did they know that we're…intimate?"

Jake inhaled. "We kept it all pretty private."

"Did anyone know?" Her serious expression tugged at him.

"A few people may have guessed something." Who knew what people might imagine, even if there had never been anything to guess? "But on the whole, we were discreet so it'll be a surprise."

Andi's shoulders tightened a bit. "I hope they won't be too upset that you're not marrying someone more... important."

"No one's more important than you, Andi. I'd be lost without you." It was a relief to say something honest, even if he meant it in a business sense, rather than a romantic one.

"I guess I should get the fancy one. If they're going to talk, let's give them something to talk about."

"That's the attitude." Jake rang the bell on the counter and the jeweler appeared again like Rumpelstiltskin. "We'll take it."

The old man beamed. "An excellent choice. I wish you both a lifetime of happiness."

Me, too, thought Jake. He'd need to think on his feet when Andi snapped out of this thing.

Four

Andi blinked as they stepped out of the dark shop into bright morning sunlight that reflected off everything from the gray cobbles to the white-crested mountain peaks that loomed over the town. The cold air whipped at her skin and she drew her warm coat about her. Out in the open she felt violently self-conscious about the huge ring on her finger, and gratefully tucked it into her coat pocket.

"The coffeehouse is just up the road." Jake took her arm. "You may not remember, but they have the best hot chocolate in the known world and you love it."

Andi's muscles tightened at the reminder that he knew more about her than she did. "Do you go there often?" It seemed odd for a king to frequent a local café. Then again she had no idea what was normal. Very strange how she remembered things like old fairy tales but not her own life.

"Of course. Got to support the local businesses."

He certainly was thoughtful. That cozy feeling of being protected and cared for warmed her as he slid his arm through hers again. How lucky she was! No doubt her memory would come back soon and—

A moped skidded past them on the narrow street. Its rider, a man in a black leather jacket, stopped and leaped off, camera in hand. "Your Highness, is it true you are engaged?" he asked, in a French accent.

Jake paused. "It is true." Andi stared in surprise at his polite demeanor.

"May I take your picture?"

Jake took Andi's hands in his. "What do you say, Andi? He's just doing his job."

Andi cringed inwardly. She didn't want anyone seeing her in her confused state, let alone photographing her. She also didn't want to make a fuss in front of a stranger. That might give the game away.

She swallowed. "Okay, I guess." She pushed a lock of hair self-consciously off her face. She hadn't had time to style it—not that she even remembered what style she usually wore—but Jake had assured her it looked lovely.

The man took about fifty pictures from different angles through a long, scary-looking lens that would probably show every pore on her face. Jake was obviously used to the attention and remained calm and pleasant. He even adjusted them into several dignified romantic poses as if they were at a professional shoot.

Almost as if he'd planned this encounter.

She fought the urge to frown, which certainly wouldn't be a good idea for the pictures. How did the photographer know they were engaged when it had only happened last night?

Jake managed to politely disengage them from the impromptu photo session and continue down the road.

He smiled and nodded at passersby, all of whom seemed quite comfortable rubbing shoulders with their monarch. But when they reached the main square she saw two more reporters, a woman with a tiny microphone clipped to her jacket and a tall man with a notepad. They greeted Jake with warm smiles and asked if congratulations were in order.

Andi tried to maintain a pleasant expression while unease gnawed at her gut.

"How does it feel to marry a king?" asked the woman, in soft Ruthenian tones.

"I'm not sure yet," admitted Andi. "Since we're not married. I'll have to let you know after the ceremony."

"When will that be?" asked the man. Andi glanced at Jake.

"We'll make an announcement when we have all the details sorted out. A royal wedding isn't something you rush into."

"Of course." The reporter was a middle-aged woman with soft blond hair. "And you've kept your promise of choosing your bride before Ruthenia's third Independence Day next week."

"The people of Ruthenia know I'm a man of my word."

Andi only just managed not to frown. He'd become engaged to her at the last minute because of some promise he made? That was awfully convenient. The knot in the pit of her stomach tightened.

The woman asked if she could see Andi's ring. Andi pulled it out and was alarmed to see it looked even bigger and brighter out here in daylight. The camera flashed several times before she could hide her hand back in her pocket again.

When Jake finally excused them, her heart was pounding and her face flushed. She let out a silent sigh of relief as he guided her into the warm and inviting coffee shop. She removed her coat and hung it on a row of iron hooks that looked hundreds of years old.

"I'm glad they didn't ask any questions I couldn't answer."

"The paparazzi are polite here." Jake took her hand and led her to a secluded table. "They know I can have them clapped in irons if they're not."

She glanced up to see if he was kidding and was relieved to see a sparkle of humor in his eye.

"The press has been helpful in letting the world know about my efforts to bring the country into the twenty-first century. It pays to keep them happy."

"How could they know about our engagement already? Did that girl you spoke to phone them?" Andi sat in the plush upholstered chair. A small fire snapped and sizzled nearby. The coffee shop had dark wood paneling and varied antique tables and chairs clustered around the low-ceilinged space that looked unchanged since the 1720s—which it probably was.

"I doubt it. They seem to know everything. It's a bit spooky at first, but you get used to it. Maybe they saw us inside the jeweler's?"

"Or maybe he tipped them off." Andi gingerly pulled her be-ringed hand from her pocket to take a menu from the elegantly attired waiter.

"Old Gregor is the soul of discretion." Jake studied his menu. Andi wondered for a second how he knew to trust Old Gregor. Had he commissioned gems for other women? But he said they'd been dating for years.

She cursed the hot little flame of jealousy that had flickered to life inside her. Why were they suddenly engaged after years of dating? Was it somehow precipitated by this promise he'd made, or had she previously refused?

For a moment Andi was hyperaware of people at tables all around them, sipping their drinks and eating. Could they tell she was missing a huge part of her life?

He shrugged. "It's their job. We live in the public eye." He reached across the table and took her hand. His strong fingers closed around hers. She squeezed his hand back and enjoyed the sense of reassurance she got from him. "You'll get used to it again."

"I suppose I will." She glanced warily about the interior of the intimate coffeehouse. "It's so unnerving not to even know what's normal. Then you can't figure out what's odd and unusual."

"It would certainly be odd for us to sit here without drinking hot chocolate." He summoned the waiter and ordered a pot of hot chocolate and a dish of cream. "And, just so you know, the waffles with summer berries are your favorite."

"Did we eat here together a lot?" The place didn't look especially familiar.

"Yes. We often brought business associates and visitors from the States here, since it's so quaint and unchanged. Now that we're engaged..." He stroked her hand inside his and fixed his dark eyes on hers. "It's just the two of us."

Andi's insides fluttered as his gaze crept right under her skin. If only she could remember what their relationship was like. It didn't sound as if they ate out unless in company, which was a bit odd. A secret affair.

It must be strange and unsettling for him to have her behaving like a different person.

Then again, he didn't seem rattled by the situation. His handsome face had an expression of calm contentment. The chiseled features were steady as the mountains outside and it was hard to imagine him getting upset or bothered by anything. Jake was obviously the kind of man who took things in stride. Her hand felt totally comfortable in his, as if he was promising her that he'd take care of her and make sure only good things happened.

Why did it feel so bizarre that such a gorgeous and successful man was all hers?

Well, of course she had to share him with a small nation, but after the lights went out he was hers alone. Hope and excitement rose through her, along with a curl of desire that matched the steam rising off the hot chocolate.

Jake kept his gaze on her face as the waiter poured the fragrant liquid into two wide round cups and then dropped a dollop of thick whipped cream on top of each one. When the waiter moved away, Jake lifted her hand to his lips and kissed it. Sensual excitement flashed through her body at the soft touch of his mouth on her skin, a promise of what would come when they were alone together.

Andi fought the urge to glance around to see if anyone had witnessed the intimate moment. She drew in a deep breath and forced herself to display the kind of cool that Jake possessed naturally. She'd better get used to being in the public eye, since she'd be spending the rest of her life in it.

If she really was marrying Jake. The idea still seemed too far-fetched and outrageous to truly believe. He gently let go of her hand and she moved it quickly to her cup and covered her confusion with a sip. The rich and delicious chocolate slid down her throat and heated her insides. Perfect.

Everything was perfect. Too perfect.

So why couldn't she escape the niggling feeling that when she got her memory back she'd discover something was horribly wrong?

Andi grew increasingly nervous as they drove back to the palace. None of the other staff knew about their engagement—at least as far as she knew. How would they react?

She climbed out of the car on shaky legs. Did she have a best friend here in whom she confided? Or was that person Jake? Tears hovered very close to the surface, but she tried hard to put on a brave face as they approached the grand doorway up a flight of wide steps.

"Good morning, sir." A black-attired man opened the door before they even reached it. "And may I offer you congratulations."

Andi cringed. They all knew already? Word spread around this tiny country like a plague.

"Congratulations, Andi. I'm not sure whether it's appropriate to tell you that, as usual, the mail is in your office."

She didn't even know she had an office, let alone where it was. She gulped, realizing that she'd be expected to do her job, regardless of whether or not she could remember how.

Either that or tell everyone that her mind had been wiped blank, and she couldn't face that. "Thanks," she managed.

She kept her hand buried deep in the pocket of her wool coat as they crossed the marble-floored entrance hall. Faces looked vaguely familiar, but she couldn't remember names or if they were friends as well as coworkers. Jake stopped to answer some questions about a phone call they'd received, and Andi hesitated, unsure which direction to walk in, or where to even hang her coat. Worse yet, a girl with lots of red hair rushed up to her, wide-eyed. "Why am I the last to know everything?"

Andi managed a casual shrug.

The redhead leaned in and lowered her voice. "I see you decided not to leave after all?"

Andi's eyes widened. "Leave?" She glanced up to see if

Jake had heard, but he was still deep in conversation several yards away.

"Stop acting innocent. I saw the suitcases you bought in town. Still, obviously something better than a new job came up."

"I don't know what you're talking about." Truer words were never spoken. Anxiety churned the hot chocolate in her stomach. Suitcases? A new job? That was odd. She needed to get to her room and see if she could find something to jog her memory.

If only she knew where her room was.

She remembered the way back to Jake's suite, and was tempted to head that way without him just to get away from the inquisitive redhead. Then again, he was apparently her boss, so that might look odd.

The ring practically burned her finger, still hidden deep inside her coat. "Let me take that for you." An older man with neat white hair crossed the floor. Andi stared. "Your coat," he continued, demonstrating the hanger in his hand. "I wonder if it's premature to call you Your Majesty?" he asked with a kind expression.

"Probably." She managed a smile while shrugging the coat off. She looked up at Jake and their eyes met. He must have seen the plea in her face as he detached himself from his questioner and strode to her side. "Let's head for my office."

As soon as they were on the stairs, she whispered that she didn't know where her room was. He frowned for a second, then smiled. "We'll go there right now."

The hallway was empty. "I don't even know anyone's name. It's the most awkward feeling. People must think I'm so rude."

"That was Walter. Worked here back when it was a hotel

and always the first to know every bit of gossip. He probably spread the word."

"This building was a hotel?"

"For a while. It had a few different lives while my family was in exile in the States. It took a lot of work to get it looking like this, and you were in charge of most of it."

Andi bit her lip, walking along carpet she may even have selected. Jake pointed to the third polished wood door in a long hallway, only a few yards from his. "That's yours. It wasn't locked when I came to get your clothes."

She tried the handle and it swung open. A neat, hotel-like room greeted her, with heavy brocade curtains and a small double bed. The dark wood furniture looked antique and impressive. She cringed at the sight of a pair of panty hose draped over the bed.

"Um, maybe I should spend a little time alone here. See if anything jogs my memory."

"Sure." Jake stroked her back softly. Her skin heated under her T-shirt as he turned her toward him and lowered his face to hers. All worries and fears drifted way for a few seconds as she lost herself in his soft and gentle kiss.

"Don't worry about anything." He pointed to a dresser. "Your phone's right there and you've always told me I'm programmed in as number one." He winked. "I'll head for my office to deal with this electrical supply situation that's cropped up. Call me if you need anything, and even if you don't."

Her fingers felt cold as he released them from his, but she couldn't help a sigh of relief as she closed the door behind him and found herself alone in the room. At last she could... fall apart.

Part of her wanted to run to the bed and collapse on it, sobbing. But another, apparently more influential, part wanted to pull open the drawers and search for signs of who she was. She tucked the stray panty hose back into their drawer, wondering if she'd taken them out when she was dressing in her evening gown. She wasn't wearing any when she'd woken up in the morning.

The drawer was rather disorganized, as if everything was just shoved in there without much thought. What did this tell her about herself? She frowned and pulled open the drawer above it. Three carelessly folded blouses and some socks gave no further encouragement about her organizational skills.

The closet door was slightly ajar and she pulled it open. An array of colorful suits hung from the hangers, along with several solid-colored dresses and skirts. At least it didn't look as messy as her drawers. She pushed some hangers apart and pulled down one of the suits. A medium blue, it was tailored but otherwise quite plain. She tried to smooth out a horizontal crease that ran just below the lapels. Another crease across the skirt made her frown. Why would a suit hanging in a closet have creases running across it?

She pulled out another suit and saw that it too had lines running through the middle. A forest-green dress also showed signs of having been folded recently, and a navy skirt and... She stopped and frowned. All the items in the closet had crease marks running across them. Not deep, sharp creases, but soft ones, as if they'd been folded only for a short time. What could that mean?

After she hung the suit back in the closet, she walked into the attached bathroom. A floral smell hovered in the air and felt reassuringly familiar. Her favorite scent? She recognized it—which meant it was a memory. Cheered, she examined the cosmetics arranged on a low shelf. There were a lot of lipsticks. She pulled one open and applied it. A rather garish orangey-pink that didn't do her complexion any favors. She put it back on the shelf and wiped her lips with a tissue.

She found the bottle of scent and removed the cap. Warmth suffused her as she sprayed some on her wrists and inhaled the familiar smell. Relief also swept through her that at least something around here felt familiar.

The scent…and Jake.

Excitement mixed with apprehension tickled her insides. How odd that they'd become engaged and she'd lost her memory in the same night. She couldn't help wondering if the two things were related.

Jake was lovely, though. He'd been so sweet and encouraging with her since she'd lost her memory. She was lucky to be engaged to such a kind and capable man. A bit odd that he was a king, but that was just one facet of him. Just a job, really. No doubt she wasn't bothered by his royal status or she wouldn't have become romantically involved with him in the first place.

She picked up her hand and looked at her big diamond ring. It was beautiful and fit her perfectly. She'd feel comfortable wearing it once she got used to it.

Once she got used to any of this.

A knock on the door made her jump. "It's me, Livia."

Andi gulped. Apparently she was supposed to know who Livia was. So far no one seemed to know about her memory except Jake and the doctor, but that was bound to change unless it came back soon. She smoothed her hair and went to open the door.

It was the same red-haired girl from downstairs. The one who'd talked about her leaving. She had a huge grin on her freckled face. "You are a dark horse."

Andi shrugged casually, as if admitting it, even though she didn't know exactly whether Livia referred to the engagement or her memory loss.

"You never breathed a word. How long have the two of you been…?" Her conspiratorial whisper sounded deafening in the quiet hallway.

"Come in." Andi ushered her into the room. Livia glanced around. Andi got the idea that she hadn't been here before, so they probably weren't the closest of friends, but maybe she could learn something from her. She managed a smile. "We didn't really want anyone to know. Not until we were sure."

Livia seemed satisfied with that answer. "How romantic. And after working together all these years. I never suspected a thing!"

"I hardly believe it myself."

"So the suitcases were for your honeymoon." Livia grinned and shook her head. "Where are you going?"

"Not sure yet." Jake hadn't said anything about a honeymoon. Surely they had to have a wedding first.

"This time make sure I'm not the last person in the palace to know. I know you're always insisting that it's part of your job to keep mum about things, but I can't believe I had to learn about your engagement on the radio."

"What did they say?"

"That you and Jake were out ring shopping in town this morning, and you told reporters you were getting married. Hey, let's see the rock!" She reached out and grabbed Andi's hand. "Wow. That's some ring. I wouldn't go on the New York City subway in that."

So Livia had come from New York, as well? That meant they'd probably known each other at least three years. Andi felt awful that she didn't even remember her.

Livia sighed. "And just imagine what your wedding dress will be like. You could probably get anyone in the world to design it for you. Some people have all the luck."

Andi was sorely tempted to point out that she had the

bad luck to not even know who she was, but a gut instinct told her not to confide in Livia. She sensed an undercurrent of jealousy or resentment that made her reluctant to trust her.

"Oh, there are the suitcases, under your bed." Livia pointed. Andi could see the edges of two black rolling cases.

"You're very obsessed with those."

"I thought you were going to take off and leave us. At least to do that interview."

Andi frowned. Had she planned a job interview somewhere?

"I was even starting to think that if we both went back to New York we could share an apartment or something. Guess I was wrong." She widened her eyes, which fell again to Andi's hand.

"You were. I'll be staying here." She smiled, and conviction filled her voice. How nice it was to be sure of something.

"I bet you will."

A million questions bounced around Andi's brain, as many about Jake and life at the palace as about herself. But she couldn't think of any way to ask them without giving the game away, and she wasn't ready to do that yet. On the other hand, at least Livia could help her find her way to her own office. That would be one less problem for her to bother Jake with.

"Why don't you walk to my office with me?"

Livia looked curious. Andi worried that she'd made a misstep. She had no idea what Livia did at the palace, and her clothing, dark pants and a blue long-sleeved peasant shirt, didn't offer any clues. "Sure."

They set out, Andi lagging a fraction behind so that Livia could lead the way without realizing it. They went along the hallway in the opposite direction from Jake's suite, and up a flight of stairs to the third floor. At the top of the stairs a blond man hurried up to them. "Goodness, Andi. Congratulations."

"Thanks." She blushed, mostly because she had no idea who he was. Luckily it was an appropriate response.

"Cook wanted me to ask you whether we should do duck or goose on Thursday for the Finnish ambassador."

"Whichever she prefers would be fine." She froze for an agonizing second while it occurred to her that Cook might be a he.

His eyes widened. "I'll let her know. I suspect you have a lot on your plate right now, what with, well, you know." He smiled. "We're all very happy for you, Andi."

She forced another smile. He'd looked surprised by her lack of decisiveness. She must usually be a very take-charge person. At least the engagement gave her an excuse to be out to lunch—literally and figuratively. She was "preoccupied."

They reached a door halfway down a corridor on the third floor, and Livia hesitated. Andi swallowed, then reached out a hand and tried the door. The handle turned but didn't open it. "Oh no. I forgot my key! You go on with what you're doing and I'll go back and get it. See you later."

Livia waved a cheery goodbye and Andi heaved a sigh. She counted the doors along the hallway so she could find her way here alone next time. Back in her room she searched high and low for the key. When she found a black handbag at the bottom of her closet, her heart leapt.

She'd already discovered that the phone in her bedroom was for business only. Not a single personal number was stored in it. She'd called each one with hope in her heart, only to find herself talking to another bank or supplier. She must have another phone somewhere.

Eager to see her wallet and find out some more about herself, she dove into the bag with her hands. A neat, small wallet contained very few clues. A New York driver's license, with an 81st Street address, about to expire. A Ruthenian driver's license ornamented with a crest featuring two large birds. A Visa credit card from an American bank, and a MasterCard from a European one.

She seemed to be living a double life—half American and half Ruthenian. But that wasn't unusual among expats. She probably kept her accounts open, figuring she'd go back sooner or later.

The bag did contain a keychain containing two keys— her bedroom and office? Other than that there was a small packet of tissues and two lipsticks. No phone. Disappointment dripped through her. Maybe she just had no life.

Except Jake.

She glanced at the business phone on the dresser and her nerves sizzled with anticipation at the thought of calling him. She felt a lot safer in his large, calm presence.

But she didn't want to be a bother. She'd wait until she really needed him.

Keys and phone in the pocket of her jeans, she set off back for the locked office. Her instincts proved correct and the smaller key opened the door. Like her bedroom, her office was neat and featureless, no photos or mementos on the desk. She'd be worried that she was the world's dullest person, except that apparently she was intriguing enough for a king to want to marry her.

She opened a silver laptop on the desk. Surely this would reveal a wealth of new information about her life——her work, anyway. But the first screen asked her to enter her password.

Andi growled with frustration. She felt like she was looking for the password to her own life and it was always just out of reach. Password, password. She racked her brain for familiar words. *Blue,* she typed in. The screen was blue. Nothing happened. *Jake?* Nothing doing. *Love?*

Nada. Apparently her computer, like her memory, was off-limits for now.

Irritation crackled through her veins. She pulled open the drawers in the antique desk and was disappointed to find nothing but a dull collection of pens, paper clips, empty notebooks. The entire office revealed nothing about her. Almost as if every trace of her individuality had been stripped away.

The way you might do if you were leaving a job.

A pang of alarm flashed through her at the thought. Had she stripped her office bare in preparation for abandoning it? She could see how getting engaged to Jake could mean her leaving her job as his assistant, or at least changing it dramatically. But surely Jake would have mentioned it?

She picked up her phone and punched in his number. Feelings of helplessness and anxiety rose inside her as she heard it ring, but she fought them back.

"Hi, Andi. How are you doing?"

A smile rose to her lips at the sound of his deep, resonant voice. "Confused," she admitted. "I'm in my office and feeling more lost than ever."

"I'll meet you there."

She blew out a long breath as she put the phone back in her pocket. It was embarrassing to feel lost without Jake at her side, but wonderful that she could call him to it at any moment. She glanced at the ring on her finger. The big diamond sparkled in the sunlight, casting little shards of light over her skin, a symbol of his lifelong commitment to her.

At least she knew what it felt like to be loved.

She flew to the door at the sound of a knock. A huge smile spread over her face at the sight of him, tall and gorgeous, with a twinkle in his dark eyes.

"I missed you," he murmured, voice low and seductive.

"Come in." Her belly sizzled with arousal and her nipples tightened just at the sight of him. "Do you always knock on my office door?" It seemed oddly formal if they'd worked together and dated for years.

A shadow of hesitation crossed his face for a split second. "I suppose I do. Would you prefer me to barge right in?"

"I don't know." She giggled. Nothing seemed to matter all that much now that Jake was here. "I guess it depends on if I'm trying to keep secrets from you."

"Are you?" His brow arched.

"I have no idea." She laughed again. "Hopefully if I do, they're not very dark ones."

"Dark secrets sound rather intriguing." He moved toward her and lifted his hand to cup her cheek. Her skin heated under his palm. "I might have fun uncovering them."

Their lips met, hot and fast, and his tongue in her mouth drove all thoughts away. She pressed herself against him and felt his arms close around her. *Much better.* Wrapping herself up in Jake was the best medicine for anything that ailed her.

His suit hid the hard muscle beneath it, but that didn't stop her fingers from exploring his broad back and enjoying the thickness of his toned biceps. Her fingertips were creeping into his waistband when a sharp knock on the door made them jump apart.

She blushed. "Do we get carried away like that often?"

Jake shot her a crooked smile. "Why not?"

A glance at the door sent her cheer scattering. "I won't recognize the person."

"I'll help you out."

She drew in a deep breath as she approached the door. "Who is it?"

"Domino." A male voice. "Just wanted to take a peek at Jake's calendar for tomorrow."

She glanced back at Jake and whispered, "I have no idea where your calendar is."

"You can peek at it in my head, Dom." Jake's voice boomed across the room.

A compact, dark-haired man in a gray suit flung the door open and entered. "Sorry, Mr. Mondragon, I didn't know you were in here. I just wondered if there was a set time for the Malaysian High Commission's arrival."

Andi listened while Jake rattled off a few planned events for the following day and tried to keep them filed in her brain in case anyone else asked her. It couldn't hurt to practice using her memory again. Still, she didn't truly breathe again until Domino backed out with a slight bow.

"I feel like the world's most incompetent assistant. Is the calendar on the computer?"

"Yup."

"It's password protected and I don't know the password. Do you know it?"

Jake looked thoughtful. "No."

"Any ideas what it might be?"

"None whatsoever. I guess there are some dark secrets between us." He lifted a brow playfully. "Maybe you have it written down somewhere."

"That's another thing." She frowned, apprehension twisting her gut as she prepared to tell him. "There's nothing personal in here at all. It's all business all the time, as if all the personal effects had been removed."

Jake blinked and his gaze swept the room. A furrow deepened between his brows; then he shrugged. "I'm not much for personal knickknacks in the office, either. Why don't we take a break and go stroll around the palace? Then at least you'll know where everything is."

Andi was a bit alarmed by the brusque way he changed the subject. One question burned in her mind. "Am I still your assistant? I mean, now that we're engaged."

"Yes, of course." Jake looked startled for a second. "I'd be lost without you arranging my life."

"Then prepare to get lost, since I can't arrange my own computer desktop right now." Tears loomed again. Apparently they'd never been very far away. "I still don't remember anything at all."

Jake took her into his arms again. His scent, familiar and enticing, wrapped around her as his embrace gave her strength. "The doctor said it would take time for your memory to return. Come on, let's go for that walk. There's no point getting upset over something you can't control."

The palace was so large that probably no one knew exactly how many rooms it had or how to get to all of them. As Jake explained, it had been the home of several dynasties of Ruthenian royals, all of whom had left their own stylistic stamp, so the building had everything from fortified turrets to elegant rows of French windows opening out onto a terrace for alfresco dancing.

As they walked about, on the pretext of discussing the decor, everyone stopped to offer their congratulations on their engagement. Some people hid their surprise, but Andi could tell it was a startling occurrence. Could they really have not noticed a romance occurring—over several years—right beneath their noses?

Five

"Jake, congratulations on your engagement." The silvery tones emerging from his phone dripped with acid. Jake glanced across his suite to where Andi reclined on the sofa looking through a tourist brochure about Ruthenia.

"Thanks, Carina." Lucky thing she couldn't see how happy he was not to be marrying her.

"Quite a surprise." Her tone was cool. "I had no idea you were involved with your assistant."

"You know how these things are. It seemed…unprofessional, but you can't halt the course of true love." He'd already explained the same to three other would-be queens, so it rolled naturally off his tongue.

"Indeed." She cleared her throat. "Daddy accuses you of toying with my affections, but I assured him that I'm a big girl and that he should still fund the new industrial development."

These veiled threats were becoming familiar, too.

"I do hope he will. We look forward to entertaining you both at the palace again soon." He was smiling when he hung up the phone. Right now everything was going as smoothly as could be expected. He was now officially off the hook for choosing the next queen of Ruthenia. No one had actually pulled support from any key projects or threatened to fund a revolution. It was probably a plus that he hadn't offended one Ruthenian big shot by choosing the daughter of another. Selecting his American assistant as his bride had left all the local families equally offended—or mollified. And so far things were working out nicely.

He couldn't understand why he'd never plotted this tidy solution together with Andi, before she lost her memory. Choosing his wife now seemed like an agenda item he'd neatly checked off.

"Why don't you join me on the sofa?" Her come-hither stare and soft tones beckoned to him.

Blood rushed to his nether regions and he stiffened. Of course there were some aspects of their engagement that should remain off-limits until Andi's memory came back. It was one thing to pretend to love your assistant, it was quite another thing to actually make love to her.

"That dinner was delicious, but I find I'm still hungry." Andi's blue eyes sparkled. She curled her legs under her and stretched one arm sensually along the top of sofa.

Her voice called to a part of him that wasn't at all practical. Jake was struck by a cruel vision of the black lacy underwear beneath her jeans and T-shirt. *She'll be angry if you sleep with her under false pretenses.*

But were they really false? He did intend to marry her.

Which was funny, as he'd never planned to marry anyone. His parents' long and arduous union—all duty and no joy— had put him off the whole institution from an early age. They'd married because they were a "suitable" match, his father the son of the exiled monarch and his mother the daughter of a prominent noble, also in exile. They'd soon discovered they had nothing in common but blue Ruthenian blood, yet they'd held up the charade for five decades in the hope they'd one day inhabit this palace and put the Ruthenian crest on their stationery again.

They were both gone by the time the "new regime" crumbled and Ruthenia decided it wanted its monarchy back. Jake had assumed the mantle of political duty, but it didn't seem fair or reasonable to expect him to take it into his bedroom, as well.

He'd much rather take Andi into his bedroom. Her lips looked so inviting in that sensual half smile. And he could just imagine how those long legs would feel wrapped around his waist....

But that was a really bad idea. When she got her memory back she'd likely be pretty steamed about the whole scenario he'd cooked up. She'd be downright furious if he took advantage of her affections, as well. Much better if they kept their hands to themselves until they could talk things over sensibly.

"Do you want me to walk you back to your room?" His voice sounded tight.

"Why? I'm not going to sleep there, am I?" She raised a brow. She seemed far more relaxed, bolder, than he'd seen her so far. She was obviously feeling comfortable, even if her memory still showed no signs of returning.

"I think you should. It's a question of propriety."

She giggled. "You are joking."

"No." He felt a bit offended. "It's a royal thing."

"So, we've never...?" She rose from the sofa in an athletic leap and strode across the room. "I don't remember the details about my own life, but I remember general stuff and I'm pretty sure that it's totally normal for dating couples to…sleep together. So I don't believe that we've been dating for years and never done more than kiss."

Jake shrugged. She had a point. If only she knew he was trying to protect her. "Okay, I admit we may have been… intimate. But now that we're engaged and it's all official and formal, I think we should play by the rules."

"Whose rules?" She raised her hand and stroked his cheek with her fingers.

His groin tightened and he cleared his throat. "Those official, hundreds-of-years-old rules that the king should keep his hands off his future bride until after the wedding."

Her mouth lifted into a wicked smile. "These hands?" She picked up his hands and placed them squarely on her hips. Heat rose in his blood as he took in the curves beneath his palms. She wriggled her hips slightly, sending shock waves of desire pulsing through him.

I'm in full control of my hands and my mind. The thought did nothing to reassure him, especially when one of his hands started to wander toward her backside. Andi pressed her lips to his and her familiar scent filled his senses. Next thing he knew his hands were straying up and down her back, enjoying the soft curves under his palms.

His pants grew tight as Andi pressed her chest against his. He could just imagine what those deliciously firm breasts must look like in her lacy bra. If he coaxed her out of her T-shirt—which would not be difficult—he could find out right away.

But that might lead to other things.

In fact, he was one hundred percent sure that it would.

He pulled back from the kiss with considerable effort. "Don't you have some…embroidery to do or something?"

"Embroidery?" Laughter sparkled in her clear blue eyes. "Do I really embroider stuff?"

He chuckled. "Not that I know of, but does a man really know what his fiancée gets up to in the privacy of her room?"

"I guess that depends how much time he spends there." She raised a brow. "Maybe we should go to my room?"

Jake froze. That seemed like a really bad idea. Which underlined what a bad idea all this kissing and cuddling was. Much better to keep things professional, with just enough hint of romance to keep the people around them convinced. At least until Andi came back to her senses.

He flinched as Andi's fingers crept beneath the waistband of his pants. He'd grown rock hard and the thought of pushing her away was downright painful. Her soft cheek nuzzled against his and his fingers wandered into her hair. She looked so different with her hair loose, much less formal and more inviting.

Her cool fingers slid under his shirt and skated up his spine. Jake arched into the sensation, pulling her tighter into his embrace. Her breathing was faster and her pink lips flushed and parted. He couldn't resist sticking his tongue into her mouth and she responded in kind, until they were kissing hard and fast again.

"Still think I should go to my room?" She rasped the question when they came up for air.

"Definitely not." He had to take this woman to bed, whether it was a good idea or not.

He reached under her T-shirt and cupped her breast, enjoying the sensation of skin and scratchy lace under his fingers. He could feel her heartbeat pounding, like his own, as anticipation built toward boiling point.

"Let's go into the bedroom." He disentangled himself from her with some effort and led her into the other room. The plain white bedcovers looked like an enticing playground and he couldn't wait to spread her out on them and uncover her step by step.

He swept her off her feet—eliciting a shriek of delight—and laid her gently on the bed.

Suddenly horizontal, Andi looked up at Jake with alarm. Her entire body pulsed and tingled with sensation. About to reach for the buttons of his shirt, her fingers stopped in midair. Their eyes met, his dark with fierce desire that made her insides tremble.

Everything about this situation felt new and different.

Jake's hands showed no hesitation as he unzipped her jeans and slid them off. Heat snapped in her veins, deepening the sense of unease creeping over her.

"What's the matter?" Jake paused and studied her face.

"I don't know. It just feels strange."

"Go with it." He lifted the hem of her T-shirt and eased it off over her head. Her nipples stood to attention inside her lacy bra, which was now exposed to view along with its matching panties. Jake's devouring gaze raked her body and Andi felt both very desirable and very, very nervous.

Jake unbuttoned his own shirt and shrugged it off, revealing a thickly muscled chest with a line of dark hair running down to his belt buckle. His powerful biceps flexed as he undid the belt and the button of his pants.

Andi's hesitation flew away. "Wait, let me do that." She rose to the edge of the bed and unzipped his pants as excitement and arousal replaced her apprehension. She pushed them down to reveal dark boxers and powerful hair-roughened thighs.

Both in their underwear, they stretched out on the cool white sheets, skin to skin. She touched his chest with a tentative finger, enjoying the warmth of his body. She traced the curve of his pec and traveled lower, to where his arousal was dramatically evident against the dark fabric of his shorts.

Jake's taut belly contracted as she trailed over it then paused.

She looked up at his face. The naked desire in his eyes further unraveled her inhibitions. She let her hands roam lower, tugging at his boxers until they slid down and his erection sprang free. She gasped, and he chuckled. Then she pulled the soft fabric down over his strong legs until he was totally naked.

"You're gorgeous," she breathed. Then she blushed, realizing that must sound silly when she'd seen him naked many times before.

"You're far more gorgeous." His slightly callused fingers tickled her skin as he ran his hand along her side, from her bra to her panties.

"But you're not seeing me as if it was the first time."

"Yes, I am," he murmured. Then he looked up. "At least that's what it feels like." Excitement danced in his dark eyes. "I could never grow tired of looking at you."

Andi swallowed. If Jake's feelings for her were anything like the intense roar of passion pulsing in her veins right now, she could understand how this could feel new and fresh even after several years.

He slid his arm behind her back and tugged her closer. Her belly flipped as it touched his, and her breasts bumped against his chest.

"Time to unwrap this present," he breathed. He propped himself on one elbow and deftly undid the clasp on her bra, releasing her breasts. She felt his breathing quicken as he tugged the lacy fabric off over her arms and lowered his mouth to one tight pink nipple.

Andi arched her back and let out a little moan as Jake flicked his tongue over the delicate skin. The sound of her own voice in the still night air startled her, and quickened her pulse further. She pushed her fingers into his thick hair and enjoyed the silky sensations roaming through her body as he licked and sucked.

"Kiss me," she begged, when she couldn't take the almost painful pleasure anymore. He responded by pressing his lips to hers with passion and kissing the last of her breath away.

Arms wrapped around him, she held Jake close. His warm masculine scent filled her senses and the heat of his skin against hers only increased her desire. Fingers trembling with anticipation, she took hold of his erection. Jake released a low moan as she ran her fingers over the hard surface, then tightened them around the shaft, enjoying the throb of pleasure that issued through him.

Had she really done this before? She couldn't believe it. Again that odd sensation of unfamiliarity almost dampened her pleasure. Everything she did was like taking a step into the dark and hoping the floor would still be there under her foot when she put it down. Where would these strange and intense sensations and urges lead her?

Jake's mouth crushed over hers once more and her doubts crumbled beneath the fierce desire to feel him inside her.

Working together they eased off her panties and he climbed over her. The inviting weight of him pressed against her chest for a moment; then he lifted himself up with his powerful arms and entered her slowly.

Too slowly.

She found herself writhing and arching to encourage him deeper. Her insides ached to hold him and her whole body burned hot and anxious with an urgent need to join with him. Her fingers dug into his back as he finally sank all the way in and she released a deep moan of pleasure into his ear.

Jake layered hot kisses along her neck and cheek as he moved over her, drawing her deeper into the mysterious ocean of pleasure that felt so strange and so good at the same time. They rolled on the bed, exploring each other from different angles and deepening the connection between them. Her hands wandered over his body, enjoying the hard muscle, squeezing and stroking him as he moved inside her.

She loved riding on top of him, changing the rhythm from slow to fast and back again as the sensations inside her built toward a dangerous crescendo. Jake was over her again when she felt herself suddenly lose control of her muscles and even her mind as a huge wave of release swept her far out of herself. She drifted in limbo as pulses of sheer pleasure rose through her again and again. Then she seemed to wash back up in Jake's arms, exhausted and utterly at peace.

"That was..." She couldn't seem to find the words. Any words, really.

"Awesome."

Jake's unroyal response made her laugh. "Exactly." Then she frowned. "Is it always like this when we...make love?"

She could swear she felt him flinch slightly. "Yup. It is."

"I guess that's good." She smiled. She must be one of the luckiest people on earth, to have a loving relationship—with really hot sex—with this ridiculously handsome man who just happened to be a king.

She stretched, still feeling delicious pulses of pleasure tickling her insides. She couldn't help wondering how she'd arrived at this juncture. How did she find herself engaged to a gorgeous monarch? Maybe she was from some kind of upper-crust family herself. It was so odd not knowing anything about yourself. She opened her eyes and peered at Jake.

"Will you tell me some things about myself?"

His sleepy gaze grew wider and a smile tilted his mouth. "Like what?"

"My background, the kind of things I like to do, that sort of stuff."

He frowned, still smiling that half smile. "Hmm, it's hard to know where to start."

Adrenaline buzzed through her at the prospect of nailing down a few details. "How about at the beginning. Did I grow up in New York?"

"No. You moved there after college." He kissed her cheek softly. "You came to work for me right after you graduated."

"What did I study in college?"

"Hmm. I can't remember exactly. I think it was something to do with literature. Or maybe French. You spoke French fluently even though you'd never been to France. I remember that."

"Oh." It wasn't so odd that he didn't know what she'd majored in. That was before she met him. "Where did I go to college?"

Jake hesitated, and frowned. "Was it U Penn? Somewhere in Pennsylvania. I'm pretty sure of that."

"You don't remember where I went to college? You're almost as bad as I am. Where did I grow up?"

Jake licked his lips. His eyes showed a mild trace of alarm. "Pennsylvania, definitely. Philly, maybe. Or was it Pittsburgh?"

"We've never been there together?" An odd knot of tension was forming in her stomach. She propped herself up in bed on one elbow.

"No, our relationship has always been pretty under wraps. The whole professional thing."

"So you haven't met my family." Again, unease niggled somewhere deep inside her.

"No. You have parents and a sister somewhere, though. You get together with them for holidays."

"In Pennsylvania?"

"I think so. You usually took the train."

"Oh." How odd that she couldn't remember anything about them. Or Pennsylvania. And it was a little disturbing that Jake seemed to know so little about her. Did they never talk about her past? "What's my sister's name?"

Jake pursed his lips for a moment. "I don't know."

"I guess I didn't talk about her that much." Maybe she and her sister weren't close. What a shame. Maybe she'd try to improve their relationship once she got her memory back. "What about my parents? Do you know their names or where they live? We could get in touch with them and see if they could jog my memory back into existence."

Jake's brow had furrowed. "I suppose we should be able to find that information somewhere."

"It's probably on my computer if I could just figure out the password."

"We'll worry about that in the morning." Jake pulled her closer to him. "Right now let's just enjoy each other."

Andi let out a sigh and sank back into his arms. "You're right. Why get stressed out over something I can't control?"

But even in his soothing embrace, there wasn't a single second when she didn't ache to recover her memory—and her history. How could you really go forward, or even live in the moment, if you don't know who you are?

After breakfast, Jake left Andi in her office to look over her files. She seemed anxious that she wasn't able to do her job since she didn't remember the details of palace life, let alone any specific events. He mused that he should have been concerned, too, since a key purpose of this whole engagement was to keep her at his side running the show, but somehow the palace was managing to tick along. And he was enjoying her company far more than he'd imagined.

How could he have worked with her for six years and not even know where her family lived? As far as he knew she was born behind the desk in his Manhattan office. And he cringed at not knowing her sister's name. For all he could remember she just referred to her as "my sister."

He strode to his current office, intent on mining it for the information he should know simply on the basis of their long acquaintance. They spent all day together—did they usually talk about nothing but work?

Andi was always excellent about keeping them focused so no time was wasted. She managed their affairs with such efficiency that there was little downtime for chin-wagging, especially since they'd moved to Ruthenia and tackled challenges higher than the legendary Althaus mountains that loomed over the palace. He'd always appreciated her professional approach to her job and to life in general.

But now he was beginning to realize he'd missed out on enjoying her company all this time. She was much more complex than he'd realized, more vulnerable and intriguing—and not just because of her missing memory. He'd never seen her as a person with emotions, with needs, before, because she'd done such an excellent job hiding that aspect of herself.

And he'd never realized she was so tempting. She'd hidden that, too.

He closed his office door and walked through to the cabinets in the file room, where the personnel files from New York were stored. Thanks to Andi's relentless organization he quickly laid his hands on her file, and the résumé she'd submitted when she applied for the job as his admin back when he was simply a venture capitalist.

A quick scan revealed that she'd graduated from Drexel University in Pennsylvania—right state, at least—with a degree in business administration and a ridiculously long list of clubs and activities to her name. Apart from some temping in Manhattan, her first job was with him. She'd graduated from North Hills Senior High School in Pittsburgh—ha, right again, maybe he wasn't so bad after all. He had to congratulate himself on being able to pick such a promising employee despite her lack of relevant work experience.

But that didn't solve his current problem of finding out about her past and helping her recover her memory.

Wait. Did he even want her to recover her memory? If she did, she'd surely remember that their relationship had been strictly professional and the whole engagement his invention.

Discomfort rose in his chest, threatening to overwhelm the sense of satisfaction—of happiness, dammit—that had suffused his body and mind since their overnight encounter.

Andi was sensational between the sheets. He'd never have dreamed that his quiet, prim assistant hid so much passion and energy beneath her suited exterior. She even looked different, like she'd forgotten to put on the mask of no-nonsense propriety she usually painted on with makeup and pinned into place with a spritz of hair spray. The real Andi—the one without the mask—was soft and sexy and downright irresistible.

Desire stirred inside him again, tightening his muscles. Blood rushed to his groin as he thought about her in his arms that morning, scented with passion as well as her usual floral fragrance. He put the résumé back in its file.

Maybe her memory wouldn't come back and they could start over from the night he'd found her dancing outside, freed of the inhibitions and anxieties built by a lifetime of experience. He couldn't help believing that the woman who'd shared his bed was the real Andi, and that she'd been hiding inside all this time, waiting for a chance to be free.

Andi let out a cry of sheer joy. She'd finally cracked the password on her computer. A cryptic penciled list in the drawer seemed like a meaningless string of words—until she started typing them in one by one.

Queen had proved to be the key that unlocked her hard drive, and possibly her whole life. Funny! She must have picked it because she knew she soon would be queen.

That thought stopped her cold for a second. Queen Andi. Didn't quite sound right. Still, she'd get used to it. And maybe Andi was short for a more majestic name, like Andromeda or something.

Her heart raced as the computer opened her account and laid a screen full of icons out before her. Yikes. So many different files, some with the names of countries, some of companies. She didn't know where to start. A sound issued from the machine, and she noticed that the email icon announced the presence of fifty-three messages. She clicked on it with a growing sense of anticipation, and scrolled back to the last one she had opened. Eticket confirmation.

Frowning, she opened the email, which revealed an itinerary for Andi Louise Blake—apparently she wasn't really named Andromeda—to travel from Munich to New York. The date listed was…yesterday.

Her blood slowed in her veins and her breathing grew shallow.

Obviously she hadn't gone on the trip, and if it was a business-related one, surely Jake would have mentioned it.

Munich—the nearest international airport, perhaps?—to New York, where she used to live...

She had been planning to leave.

Head spinning, she sat back in her chair. Why would she leave, if she was in love and about to get engaged?

She should just ask Jake about this. Why get all worked up when it could be a business trip that just got canceled at the last moment, maybe due to her loss of memory, or their engagement?

Andi glanced down at her ring with a growing sense of unease. She never had figured out why her clothes were creased as if they'd been packed. She must have changed her mind and unpacked at some point, but when? And why did Jake not know about her plans to take off?

Had she issued an ultimatum and forced him into proposing to her?

She swallowed, then started to chew on a nail. Her stomach curled up into a tight ball. Maybe she should see what else was going on in her email before she spoke to Jake.

It was hard to read with so much nervous energy leaping through her system. Her eyes kept jumping around on the screen. Most of the emails were business related—responses to invitations, scheduling questions, orders for supplies and that kind of thing.

Then one titled What's going on? from a Lizzie Blake caught her eye. Blake—the same last name as her. What *was* going on? She clicked on it with her heart in her mouth.

Andi, I know you told me not to email personal stuff to this account, but I've tried calling you and you won't call back. We saw a news story on TV yesterday saying that you're going to marry Jake Mondragon, your boss. Is this true? How come you didn't tell us? I thought you were getting ready to quit from the way you've been talking lately. Mom is pretty upset that you'd keep something like this from us. I remember you saying years ago that your boss was hot, but you never mentioned dating him, let alone getting engaged. Anyway, get in touch ASAP and let me know if I need to find a dress for a royal wedding. XX Sis.

Andi sat back, blinking. She had a sister called Lizzie. Who knew absolutely nothing about her relationship to Jake. And who'd been calling her but not getting through. She *must* have another phone somewhere that she used for personal calls.

She scanned the rest of the emails, but nothing else looked truly personal.

Where would she keep another phone? Brain ticking fast, she hurried back to her bedroom, glad she didn't run into anyone in the hallway—especially Jake.

A pang of guilt and hurt stung her heart. She was avoiding him. Only this morning they'd lain in each others arms and she'd enjoyed such contentment and bliss that she hadn't even minded about her memory being gone.

Now she was racked with suspicion and doubt. She locked her bedroom door behind her and started to go through the closet and drawers again. Finally, in the pocket of a black pair of pants she found a small silver phone. The pants showed signs of being recently worn—slightly creased across the hips and behind the knees—so maybe she had them on just before she lost her memory.

She flipped the phone open and pulled up recent messages. There were three from Lizzie and one from her mom, who sounded noticeably upset. Her voice, with its hint of tears, struck a sharp and painful chord deep inside her. On instinct Andi hit the button to dial the number.

"Andi!"

"Mom?" Her voice shook slightly. "Is it really you?"

"Of course it's me. Who else would be answering my phone?" A bright laugh rang in her ear. "What the heck is going on over there?"

Andi drew in a steadying breath. "I don't really know, to be honest. I lost my memory."

"What?"

"Jake found me dancing around outside and I couldn't remember anything at all. I didn't even remember you or Lizzie until I saw her email and found the messages on my phone."

"Oh, my gosh, that sounds terrifying. Are you okay?"

"More or less. It's been strange and kind of scary, but I'm not sick or injured or anything."

"That's a blessing. Has your memory come back?"

Andi blinked. A blurry vision of a face—an energetic woman with short light brown hair and bright blue eyes filled her brain. "I think it's coming back right now. Do you have blue eyes?"

"Of course I do. That's where you got them from. You forgot my eye color?"

"I forgot you even existed. I didn't know my own name." Other images suddenly crowded her brain: a man with gray hair and a warm smile, a blonde with long curls and a loud laugh. "But it's coming back now that I hear your voice." Excitement crackled through her veins. Finally she had an identity, a past. The details crashed back into her brain one after the other—her childhood home, her school, her old dog Timmy...

"Are you really engaged to your boss?" Her mom's voice tugged her back to the present.

Andi froze. That part she didn't remember. "He says we got engaged right before I lost my memory. I don't remember it."

"Do you love him?" The voice on the phone was suddenly sharp.

"Oh, yes. I've always loved him." The conviction rang through her whole body. "I've loved him for years."

"You never said a thing. I had no idea you were even involved with him."

Andi blinked rapidly. The memories flooding her brain were curiously devoid of any romantic images of her and Jake. She had plenty of memories of working with him, but as she mentally flipped through them looking for signs of their relationship a strange and awful truth dawned on her. "That's because I wasn't involved with him."

Six

Her mom's confused and anxious reaction prompted Andi to make excuses and hang up the phone. She needed someone who could answer questions, not just ask them. Instinct told her to call her sister, Lizzie.

"Your Majesty!" Her sister's now-familiar voice made her jump.

"Lizzie, you wouldn't believe what's been going on."

"You're right. I don't, so you'll have to break it down into tiny pieces for me. Are you really marrying your boss?"

Andi bit her lip. "I don't know. It's the weirdest thing, I lost my memory and ever since then we've been engaged. But my memory's coming back now—since I found your phone messages and spoke to Mom—and I don't remember anything at all about being engaged to him."

"You never even told me you were dating him."

"I don't remember anything about that, either. I do recall being seriously attracted to him for, oh, years and years, but not that anything actually came of it. Now suddenly I seem to be engaged to him and I have no idea what's going on."

"How does he explain the situation?"

Andi blew out. "I don't know. I haven't spoken to him about it yet. My memory only just started coming back and he doesn't know yet."

"Do you remember him asking you to marry you?"

She thought for a second. "No. I don't remember everything, though. There's a gap." She raised a hand to her head where she could still feel a slight bump. "I must have fallen and banged my head, or something." She paused, remembering the etickets she'd seen on her computer. "Did I say anything about coming back to the States?"

"For Christmas, you mean?"

Andi wondered how much to reveal, then decided things were so complicated already that she might as well be truthful. "For good. I think I was planning to leave here. I had tickets back to New York."

"And you don't remember why?"

I do.

The realization was seeping back into her, almost like blood rushing to her brain. She had intended to leave. She wanted to go because she was tired of adoring Jake while he flirted with other women in the name of business.

Because she loved him and knew she could never have him.

A sharp pain rose in her middle around the area of her heart. How had six years of yearning turned—overnight— into a fantasy engagement?

It didn't add up. There was a missing piece to the puzzle and she had no idea what it was.

"So are you marrying him, or what?" Lizzie's amused voice roused her from her panicked thoughts.

Her eyes fell on the big ring, flashing in the afternoon

sunlight pouring through the large office window. "Yes." Then she frowned. "At least I think so."

"Well, I saw it in the *National Enquirer,* so it must be true, right?" Lizzie's voice was bright with laughter. "There's a picture of you with a rock on your finger the size of my Mini Cooper. Is that thing real?"

Andi stared at the glittering stones. She was pretty sure it was a real diamond, but was it a real engagement ring? "Sure. It's from a jeweler here in town. Jake bought it for me yesterday."

"Sounds pretty official to me. Is he good in bed?"

Andi's mouth fell open.

"Come on, I'd tell you. Or do royal romances not involve any sex?"

Her teasing voice brought a smile to Andi's lips. "He's amazing."

"Ha. I had a feeling. I've seen pictures of him and he's seriously handsome. I love the dark flashing eyes. Is he romantic?"

"Very." She could almost feel his arms around her right now, holding and steadying her. "He's been so sweet with me since I lost my memory. We've managed to keep it a secret so far. You and Mom and the doctor he called are the only other people who know."

"Why keep it a secret?"

"I guess because I felt so vulnerable. Like everyone around me knows more about me than I do. I didn't want anyone to know. It's all coming back now, though. Not all the tiny details yet, like work stuff I have to do, but the bigger things like who I know and where I'm from and…"

How much I've always loved Jake.

Were they really going to be married and live happily ever after? It seemed too much to hope for.

"So you're going to be a queen. Will I have to curtsy to you?"

"Gosh, I hope not." Andi laughed. "What a strange idea. I can't quite see myself with a crown on."

"You'd better get used to the idea. Can I be your maid of honor? Or maybe they don't have them in Ruthenia."

"I have no idea. I've never planned a wedding here and apparently I haven't paid close enough attention at the few I've attended." Images of Jake's other would-be brides crowded her mind. Alia and Maxi and Carlotta and Liesel... there were so many of them. Rich and beautiful and fawning all over him. Why, out of all the glamorous and powerful women available to him, had Jake chosen her?

It was time to track him down and ask some questions.

After promising to call Lizzie back and tell her the details, Andi went into the bathroom and looked in the mirror. Her cosmetics were strung out along a shelf, which was not how she used to keep them. She also remembered that she nearly always tied her rather wispy hair up in a bun and slicked it down with gel—she was always experimenting with different brands as the Ruthenian climate was surprisingly humid. Now her hair lay loose around her shoulders, and her face looked oddly colorless without the lipstick and blush she usually donned.

A glance in her closet reminded her she was a hard-core suit wearer. She felt it was important to project a professional image, and she liked bright colors as they seemed assertive and positive. Right now she had on a rather uncharacteristic pastel yellow blouse and a pair of slacks and her hair wafted around her shoulders. People must have noticed the difference.

Part of her felt embarrassed that she'd been walking around the palace looking like a paler, less polished version of herself. And part of her wondered whether Jake actually preferred the less made-up look. He'd chosen the super-casual jeans and T-shirt she'd worn all the previous day. She blushed as she remembered he'd also chosen the racy lingerie. A glance in her underwear drawer confirmed that cotton briefs and no-nonsense bras were more her style.

Still, if Jake liked lacy lingerie and jeans, she could adjust. She couldn't resist smoothing just a hint of blush on her cheeks. They were a bit pale with shock. But she used a clear gloss instead of lipstick and left her hair loose—maybe it didn't look so bad after all.

With a deep breath, she set off for his office. Her pulse rate roared like a runaway truck by the time she finally plucked up the courage to peek around the open door. Jake was in conversation with a man she instantly remembered as the minister of economics. Jake looked up when she entered the doorway, and an expression flickered across his face—shock?—almost as if he suddenly knew her memory was back.

Andi struggled not to fidget as the conversation continued for another couple of minutes—something urgent to do with trade tariffs. Her nerves were jumping and her palms sweating.

In his dark suit, with his usual air of unhurried calm, Jake seemed perfectly poised and in control of any situation. She, on the other hand, had no idea what their situation really was. She could remember nearly everything about her life—except a romance with Jake.

He finally closed the door behind the economics minister and turned to her. Again she could see in his face that he knew something was different.

"My memory is coming back." She floated the words out, as if on a string, wondering what his response would be. Would he take her in his arms with a cry of joy?

Jake didn't move an inch. "That's great." He seemed to be waiting for her to reveal more.

"It started when I saw an email from my sister. Then I phoned my mom. That jogged something in my brain and the memories started bubbling up."

"What a relief." His voice was oddly flat. He still made no move toward her.

Andi's eyes dropped to her ring, which seemed to sting the skin underneath it. "It's strange, I remember working with you for years, but I don't…" Her voice cracked as fear rose in her chest. "I don't remember anything about us." She faltered. "I mean us being…romantically involved."

Jake stepped up to her and took her hand. Her heart surged with relief and she was about to smile, but his deadly serious demeanor stopped her. "I'll be completely honest with you."

"About what?" Her pulse picked up and a sense of dread swelled inside her.

"We weren't involved. Our relationship was strictly professional until two days ago."

"We weren't dating? Not even in secret?" Her heart hammered against her ribs.

"No."

Andi swallowed hard and her rib cage tightened around her chest. The ostentatious ring suddenly seemed to weigh down her hand and drain her strength. "So, the engagement is fake?" Her voice came out as a rasping whisper, filled with every ounce of apprehension and terror she felt. "It was all pretend?"

Jake tilted his head. "No."

Andi wanted to shake him. "Could you be more explicit?"

He frowned. "It's hard to explain. You were going to leave, and I didn't want you to. I was under pressure to choose a bride, and then you lost your memory. Things fell into place and I realized you're the ideal woman to be my wife."

She blinked, trying to make sense of his words. "So we are engaged?"

"Absolutely." His dark eyes looked earnest.

Then a cold sensation crept over her. "But you're not in love with me."

He swallowed. "Love is something that grows over time. I'm confident that we'll enjoy a happy and successful marriage. The important thing is to provide stability for Ruthenia, and as a team we can do just that."

Andi struggled for breath. The man of her dreams, whom she'd fantasized about and mooned over for six long years, wanted to marry her.

Because she'd be a key member of his team.

A cold laugh flew from her lips. "Wouldn't it have been easier to just offer me a higher salary?"

He raised a brow. "I tried that."

"And I said no? Wait. Now I remember saying no. You were so sure you could talk me around, just like you always do." Her vision blurred as tears rose to her eyes. "And you really thought I'd go along with this crazy plan?"

"You're sensible and practical. I knew you'd see the sense in it."

"In spending my life with a husband who doesn't love me? You never even noticed I was female." A flashback to their lovemaking filled her brain. He'd noticed it then. But maybe he'd just pretended she was one of the glamorous socialites that usually buzzed around him. He'd had no shortage of girlfriends in the time she'd worked for him.

"My parents married because their families were both exiled Ruthenian nobles. They were married nearly fifty years."

His parents had died before she met him. She knew little about them except that they were part of New York society. "Were they happy?"

He hesitated. "Of course."

"You don't sound convinced. Did they love each other?"

"It was a successful marriage, and they achieved their lifelong goal of producing an heir who'd be ready to take the throne of Ruthenia when the time came."

"Lucky thing you were cooperative. It would be a shame to throw away fifty years of your life and have your son insist he was going to be a pro skateboarder. Did you really think I'd just go along with your plan?"

"Yes."

His calm expression exasperated her. He still thought she was going to go along with his scheme. He obviously didn't care about her feelings at all. "We slept together." Her body still sizzled and hummed with sensual energy from that amazing night.

The passion they'd shared might have been fake on his side, but on hers it was painfully real.

"I didn't intend for that to happen." His expression turned grim. "I understand that you must be furious with me for taking advantage of your situation."

"You're right. I am." Devastated would have been a better word. Their lovemaking wasn't the fruit of a long-term and loving romance, at least not for him. On her side she'd probably had enough romance in her head to last a lifetime.

He must have found it hilarious that she fell into his arms so easily. "Didn't you think it was wrong to sleep with an employee?"

His eyes narrowed. "Yes. I didn't intend to sleep with you until I'd explained the situation."

"Until you'd explained to me that you needed a wife and I was handy?" She still couldn't quite believe he took her so totally for granted.

Obviously he had no respect for her feelings and wishes. A chill swept through her and she hugged herself.

"You were confused after losing your memory. I didn't want to complicate matters when I knew you were in no state to make an important decision."

"So you just made it for me."

He drew in a breath. "You know me well enough to trust my judgment."

She struggled to check her anger. "I trust your judgment perfectly in matters of business, but not where my personal life is concerned. You already knew I intended to leave because I wasn't feeling fulfilled."

No need to say she couldn't stand to see him marry another woman. He'd assume she was thrilled that he'd made a coldhearted and clinical decision to marry her. "It's downright arrogant of you to assume I'd marry you."

"I know you're capable of rising to any challenge."

"But what if I don't want to?" Her voice rose a little and she struggled to check tears. A romance with Jake was such a heartfelt wish. Suddenly it had become a duty.

No doubt sex with her was supposed to seal the pact in some way.

What a shame she'd enjoyed it so much. Right now she wanted to chastise her body for still craving his touch. She should hate him for what he'd done when she needed his help the most.

Jake still stood there, calm and regal, chin lifted high.

A sinister thought crept over her. If he could plan something so outrageous as marriage to a woman who didn't know who she was, perhaps he contrived to put her in such a vulnerable position.

"Were you responsible for me losing my memory?" If he'd gone this far in his deception, who knew what he could be capable of?

"No." His answer was decisive.

She wanted to believe him—and hated herself for it.

"Then what did happen?" So many pieces were still missing.

"I don't know how you lost your memory. I found you outside dancing around on the grass in the moonlight."

Andi blushed. Had she done anything embarrassing? She couldn't remember a single thing about that night. Though now that he mentioned it, she did remember telling him she was going to leave. A cold sensation slithered through her. She was leaving to protect her heart.

Right now her heart was being flayed open. Jake's desire to keep her had nothing to do with him wanting her as his fiancée, or even his friend, and everything to do with keeping his office running smoothly.

And he'd seduced her into his bed on the pretext that they'd been dating for years.

Her insides still hummed with sense memories that would probably torment her forever. She'd thought they were making love—and her whole spirit had soared with the joy of it—but he was just cementing a deal.

On instinct she pulled the big ring from her finger. It wedged a bit over the knuckle, but she managed to get it off. "Take this back."

His eyes widened. "Oh, no. You must wear it."

"I don't have to do anything." She shoved it forward. "It's not real."

"I assure you those stones are genuine and worth a large sum of money."

Andi's mouth fell open, then closed shut. How could he not understand a word she was saying? She walked to his desk and put the ring down on the polished surface. It looked odd there, sparkling away amongst the piles of papers.

"I don't intend to wear or own any kind of engagement ring unless I'm actually engaged. And since we're not really engaged or even involved, I don't want anything to do with it." Tears threatened in her voice. She crossed her arms, and hoped it would hide the way her hands were shaking.

"But we are engaged." Jake's words, spoken softly, crept into her brain and heart. "I really do want to marry you."

Andi blinked, trying to catch her breath. How could a dream come true in such a horrible, distorted way?

The odd expression in his eyes almost made her consider it. There was something like…yearning in their dark depths.

Then again, she was obviously good at dreaming stuff up.

Now that her memory was back she knew—in the depths of her aching soul—that she'd loved Jake for years, pined for him and hoped that one day he'd see her as something other than an efficient assistant. She'd adored him in silence, occasionally allowing herself to fantasize that things might one day be different if she waited patiently for him to notice her. Their time as an engaged couple was the fulfillment of all secret hopes—and now she'd woken to find herself living a mockery of her cherished dreams.

Anger flared inside her, hot and ugly. "You honestly think I would continue with this charade that you sprung on me when I was at my most vulnerable? To let people think that we love each other when we're nothing more than boss and assistant, as always?"

"We'll be equals, of course, like any couple."

He said it simply, like he really believed it. But then Jake could convince anyone of anything. She'd watched him in action for too long. "I'm not sure that many couples are equals, especially royal ones." She'd be the official wife, sensibly dressed and courteous as always. The one who got left behind with her embroidery—not that she did embroidery—while he was out having affairs with other women.

"I need to leave, and right now." If she continued with this pretense for even another hour, she'd get sucked into hoping their official engagement might turn into true romance. Even with every shred of evidence pointing to that being impossible and hopeless, she'd already proven herself to be that kind of softheaded, dreaming fool.

"The story's gone around the world already."

She steadied herself with a breath. All her relatives knew, probably all her old friends. Everyone she'd ever known, maybe. "You'll just have to explain that it was all a big lie. Or a joke." Her voice cracked on the last word. It did feel like a cruel joke at her expense. She'd never experienced such feelings of happiness and contentment as during the last couple of days as Jake's fiancée. Their night of lovemaking had raised the bar of pure bliss so high that she'd likely never know anything like that again.

"I'm going to pack my bags." She turned for the door. Her whole body was shaking.

Jake caught hold of her arm and she tried to wrench it away, but his grip was too strong. "The people of Ruthenia are counting on you. I'm counting on you."

His words pierced her soul for a second, but she summoned her strength. "I'm sure the people of Ruthenia can find something else to count on. Television game shows, perhaps."

"We're going to be on television tonight. To talk about celebrating our engagement during the Independence Day celebrations."

Andi froze. "Independence Day. That's what this is all about, isn't it?" She turned and stared at his face. A memory of Jake's public promise to choose a wife formed in her mind. "You committed to picking a bride before Ruthenia's third Independence Day." She squinted at him, looking for signs of emotion in his face. "Your deadline had come right up on you and you had to pick someone or you'd be a liar. And there I was, clueless as a newborn babe and ripe for duping."

"Andi, we've been partners for years. It's not that big a leap."

"From the office to a lifetime commitment? I think that's a leap. You can't just get a plane ticket and leave a marriage." She lifted her chin as anger and hurt flashed over her. "Though apparently I can't just get a plane ticket and leave my job with you, either." Fury bubbled up inside her. "Do you think you can control everything and everyone?"

"I'm not trying to control you, just to make you see sense. We're a great team."

"I've never been into team sports. When I marry, it will be for love." Her heart ached at the thought that she'd loved Jake almost since the day she met him.

Though right now she hated him for tricking her into a relationship that meant nothing to him.

"Think it over, Andi. Be sensible."

"I am sensible. That's why I know this would never work."

Jake's expression grew impenetrable. "Stay until after Independence Day, at least."

"You think I'll change my mind? Or maybe you think I'll just be guilt-tripped into marrying you by seeing all those smiling Ruthenian faces. What if people don't like the idea of you marrying your lowly assistant? They'd probably rather see you marry some Ruthenian blue blood with twelve names."

"They'll all know I made the right choice."

His words hung in the air. *The right choice.*

Impossible.

Still, his quiet conviction both irked and intrigued her.

She stared hard at his chiseled face. "You really do want to marry me?"

He took her hands in his. Her skin tingled and sizzled, and she cursed the instant effect he always had on her. "I do want to marry you."

Those accursed hopes and dreams flared up inside her like embers under a breath.

He doesn't love you. Don't get carried away.

Still, maybe something could come of this crazy situation. Could she live with herself if she didn't at least try to make it work?

She inhaled a shaky breath. "If I agree to stay until Independence Day, then decide it won't work, you'll let me go?"

His expression clouded. "Yes."

She wasn't sure she believed him. Jake didn't often admit, or experience, defeat. But she could always sneak away this time.

Or stay here for the rest of her life.

Her heart thumped and her stomach felt queasy. "I can't really believe this is happening. We'll sleep in separate rooms?"

"If you prefer." His cool reply sounded like a challenge. He probably intended to seduce her again. She silently determined not to let him.

"Independence Day is three days away." Could she stand to be Jake's unloved but practical fiancée for seventy-two hours? She really didn't want to let everyone down and ruin the Independence Day celebrations. She could look at it as her job, as long as there was no kissing or sex involved.

And then there was that insane hope that they really could live happily ever after.

Jake picked up the ring from among the papers on his desk. "You'll need this."

Andi eyed it suspiciously. Putting the ring back on would mean agreeing to his terms. Clearly he expected her to, and why wouldn't he? She'd always done everything he asked in the past.

He picked up her hand without asking permission. Her skin heated instantly at his touch and she made the mistake of looking up into his face. His dark gaze dared her to refuse him—and she knew in that instant that she couldn't.

Why did he still have so much power over her?

She was disoriented right now. Confused. Her memory slipping and sliding back into her head while she tried to take in the strange new reality of Jake wanting to marry her.

Wanting to *marry* her.

It should be a dream come true—so why did it feel more like a waking nightmare?

Seven

The following afternoon, Andi adjusted the collar of her new and fabulously expensive dress. Fit for a queen. The rack of designer clothes had arrived with a coordinator from Ruthenia's most snooty bespoke tailor to help her choose the right look and make any necessary alterations.

She'd tried not to tremble when the seamstress stuck pins in around her waist and bust. Now the freshly sewn green fabric draped over her like a second skin of luxurious silk.

But did she look like a future queen? She'd be paraded on TV as one tonight. RTV was setting up cameras in the ballroom to interview her and Jake. She'd tried to beg off and delay any public appearances until after she'd made her decision, but endless calls from the television station had hounded her into it and at this point she'd appear snooty and uncooperative if she said no again.

"Earrings." A representative from the jeweler where

they'd bought the ring opened a case filled with sparkly gems. Andi hadn't even noticed her come in, but then people were coming and going in a constant scurry, preparing for the evening shoot. The earrings blurred into a big shiny mass.

"You choose." Andi didn't even want to look at them. Better to let these professionals decide whether she looked like a future queen or not.

She certainly didn't feel like one.

Was it her job to act this part? It felt more like her patriotic duty. Which was silly since she was American, not Ruthenian. At least until she married Jake.

If she married Jake.

She tried to keep her breathing steady as the girl clipped big emeralds to her ears and murmured, "Perfect." The seamstress nodded her approval and beckoned across the room.

A middle-aged woman with a blond pompadour and a rat-tail comb approached with a gleam in her eye. She picked up a strand of Andi's limp hair between her thumb and finger and winced slightly. "Don't worry. We can fix it."

Thirty minutes later her hair hung around her shoulders in plump curls that everyone assured her looked "lovely." The woman staring back at her from the mirror, wide-eyed and pale beneath her carefully applied makeup, didn't even look like her. She'd barely managed to remember who she was, and now she was being turned into someone else.

"Andi, can you come in for a moment? They want to check the lighting."

She steadied herself and walked—slowly in her long, rather heavy dress—toward the formal library where the cameras were set up.

Jake was nowhere to be seen.

It's your job, she told herself. Just be professional. Being a monarch's fiancée definitely felt more like a career assignment than a romantic dream come true.

Strangers' hands shuffled her into place under blistering hot lights that made her blink. More powder was dotted on her nose and fingers fluffed her curls. Out of the corner of her eye she could see the local news anchor going over some notes with a producer. What kind of questions would they ask?

I won't lie.

She promised herself that. This whole situation was so confusing already; she had no intention of making it worse by having to keep track of stories. She'd try to be tactful and diplomatic, of course.

Just part of the job.

A sudden hush fell over the room and all eyes turned to the door. His majesty. Jake strode in, a calm smile on his face. Andi's heartbeat quickened under her designer gown. Fear as well as the familiar desire. Would she manage to act the role of fiancée well enough to please him?

She cursed herself for wanting to make him happy. He hadn't given her feelings any thought when he'd tricked her into wearing his ring.

Their eyes met and a jolt of energy surged through her. *I really do want to marry you.* His words echoed in her brain, tormenting and enticing. How could she not at least give it a shot?

A producer settled them both on the ornate gilt-edged sofa under the lights, in full view of three cameras. Andi felt Jake's hand close around hers, his skin warm. She almost wished he wouldn't touch her, as she didn't want him to know she was shaking and that her palms were sweating.

No aspect of her job had ever made her so terrified. She'd greeted foreign dignitaries and handled major international incidents without so much as a raised pulse. Why did every move she made now feel like a matter of life and death?

Silence descended as the interviewer moved toward them, microphone clipped to her blue suit. Andi's heart pounded.

I won't lie.

But Jake didn't have to know that.

"Your Majesty, thank you so much for agreeing to this interview." Jake murmured an assent. "And for allowing us to meet your fiancée." The journalist smiled at Andi.

She tried not to shrink into the sofa. Yesterday morning she'd been totally comfortable and happy as Jake's fiancée. It had felt as natural as breathing. But now everything was different and she'd been dropped into the middle of a movie set—with no script.

The reporter turned her lipsticked smile to Andi. "You're living every young girl's dream."

"Yes," she stammered. *Except in the dream the prince actually loves you.* "I still can't believe it."

No lies told so far.

"Was the proposal very romantic?"

Andi grew hyperconscious of Jake's hand wrapped around hers. She drew in a breath. "I was so stunned I don't remember a word of it."

The reporter laughed, and so did Jake. Andi managed a smile.

"I guess the important part is that you said yes." The reporter turned to Jake. "Perhaps you could tell us about the moment."

Andi stared at Jake. Would he make something up? He'd lied to her when he'd told her they were engaged. Unless a king could become engaged simply by an act of will.

"It was a private moment between myself and Andi." He

turned to look at her. Then continued in a low voice. "I'm very happy that she's agreed to be my wife."

Until Independence Day. He was obviously confident he'd convince her to stay after that, but as she sat here under the lights with people staring at her and analyzing every move she made, she became increasingly sure she'd couldn't handle this.

It would have been different if Jake wanted to marry her for the right reasons and she could look forward to true intimacy and companionship, at least when they were alone together.

But she'd never been enough for him before, and she was painfully sure that she wouldn't be enough for him now—ring or no ring.

"What a lovely ring." Andi's hand flinched slightly under the reporter's gaze. "A fitting symbol for a royal romance."

Yes. All flash and pomp. "Thanks. We bought it right here in town. The local village has such skilled craftspeople."

"I think it's charming that you chose the work of a Ruthenian artisan, when you could so easily have bought something from New York or Paris."

"Both Andi and I are proud of Ruthenia's fine old-world craftsmanship. It's one of the few places where attention to detail is more important than turning a quick profit. Some people might see our steady and deliberate approach to things as a hindrance in the modern world of business, but I see them as strengths that will secure our future."

Andi maintained a tight smile. He was turning their engagement interview into a promotional video for Ruthenia. Something she would have heartily approved of only a few days ago, but now made her heart contract with pain.

With his "steady and deliberate" approach to marriage,

he expected her to devote her life to Ruthenia and fulfill the role of royal wife, whether he loved her or not.

Andi startled when she realized the reporter was staring right at her. She'd obviously just asked a question, but Andi was so caught up in her depressing ruminations that she hadn't even heard it. Jake squeezed her hand and jumped in. "Andi will be making all the wedding arrangements. In our years of working together she's proved that she can pull off the most elaborate and complicated occasions."

He went on to talk about Ruthenian wedding traditions and how they'd be sure to observe and celebrate them.

What about my family traditions? Andi remembered her cousin Lu's wedding two summers ago. A big, fat Greek wedding in every sense of the word. What if she wanted to celebrate her mom's Greek heritage as well as Jake's Ruthenian roots?

Not a chance. Just one more example of how her life would slide into a faded shadow of Jake's.

But only if she let it.

Resolve kicked through her on a surge of adrenaline. She didn't have to do anything she didn't want to. "Of course, we'll also honor our American roots and bring those into our planning. I have ancestors from several different countries and we'll enjoy bringing aspects of that heritage into our wedding."

The reporter's eyes widened. Jake was so big on being all Ruthenian all the time, trying to prove that despite his New York upbringing, every cell in his blue blood was Ruthenian to the nucleus. Right now she couldn't resist knocking that. If he wanted a Ruthenian bride there was no shortage of volunteers.

But he'd chosen an American one. She smiled up at him sweetly. His dark eyes flashed with surprise. "Of course. Andi's right. Our American background and experience have enriched our lives and we'll certainly be welcoming many American friends to the wedding."

Andi felt his arm slide around her shoulders. She tried not to shiver at the feel of his thick muscle through her dress. "And now, if you don't mind, we have a lot to do to prepare for the Independence Day celebrations this week. Our third Independence Day marks a turning point for our nation, with our gross national product up and unemployment now at a fifty-year low. We hope everyone will join us in a toast to Ruthenia's future."

He circled his arm around her back, a gesture both protective and possessive. Andi cursed the way it stirred sensation in her belly and emotion in her heart. The reporter frowned slightly at being summarily dismissed, but made some polite goodbye noises and shook their hands.

Andi let out a long, audible sigh once the cameras finally turned off.

Jake escorted her from the room, and it wasn't until they were in the corridor outside that he loosened his grip on her arm slightly. "Nice point about our American heritage."

She wasn't sure if he was kidding or not. "I thought so." She smiled. "I'm kind of surprised you decided to pick an American wife. I was sure you'd marry a Ruthenian so you could have some ultra-Ruthenian heirs."

An odd expression crossed his face for a second. Had he forgotten about the whole royal heir thing? This engagement scenario seemed rather by-the-seat-of-the-pants; maybe he didn't think it through enough. Did he really want a Heinz 57 American girl from Pittsburgh to be the mother of Ruthenia's future king?

"Being Ruthenian is more a state of mind than a DNA trait." He kept his arm around her shoulders as they marched along the hall.

"Kind of like being king?" She arched a brow. "Though I

suppose that does require the right DNA or there'd be other claimants. The only way most Ruthenians can claim the throne is by marrying you. I guess I should be honored."

Jake turned to stare at her. She never usually talked back to him. Of course she didn't—he was her boss. Maybe once he discovered the real, off-hours Andi had a bit more spunk to her he'd lose all interest in hoisting her up onto his royal pedestal.

"I don't expect you to be honored." Humor sparkled in Jake's dark eyes. Did nothing rile him? "Just to think about the advantages of the situation."

"The glorious future of Ruthenia," she quipped.

"Exactly."

"What if I miss Philly cheesesteak?"

"The cook can prepare some."

"No way. She's from San Francisco. She'd put bean sprouts in it."

"We'll import it."

"It'd go cold on the plane."

"We'll fly there to get some."

"Is that fiscally responsible?"

He laughed. "See? You're a woman after my own heart."

"Cold and calculating?" She raised a brow.

"I prefer to think of it as shrewd and pragmatic." He pulled his arm from around her to reach into his pocket and she noticed they were at the door to his suite. She stiffened. She did not want to go in there and wind up in his bed again. Especially if it was the result of some shrewd and pragmatic seduction on his part.

The intimacy they'd shared left her feeling tender and raw. Probably because she'd always loved him and the act of making love only intensified everything she'd already felt. Now that she knew he didn't love her—that it was a mechanical act for him—she couldn't bear to be that close to him again.

"I guess I'll head for my room." She glanced down at her ridiculously over-the-top interview dress. "Am I supposed to give this dress to someone?"

"You're supposed to wear it to the state dinner tonight."

State dinner? She didn't remember planning any dinner. In fact she remembered deliberately not planning anything for the first few days after she intended to leave. "Maybe my memory isn't fully back yet, but I…" It was embarrassing to admit she still wasn't in full control of her faculties.

"Don't worry, you had nothing to do with it. I pulled the whole thing together to butter up all the people cheesed off by our engagement."

"That's a daring use of dairy metaphors."

Jake grinned. "Thanks. I'm a man of many talents."

If only I weren't so vividly aware of that. She sure as heck wished she'd never slept with him. That was going to be very hard to forget.

"So let me guess, all your recently jilted admirers, and their rich and influential daddies, will be gathered around the table in the grand dining room to whisper rude remarks about me." Her stomach clenched at the prospect.

"They'll do no such thing." Jake had entered the suite and obviously expected her to follow. He'd totally ignored her comment about heading for her room. "They wouldn't dare."

That's what you think. Powerful people could afford to be blissfully ignorant about what others thought, since no one would dare say anything to their face. She, on the other hand, was more likely to get a realistic picture of their true feelings since people didn't bother to try to impress a mere assistant.

But would they act differently now they thought she was engaged to Jake?

She glanced down at her perfectly tailored dress. It might be interesting to see how they behaved now the tables were turned and she was the one about to marry a king.

And it would certainly be educational to see how Jake behaved in their midst now that he was officially engaged to her.

"You look stunning." Jake's low voice jolted her from her anxious thoughts. His gaze heated her skin right through the green silk as it raked over her from head to toe, lingering for just a split second longer where the bodice cupped her breasts.

"Thanks. I guess almost anyone can look good when they have a crowd of professionals available to take charge."

"You're very beautiful." His dark eyes met hers. "Without any help from anyone."

Her face heated and she hoped they'd put on enough powder to hide it. Did he mean it or was he just saying that to mollify her? She didn't really believe anything he said anymore.

On the other hand, maybe he'd come to see her in a new light since he started considering her as wife material. She did feel pretty gorgeous under his smoldering stare.

"Flattery will get you everywhere." A sudden vision of herself in his bed—which was less than forty feet away—filled her mind. "Okay, maybe not everywhere. How long do we have until dinner?" She wasn't sure hanging around in his suite was a good idea. It might be better to spend time in more neutral territory.

"About half an hour."

"And who arranged this dinner if I didn't?" Curiosity goaded her to ask the question. The palace seemed to be running pretty well without her input, which should make her feel less guilty about leaving, but it irked her somewhat, too.

"Livia. She's been really helpful the last few days. Really stepped into your shoes."

"Oh." Andi stiffened. Why did it bother her that Livia might be after her job? She was planning to leave it, after all. Still, now that she remembered more of her past, she knew Livia had always felt somewhat competitive toward her, and resentful that Andi was hand in glove with Jake while she did the more routine work like ordering supplies and writing place cards.

She couldn't help wondering if Livia might now be resentful that Jake planned to marry her—talk about the ultimate promotion.

If you were into that sort of thing.

"Champagne?" Jake gestured to a bottle chilling in a silver bucket of ice. He must have had it brought here during the interview.

"No thanks." Better to keep her head. She had a feeling she'd need it. "But you go ahead."

"I couldn't possibly drink alone. And it's a 1907 Heidiseck."

"Are you sure it's not past its sell-by date?"

He chuckled. "It was recovered from a ship that was wrecked on its way to deliver champagne to the Russian Imperial family. It's been brought up from the bottom of the sea and tastes sublime even after decades of being lost."

"Very appropriate, considering the history of Ruthenia."

"That's what the friend who gave it to me thought. Won't you join me in a toast to our future?" His flirtatious glance tickled her insides.

She took a deep breath and tried to remain calm. "Not until I've figured out whether I want us to have a future."

Jake tilted his head. "You're very stubborn all of a sudden."

"That's because we're discussing the rest of my life, not just some seating placements or even a corporate merger."

"I like that about you. A lot of women would jump at the chance to marry me just to be queen."

Or just because you're embarrassingly attractive and shockingly wealthy. She tried to ignore those enticements herself.

Jake lifted a brow. "That doesn't mean much to you, does it?"

"I've never had the slightest desire to be called Your Majesty."

"Me, either." He grinned. "But if I can learn to put up with it, I'm sure you could handle it, too."

"Did you always know you'd be king one day?" She'd wondered this, but never dared ask him.

"My parents talked about it, but I thought they were nuts. I planned to be a king of Wall Street instead."

"And now you're doing both. I bet your parents would be very proud. It's a shame they weren't alive to see you take the throne." She knew they'd died in a small plane accident.

"If they were alive they'd be ruling here themselves, which would have been just fine with me."

"You don't like being king?" She couldn't resist asking.

"I like it fine, but it's a job for life. There's no getting bored and quitting. Sometimes I wonder what I would have done if I'd had more freedom."

"You were brave to take on the responsibility. Not everyone would have, especially with the state Ruthenia was in when you first arrived."

"I do feel a real sense of duty toward Ruthenia. I always

have, it was spooned into me along with my baby food. I couldn't turn my back on Ruthenia for anything."

She didn't feel the same way. In fact she could leave and never look back—couldn't she? She hadn't been raised to smile and wave at people or wear an ermine robe, but she had always felt a strong sense of commitment to her job— and her boss.

Who stood in front of her tall and proud, handsome features picked out by the light of a wall sconce. She admired him for stepping up to the responsibilities of getting Ruthenia back on its feet, and committing himself to help the country and its people for the rest of his life.

She should be touched and honored that he wanted her help in that enterprise, regardless of whether he loved her.

Still, she wasn't made of stone. Something she became vividly aware of when Jake reached for her hand and drew it to his lips. Her skin heated under his mouth and she struggled to keep her breathing steady.

He's just trying to seduce you into going along with his plan. It doesn't mean he really loves you—or even desires you.

Her body responded to him like a flipped switch, but then it always had, even back when he saw her as nothing more than an efficient employee. Heat flared in her belly and her fingertips itched to reach out and touch his skin.

But she'd resisted six long years and she could do it now.

She pulled her hand back with some difficulty. Her skin hummed where his lips had just touched it. A quick glance up was a mistake—his dark eyes fixed on hers with a smoldering expression that took her breath away.

But she knew he was an accomplished actor. You had to be to pull off international diplomacy, especially when it involved placating all the outrageous characters he dealt with in Ruthenia.

"You're very suspicious." His eyes twinkled.

"Of course I am. I woke up from amnesia to find myself engaged to my boss. That kind of thing makes a girl wary."

"You know you can trust me." His steady gaze showed total confidence.

"I thought I could trust you." She raised a brow. "Over the last day I've learned I can't trust you. You used me to your advantage, without consulting me."

His expression darkened. "I couldn't consult with you because you didn't know who you were."

"You could have waited until my memory came back and we could discuss it calmly." *Instead you decided to convince me between the sheets.* He'd undermined all her inhibitions and drawn her into the most intense and powerful intimacy.

Too bad it had worked so well.

"Time was of the essence. Independence Day is coming right up."

"And you couldn't disappoint the people of Ruthenia."

"Exactly. I knew you'd understand."

She did. The people of Ruthenia and his own reputation were far more important than her feelings.

Did he even know she had feelings?

She had three days to put him to the test.

Eight

Andi would have liked to sweep into the dining room and smile confidently at the gathered Ruthenian dignitaries and their snooty daughters, then take her place at the head of the table.

But it didn't work like that.

The toe of her pointed shoe caught in the hem of her dress on her way into the anteroom and she pitched through the doorway headfirst. Jake, walking behind her, flung his arms around her waist and pulled her back onto her feet before she fell on her face into the Aubusson carpet. It was not an auspicious entrance into high society.

Her face heated, especially when she saw the looks of undisguised glee on Maxi's and Alia's faces.

Jake laughed it off and used the occasion to steal a kiss in front of the gathered audience. She was too flustered to attempt resistance, which would have looked rude and strange anyway, since as far as everyone knew they were madly in love.

The kiss only deepened her blush and stirred the mix of arousal and anguish roiling in her gut.

"Congratulations!" A portly older man with medals on his jacket stepped forward and bowed low to Andi. She swallowed. This was the Grand Duke of Machen. He didn't have any marriageable daughters left, so he was one of the few non-hostile entities in the room. He turned to Jake. "We're all thrilled that you've finally chosen a bride to continue the royal line."

The royal line? Andi's muscles tightened. As Jake's wife she'd be expected to produce the future king or queen. Which meant that even if it were a marriage of convenience, there would be some sex involved. She'd already learned that making love with Jake touched something powerful and tender deep inside her. Not something she could do as a matter of routine. Could he really expect that of her? It was different with men. They could turn off their emotions and just enjoy the pure physical sensations.

If only she could do that.

A glance around the room revealed that not everyone was as thrilled as the grand duke. Maxi's father Anton Rivenshnell looked grim—salt-and-pepper brows lowered threateningly over his beady gray eyes. Maxi herself had abandoned her usual winning smile in favor of a less-flattering pout.

"I suppose an American bride seemed a natural choice when you spent your entire life in America," growled Rivenshnell, his dark suit stretched across an ample belly. "Though this is naturally a disappointment for the women of Ruthenia."

Jake seemed to grow about a foot taller, which, considering his already impressive height of six-one, made him a little scary. "Andi has demonstrated her commitment to Ruthenia over the last three years, living and working by my side. She is one of the women of Ruthenia."

Ha. Andi couldn't help loving his spirited defense of her. "I've never been so happy as I am here." The honest truth. She wasn't going to lie. "I've spent every day enjoying the people and the beautiful countryside, and I've come to love Ruthenia as my home."

"And you fell in love with your boss, too." The grand duke's laugh bellowed across the room.

"Yes." She managed a shaky smile. Again, it was the truth—but no need for Jake to know that. As far as he was concerned she was just fulfilling her part of the arrangement.

Andi felt very self-conscious as they were ushered into the dining room by a rather smug Livia. This was the first time she'd attended one of these affairs as a guest, not one of the staff members hovering along the walls ready to serve the diners and tend to Jake's needs. Livia shot her at least three meaningful glances, though she couldn't actually tell what they meant.

At least she managed not to fall on her face on her way to the end of the table, where she was seated far, far away from Jake, probably in between two daddies of rejected girls.

Jake was seated between Alia and Maxi, just as she'd sat him before she lost her memory. Then she'd done it as a joke, to torment him with his two most ardent admirers and hopefully put him off both of them. Now he must have planned it himself, for reasons she could only guess at.

Did he intend to have affairs with each of them now that he was no longer on the hook to make one his queen? Surely quiet little Andi wouldn't object.

The very thought made her seethe. Still, she didn't

remember Jake ever cheating on one of his many girlfriends. On the other hand, he rarely dated the same one for long enough to get the chance. As soon as a girl showed signs of getting serious, he brought an abrupt end to things.

Andi had rather liked that about him. He never continued with a relationship just because it was there. He was often blunt and funny about the reasons he no longer saw a future with a particular girl. And it always gave her fresh hope that one day he'd be hers.

And now he was. At least in theory.

Irritation flickered through her at the sight of Alia brushing his hand with her long, manicured fingers. Jake smiled at the elegant blonde and spoke softly to her before turning to Maxi. The sultry brunette immediately lit up and eased her impressive cleavage toward him. Jealousy raged in Andi's gut and she cursed herself for caring.

"Your parents must be delighted." The gruff voice startled Andi, who realized she was staring.

"Oh, yes." She tried to smile at the white-haired man by her side. Up close she could see he was probably too old to have a jilted daughter, so that was a plus.

Her parents would be happy if she married Jake. At least she imagined so. How would they feel if she refused to marry him?

"Have they visited Ruthenia before?"

"Not yet. But I'm sure they'll love it here."

"I imagine they'll move here." His blue eyes twinkled with…was it warmth or malice?

"They have their own lives back in Pittsburgh, so I don't think they'll be leaving."

"But they must! Their daughter is to be the queen. It would be tragic for a family to endure such separation."

"It's quite common in the U.S. for families to live hundreds or even thousands of miles apart."

"In Ruthenia that would be unthinkable."

"I know." She shrugged. Was he also implying that having such a coldhearted and independent American as their queen was unthinkable? "But they have jobs they enjoy and friends where they live. I'm sure they'll come visit often."

"They've *never* visited you here? How long have you been here?"

"Three years, but it's an expensive trip and…" He was making her feel bad, and she had a feeling that's exactly what he intended. "Have you ever visited the States?" She smiled brightly. Every time she looked up, someone was peeking at her out of the corner of their eye. Including Livia. She was beginning to feel under siege.

Jake shot her a warm glance from the far end of the table. Even from that distance he could make her heart beat faster. He looked totally in his element, relaxed, jovial and quite at home in the lap of luxury, surrounded by Ruthenian nobles.

Whereas she felt like a scullery maid who'd wandered into the ballroom—which wasn't a million miles from the truth. In all her dreams of herself and Jake living happily ever after, they lived happily in a fantasy world of her own creation. While life in the Ruthenian royal palace was definitely someone's fantasy world, it wasn't hers, and Jake was clearly making a terrible mistake if he thought this could work.

Jake beamed with satisfaction as staff poured the coffee. Andi looked radiant at the far end of the table, resplendent in her regal gown and with her hair arranged in shiny curls that fell about her shoulders. Ruthenia's haughty beauties disappeared into the drapery with her around. He'd tried to reassure them that his marriage was a love match and not a deliberate insult to them and their families. He couldn't afford to lose the support of Ruthenia's most powerful businessmen. Noses were definitely bent out of shape, but no one had declared war—yet.

A love match. He'd used the term several times now, though never within earshot of Andi. He couldn't say something so blatantly untrue right in front of her—at least not now that she had her memory back. He knew nothing of love. Raised by a succession of nannies while his parents traveled, he'd been groomed for duty and honor and not for family life and intimate relationships. Love seemed like something that happened in poems but not in real life, and he didn't want to promise anything to Andi that he couldn't deliver.

He was hotly attracted to her and admired all her fine qualities, and that was almost as good. Many people married for love and ended up divorced or miserable. It was much more sensible to go into a lifetime commitment with a clear head and a solid strategy.

Andi seemed concerned about the lack of love between them once her memory returned and she knew they hadn't been involved. His most important task over the next two days was to convince her they were meant to be together, and surely the best way to do that was to woo her back into his bed. The warm affection they'd shared stirred something in his chest. Maybe it wasn't the kind of love that inspired songs and sonnets, but he ached to enjoy it again.

It took some time for the guests to filter out the front door, and he kept half an eye on Andi the whole time in case she should decide to slip away. She looked tense, keeping up her end of every conversation but looking around often as if checking for escape routes. He'd been so busy rebuilding the relationships he'd worked hard to cement in the past three years by dancing with different girls that he hadn't danced with Andi. There was plenty of time for him to catch up with her after the guests left.

He kissed Alia on the cheek and ignored the subtle squeeze she gave his arm. He slapped her father on the back and promised to call him to go over some business details. So far, so good. Now where was Andi? She'd managed to slip away as the Kronstadts made their exit.

Irritation and worry stirred in his gut along with a powerful desire to see her right now. He strode up the stairs from the foyer and intercepted her in the hallway outside her room.

He slid his arms around her waist from behind—just as he'd done when she dove unceremoniously into their company earlier. A smile spread across his mouth at the feel of her soft warm body in his arms, and he couldn't wait to spend the night together.

But she stiffened. "I'm tired, Jake."

"Me, too." He squeezed her gently. "We can sleep in each other's arms."

"I don't think that's a good idea." She unlocked her door and he followed her in, arms still wrapped around her. Her delicious scent filled his senses. He twirled her around until they were face-to-face—and noticed her face looked sad.

"What's going on, Andi? You did a fantastic job this evening."

Her mouth flattened. "We should close the door, for privacy."

"Sure." That was a promising start. He turned and pushed it shut. "Why do you look unhappy?"

"Because I can't do this. I don't fit in here. I feel like an intruder."

"That's ridiculous. You fit in here as well as I do."

"I don't. I felt out of place and people kept going on about me being American. They obviously don't like the idea of you marrying a foreigner."

"Monarchs nearly always marry foreigners. That's how the British royal family ended up being German." He grinned. "They used to import brides from whichever country they needed to curry diplomatic favor with. It's a time-honored tradition."

"I don't think marrying me will get you too far with the White House."

"Oh, I disagree." He stroked her soft cheek with his thumb. "I'm sure any sensible administration would admire you as much as I do."

Her eyes softened for a moment and a tiny flush rose to her pale cheeks. But she wouldn't meet his gaze.

He placed his hands on either side of her waist. She had a lovely figure, a slender hourglass that the dress emphasized in a way her stiff suits never could. The tailored bodice presented her cleavage in a dangerously enticing way, and a single diamond sparkled on a fine chain between her small, plump breasts.

A flame of desire licked through him. "You were the loveliest woman in that room tonight."

"You're sweet." There was no hint of sparkle or a smile in her eyes. She didn't seem to believe him.

"You know I'm not sweet." He lifted a brow. "So you'd better believe me. Every minute I danced with those other girls, I wished I was dancing with you."

But you weren't.

He'd danced with those women because it was good for the nation's economy to keep their families on his side. Maybe he'd desired them, too, but that wasn't why he twirled them around the floor. Andi knew that business would always come first with Jake. She's always known that, and admired it. But now that she contemplated the prospect of spending the rest of her life with a man who didn't love her, it seemed like a mistake.

Mostly because she loved him so much.

The press of his strong fingers around her waist was a cruel torment. Her nipples had thickened against the silk of her bodice, aching for his touch. The skin of her cheek still hummed where he'd brushed his thumb over it.

She even loved him for the fact that he'd marry a woman he didn't love just for the sake of his country. That kind of commitment was impressive.

Unless you were the woman he didn't love, and had to watch from the sidelines, or even under the spotlight, while he gave his heart and soul to Ruthenia and its people.

His presence dominated her room, with its neat, impersonal decor. He was larger than life, bolder, better-looking and more engaging than any man she'd ever met. Wasn't it enough that he wanted to marry her?

Why did she think she was so special she deserved more than he offered? Maybe it was the independent-minded American in her who wanted everything. It wasn't enough to be queen and have a handsome and hardworking husband—she had to have the fairy-tale romance, as well.

Jake leaned in and kissed her softly on the mouth. Her breath caught at the bottom of her lungs as his warm, masculine scent—soap and rich fabrics with a hint of male musk—tormented her senses. Her lips stung with arousal as he pulled back a few inches and hovered there, his dark gaze fixed to hers.

Her fingers wanted to roam under his jacket and explore the muscles of his back and she struggled to keep them still at her sides. If she let him seduce her she was saying "yes" to everything he offered.

Including sex without love.

Yes, they'd had sex once already, but at the time she'd been under the delusion that he loved her and had proposed to her out of genuine emotion. Which was very different from the business arrangement he'd presented to her earlier.

His lips lowered over hers again, but she pulled back, heart thumping. "Stop, Jake. I'm not ready."

His eyes darkened. "Why not?"

"It's all happening too fast. I still barely know who I am. I can't think straight with you kissing me."

"Maybe I don't want you to think straight." A gleam shone in his seductive dark eyes.

"That's what I'm worried about." She tugged herself from his embrace, and almost to her surprise, he let her go. "I don't want to rush into this and realize a year or so from now that it was a huge mistake."

"I'll make sure you never regret it."

"I think that's quite arrogant of you." She tilted her chin. She'd never spoken to him like this before and it scared her a little. How would he react? "You seem to think you know exactly what I feel, and how I'll react."

"I know you very well after six years together." His warm gaze and proud, handsome face were dangerous— both familiar and alluring.

"But those were six years together in a professional relationship, not a marriage." For a start, he'd never barged into her room with his arms wrapped around her waist.

"I don't really see the difference." He looked down at her, slightly supercilious.

Indignation surged inside her, battling with the infuriating desire to kiss his sensual mouth. "That's the problem. It is different. As your assistant I have to follow certain rules of behavior, to always be polite and not express my opinion unless it's directly relevant to our work. To be on my best behavior and keep my emotions to myself. Maybe I'm not really the person you think I am at all." Her voice rose and she sounded a little hysterical.

Which was probably good, since he seemed to think she was some kind of well-mannered automaton who could easily approach the rest of her life as a kind of well-paid job with excellent benefits and perks.

"So the real Andi is very different from the one I know?"

She let out a long sigh. "Yes." She frowned. Who was the real Andi and what did she want? For so long she'd wanted Jake—while knowing in her heart that he would never be hers—that it was hard to think straight. "I don't know. But that's why we need to take it slow. You don't want to marry me and then find out I'm not the faithful and loyal helpmeet you imagine."

"I'd love to get to know your wild side." His eyes narrowed and a half smile tilted his mouth.

"I'm not sure I have one."

"You do." His smile widened, showing a hint of white teeth. "I've seen it."

Her face heated. "I still can't believe you slept with me under false pretenses." Her body stirred just at the memory of being stretched against him, skin to skin.

"They weren't false. We really are engaged."

She crossed her arms over her chest, and tried to ignore the tingling in her nipples. "I beg to differ. You hadn't asked the real me to marry you. You just assumed that I would. Not the same thing at all."

"But you seemed so happy about it." His expression was sweetly boyish for a moment, which tugged at a place deep inside her. "I thought you truly wanted us to be together."

I did.

She blinked, trying to make sense of it all. Jake's sturdy masculine presence wasn't helping one bit. She was painfully aware of the thickly muscled body under his elegant evening suit and how good it would feel pressed against hers.

He picked up her hand and kissed it. A knightly gesture no doubt intended to steal her heart. She shivered slightly as his lips pressed against the back of her hand, soft yet insistent.

During the nightmare of not knowing who she was, the one source of relief and happiness was Jake. He'd been the rock she could lean on and draw strength from while everything else around her was confusing and mysterious. She had been happy then, at least during the moments that the rest of the world fell away and they were alone together, lost in each other.

Could that happen again?

"I think we should spend some time together away from the palace." Getting out of their everyday work environment would be an interesting test of their relationship. They really hadn't spent leisure time together. Of course Jake didn't exactly have free time, unless you counted junkets with investors and state dinners. She didn't either, since she'd always devoted every minute to her job. She never went on the staff trips to the local nightclub or their weekend jaunts to Munich or Salzburg. As Jake's assistant she'd always felt herself too needed—or so she'd told herself—to disappear for more than an hour or two.

Jake stroked her hand, now held between both of his. She struggled to keep herself steady and not sink into his arms. "Is there someplace near here that you've always wanted to go?"

He tilted his head and his gaze grew distant. "The mountains."

"The ones you can see out the window?"

"Yes. I've always wanted to climb up and look down on the town and the palace." He shrugged. "There's never time."

"There isn't time right now, either." She sighed. "I don't suppose you really can get away from the palace right before Independence Day." Her request for time alone seemed silly and petty now that she thought about it. He had a lot of work to do and people would be arriving from all over the world in the run-up to the celebrations.

"Then we'll have to make time." He squeezed her hand.

An odd sensation filled her chest. He was willing to drop everything on a whim to get away with her? "But who will greet the arriving guests? We'd be gone for hours." There was a large group of Ruthenian expats arriving from Chicago, including three prominent businessmen and their families who had been invited to stay at the palace.

"I'm sure the staff can manage. Livia's proving very capable."

A slight frisson of anxiety trickled through her. Why did the idea of Livia quietly taking over her job make her so uncomfortable? Surely it was ideal.

"And how would we get there?"

"My car." Amusement twinkled in his eyes. "I can still drive, you know, even though I rarely get the chance."

"No driver or attendant?"

"Not even a footman. And we'll leave our PDAs behind, too. No sense being halfway up a mountain texting people about trade tariffs."

Andi laughed. He really was prepared to drop everything just to make her happy. Selfish of her to want that, but it felt really good. And the mountains had always called to her. Right now the slopes below the snow-covered peaks were lush with grass and wildflowers. "We'd better bring a picnic."

"Of course. Let the kitchen know what you want and tell them to pack it in something we can carry easily."

Andi blinked. This would be a test for her of how she could handle the transformation from staff to employer.

Or as Jake's wife was she just a high-level member of staff? The situation was confusing.

She pulled her hand gently from his grasp. "When should we go?"

"Tomorrow morning. I've learned to seize the moment around here. If we wait any longer we'll get sucked into the Independence Day activities."

"I guess we should call it an early night." She hoped he'd take a hint and leave.

"But the morning is still so far off." A mischievous twinkle lit Jake's eyes.

"It's after midnight."

"One of my favorite times of day. Maybe we should go dance around on the lawn outside." His gaze swept over her elegant dress—and sent heat sizzling through the defenseless body underneath it. "You're dressed for it."

"I don't think so. I might lose my memory again." *Or just my heart.*

She did not want anything sensual to happen between them until she'd had a chance to wrap her mind around the whole situation and make some tough decisions. Jake's touch had a very dangerous effect on her common sense, and this was the rest of her life at stake here.

"Just a stroll in the moonlight?" He took a step toward her. Her nipples thickened under her bodice and heat curled low in her belly.

"No." She'd better get him out of here and away from her while she still could. It wasn't easy saying no to something you'd dreamed of for six long years. "We'll be doing plenty of walking tomorrow. Conserve your energy."

"What makes you think I need to?" He lifted a brow. Humor sparkled in his eyes.

Andi's insides wobbled. Was he really so attracted to her? It was hard to believe that he'd gone from not noticing her at all, to trying every trick in the book to lure her into his bed.

Then again, he was known for his ability to close a deal by any means necessary.

It was more important right now to learn whether he could respect her wishes, or not. This was a crucial test.

"Goodnight, Jake." She walked to the door and opened it. "I'll see you in the morning." Her pulse quickened, wondering if he'd protest and refuse to leave.

"Goodnight, Andi." He strolled to the doorway and brushed a soft kiss across her lips. No hands, thank goodness, though her body craved his touch. He pulled back and stepped into the hallway.

Her relief was mingled with odd regret that she wouldn't be spending the night in his strong arms.

He'd passed her test.

Then he turned to face her. "I have a bet for you."

"A bet? I'm not the gambling type."

"I didn't think you were." His mouth tilted into a wry smile. "But I bet you that tomorrow night you'll sleep in my bed—with me."

Her belly quivered under the force of his intense gaze, but she held herself steady. "What are the odds, I wonder?"

"I wouldn't advise betting against me." He crossed his arms over his powerful chest.

"Normally, neither would I." She couldn't help smiling.

His confidence was rather adorable. "But I think it's important to keep a clear head in this situation."

"I completely agree." He flashed his infuriating pearly grin.

His arrogance alone made her determined to resist. Apparently she'd be the one with a test to pass tomorrow.

Nine

Andi watched as two footmen loaded their picnic lunch—impractically packed in two large baskets—into the trunk of Jake's black BMW sedan. The cook had acted as if Andi was already mistress of the house. No questioning of her ideas or complaining that they were low on certain ingredients, as she usually did.

Livia managed to pass on a couple of comments from the staff gossip—including that everyone knew Jake had slept alone the previous night. Andi blushed. Of course everyone knew everything in the palace, especially the maids. Livia obviously wasn't intimidated by Andi's new status and she made it clear that Jake would have had company in bed if she were in Andi's shoes.

In the old days it would be expected for her to wait until the wedding night. Now it was quite the opposite. People would wonder what was wrong if she persisted in sleeping alone.

She'd dressed in those jeans Jake liked and a pale pink shirt she'd bought on a whim, then decided it wasn't professional enough. Her hair was in a ponytail—not as formal as the bun—and she'd forgone all makeup except blush and lip gloss.

Apparently she wanted him to find her attractive.

This whole situation was very confusing. She wanted him to want her—but only for the right reasons.

Jake strode down the steps, talking on his phone. He'd abandoned his usual tailored suit for a pair of dark jeans and a white shirt, sleeves rolled up over tanned arms. He smiled when he saw her, and her stomach gave a little dip.

Pulling the phone from his ear he switched it off and handed it to one of the footmen. "Kirk, please hold this hostage until I get back. I don't want any interruptions." He turned to Andi. "Did you leave yours behind, too?"

"It's on my desk. I can handle the challenge of being incommunicado all afternoon."

"What if you need to call for help?" asked Kirk.

"We're quite capable of helping ourselves." Jake held the passenger door open for Andi. She climbed in, anticipation jangling her nerves. She couldn't remember being anywhere all alone with Jake. She felt safe with him though. He'd be a match for any wolves or bears or whatever mythical creatures stalked the mountains of Ruthenia.

He climbed in and closed the door. In the close quarters of the car he seemed bigger than usual, and his enticing male scent stirred her senses. His big hand on the stick shift made her belly shimmy a little. "How do you get so tanned?"

"Tennis. We should play it sometime."

Of course. He played with any guests who showed an interest, and invariably won. He was far too naturally competitive to be diplomatic while playing a sport.

"I haven't played since college."

"I bet you were good." He shot her a glance.

"I wasn't too bad." Her nerves tingled with excitement at the prospect of playing with him. There was something they had in common. Of course he'd beat her, but she'd enjoy the challenge of taking even a single point off him. "We'll have to give it a try."

If I stay.

They pulled out of the large wrought-iron gates at the end of the palace driveway and past the old stone gatehouse. Andi waved to the guards, who nodded and smiled. Somehow living here as Jake's…partner didn't feel all that odd right now.

It felt downright possible.

"Do you know which roads to take to get to the foot of the mountain?"

"I know which roads to take to get halfway up the mountain, and that's where we're headed."

"Don't like climbing?"

"I love it, but why not climb the high part?"

Andi laughed. "That sounds like a good approach to life in general."

"I think so."

They drove through the ancient village, where some of the buildings must be a thousand years old, with their sloping tile roofs and festoons of chimneys. The road widened as they left the village and headed through a swathe of meadows filled with grazing cows. The sun was rising into the middle of an almost cloudless sky and the whole landscape looked like a 1950s Technicolor movie. She almost expected Julie Andrews to come running down a hillside and burst into song.

"What would you have done if you were born to be king of somewhere really awful?"

Jake laughed. "Everywhere has its merits."

"Antarctica."

"Too many emperors there already—the kind with flippers. But I see your point. Still, a lot of people said Ruthenia was too badly broken to be fixed. Years of decline during and after the fall of communism, no work ethic, low morale and motivation. And it's turned on its head in three short years since independence. You just have to believe."

"And work hard."

"No denying that. But when you have concrete goals and a good road map, almost anything is doable."

The sunlight pouring through the windshield played off his chiseled features. His bone structure alone contained enough determination for a small, landlocked nation.

He'd been totally up-front about his goals and road map where she was concerned. The goal was obviously a long and successful marriage that would help him as a monarch, and the road map apparently included seducing her into his bed tonight.

She was not going to let him do that. Her judgment was already clouded enough by his sturdy, masculine presence in the car next to her.

The car started to climb steadily, as the road wound around the base of the mountain. It looked much bigger from here, the snow-capped peak now invisible above a band of conifers that ringed the mountain's middle like a vast green belt. The road petered out into a steep farm track past a group of cottages, then finally ended at a field gate about a mile farther on.

"We're on our own from here." Jake climbed out and popped the trunk. "And since we don't have sherpas, we'd better eat lunch close by. These baskets look like they were designed for royal picnics in the nineteenth century."

"They probably were." Andi touched the soft leather

buckles on the big, wicker rectangles. She and Jake carried one together through the gate and into the field. Distant sheep ignored them as they spread their blanket under a tree and unpacked the feast.

Jake took the lid off the first dish. "Cabbage rolls, very traditional." He grinned. She had a feeling he'd appreciate her picking a Ruthenian dish. The spicy meat wrapped in soft boiled cabbage was as Ruthenian as you could get, and there was a jar of the hot dipping pickle and onion sauce served with it at Ruthenian inns. Jake picked up a perfectly wrapped cabbage roll and took a bite. "Ah. New Yorkers have no idea what they're missing out on. We really should market this for the States."

"Do you ever stop thinking about business?" She raised a brow.

"Truthfully? No. But then you know that already." His eyes twinkled as he took another bite.

At least he was honest. Andi reached into another dish and pulled out one of the tiny phyllo pastry wraps filled with soft, fresh goat cheese. This one came with a dish of tangy beetroot sauce. She spooned the sauce onto her pastry and took a bite. Like many things in Ruthenia it was surprising and wonderful. "These would definitely be a big hit. Perhaps a Ruthenian restaurant in Midtown."

"To give the Russian Tea Room a run for its money?" Jake nodded and took a phyllo wrap. "I like the way you think. You can't deny that we're a good team."

Her heart contracted a little. "Yes." A good team. They were that. But was that enough? She wanted more. She wanted...magic.

The midday sun sparkled on the roofs of the town far below them. "Why didn't they build the castle up here? It would have been easier to defend."

"It would also have been really hard getting a cartloads of supplies up and down that steep track."

"I guess the peasants would have had to carry everything."

"And maybe they would have staged a revolt." Jake grinned, and reached for a spicy Ruthenian meatball. "Easier to build on the flat and put a town nearby."

"As an imported peasant I have to agree."

Jake laughed. "You're the king's fiancée. That hardly makes you a peasant."

"Don't think I'll forget my humble peasant origins." She teased and sipped some of the sweet bottled cider they'd bought. "I'm the first person in my family to go to college, after all."

"Are you really? What do your parents do?"

Andi swallowed. So odd that they hadn't talked about her past or her family before now. Jake had never been interested. "My dad works at a tire dealership and my mom runs the cafeteria at a local elementary school."

Jake nodded and sipped his cider. Was he shocked? Maybe he'd assumed her dad was a lawyer and her mom a socialite. Discomfort prickled inside her. "Your ancestors would probably be scandalized that you're even thinking of marrying someone like me."

"I bet the old Ruthenian kings married the miller's daughter or a pretty shepherd girl from time to time."

"Maybe if they could spin straw into gold," Andi teased. "Otherwise they probably just had affairs with them and married girls who came with large estates and strategically located castles."

He laughed. "You're probably right. But you can spin straw into gold, can't you?"

"I find that spinning straw into freshly minted Euros is more practical these days." She bit off a crunchy mouthful of freshly baked Ruthenian pretzel, fragrant with poppy seeds. "Gold makes people suspicious."

Jake smiled. Andi really did make gold, at least in his life. "If only people knew that you're the dark secret behind the salvation of the Ruthenian economy. Sitting up there in your office at your spinning wheel."

"They probably figure I must have mysterious powers. Otherwise why wouldn't you marry a Ruthenian glamour girl?"

"Those Ruthenian ladies are all a handful. None of them grew up in Ruthenia, either. I'd like to know what they're doing in those Swiss finishing schools to produce such a bunch of spoiled, self-indulgent princesses. They're far too much like hard work, and you'd certainly never catch them doing any real work." And none of them had Andi's cute, slightly freckled nose.

She looked pleased. "They can't all be like that."

"The ones who aren't are off pursuing careers somewhere—probably in the U.S.—and aren't hanging around the palace trying to curry favor with me."

"You could have staged a campaign to invite all Ruthenian expats to come back and compete for your hand."

Jake shuddered at the thought. "Why would I want to do that when you're right here?" He took a bite of a pretzel. "You've already passed every possible kind of test life in Ruthenia has thrown at you and proved yourself a star."

She blushed slightly. "I wouldn't say that."

"I would." His chest filled with pride that Andi had managed the big shift in lifestyle with such grace and ease. She'd eased the transition for him in so many ways that he'd probably never even know. No one could deny they were a powerful team. "Let's drink to us."

She took a glass with a slightly shaky hand. "To us."

"And the future of Ruthenia." Which would be a very bright one, at least for him, with the lovely Andi at his side. He'd seen another side of her since her memory came back—a feistier, more independent Andi than the one who'd worked so tirelessly as his assistant. He liked her all the more for being strong enough to stand up to him.

And the chemistry between them...if that's what it was. He couldn't put it into words, but the very air now seemed to crackle with energy when they got a little too close. He hoped she felt it, too—and suspected she did. Her cheeks colored sometimes just when he looked at her, and there was a new sparkle in her lovely blue eyes—or maybe it had always been there and he'd just never noticed it before?

Obviously he'd been walking through life with blinkers on where Andi was concerned. Thank heavens he'd finally realized what he'd been missing out on all these years.

After they'd finished eating they packed the baskets back in the car and set off up the grassy slopes on foot. The meadows grew steeper as they climbed, and the view more magnificent. They could see over the ancient forest on the far side of the town, and to the hills beyond, with villages scattered in the valleys, church steeples rising up from their midst. Jake's heart swelled at the sight of his beautiful country, so resilient and hopeful.

"Thank you for bringing us up here." He wanted to touch her, to hold her and kiss her and share the joy that pulsed through him, but Andi managed to remain out of reach.

After about an hour of steady climbing, they reached a small round tower, almost hidden in a grove of trees.

"Yikes. I wonder if the witch still has Rapunzel imprisoned in there." Andi peered up at the gray stones, mottled with moss and lichens.

"It's a lookout post," he replied. "I've seen it on the old

maps. They would watch for soldiers approaching in the distance, then signal down to the palace—which was a fortified castle back then—with a flag that let them know what was happening. Let's go inside."

He strode ahead into the arched doorway. Andi followed, rather more hesitant.

"There was probably a door, but it's gone," she said as she peered up into the tower. Any ceiling or upper floors were also gone, and the stone walls circled a perfect patch of blue sky. "It would make a great play fort for kids."

"We'll have to refurbish it for ours." Jake smiled. He'd never given much thought to having children, but the prospect of sharing family life with Andi stirred something unexpected and warm inside him.

Andi's eyes widened.

"Have I shocked you?"

"Maybe. It's all just a bit…sudden."

Jake shrugged. His changed relationship with Andi felt surprisingly natural, as if it had been in the cards the whole time without him knowing it, almost in the same way he was destined to return to Ruthenia.

But one thing still pricked at him. She'd been planning to take off—to abandon him and Ruthenia in search of… what? "Why were you going to leave?"

She startled slightly. "I already told you. I didn't see any future in my job and I felt it was time to move on."

He frowned. He couldn't help but feel there was more to it than that. "What were you going to do, back in the States?" He walked toward her. Sunlight pouring through the open roof illuminated her hair with a golden halo and cast sunbeams over her slender form.

"Um, I was thinking of starting my own business."

Shock and hurt surprised him. Her leaving still felt like

a personal betrayal. "Intriguing. What kind of business?" She could start her business here.

"Event planning. I intended to find a job at an event-planning company, then gradually branch out on my own."

"You've certainly got the experience for it."

"I know." She lifted her chin. "I must have planned hundreds of events over the last six years."

She wanted to be independent, in charge of her own destiny. He admired that. "As queen you'll have significant responsibilities. You'll be an important person in your own right. People will request your presence for events I can't attend." He knew she'd find it fulfilling.

"It's hardly the same." She lifted her chin. "I'd still be working for you."

"Working *with* me." He took a step toward her. "As equals." Another step. She hadn't moved. He reached out and took her hand. His skin hummed as their fingers met.

"You shouldn't," she breathed, tensing at his touch. "I really was planning to leave, and I still might."

His chest tightened, though he didn't really believe her. "You'll have a wonderful life here. You already know that. You'll never be bored and you can run all the businesses you want, as well as being queen." He stroked her hand with his thumb. Her skin was so soft.

"I still don't believe that staying is the right thing to do."

"I'll convince you." Pride mingled with emotion coursed through him as he raised her hand to his mouth and pressed his lips to her palm.

She gasped slightly and tried to pull her hand back, but he held it fast.

Her lips quivered slightly as his moved closer. Her delicious scent tormented his senses. He eased toward her until their chests were almost touching. She still hadn't moved. He could see in her darkening gaze that she felt the same fierce attraction he did. She wanted him every bit as much as he wanted her, despite her foolish worries and reservations. He'd just have to prove to her that her future should be right here, with him.

His lips closed over hers in a single swipe that drew them together. She arched into him, and he felt her nipples tighten inside her blouse as her fingertips clutched at his crisp shirt. She kissed him back hard, running her fingers into his hair and down his collar.

Jake sighed, reveling in the glorious sensation of holding Andi tight in his arms and kissing her doubts away.

She shuddered as his hand slid over her backside and down her thigh. Her knees buckled slightly as he touched her breast with his other hand, squeezing gently through her soft blouse.

No denying the energy between them. It had a life force of its own and drew them closer and bound them more tightly together every time they touched.

She shivered as his hand roamed under her blouse and his fingers brushed her taut nipple through her bra. At the same time his tongue flicked hers in a way that made her gasp.

Jake grimaced. He'd grown painfully hard. The sheer pleasure of kissing Andi was rather undermined by the powerful urge to strip off her clothes and make mad, passionate love to her right here, right now.

But he didn't want to drive her away. He'd already pushed too far too fast and he needed to let her come to him—to leave her wanting more.

He eased his mouth from hers and left her blinking in the half light of the tower as he pulled back. "Let's not get carried away. It's not too comfortable in here."

When he took things further, he needed to be sure she'd say yes. It was a delicate dance and he didn't entirely want her to know how much power she had over him. She could use it against him. The last nights alone had been painful and he had no intention of prolonging the torment by coming on too strong. He couldn't risk losing her now.

They walked a little higher up the mountain, then decided they'd scaled lofty enough heights for one day and turned for home. A bit out of character for him. Normally if he started something he had to take it as far as it could go.

In the car on the way back he realized he was going to forfeit his bet. Yes, he could seduce her on a whim—her reaction in the tower proved that. But he no longer wanted to. He wanted her heart and mind entwined with his, not just her body, so winning a bet seemed meaningless in the grand scheme of things.

It was a sign of maturity to forfeit a battle in order to win the war. He kissed her good-night with chaste tenderness, and watched her walk away to her own room with regret and desire singing in his blood.

Andi couldn't help a tiny twinge of guilt when she awoke in the morning and remembered that she'd made him lose his bet.

The kiss in the tower had shocked and scared her. How easily she fell into his arms, panting and moaning and letting him know just how easily her control evaporated around him. If he hadn't broken off the kiss she'd probably have made love to him right there on the moss-covered stones.

All that talk about their children and her future as queen had mingled with his powerful touch to throw her into a swoon of excitement, and at that point she might have agreed to anything just to feel his body against hers.

Not good.

She needed to think with her head, and not with her heart. Or any other parts of her body. Jake was still Jake—all business, all about Ruthenia, practical and not personal. He'd never for one instant hinted that he loved her. He was too much of a gentleman to lie about something like that.

She shivered, despite the morning sun. Why did she have to be so crazy about him?

It was the last day before the Independence Day celebrations turned Ruthenia into a countrywide party. She knew they'd both be flat-out busy today making last-minute plans and it should be easy to avoid him.

At least until tonight.

A tiny ray of pride shone through her anxiety. She'd managed to resist him after all, which meant she could still be clearheaded about her choice to stay or go. After the kiss in the tower she hadn't been so sure.

She showered and dressed, hoping she could manage not to be alone with him too much today. Her schedule—so recently abandoned—was packed with things to organize for the festivities. Plans made long before his crazy idea of marrying her, and which she couldn't really trust to anyone else.

Or that she didn't want to.

"Hey, Andi." A voice through the door made her jump. Not Jake's voice. Livia's. "Want me to take over for you so you can spend the day with His Majesty?"

"Not at all. I have everything covered." She hurried to the door and pulled it open, glad she'd painted on her usual business face. "I'll run through the guest list and make sure plans are in place to receive all the dignitaries arriving today. If you could check the menus and make any adjustments based on availability, I'd appreciate that."

A smile pulled at Livia's mouth. "You don't have to do all this stuff anymore, you know."

"This is the biggest occasion in Ruthenia's history—since independence, anyway, and I intend to pull my weight." And keep as busy and as far away from Jake as possible.

"I can handle it." Livia crossed her arms.

"I'm sure you have plenty of other things to handle." Would Livia offer to handle Jake, as well? Andi felt sure she'd be happy to take charge of his very personal needs, if requested. A twinge of jealousy tweaked her. "I have some phone calls to make."

She spent the day running from her office to the various meeting rooms and dining rooms, making last-minute changes to travel schedules and setting up tours of the local area for the visitors. Around lunchtime, visitors started to trickle in, arriving in their diplomatic cars and in hired limos, and she welcomed them to the palace.

Of course she welcomed them as Jake's fiancée, and the congratulations rang painfully in her ears as guest after guest remarked on how happy they were for the royal couple.

Jake looked rather pleased and proud, but then maybe he always looked like that. Twice he managed to slide his arm around her in situations where it would have been embarrassing to resist. Once in front of the French ambassador, and another time while greeting the Taiwanese cultural attaché. She cursed the way her skin hummed and sizzled under his touch, even through her tailored suit.

The big ring glittered on her finger, like a sign saying, Property of the Palace.

But Jake didn't own her. She hadn't agreed to marry him, simply to stay until after the celebrations.

At least that's what she tried to tell herself.

Feelings of foreboding and guilt, that she'd let down the

entire country as well as Jake, gathered in her chest like a storm. Could she really leave?

If it meant escaping a lifetime of heartache, yes.

Ten

This was it, his last chance. Jake eyed Andi from the far end of the long table, over the sparkling crystal and polished plates of the state dinner. Tomorrow was Independence Day and he could feel in his gut that he still hadn't convinced her to stay.

Why was she so stubborn?

She knew how many women would give a limb to be in her position, but she didn't seem to value the role of queen at all. Andi wasn't interested in wearing inherited diamonds or dressing up in silk and lace. She didn't care about dining with international luminaries or being called Your Majesty. She cared about people, regardless of whether they were important or not.

All of which only made him like her more.

And then there was that face. Curious and intelligent, with that active mouth and slightly upturned nose. Those sharp blue eyes that never missed anything.

And her slim but strong body, which beckoned him from beneath her fitted golden dress. Tonight he would claim her and sleep with her in his arms, assured that she'd never leave him.

He danced with her three times—heat crackling through his veins—while the jazz quartet played in the ballroom. In between, while dancing with other women, he barely took his eyes off her.

"I'm afraid Andi and I must retire," he announced, after the shortest decent amount of time. He didn't want to give her a chance to escape. "We've got a big day tomorrow, so I'm sure you'll excuse us."

He strode toward her and took her arm, then swept her out of the ballroom. She stiffened once they exited the soft lighting and sensual music, and entered the gilt-trimmed hallway.

"I'm exhausted," she murmured, avoiding his gaze.

"No, you're not." Not yet. He slid his hand along her back and saw the way her nipples peaked under the fine silk of her gown. A flush spread from her cheeks to her neck.

Desire flashed through him at this fresh confirmation that she wanted him as badly as he wanted her.

And he was going to make sure neither of them was disappointed.

"You're coming with me." He tightened his arm around her waist and marched her along the hallway.

"You can't make me." She whispered while her flushed cheeks and dark, dilated pupils argued with her words.

"I'm not going to make you do anything." Her hand felt hot in his, and desire whipped around them, distinct and intoxicating. It had been building all day. All week. For the past six years—though he'd been too wrapped up in business to notice it until now.

He opened the door to his suite and tugged her inside.

Then closed and locked it. Her mouth opened in protest, lips red, and he kissed her words away.

She struggled slightly—a token resistance he'd expected—before she softened and her arms closed around him as he knew they would. Once again he felt her fingertips press into the muscle of his back—claiming him—and he grew hard as steel against her.

Andi's soft body felt like a balm to his aching soul. Her mouth tasted like honey and sunshine, and her skin was warm and soothing. His fingers roamed into the silk of her hair and down over her gentle curves.

She writhed, and a gentle sigh slid from her lips as he cupped her breast. He could feel the connection between them, invisible and powerful, and he knew she could feel it, too, when she let down her resistance.

Her dress came off easily, via a simple zipper concealed behind a row of false buttons. Pleasure rippled through his muscles as the luxurious fabric pulled away, revealing soft lace and even softer skin.

Groaning, he settled her onto the bed and pressed a line of kisses over her chin and neck, then down between her breasts and over her belly, which twitched as he roamed lower, burying his face in the lace of her panties.

He felt her fingertips in his hair and heard her low moan as he sucked her through the delicate fabric and enjoyed the heat of her arousal. Her legs wrapped around his shoulders, pulling him closer into her and he licked her to a state of silky wetness before slipping the delicate lingerie down over her smooth thighs.

"You're so beautiful." He murmured the words as his eyes feasted on her lush nakedness. All wide, blue-eyed innocence, her gaze met his for a second before she reached for him and pulled him over her, kissing him with ferocity that snatched his breath and tightened his muscles.

Struggling together they removed his formal suit, baring his hot skin. Aroused almost to the point of insanity after these past days of torture, he couldn't wait to be inside her.

And the feeling was mutual. Andi raised her hips, welcoming him as she breathed hot kisses over his face and neck. Sinking into her again was the best feeling he'd ever had. He guided them into a shared rhythm that made Andi gasp and moan with pleasure.

He wanted Andi at his side—and in his bed—for the rest of his life. She was perfect for him in every way. Brilliant, beautiful, sensual and loyal.

He eased them into another position that deepened the connection between them and made beads of delicious perspiration break out on Andi's brow. Her breathing was ragged and her lips formed an ecstatic smile. Pleasure swelled in both of them, thickening and deepening and growing into something new—their future together—as they moved together, clinging to each other with fevered desperation.

Jake held his climax off for as long as he could, until Andi's cries reached a pitch of pleasured anguish that sent him over the edge. They collapsed onto the bed together, panting and laughing, then relaxed into a sleepy embrace.

A sense of deep contentment settled over him, along with the languid desire unfurled in his limbs. Emotions he couldn't name flickered through him and illuminated his visions of the happy future they'd share, as he drifted off to a peaceful sleep.

Andi watched Jake's chest rise and fall, while silver beams of moonlight caressed his skin through a crack in the curtains. Her heart swelled with painful sensation.

It had been so easy. She'd told him she was tired and that

she wanted to go to bed. Did he care? No. He had his own agenda and her needs were irrelevant.

He also knew she never had a prayer of resisting him. How could one person have so much power over her? He'd ruled her life for six years. Six years during which the joy of being with Jake was mingled readily with the sorrow of knowing their relationship was strictly business.

Now he'd followed through on his promise to seduce her into his bed. He'd driven her half mad with sensation— just because he could—and now he slept like a newborn, without an ounce of recrimination.

If only life could be that simple for her.

He didn't care if she loved him or not. That didn't matter to him one bit. He needed a wife and she was a promising candidate with a good résumé. Tried and tested, even, in more ways than one.

Jake probably didn't want to love anyone. Emotions were complicated and messy, and he wouldn't like anyone else having that kind of power over him. No doubt he preferred to keep things clearheaded and businesslike.

At least for one more day, she could manage to do the same. She couldn't bear to think ahead any further than that right now.

The next morning, Andi helped Jake host a palace breakfast for nearly fifty guests. Then they rode through the town in an open carriage with a procession of schoolchildren in front and the town's marching band behind them. Flags waved from windows and hands and the whole country seemed alive with enthusiasm and energy.

At one point Jake slid his hand into hers and warmth flared in Andi's chest at the affectionate gesture. But she turned to look at him and he was waving out the window with the other hand. No doubt the romantic gesture was just intended to look picturesque to the gathered crowds.

Her heart ached that she wanted so much more than a relationship put on for show.

Back at the palace a feast filled long tables on the patio outside the ballroom. She had her work cut out for her chatting with female guests—each of whom congratulated her on her engagement and wished her every happiness.

Are you happy? she wanted to ask each of them. Did these elegant women in their designer clothes enjoy close and loving relationships with their important husbands? Or were they content to follow along and smile, enjoying the gourmet food and expensive shoes that came with the job?

She envied the few women who were there in their own right as ambassadors or dignitaries of sorts. In charge of their own destinys and not dependent on anyone.

Whenever she glimpsed Jake, he looked right at home amidst the glamorous crowd, smiling and talking and laughing—in his element.

By midafternoon Andi felt exhausted. Last night's late-night shenanigans hadn't helped. As servants cleared the coffee cups and the guests wandered out onto the lawn, she slipped back into the palace for a moment's breather.

"Hey, Your Majesty." Livia's voice startled her as she hurried along the corridor. "Playing hooky?"

"Getting something from my room." She just wanted to be alone.

"Don't you have servants for that?" Livia's brown eyes twinkled with mischief as she caught up with Andi and followed close by her.

"I'm used to doing things for myself."

"It must be hard to make the leap from PA to princess. Though I think I could manage it." She crossed her arms.

"Shame Jake didn't notice me first. Still, maybe it's not too late." She raised a brow. "I don't imagine kings usually stick to one woman for the rest of their lives."

"Have you lost your mind?" Andi's temper finally snapped. She ran up the stairs, hoping Livia would not follow.

Livia laughed, climbing right behind her. "Oh, dear. We have turned into a princess, haven't we? I'm just saying what I've observed. It must be difficult watching your fiancé dance with other women almost every night. It takes a special person to put up with that, I'd imagine."

"It's just part of his job."

"And I suppose that putting up with it is part of yours." Livia followed her down the hallway to her own door. "Oh, dear, will I get fired for speaking my mind?"

Her voice grated on Andi's nerves. "Quite possibly."

"You must feel pretty powerful right now."

Not in the least. She wanted to cry. If she was just Jake's assistant she'd have had no difficulty issuing Livia some task, then talking later to Jake about how she wasn't working out. Now, somehow, everything seemed more loaded.

More personal.

"Don't you have a job to do?" Andi turned to her. "There's a big event going on and you should be running it."

"You should be attending it, so I guess we're both skiving off. I'm leaving anyway. Off to New York." She grinned and crossed her arms.

Curiosity goaded Andi. "You have a job there?"

"You'd know all about it. It's the one I told you about that you tried to steal from me. I guess it's lucky for both of us that I tripped you on those stairs in your silly dress."

"What?" Shock washed over her. "Is that when I hit my head?"

"Oh, did I just say that out loud?" She shook her head, making her red curls dance. "Must be loopy from packing. Certainly was lucky, though! I'd have said 'have a nice trip' if I'd known I was sending you into King Jake's affectionate arms. I saw you dancing around like a loon and him coming to your rescue."

Andi stared at her. "I think you should leave right this minute before I tell someone you tried to hurt me."

Livia just laughed. "I couldn't agree more. I'm looking forward to leaving this sleepy backwater and getting back to the big city. Ah, freedom!"

Anger flashed through Andi as Livia waltzed away. None of this would have happened if it wasn't for her interfering jealousy!

She couldn't help being jealous of Livia, now. If Andi married Jake she'd never get to live in New York again. Never be mistress of her own destiny again, with plans and hopes and dreams that could change on a whim.

She'd have duties. Responsibilities. She'd have to be loyal and faithful, serving Ruthenia and Jake until the end of her days.

While Jake danced and flirted and chatted with other women, day after day, night after night.

At least Livia wouldn't be around to taunt her anymore.

In the bathroom she splashed water on her face. She looked pale and haunted, so she slapped on a bit of her familiar blush. But even that couldn't pick up her spirits right now, though. She'd been in the public eye all day, and even though Jake was right there at her side for much of the time, it felt as if they were a thousand miles apart—her craving affection and love, and him needing a royal spouse to put on for ceremonial occasions, much like his sash and scepter.

Last night's intimacy didn't make things better. The closeness they'd shared for those brief hours seemed so distant now, like it wasn't real at all. The memory of his embrace still made her heart beat faster, which only made it hurt more that he didn't love her.

Were her suitcases still here under the bed? Sudden curiosity prompted her to look. They were. She'd only committed to stay through the end of today. After that she could pack her things—again—and get back on the track she'd planned before Jake derailed her for his own professional needs.

A wife by Independence Day. That's all he'd needed. If she wasn't around, he might well have asked Livia. It probably didn't matter all that much to him as long as she did her job.

Still, she did have a job to do for today. She dabbed on a little of her favorite scent, hoping it would lift her spirits. Didn't work.

Lying in his arms last night had been so bittersweet. A dream come true, but with the knowledge that it was just a dream. He'd slept with her to win her over to his side, much as he'd done while her memory was gone.

Any pleasure she'd enjoyed withered away when she remembered that.

She dabbed a bit of powder on her nose—it suddenly looked red—and steeled herself to go back downstairs again. She'd pushed herself through enough long and tiring events over the past six years; she could manage one more, even if her heart was breaking.

"Where's your fiancée?" Maxi sidled up to Jake as a waiter refilled his champagne glass.

"Andi's around somewhere. It's a big crowd." Where was she? He'd been so wrapped up in their guests he'd only glimpsed her a couple of times through the crowd. Still, they'd spent a full hour together this morning being dragged through the town in the ceremonial carriage. Andi had been quiet, which was fine with him. He liked that she didn't have to chatter on all the time like some women. He hadn't stopped thinking about her all day, wanting to see her smile, her frown, hear her laugh and even her scolding. She was becoming an obsession.

"Daddy has a proposition for you."

"Oh?" Jake sipped his freshly filled glass.

Maxi nattered on about some proposed factory project in the eastern hills. He was used to listening with one side of his brain and making the right noises, while using the other side of his brain to plan ahead.

Tonight he needed to let Andi know how much she meant to him. He'd told her with his body, but Andi was a pragmatist and he knew she'd want to hear it in words.

I love you.

The truth rang through him like the old church bell tolling in the distance. Maybe he'd known it all along but not realized it until right now. The reality of it left him stunned and filled with a powerful sense of joy.

He loved her and he had to let her know that.

"What?"

He didn't realize he'd said the words aloud until he looked into Maxi's startled face. Her lipstick-painted mouth stretched into a wide smirk. "Thank you, Jake, I'm touched."

He schooled his face into a neutral expression. "Don't take it personally." He raised a brow. "I'm talking about the development project." He must be losing it. Andi had cracked open some tender new part of him that didn't quite know how to act. He was so used to being all business all the time that it was hard to switch off that part of him and just be.

Andi certainly didn't have trouble reining her emotions in. She acted as if she was trying to decide whether to accept a promotion or not. It stung that she had no personal feelings for him at all. He could be alarmed that one slender woman had such a strong hold over him—instead he just wanted to kiss her again.

Andi stood there for a moment, incredulous. A cold, empty space opened up inside her. If Jake loved Maxi, why didn't he just marry her?

She stepped backward, shrinking back into the crowd before Maxi noticed her. Jake couldn't love Maxi, could he? She was insufferably arrogant and annoying—he'd said so himself. Unless he was just trying to throw her off the scent.

Maybe he didn't really love Maxi but just said that to her to keep her favor now that he intended to marry someone else. Maybe he was going around telling every girl in Ruthenia that he loved them and if only he didn't need a wife who can type and file efficiently…

Her mind boggled.

Jake was a master manipulator; that was how he accomplished so much and managed to get so many people on his side. Now he was masterminding his marriage, and his relationships with every beauty in the nation, with the easy grace she'd always admired.

Except that now she was its victim. So easy to seduce. Such a quiet and willing accomplice. Ready to sacrifice her life in his service.

Except that she had no intention of making that sacrifice.

She'd tell him why she was leaving, and give him a chance to reply, but nothing he said could now change her decision to get away before she signed up for a lifetime of heartache.

She made it through the grand afternoon tea and an enormous dinner. She barely saw Jake at all, so the hardest part was accepting the continued stream of congratulations on her engagement. She wanted to tell them, "I'm not marrying him!" but she didn't. Too well trained in royal decorum for that.

No. She waited until the last guests had left or gone to bed and she was alone with Jake. She let him lead her to his suite, steeling herself against the false reassurance of his hand around hers or his warm smiles.

Once inside she closed the door. "Independence Day is over, and I'm leaving."

Jake's expression turned dark. "You can't be serious."

"I am, and I'll tell you why." She straightened her shoulders and dared herself to look him right in the eye. He might have power over her, but she was stronger. "You don't love me."

"I do. I love you. I've been meaning to tell you." His expression was the same as always, bright and good-humored. Like none of this really mattered.

"But you forgot?" She forced a laugh, though inside she was crumbling to pieces. "You have been busy, of course. I overheard you telling Maxi you loved her. Perhaps you got us confused for a moment."

Jake smiled. "That's exactly what happened. I said it to you in my mind and it came out of my mouth in front of Maxi."

"You must really think I'm a total idiot." Anger snapped through her at his ludicrous response. "I know I've been pretty gullible, believing that we're engaged when we're not, and going along with your oh-so-convenient plan to get engaged in time for the big day, but it's all stopping right here."

"Andi, be sensible. It's been a long day."

"I'm tired of being sensible. I've been sensible to the point of madness lately, smiling at strangers while they congratulate me on an engagement I fully intend to break off. It's enough to drive almost anyone stark mad."

"I do love you." Jake's dark eyes fixed on hers and the intense look in them almost made her weaken.

Almost, but not quite.

"No you don't!" Her voice rose. "I don't think you even know what love is. All your relationships are carefully orchestrated for maximum effect. You stage manage us just like the seating plans at your dinners, swapping and changing people to curry favor when needed."

"I'm not trying to curry favor with you."

"Obviously not. I was seated as far as possible from you all day." She enjoyed the retort. "Maybe royal couples are supposed to be kept apart so they don't get tired of each other."

"You know that's just convention. You and I already have a close, intimate relationship."

"No, we don't." She cursed the way his words made her chest swell. "Just because you've seduced me into bed does not mean we're intimate. You think you can fix everything with sex. If you pleasure me in bed then somehow it will turn into a love that isn't there. It doesn't work like that. True intimacy is based on trust, and I don't trust you."

He stared at her, the good humor draining from his face. "I know I broke your trust. I promise you I'll never do anything to lose it again."

"Once lost, trust cannot be regained. Whether you love Maxi or not, I really don't care, but either way, I can't trust you and I won't live my life with someone when I don't know if I can believe what they say. It's too late."

Just the fact that she could even suspect him of carrying on with another woman made marriage to him a recipe for disaster.

"I want a normal life that isn't under any spotlights. I'd like to marry an ordinary man who doesn't have glamorous women kissing up to him all day." Did she? She couldn't imagine being involved with anyone after having her heart pummeled by this whole experience. She needed to get out of here before she burst into embarrassing tears.

"I've told you I love you." His features hardened and his eyes narrowed. Silence hung in the room for an agonizing moment. "I've given you ample proof that I care about you and think you're the perfect wife, yet you persist in wanting to leave. Leave then." His gaze pierced right through her. "I won't hold you here."

Andi swallowed. Now he was dismissing her.

Isn't that what she wanted? She'd already told him there was no chance. "I can't be the perfect wife for a man who really just wants a permanent assistant."

"Naturally." He seemed to look down on her along the length of his aristocratic nose. His eyes flashed dark fire. "I don't want you to marry me against your will."

"Good, because I don't think that would be right for either of us." Was she trying to convince him, or herself? "It's important to marry someone you care about. Someone you love." Her voice cracked on the word love.

Once she'd have thought she had enough love in her for Jake to sustain both of them, but lately she'd learned different. She couldn't stand by as the faithful wife while he continued to flirt with and cajole other women, even if it was just for "business" reasons. Not if she didn't know that alone, in bed, he was all hers, heart and soul.

She needed a man she'd believe when he said, "I love you."

"Goodbye, Jake." Her whispered words hovered in the night air of his dimly lit room. She pulled the big engagement ring from her finger and left it on the table.

He didn't respond. Obviously she was worth nothing to him now that she'd scuppered his neat plans. No more protestations of love, or even of how useful their union would be to Ruthenia.

Nothing but his icy glare.

Andi let herself out of the room and hurried along the corridor, grim sensations of regret trickling over her like cold water. She half hoped—and feared—that she'd hear the door open and sense Jake's powerful stride covering the carpet after her.

But nothing disturbed the small, nighttime noises of the palace.

She had to leave right now, even though there were no trains until morning. She didn't want to see him ever again.

Tears streamed down her face as she shoved her clothes back into her two suitcases for the second time in a week. How had she let herself get sucked into such an insane situation? Something about Jake Mondragon undermined all her good sense and left her gasping and starry-eyed. She'd already spent years hoping he'd suddenly fall madly in love with her, which was no doubt why his ridiculous and unsuitable engagement idea had been so easy to put over on her.

Her face heated at the thought of how happy she'd been back when she had no idea that their whole engagement wasn't genuine. He'd smiled at her and kissed her and held her like they were madly in love, knowing all along that the whole thing was a lie.

How humiliating.

She threw her hairbrush into her suitcase with a pleasant thud. Almost done with the packing. Her clothes would be really crumpled now after being shoved in so haphazardly, but she could iron them out again.

Shame she couldn't do that with her heart. She suspected it would be crushed and creased for a long time. Possibly forever.

There was still one thing hanging in the closet. The long, floaty pale dress she'd been wearing the night she lost her memory. She let out a long breath as she remembered why she had it on. She'd brought it with her to Ruthenia thinking she'd need something smart and beautiful to wear at parties now that her boss was a king. She'd chosen it after much giggling deliberation with a girlfriend, because it made her feel like Cinderella at the ball.

She'd never worn it before that night. Since she was staff, she didn't actually attend the parties. A crisp black suit had proved to be the most suitable evening attire as she hovered around the edges of the festivities, making sure everything was running smoothly and attending to Jake's every need. Her Cinderella fantasies had remained locked in the closet, just like the dress.

She'd taken it out that one night, just to see what it would feel like to wear it. The whole palace was wrapped up in the party happening in the dining room and ballroom, so no one noticed when she walked down the stairs, tiptoeing carefully in the silver sandals she'd bought to match the dress and never worn before.

She'd walked to one of the narrow casement windows and looked out. Pale moonlight glanced off the mountains in the distance and bathed the green valley in its soft glow. She'd grown to love the rugged countryside and its fiercely independent and engaging people. The palace and its nearby town were her home now, after three years. Leaving felt like stepping out of her own life and into a big, scary unknown.

Inspired by her pretty dress, she'd wanted to take one last walk around the grounds in the moonlight, just to let her imagination run free and think about what might have been before she left for the last time. The weather was surprisingly warm for so early in the spring and the soft grass, silver with dew, begged her to walk across it.

She'd crossed the wide terrace and taken off her sandals, not wanting to get the soft leather wet or have the heels sink into the lawn. Had Livia really tripped her? That's when her memory stopped. Sometimes the steps were slippery, the stone worn smooth by the passage of feet over two hundred or more years since they were built. She could see them from her window right now.

But she would never walk down them again. No detours this time. She had to get out of here and away from Jake.

She'd since worn far more fabulous and expensive dresses, tailored right on her body by Ruthenia's finest seamstresses, and she knew that they felt like the world's stiffest armor as she moved through her ceremonial duties next to a man who didn't love her.

She turned and scanned the room to see if she'd missed anything.

Her belongings had fit so neatly into her two bags, almost as if they'd just been waiting to pack up and go. Her heart sank at the sight of her empty dressing table, the gaping closet with its almost vacant hangers. Soon someone else would live in the room, and she'd never see it again.

Now all she had to do was get out of here without being seen. She couldn't bear to explain the situation to anyone. They'd be so shocked and disappointed. Disgusted even, at how she wouldn't slot into Jake's plans for the good of the nation.

Guilt snaked through her heart, or maybe it was just grief at what she was leaving behind. The memory of Jake's face—hard and angry—would stay with her forever. She shivered and turned to pick up her bags.

Even though it was well after midnight, she'd need to sneak down the back stairs. The cleaners sometimes worked late into the night, especially after a major event. If she could make her way to the rear entrance without being seen, she could cut across the gardens to the old barnyard and take one of the runabout cars kept near the old stables for staff to share on errands.

She grabbed the handle of each bag and set off, pulse pounding. No looking back this time. The pretty dress could stay right there in the closet, along with all her romantic fantasies. They'd caused her nothing but pain.

From magical fairy-tale engagement to shocking scandal overnight. She'd have to keep her head down for, oh, the rest of her life.

She let herself into the old staircase, dimly lit by aging sconces, and hurried down the steep, winding steps, bags thumping unsteadily behind her like chasing ogres no matter how high she tried to life them.

She held her breath as she opened the heavy wood door at the bottom. It led out into the back kitchen, which was rarely used, only if they were catering a truly enormous feast—like the one today. Freshly scrubbed pots and baking trays covered the sideboard and big bowls of fruit stood on the scrubbed table ready to be sliced for breakfast, but the lights were low and she couldn't see anyone about.

Lowering her bags onto their wheels, she crept across the flagstone floor.

One the far side of the old kitchen, she could see the

door that led directly out into the kitchen garden. Before she took a step into the room, a burst of laughter made her jump. She froze, heart pounding, peering into the shadows. Voices reached her from the next room, the passage to the modern kitchen. She didn't recognize them, but the palace often hired extra caterers for big events. Were they already up, making breakfast?

She shrank back into the stairwell, but after an anxious minute, no one had appeared, so they obviously hadn't heard her. Bags lifted by her straining biceps, she crept across the floor. She lowered her bags for a moment and tried the handle—old, but well-oiled, the door slid quietly open, and cool night air rushed in.

She drew in a breath, then stepped out and closed the door quietly behind her. The click of the latch struck an ominous chord in her chest. She'd left the palace forever. She should feel happy that she'd escaped the building without being seen. Instead, she felt like a thief, leaving with stolen goods.

Which was ridiculous. She'd given years of her life to this place. Was that why it hurt so much to leave? And she wasn't gone yet. She still had to get across the grounds and past the sentries at the gatehouse.

She scanned the walled garden—a gloomy well of shadows in the cloudy moonlight—then hefted her bags past the menacing dark rectangles of the large herb beds. An arched doorway on the far side led to the stable yard, where the staff cars were parked. The ancient door creaked on its hinges as she pulled it open, and she shot a glance behind her. A lightbulb flicked on in one of the upper windows, and she held her breath for a moment. Was it Jake's window? Would he come look for her?

She cursed herself when she realized that it was on the upper, staff-only floor. Why would Jake come looking for her? He'd told her to get lost. Which was exactly what she'd wanted.

Wasn't it?

Heaviness lodged in her chest as she crept across the paved stable yard. She retrieved a key from the combination-locked box in the wall—they'd be sure to change the code tomorrow—climbed into the nearest car and started the engine.

Andi glanced up at the house to see if anyone would look outside, but no one did. Cars did come and go at all hours when the house was full of guests and there were meals to prepare. She didn't turn the lights on right away.

A sharp pang of regret shot through her as she pulled onto the wide gravel drive for the last time. A ribbon of silver in the moonlight, it led through an allée of tall trees. It was hard to believe she'd never see this beautiful place again. She certainly wouldn't be welcome back for return visits.

And she'd never see Jake again. She should be happy about that, considering what he'd done, but all the years they'd spent working side by side—and that she'd spent mooning over him and hoping for more—weighed on her mind. He was a good man at heart and she didn't wish him ill.

Don't think about him.

There was still one more gauntlet to run—the gatehouse. The guards didn't usually pay too much attention to cars leaving the palace, especially familiar staff cars, so she hoped they'd simply wave her through. She cringed, though, when she saw a uniformed figure emerge from the stone gatehouse and approach.

She cleared her throat and rolled down the window. "Hi, Eli, it's only me. Picking up a friend." The lie was the first thing that sprang to mind.

Eli simply smiled and gave her a little salute. She raised her window and drove out the palace gates for the last time, blinking back tears. In the morning, Eli and everyone else would know she'd run off into the night.

The town was deserted as she drove through it. She parked on a quiet street so she could walk the last stretch to the station. No need to advertise where she'd gone, since it would probably be hours until the first train of the morning. The staff cars were all identical Mercedes wagons and easily recognizable, and she didn't want to be too easy to find.

Not that anyone would come looking for her. She left the keys in the glove compartment. Petty crime was almost nonexistent in the town as everyone knew each other too well.

She groped in her bag for dark sunglasses. No need for strangers to see her red and puffy eyes. She wrapped a blue scarf around her head and neck. It wasn't cold but she didn't want anyone to recognize her if she could help it.

All she had to do was wait for the early-morning train to Munich, then book a flight to New York.

Her original plan had been to head to Manhattan and stay at the 92nd Street Y and temp until she could find an apartment and a job. She'd even had that promising interview set up. So, there'd been a hitch in her plans, involving all her lifelong dreams coming true and then turning into a nightmare, but she'd just have to get back on track and start rebuilding her life.

She glanced up and down the dark empty street before hurrying past the old stone buildings toward the ornate nineteenth-century train station at the edge of town.

She'd intended to leave Jake behind, and now she was doing it.

So why did it still hurt so much?

Eleven

Jake paced back and forth in his bedroom, anger and pain firing his muscles into action. His wounded pride sparked fury inside him. He'd been mad enough to lose his heart to a woman, and now she flung it back in his face.

No one had ever treated him so coldly. He'd offered her his life and she'd turned him down. He should despise her for being so heartless and cruel.

So why did the thought of facing even one day without her make his whole body ache?

He'd have to announce to the whole country—to the world—that their engagement was over. People would wonder why she left and gossip would echo around the villages for months.

But he didn't care about any of that. It was the prospect of nights without Andi's soft body in his bed. Of days lacking her bright smile. Long evenings without her thoughtful conversation.

He couldn't force her to marry him against her will. Lord knows he'd come close enough by thrusting this whole engagement on her when she was indisposed by her lack of memory.

Shame trickled over him that he'd taken advantage of her so readily. She'd been so willing—in her lack of knowledge about their true past—and it had been so wonderful. A natural extension of their happy working relationship.

Idiot. Having sex with your assistant had nothing to do with work. Why had he tried to convince himself it was okay? If he really wanted to marry her he should have waited until she got her memory back, courted her like a gentleman—or at least a conventional boyfriend—then proposed to her.

Maybe he thought that as a king he was so special he didn't have to follow any of the conventions of romantic love? He certainly put a lot of energy into following other conventions, so why had he veered so badly off course with Andi?

He halted his pacing at the window. He'd been keeping an eye out for lights from a car traveling up the driveway, but had seen none. She was probably still here in the palace.

But she'd already rejected him and it was too late to change her mind. She needed a man she could trust, and in taking advantage of her amnesia, he'd given her good reason to never trust him again.

He'd given up a lot to take on his role as king of Ruthenia. Now he'd just have to learn how to live without Andi, as well.

Andi flinched as the ticket agent looked at her. She'd removed her dark glasses because, well, it was still dark outside. But there was no flicker of recognition in his eyes.

Without extravagant jewels and fancy dresses she just slipped right back into the regular population.

As the platform filled with people waiting for the first train, she shrank inside her raincoat, raising the collar. The occasional stare made her want to hide behind a column. Soon enough they'd all know who she was and what she was doing.

She climbed onto the train without incident. Had she thought Jake would send the cavalry after her? The Ruthenian hills were notably free of galloping horsemen and the roads almost empty of cars as the train pulled away from the town at 7:43 a.m.

Perhaps he was secretly relieved to see her go. He could blame her for breaking off the engagement and carry on with his merry life as an eligible royal bachelor, with gorgeous women kissing up to him at every opportunity.

Her heart still ached with jealousy at the thought of Jake with another woman. Which was totally ridiculous since she'd just rejected him.

The train picked up speed outside the town and flew through the open fields and villages with their tall steeples, clustered at the foot of the proud mountains. She'd never even heard of Ruthenia until she met Jake, but it had come to feel like home and she was going to miss it.

She pulled a book from her bag, but the words blurred before her eyes and she couldn't concentrate. Tears threatened and she pushed them back. Was she making a terrible mistake? Would Jake have grown to love her?

She'd never know now, but it was too late to turn back.

It was midmorning by the time she reached the border crossing between Ruthenia and Austria. She held her breath while the border guards walked through the train checking passports.

The young, clear-faced guard looked at her passport, then pulled out his phone. He spoke rapidly in German and made a sign to another guard on the platform. The two elderly ladies seated on the bench opposite her glanced at each other. Andi felt her heart rate rise.

"I don't have anything to declare." She gestured to her two suitcases. "You can look through them."

"Will we be moving soon?" Her voice sounded shaky. Sitting here made her feel anxious, like she wanted to get up and run. Was Jake behind this? She cursed the pinch of hope that jangled her nerves.

Unlikely. She'd never seen him look so furious as he did last night. If only she could make that memory go away.

Jake's car swerved on a gravel patch in the road and he righted it quickly, coming around another of those hairpin turns on the mountainside. He probably should have taken the train, like Andi. It was the most direct route as it cut right through one of the larger mountains.

But he didn't want anything to hold him up. He also didn't want other people around. This was between him and Andi.

His pride still hurt at her forthright rejection, but something inside him couldn't let her leave like this. She'd said she didn't trust him, and that hurt more than anything. He'd broken her trust. He'd tried to keep her at his side using seduction and bargaining.

When he told her he loved her, she simply didn't believe him.

She thought his declaration was just more words. She didn't understand that his feelings for her had transformed him.

Swinging around another tight corner, he felt a twinge of guilt about using the border guards to hold the train.

Another aspect of royal privilege he'd abused. Still, it was an emergency situation. Once she got back to the U.S., she'd be gone from his world, and he knew in his heart that he'd never get her back.

Then he'd spend the rest of his life missing her and kicking himself for losing the only woman he wanted.

He drove through the Dark Forest at warp speed, adrenaline crackling through his muscles, and emerged into the open plain on the other side just before noon. He'd had to stop on the way for one simple, but important, errand. This time he intended to get everything right.

He spotted the long train at the border crossing from quite a distance away. Luckily the road ran almost directly across the tracks near the village, so he pulled onto the verge and jumped out. Bright morning sun shone off the dark blue-and-gold surface of the cars and turned each window into a mirror. Which car was Andi in? And would she even talk to him after how he'd behaved at their last meeting? Every cell in his body, every nerve pulsed with the desperate need to see her and make things right.

The train was an old one, with individual compartments seating about six people each. The first three he peered into contained no familiar face, but in the fourth, opposite two older women in wool berets, sat a pale-faced and anxious-looking Andi.

He grasped the cool handle and inhaled. She looked up as he pushed the door open and he heard her gasp.

"I can't live without you, Andi."

He hadn't planned what to say. He'd done too much planning lately. "I really do love you." He prayed that the truth would ring through in words that now sounded hollow from overuse. "I didn't realize it myself. I've never known love before. I was raised to think with my head and not my heart. I spent so much time convincing myself I wanted to marry you because it was a sensible decision, because our marriage would be good for Ruthenia. The truth is that now my desire to keep you has nothing to do with Ruthenia. I want you for myself and I can't imagine spending the rest of my life without you."

Tears welled in her eyes for a moment and his heart clutched.

The two women opposite her suddenly rose, grabbing their carryalls, and hurried toward the door where he stood. "Please excuse us," one puttered in Ruthenian. He'd forgotten they were there. He stood aside to let them pass, eyes fixed on Andi.

She hadn't moved an inch, but color rose to her pale cheeks.

Hope flared in his chest. "I admit that our engagement began for the wrong reasons. I'm ashamed about that." Guilt stung him. "All I knew was that I enjoyed your company, and that once I kissed you…" He blew out a breath. "Once I kissed you, nothing was ever the same again."

He saw her swallow, fighting back tears that made her blue eyes glisten.

He ached to take her in his arms and kiss away her tears. The few inches between them seemed an agonizing gulf. "I need you, Andi."

Her lips didn't flinch. Her silence hurt him, but she hadn't told him to go. There was still hope.

He reached into his pocket and drew out the item he'd picked up on the way here. The simple ring, the one she'd chosen in the shop that morning.

He knelt on the floor of the train car and pulled the ring from the box. "Andi, I know this is the ring you wanted. I made you get the other one because it was showier. I realize I was making decisions for you and trying to turn you into someone you don't want to be. I'd like to go right back to the beginning and start over."

She hesitated for a moment, eyes fixed on the ring.

His heart clenched. She'd already told him that she didn't want to be his wife. She didn't want a life of royal duty and an existence in the public eye. But that wasn't all he offered. How could he make her see that despite all the trappings of royalty, he was just a man? A man who loved and needed her with every fiber of his being.

"Andi, right now I wish I wasn't a king." It took effort to stop his hands from reaching out to her. "That I could promise you an ordinary life, in a comfortable house in some American suburb, where our children could attend the local school and play in Little League. The truth is I can't. I'm already married to Ruthenia and that's my destiny. I can't turn away from it any more than I could turn back the river flowing through the mountains."

He saw her throat move as she swallowed. Her hands shifted slightly, clutching at each other through her black gloves. How he longed to take them in his own hands.

"But I need you, too, Andi. Not because you can help me run the country or the palace, but because you're the woman I want to share my life with. That I need to share my life with."

Emotion flickered across her lovely face and made hope spark inside him. "I do love you, Andi. I love you with all my heart and soul, with parts of me that I never knew existed. I tried to ignore the new tender feelings starting inside me because they scared me. It was easier to talk myself into using practical reasons to keep you. To convince myself I was still in full control of my emotions, that I didn't truly need you, or anyone else." He drew in a ragged breath. "But I do need you."

He paused, emotions streaming through his brain and

mind. How hard it was to put into words things that he could only understand at gut level. "I didn't know until now that I've been living a half life, devoid of emotion and even of true joy. In your arms I've found happiness I never knew existed."

He blinked, embarrassed by his frank confession. "I know you no longer believe me when I tell you I love you." He shook his head. "I don't blame you. Those words have lost their power. They've been used too many times. I don't know how to express what I truly feel except to say that my life is empty and hollow without you. Please don't leave me, Andi."

Andi blinked, eyelashes thick with tears. The raw emotion in his voice stunned her. He was always so calm, so controlled, so in charge of every situation. Right now she could sense that every word he said was true.

No guile, no charm, no winning ways—just a heartfelt plea that shook her to her core.

She hadn't dared to utter a single word until now, and when she opened her mouth, the painful truth emerged. "I love you, Jake. I've always loved you." Why hide anything now? "I've loved you almost since the first day I came to work for you. You're kind and fair and thoughtful, and tough and strong when you need to be. I've admired you every day and dreamed about you every night."

Putting her thoughts into words took effort, but it was a relief to finally get them off her chest. "So you see, when my memories—and the resulting inhibitions—were erased, I fell so easily into the kind of relationship I've always dreamed of. I'm sure it was frightening to know that someone you've worked so closely with for years had those kind of feelings."

She shivered slightly. "I didn't want you to ever find out.

That's one of the main reasons I wanted to leave. It was all wrong from the start."

"But it's not wrong." Jake kept his gaze fixed on hers. "I was wrong to take advantage of you, but we're meant to be together. I don't want a ceremonial wife *or* an assistant. I want someone who'll remind me I've never been up the mountain, and who'll take me there. I don't want someone who'll take good minutes on my life, I want someone to live it with me and make it fuller and richer than I ever imagined."

Unable to hold still any longer, Andi reached out to him and clasped his hands. He was still holding the ring, the pretty, simple diamond she'd liked, and the fact that he'd brought it touched her deeply. "I was already cursing myself for leaving you—and Ruthenia. I felt like I was leaving a big chunk of my heart behind." She hesitated and drew in a breath. "I don't want to leave you behind."

"Then don't. I'll come with you. Ruthenia can get along without me for a while." He rose from the floor and sat on the seat beside her. "We should visit your parents. It seems only right that I should ask them for your hand in marriage." A twinkle of humor brightened his eyes. "And maybe I'll have better luck with them."

He held up the ring between finger and thumb. "Though it would be nice to put this ring somewhere safe, like your finger, so it doesn't get lost while we're traveling."

The ring blurred as Andi's eyes filled with tears. She pulled off her gloves and held out her bare hands, which trembled. "I will marry you, Jake." Her voice cracked and a violent shudder rocked her as the cool metal slid over her finger. The act felt far more powerful and meaningful than the first time, when she didn't even know who she was. "I do want to spend the rest of my life with you."

Now that Jake had poured out his feelings, everything

felt different. She no longer had any doubt that he loved her as much as she loved him. Sun poured in through the large railcar window, and the world outside seemed bright with promise. "I love the idea of going to see my family. They'll be thrilled to meet you. If this train ever gets moving again, that is."

Jake grinned. "Let's see what we can do about that. But, first things first." He slid his arm around her back and pulled her close. Andi's eyes slid shut as their lips met and she kissed him with all the pent-up passion and emotion she'd planned to lock away for the rest of her life. Relief and joy flooded through her and her heart exploded with happiness at the feel of his strong arms around her. When they finally pulled apart, blinking in the sun, she had a strange sensation of her life starting afresh from this moment.

"I love you, Jake." At last she could say it out loud without a hint of embarrassment or doubt. She'd waited years for this moment and it was sweeter than she'd ever dreamed.

"Not as much as I love you." Jake's eyes sparkled.

"You're so competitive."

"So are you." He grinned. "One more reason why we're perfect for each other." Then he pulled out his phone. "Now, let's see if we can get this train moving."

Epilogue

"Of course you need an assistant." Jake leaned in and kissed Andi's neck.

Piles of envelopes and résumés covered her desk. The prospect of going through them seemed more than daunting. "But we already have a full staff. And three nannies."

"You need someone just for you." He eased his thumbs down her spine. "So you can come up with a crazy plan for the weekend, and put her to work making it happen while you and I go for a stroll on the mountain."

"That's too decadent."

"It's an important part of any monarch's job to be decadent."

Andi laughed. "Says who?"

"The paparazzi. They don't want to cover a bunch of dull worker bees."

"True." She giggled. "They did have fun taking those ridiculous shots of me sailing when I was eight months pregnant."

"See? You're helping people earn their livelihood. And what about the tourists? They want glamour and excitement, romance and majesty, not a queen who licks her own envelopes."

"I can think of better things to lick." She raised a brow.

"Now that you put it that way, I think I'll cancel this afternoon's meeting on foreign policy."

"Don't you dare." She shot him a fierce glare. "Just save your energy for later." She stroked a finger over his strong hand, where it rested on her desk.

"Have I ever run out of energy?" He growled the question in her ear.

"Never. Now I know where our son gets it from." Little Lucas was a tireless eighteen-month-old bundle of energy. They'd managed with just two nannies until he learned to walk; after that, three—plus Andi—were required to keep up with him.

A joyful shriek outside the door alerted her that his morning nap must be over. Jake dodged to the side as little Lucas barreled into the room, blond curls bouncing. "Mama, read me a story!"

"Of course, sweetie."

"See? You need an assistant so you have someone to read through all these résumés for you while you read Lucas a story." Jake chuckled.

"You're hired." She winked and gathered Lucas into her arms. "Lucas and I have an appointment with Thomas the Tank Engine."

"And James the Red Engine." Lucas's serious face reminded her so much of Jake's sometimes, despite the pudgy dimpled cheeks.

"This sounds like a very important meeting. Perhaps I should attend, too."

"Most definitely. Foreign policy can wait. Tell them

Ruthenia just wants to be friends with everyone." Andi swept Lucas up in her arms as she stood.

"A very sensible approach. We'll just have a big party with cupcakes and tell everyone to play nicely." Jake squeezed Lucas's little hand.

"Chocolate cupcakes, 'kay, Daddy?"

"Hmm. Not sure. We might have to put a committee together to discuss the finer details."

"How 'bout rainbow sprinkles?" Lucas's bright blue eyes stared at his dad.

"If rainbow sprinkles are involved I'll just have to issue an executive order."

Lucas clapped his chubby hands together.

Andi shrugged. "I do like to be surrounded by men who can make important decisions without a lot of fuss. Really takes the pressure off. Where's the book?"

Lucas pointed at his nanny Claire, who stood in the doorway with a stack of paperbacks and a freshly made snack on a plate.

"Let's head for the garden." Andi moved to the door. "Claire, can you call ahead and have some blankets spread on the lawn? And maybe bring out Lucas's trike and stick horse." She tickled under his chin and he giggled. Then she glanced up at Jake. "See? I am getting better at not doing everything myself."

"Your efforts are admirable. And much needed since you'll soon be in the third trimester and Lucas isn't getting lighter." He picked his son up and held him in his arms. Lucas clapped both chubby palms against his cheeks and laughed aloud. "What if his sister has as much energy as he does?"

"Then we'll need six nannies. If we keep having kids there will be zero unemployment in Ruthenia."

Lucas arched his back, signaling his desire to be free on

his fast-moving feet. Jake put him gently down and they both watched as Lucas tore off down the corridor with Claire running after him. "How do people manage a toddler without a nanny while they're pregnant?" Already she could get a little short of breath climbing stairs without carrying anyone.

"I don't know. I always had a nanny." He winked.

"It's amazingly easy to get used to being spoiled rotten. Where's my dish of peeled grapes?"

They both laughed. They knew they worked hard, for much longer hours than most people. Andi had come to enjoy the routine round of entertaining. It felt good to bring people into their home and make them feel welcome. As the host she took special pleasure in making sure everyone had a good time, quite different than when she simply had to make sure the events ran smoothly.

Her parents had fallen in love with both Ruthenia and Jake. With her father newly retired and her mom only working during the school year, they'd allowed Jake and Andi to give them a quaint house right in the town as a "vacation home," insisting they wanted to visit regularly without being on top of the couple.

Andi's sister and her husband flew in for the wedding, and their little daughter was a flower girl in the majestic old town church where they said their vows. They now also came to visit regularly, and the sound of little Lucy's childish laughter bouncing off the palace walls had urged Andi and Jake into parenthood.

Since Lucas was born the palace no longer felt like a place of business where people slept, but was fully a family home, where people also worked.

The difference was subtle, but transformative. Jake slid his arms around her waist. "Would you like me to carry you downstairs, Your Majesty?"

"That won't be necessary." She wriggled against him, enjoying the flash of heat that always sparked between them when they touched. "But you can kiss me."

His lips met hers and her eyes slid closed. She could always lose herself in his kiss. She'd dreamed of it so long and come so close to never tasting him again. Her fingers played over the muscle of his chest through his tailored shirt.

She pulled back, lips humming with desire. "Hold that thought. I have a story to read and you have to bring about peace in our time. I'll see you tonight."

"And every night." His soft glance was loaded with suggestion.

She glanced down at her hand, where the simple diamond ring she'd first chosen sparkled behind her engraved wedding band. A smile crept over her mouth. "For the rest of our lives."

* * * * *

CLAIMING HIS ROYAL HEIR

BY
JENNIFER LEWIS

For Lilly, my good friend and companion
in many adventures.

Acknowledgements:

Many thanks to the lovely people who helped improve
this book while I was writing it: Anne, Jerri, Leeanne,
my agent Andrea and my editor Charles.

One

"Your son is my son." The strange man looked past her into the hallway, searching.

Stella Greco wanted to slam the front door in his face. At first she'd wondered if he was a strip-a-gram like the one her friend Meg hired for her surprise party two years ago. But the expression on this man's face was too serious. Tall, with unruly dark hair that curled around his collar, stern bronzed features and stone-gray eyes, he filled her doorway like a flash of lightning.

Now his words struck her like a harsh bolt. "What do you mean…your son?" Her mother lion instincts recoiled against him. "Who are you?"

"My name is Vasco de la Cruz Arellano y Montoya. But I go by Vasco Montoya when I'm abroad." A smile flickered at the corner of his wide, sensual mouth, but not enough to reassure her in any way. "May I come in?"

"No. I don't know you and I'm not in the habit of letting unknown men into my house." Fear crept up her spine. Her son didn't have a father. This man had no business here. Could she simply shut the door?

The sound of nursery-rhyme music wafted toward them, betraying the presence of her child in the house. Stella glanced behind her, wishing she could hide Nicky. "I have to go."

"Wait." He stepped forward. She started to push the door shut. "Please." His voice softened and he tilted his head. A lock of dark hair dipped into his eyes. "Perhaps we could go somewhere quiet to talk."

"That won't be possible." She couldn't leave Nicky, and she certainly didn't intend to bring him anywhere with this man. She prayed Nicky wouldn't come crawling down the hallway looking for her. Every maternal instinct she possessed still urged her to slam the door in this man's too-handsome face. But apparently she was too polite. And there was something about this strange man that made it hard. "Please leave."

"Your son…" He leaned in and she caught a whiff of musk mingled with leather from his battered black jacket. "My son…" his eyes flashed "…is heir to the throne of Montmajor."

He said it like a proclamation and she suspected she was supposed to fall down in surprise. She kept a firm hold on the door frame. "I don't care. This is my private home and if you don't leave I'll call the police." Her voice rose, betraying her fear. "Now go."

"He's blond." His brow furrowed as he looked over her shoulder again.

Stella spun around, horrified to see Nicky scooting along the floor with a huge grin on his face. "Ah goo."

"What did he say?" Vasco Montoya leaned in.

"Nothing. He's just making sounds." Why did people expect a barely one-year-old to be speaking in full sentences? She was getting tired of people asking why he couldn't talk properly yet. Every child developed at his own pace. "And it's none of your business, anyway."

"But it is." His eyes remained fixed on Nicky, his large frame casting a shadow that fell through the doorway.

"Why?" The question fell from her lips as a frightening possibility occurred to her.

"He's my son." He peered at her boy.

She swallowed. Her gut urged her to deny his claim. But she couldn't—not really. "What makes you think that?"

The intruder's gaze stayed riveted on Nicky. "The eyes, he has the eyes." Nicky stared back at him with those big gray eyes she'd tried to attribute to her maternal grandmother. Her own eyes were a tawny hazel.

Nicky suddenly darted past her, reached out a chubby hand and grabbed one of Vasco's fingers. The big man's face creased into a delighted smile. "It's a pleasure to make your acquaintance."

Stella had snatched Nicky back into the hallway and clutched him to her chest before she took a breath.

"Ga la la." Nicky greeted the man with a smile. Somehow that just made it worse.

"This is a gross invasion of my privacy. Of our privacy," Stella protested, clutching her son tighter. A horrible feeling in the pit of her stomach told her this really was the father of her son. She lowered her voice. "The sperm bank assured me that donor identity was confidential and that my information would never be shared with anyone."

His eyes met hers—ocean-gray and fierce. "When I was young and foolish I did a lot of things I now regret."

She knew Nicky had the right to contact his father once he came of age, but she'd been assured the father did not have the same rights.

"How did you find me?" She wanted her child to be hers alone, with no one else around to make demands and mess things up.

If this even was the father. How could he know?

He cocked his head. "A donation or two in the right pocket reveals most things." He had a slight accent, not a strong one but a subtle inflection warming his voice. He certainly had an old-world sense of entitlement and the importance of bribery.

"They gave you the names of the women who bought your samples?"

He nodded.

"They could have lied."

"I saw the actual records."

He could be lying right now. Why did he want Nicky? Her son wriggled against her, squawking to be put down, but she didn't dare release her grip.

"He might not be yours. I tried sperm from several donors." She clutched Nicky close. Now she was lying. She'd become pregnant the first cycle.

He lifted his chin. "I saw your records, too."

Her face heated. "This is outrageous. I could sue them."

"You could, but it doesn't change the one really important fact." He looked down at Nicky and his harsh gaze softened. "That's my son."

Tears sprang to her eyes. How could a perfectly ordinary day turn into a nightmare so fast?

"You must have fathered loads of children through the bank. Hundreds even. Go find the others." She grasped at straws.

"No others." He didn't take his eyes off Nicky. "This is the only one. Please may I come in? This is no conversation to have in the street." His tone was soft, respectful.

"I can't let you in. I don't truly have any idea who you are and you freely admit that you're here because of information you obtained illegally." She straightened her shoulders. Nicky wriggled and fussed in her arms.

"I regret my mistake and wish to make amends." His wide gray eyes implored her.

An odd tender feeling unfurled in her stomach. She shoved it back down. Who was this man to play on her feelings? With his looks, he was probably used to women rolling over every time he asked. Still, she couldn't seem to shut the door on him.

"What's his name?"

The stranger's question, asked with a tender half smile at Nicky, startled her.

She hesitated. Telling him Nicky's name would give him the right to call him by it. Almost an invitation. But what if he was Nicky's real donor? His father…the word made her quake deep inside. Did she have the right to drive him away?

"Can I see some ID?" She was stalling as much as anything. A man capable of paying for information could pay for fake ID. But she needed time to think.

He frowned, then reached into his back pocket and pulled out a money clip. He plucked a card from it. A

California driver's license. "I thought you were from Mont…" What was the name he'd said again?

"Montmajor. But I lived in the U.S. for a long time."

She peered at the picture. A slightly younger, less world-weary version of her visitor stared back. Vasco Montoya was indeed the name on the card.

Of course, you could buy driver's licenses on every street corner these days, so it didn't prove anything. She hadn't seen the donor's name at any time, so she still had no idea if Vasco Montoya was the man whose frozen semen she'd paid for.

It was all so…ugly. People had laughed when she told them how she planned to conceive her child. Then they'd frowned and clucked about turkey basters and told her to just go find a man. She'd wanted to avoid that complication. Frozen semen seemed safer at the time.

"Which sperm bank did you donate to?" Maybe he was bluffing.

He took his license back from her trembling fingers and shoved his money clip back in his pocket. "Westlake Cryobank."

She gulped. The right place. She hadn't told anyone, not even her best friend, where she went. Somehow that made the whole clinical procedure easier to forget. Now this tall, imposing male was here to shove it back in her face.

"I know you don't know me. I didn't know how to approach you other than to come in person and introduce myself." His expression was almost apologetic, accompanied by a Mediterranean hand gesture. "I'm sorry to shock you and I wish I could make this easier."

He shoved a hand through his dark hair. "You know my name. I've made my fortune in gemstone mining.

I have offices and employees all over the world." He pulled another card from his money clip. She took it with shaky fingers, which wasn't hard, since she still held Nicky clamped to her chest with the other arm.

Vasco Montoya, President
Catalan Mining Corporation

Catalan. The word struck her. She'd chosen her donor partly because he'd proudly proclaimed his Catalan ancestry. It seemed exotic and appealing, a taste of old Europe and a proud culture with a glorious literary history. She'd always been a sucker for that kind of thing.

And those eyes were unmistakable. The same slate-gray—with a hint of stormy ocean-blue—as her son's.

"I don't want to hurt you. I just want to know my son. As a mother, I'm sure you can imagine what it would be like to have your own child out there, walking around, and you've never met him." Again his gaze fixed on Nicky, and powerful emotion crossed his face. "You would feel like part of your heart, of your soul, is out there in the world, without you."

Her heart clenched. His words touched her and she recognized the truth in them. How could she deny her son the right to know his own father? Vasco's attitude had softened, along with his words. Her maternal instincts no longer screamed at her to shove him back down her steps. Instead she felt an equally powerful urge to help him. "You'd better come in."

Vasco closed the front door and followed Stella Greco down the hall and into a sunny living room with colorful toys scattered on the wood floor and on the plump beige sofa.

Strange emotions and sensations tightened his muscles. He'd come here from a sense of duty, keen to tie up a loose end that could cause succession problems in a future he didn't want to think about.

He'd wondered how much money she'd take to give him the child. Most people had their price, if it was high enough, and he knew he could promise the boy a good life in a loving environment.

Then those big gray eyes met his, wide with the innocent wonder of childhood. Something exploded in his chest at that moment. Recognition, at a gut level.

This was his son and already he felt a connection with him stronger than anything he'd ever experienced. She'd put the boy down and the toddler had crawled up to him. While his anxious mother watched, Vasco crouched and held out his finger again. His heart squeezed as the toddler took a tight hold of it.

"What's his name?" She never had answered his question.

"Nicholas Alexander. I call him Nicky." She said the words slowly, still reluctant to let him into their private world.

"Hello, Nicky." He couldn't help smiling as he said it.

"Hi." Nicky's grin showed two tiny white teeth.

"He said hi." Stella's face flushed. "He said a real word!"

"Of course he did. He's greeting his father." His chest swelled with pride. Though he could take no credit for Nicky other than providing half his DNA. Shame crept through him at the callous act of donating something as precious as the building blocks of life for a few dollars.

At the time he'd been glad to throw away the royal seed as he'd rather have died than dip into the royal coffers.

He glanced at Stella. He'd had his reasons for donating his sperm ten long years ago, but what were her reasons for buying it? His preliminary research told him Stella Greco worked at the local university library, restoring books. He'd expected a pinched spinster type, older and forbidding. What he found instead was a total surprise.

She was pretty, too pretty to need to purchase sperm at a store. Her hair was cut in a shiny, golden-brown bob. Freckles dotted her neat nose and her hazel eyes were wide and kind. He'd be surprised if she was even thirty, certainly not old enough to get desperate over her biological clock expiring. Did she perhaps have a husband who was infertile?

He glanced at her hand and was relieved to see no ring. He didn't need another person in the mix. "You must move to Montmajor with Nicky." Thoughts of paying her to give him the child seemed foolish, now. If he'd connected so forcefully with his own flesh and blood in only a few seconds, the maternal bond was not something that could be dissolved by any amount of cold cash.

"We're not moving anywhere." Still standing, she hugged herself. The living room of the little Arts and Crafts bungalow was small but pleasant. She wasn't rich. He could tell that from the simple furnishings and the tiny blue car parked outside.

"You'll have a comfortable home in the royal palace

and you'll want for nothing." The palace he loved with his soul, and that he'd once been cruelly driven from, was the perfect place. She'd know that once she saw it.

"I like California, thank you. I have a good job restoring rare books at the university, and I love our little house here. The schools are excellent and it's a nice, safe, friendly community for Nicky to grow up in. Believe me, I did a lot of research."

Vasco glanced around. Sure, the house was pleasant, but the sound of nearby traffic marred the peace and California was filled with temptations and traps for a young person. "Nicky would be far better off in the hills and fresh air of Montmajor. He'd have the best teachers."

"We're staying here, and that's final." She crossed her hands over her chest. She wasn't tall, maybe five foot five, but she had an air of authority and determination that amused and intrigued him. He could tell she had no intention whatsoever of changing her carefully thought-out plans.

Luckily, he had decades of experience in negotiation, and rarely failed. He could offer financial incentives or other temptations she'd be loath to resist. Although she might not have her price in purely financial terms, everyone had dreams and if he could tap into those she'd eventually be persuaded.

Or he could seduce her. Now that he'd seen her this possibility held tremendous appeal. Seduction offered the benefits of instant intimacy and unlimited enjoyment. Definitely something to consider.

But this wasn't the right time. His appearance was a shock and she needed a chance to digest the idea that her son's father would be involved in his life. He'd give her a day or two to accommodate herself to the new reality of his presence.

Then he'd return and entice her into his arms and his plans.

"I'll bid you adieu." He made a slight bow. "Please do some research into me." He gestured at his business card, held between his fingers. "You'll find that everything I've told you about myself is true."

She frowned, which caused her nose to wrinkle in a rather adorable way.

Stella blinked. She looked surprised that he'd chosen to leave without securing a deal. "Great."

"I'll be in touch to discuss matters further."

"Sure." She tucked a strand of hair behind her ear. Suspicion hovered in her eyes. He suspected she'd be locking all the doors and windows tonight. He had to admit that she seemed an excellent and protective mother to his child.

Little Nicky sat on the floor, engrossed in putting plastic rings onto a fat plastic stick. Emotion filled Vasco's chest at the sight of the sweet young boy that was his flesh and blood. "Nice to meet you, Nicky."

The toddler glanced up, obviously aware of his own name. "Ah goo."

Vasco grinned, and Nicky grinned back. He looked at Stella. "He's wonderful."

"I know." She couldn't help smiling, too. "He's the most precious thing in the world to me. I think you should know that."

"Trust me, I do. And I respect it." Which is why he intended to bring Stella back to Montmajor along with Nicky. A boy should be with his mother as well as his father.

As he fired up the engine of his bike, now hot from standing in the California sun outside Stella's house, he congratulated himself on a successful first encounter with his son's mother. She'd started by wanting to throw him out, and ended by giving him her phone number.

He gunned the engine and took off up the hill toward the Santa Monica freeway. A very promising start.

Stella bolted the door as soon as Vasco was gone. She wanted to let out a huge sigh of relief, but she couldn't. It wasn't over.

It wouldn't ever be over.

Her son's father—the one she never wanted or needed—had come into both of their lives and if he checked out after testing they'd never be the same again. The best she could hope for was that he'd go back to wherever he came from—Montmajor, was it? She'd never even heard of the place—and leave them in relative peace.

She wanted to believe that he was an impostor and that his country was the invention of an overactive imagination. He certainly looked like something out of a Hollywood movie with his worn leather jacket, faded jeans and scuffed leather boots. His looks were pure glam.

He didn't look like a king of anything at all, except maybe King of the Road. Especially since she'd seen him climb on a big, black motorbike right in front of her house. What kind of king went around on a hog?

Maybe he was a fake. Or some kind of crazy. California had enough of those.

Whoever he was, something told her he was Nicky's father. His hair was dark, almost black, and his skin tanned and scorched by the sun, but his eyes were unmistakably Nicky's. Slate-gray and intense, they'd surprised the nurses at the hospital who insisted a blond baby should have blue eyes. They'd never changed color and they were the first place she could read his mood.

Vasco's eyes were hooded by suspicious lids and dark lashes, while Nicky's still had the bold innocence of childhood, but they were the same eyes. Vasco Montoya was Nicky's father.

She settled Nicky into his high chair with some Cheerios and a cup of watered-down apple juice.

She hated that they'd had the whole conversation in front of him. How much could a one-year-old comprehend? Just because he didn't say much didn't mean he couldn't understand at least some of what was going on.

Two

A faint ray of sunlight snuck through the wall of miniblinds in the office of the customer relations manager at Westlake Cryobank. Stella watched the wand of light stretch across the neat gray desk toward the woman behind it. The finger of accusation?

Three days had passed since Vasco Montoya had appeared in her life, and she hadn't heard from him again. Maybe the whole thing was a dream—or rather, a nightmare—and nothing would come of it. She'd been preoccupied with "what ifs" and spent hours online reading about other people's experiences with absent fathers reappearing in their lives. Her brain was boggling with possibilities and problems, and now he'd vanished.

Still, she needed to know where she stood.

"As I said, madam. We assure confidentiality for

all our clients." The woman's voice was crisp and businesslike, her hair styled into a golden blond helmet.

"So how do you explain the arrival of this man on my doorstep?" She flung down the page she'd printed from a website on sapphire mining. An interview with Vasco Montoya, head of Catalan Mining and—as he'd claimed—king of the sovereign nation of Montmajor. Apparently he'd grown his business from a small mine in Colombia to an international concern with billions in assets. In the picture, he wore a pinstriped suit and a pleased expression. Why wouldn't he? He was the man who had everything.

Except her son.

The woman swallowed visibly, then shone a fake smile.

It's her, I can feel it. He probably seduced her into it. Rage swelled in her chest. "He knows where I live and that I used his donation. He wants us to move back to his country with him." The idea was laughable—except that it wasn't funny. "How much did he pay you?"

"It's not possible for him to obtain the information from us. All our records are kept in a secure, offsite location."

"I'm sure they're computerized, as well."

"Naturally, but…"

"I don't want to hear any *buts*. He said that he paid money to obtain the information, so you have a leak in your security somewhere."

"We take the greatest precautions and we have top-notch legal advice." Her words contained a veiled threat. Did they expect her to sue? That wouldn't help.

She sat back in the hard plastic chair. "I guess what I really want to know…" She thought of Nick, happily playing at the university day care. She'd hurried to Westlake after dropping him off early. "Does he have any rights, or did he sign those away when he donated the sperm?"

"Our donors do sign away all rights. They have no say in the child's future and no responsibility to support it."

"So I can tell this man that, legally, he's not my son's father."

"Of course."

Relief trickled through her. "Has he fathered any other children?"

"That information is confidential." The cool smile again. "However I can tell you that Mr. Montoya has pulled his donations and will not be doing further business with Westlake Cryobank."

"Why? And when did he do this?"

"Just last week. It's not unusual for a donor to find themselves in a new situation—married, for example— and to decide to withdraw themselves from our database."

"But how did he find my identity?"

She could hear her own breathing during the silence that followed.

Debbie English tapped on her keyboard for a minute, then leaned back in her chair. "Okay, I can't see there's any harm in telling you that you are the only one who used his sample."

"So if he hacked into your database…"

"Impossible." The woman's face resembled a finely made-up stone wall.

She drew in a breath. "Why was I the only one in ten years who used his sample?"

"We have a very large database. More than thirty thousand donors. Just glancing at his file, I can see that he's not American, and that he wrote in Catalan ancestry rather than checking a box for a more popular heritage. Those things alone might have turned buyers off. We advise our donors to…" Debbie English's voice trailed on and she remembered the excitement and confusion of her trip to Westlake Cryobank.

There it was again. His Catalan ancestry—unusual and intriguing to find in the prosaic database—had attracted her. Probably most people didn't even know what Catalan meant, or thought it was somewhere in China. She knew it was a unique culture with its own language and customs, a mixture of French and Spanish, charming and romantic with strong roots in a colorful past.

Just like Vasco Montoya.

"PACIFIC COLLEGE IN FUNDING CRISIS AFTER STATE SPENDING SLASHED."

The article headline caught Stella's eye as she marched past the newsstand on her way from the parking lot to the library. Rushed and scattered by her unsatisfactory visit to Westlake Cryobank, she had to stop and read it three times. She was sitting out in the garden on her swing seat while Nicky napped in the stroller after a walk. Three days had passed since Vasco Montoya had appeared in her life, and she'd heard nothing.

Pacific College was her employer.

She handed over some coins and scanned the article about a fifty percent cut in state spending on the small liberal arts college. Fifty percent? The college president was quoted saying that he planned to protest and also to raise money from the private sector, but that programs would have to be cut.

In her office, there was a message on her phone asking her to visit Human Resources at her earliest convenience. She sank into her chair and her breathing became shallow.

A knock on the door made her jump and she half expected to see Vasco Montoya respond to her murmured, "Come in."

"Hi, Stella." It was Roger Dales, dean of the fine arts department. Her boss. "I just want you to know how sorry I am."

"What do you mean, you're sorry."

"You haven't heard from HR?" He sounded surprised.

"I had an…outside appointment this morning. I just got in. I saw an article about funding cuts but I haven't had time to…" She hesitated, a sense of doom growing inside her. "Am I fired?"

He came into the room, a whiff of pipe smoke clinging to his tweed jacket, and closed the door behind him. "We've lost all funding for the books and prints archives. It's devastating news for all of us." He hesitated, and she saw the regret in his eyes. "I'm afraid your job has been eliminated."

Words rose to her lips, but not ones she'd want to say to a college dean. An odd fluttering, panicky sensation gripped her stomach.

"As Human Resources is no doubt about to tell you, you'll receive two weeks' pay and your benefits will continue until the end of the month. I'm sorry there isn't a better severance package but with the current financial situation…"

His words continued but her brain ceased to register them. Two weeks' pay? She had some savings but not enough to last more than six months, and that's if nothing went wrong with the car or their health or—

"If there's anything I can do, please don't hesitate to call me."

"Do you know of anyone looking for a rare book restorer?" Her voice had an edge that she hadn't planned. Jobs like this were scarce at the best of times.

"Perhaps you could approach some private libraries."

"Sure. I'll try that." She'd lose the university day care, too. Now she'd have to pay for child care or renovate precious and fragile items on her kitchen table while Nicky crawled around her feet.

Disbelief warred with shock and confusion as he opened the door and slipped from her office. How could her whole life fall apart so fast?

Stella spent three days sending out carefully composed résumés to every university library, museum and private library she could dig up on the internet. When one in Kalamazoo, Michigan, offered her an interview, she realized that even applying for a job with a very young child was challenging. She couldn't take him with her, but he was too young to leave for more than a few hours with even her most devoted friends. Her mom had died three years ago in a skiing accident, leaving her with no close family to count on.

"Maybe I should call Vasco and tell him I need him to babysit," she joked on the phone to her pal Karen, who sat for her occasionally during the day, but worked nights as a bartender in a downtown club, leaving her own three- and eight-year-olds with her mom.

"That would be one way to get rid of him. In my experience men lose interest in anything that involves changing diapers."

"Why didn't I think of that before? I should have invited him in and handed Nicky to him after a poop."

"Has he called?"

"No." She frowned. Now that he'd gone several days without calling, she was actually ticked off at him. Who was he to waltz into her life—and Nicky's—and announce his right to be there and then just disappear without a trace?

"Hmm. He did sound a bit too good to be true. Tall, dark, handsome, leather-clad and royal?"

"Trust me, none of those things appeal to me."

"Yes, I know. You prefer short, fickle redheads."

"Trevor had sandy hair, not red."

"Same diff, sweetie. Either way, he seems to have put you off men for good. Have you even dated since you guys broke up?"

"I don't have time for dating. I'm busy with Nicky." And work, she would have said until two days earlier. She'd been told, very gently, to collect her belongings immediately after her HR discussion. Apparently newly laid-off employees were not encouraged to mess with rare books.

"It's been nearly three years, Stell."

"I'm not interested. I have a very full life and the last thing I need is a man to screw it up for me."

"The right man will come along. Just don't be so busy slamming the door in his face that you don't recognize him when he does. Hey, look at it this way. Vasco already wants you to move to his country—that's a bit of a change from Trevor who wasn't even ready to live with you after eight years."

"Vasco wants Nicky to move to his country. He couldn't care less about me. Besides, he hasn't called. Maybe I'll never hear from him again." Annoying how his face had imprinted itself in her mind. She kept seeing those steel-gray eyes staring at her from everywhere.

"Oh, he'll call. I have a feeling." Karen laughed. "The question is, what will you say to him?"

Stella drew in a breath. "I'll let him spend time with Nicky if he wants, and let them get to know each other. It would probably be best for Nicky to have a relationship with his father."

"Aren't you worried he'll try to take over and tell you what to do?"

"He can't. He doesn't have any legal rights. I could tell him to go away at any time."

"He doesn't seem like the type who takes orders. But here's a thought, wouldn't a European royal have a large collection of old books that need fixing up? You might be able to find some nice work through him."

"Oh, stop. My job search is a disaster. Everything's so far away and the pay is dismal. Barely enough to pay for diapers, let alone support us both. Soon I'll be asking people if they'd like fries with that—hang on, there's someone at the door." The familiar chime sounded and the glass pane darkened as a large silhouette loomed outside.

Stella's stomach contracted. Although she couldn't

see much through the dimpled glass, she knew—every single part of her knew—that Vasco Montoya stood on her doorstep.

Three

Stella said goodbye to Karen and shoved the phone in her pocket. To her annoyance she found herself smoothing her hair as she walked up the hallway to the door. Ridiculous! Still, she might as well be civil since she'd decided that if he was Nicky's father she couldn't in good conscience try to keep him entirely out of Nicky's life.

She'd always wished for the kind of family you saw on TV, with the smiling mom and dad doting on their kids. Instead she had the awkward and hard to explain reality of a dad who had disappeared when she was a baby and never gotten in contact again. There'd always been a gap in her life, a thread of pathetic hope that he'd remember her—that he'd love her—and come back for her. When her mom died suddenly when Stella was in her twenties she'd even tried to look for him, until friends persuaded her that might bring more heartache rather than the resolution and affection she craved. They'd told her she was too nice, too anxious to please, too hopeful that she could put everything right and make everyone happy, when sometimes that wasn't possible.

Didn't stop her from trying, though, which was probably why she couldn't drive Vasco Montoya away without at least finding out the truth. Deep down she just wanted everyone to be happy.

She pulled open the door to find him standing there—even taller and more infuriatingly handsome than she remembered—his arms laden with wrapped gifts and a big spray of flowers.

"Hi, Stella." His mouth flashed a mischievous grin.

She blinked. "Hello, Vasco. Please come in." Mercifully she sounded calmer than she felt. What did he have in all those shiny packages?

"These are for you." His gray gaze met hers as he handed her the bouquet. Her heart jumped and she snatched them from him and turned down the hallway. The arrangement was beautiful—a mix of wildflowers and exotic lilies. The scent wafted to her. "I'll just put these in water."

"Where's Nicky?"

"He's upstairs having a nap. He'll wake up soon." She wanted him to know she wasn't going to disturb her son's routine for an unscheduled visit.

"That's fine. It gives us a chance to talk."

She filled a green glass vase with water and slid the flowers into it. Later she'd take the time to trim the stalks and arrange them. Right now her hands were shaking too much. "Would you like some…tea?"

It was impossible to imagine Vasco Montoya sipping tea. Swigging rum from an open bottle, maybe.

He smiled as if he found the idea amusing, too. "No, thanks." He unleashed the pile of packages onto the kitchen table, then pulled out a small rectangular present wrapped in dark red paper and ornamented with a slim white ribbon. "This is also for you."

She took the present from his outstretched hand, then realized she was frowning. Obviously he was trying to curry favor with her, which rubbed her the wrong way. "You shouldn't have."

"I've done a few things I shouldn't have." Humor danced in his eyes. "I'm trying to put that right. I appreciate your giving me the chance to try."

She softened a bit, more from his hopeful expression than his words. "Should I open it now?"

"Please do." He sat in a kitchen chair, apparently relaxed despite the strange situation.

Her hands shook a bit as she plucked at the ribbon and carefully pulled the wrapping paper off by lifting the tape. She was constitutionally unable to rip paper. Probably an occupational hazard.

The wrapping peeled back to reveal a black paper book jacket with an abstract picture. Her eyes widened as she realized that she now held in her hands a 1957 first edition of Jack Kerouac's Beat Generation classic *On the Road*.

"I know you like books."

"Where did you get this?" This edition retailed for nearly ten thousand dollars. In near-mint condition like this, possibly far more.

"A friend."

"I can't accept it. It's far too valuable." Still, she

couldn't help turning it over to look at the back, and peer inside. The pages were in such good condition, no yellowing or wear, that it must have been in a box for over fifty years.

"I insist. I like finding the right gifts for people."

She stared at him. How could he know about her interest in that era—music and art as well as literature— and that her life revolved around rare books?

His easy grin revealed that he knew he'd scored a hit. "I know you restore books, so I had to give you one in perfect condition or it would be like handing you work." He had dimples in his right cheek and chin when he smiled.

"How did you know what I do?"

He shrugged. "I searched for your name on Google."

"Oh." She'd done the same thing with his, which had informed her that not only was he the king of a tiny country in the Pyrenees, but that he'd amassed a fortune in the mining industry over the last ten years. At least he could afford the gift.

It seemed a shame to even touch the cover, when she knew how every fingerprint caused fabric and paper to deteriorate. Still, what was the point of a book if not to be looked at and enjoyed? "Thank you."

Still, there were a lot of unanswered questions, most of them hard to ask and undoubtedly awkward to answer. Like this one: "Would you be willing to take a paternity test?"

"Absolutely."

"Oh." For some reason she'd expected him to resist. "I found a lab locally. They said you and Nicky have to go in and they'll take swabs from your cheek."

"I'd be glad to." His expression was perfectly serious.

"Why did you donate your sperm?" She was on a roll now.

For once he looked uncomfortable. He leaned forward, frowned, shoved a tanned hand into his hair. "It's complicated. Mostly it had to do with being turned away from the land and family that meant everything to me, and finding myself here in the land of plenty without fifty dollars to my name. Not very heroic, huh?"

She shrugged. His honesty appealed to her. "I suspect money trouble is a pretty common reason. Most of the donors seemed to be college students. I guess it's a painless way to earn some extra cash."

"Sure, until you grow up and realize the consequences."

He regretted it now. Somehow that hurt. "Your donation has brought the greatest joy into my life. Don't wish that away."

He tilted his head, thoughtful. "You're right. Nicky was meant to be here. It's just a strange situation to find oneself in." A smile lit his eyes.

Stella's toes curled as a hot sensation unfurled in her belly. She wished he'd stop looking at her like that. As if he'd found the woman of his dreams, or something.

Definitely *or something*.

"I've decided that you and Nicky should visit Montmajor. Then you can see and decide for yourselves whether it's the right place for you to live." His easy pose and confident expression suggested that he already knew what their decision would be.

The urge to say no was flattened by the reality of her bleak economic prospects in California right now. "That sounds like a good idea."

His eyes widened. Apparently he'd expected at least

some resistance. "Fantastic. I'll arrange the flights. Is next week too soon to leave?"

Should she pretend she needed to "take time off work" or did he already know her job was gone? She didn't want to appear too much of a pushover. "Let me check my book."

She rose and walked into the living room, where she pretended to flip through her datebook, which was alarmingly empty. As she walked back into the kitchen his gaze drifted over her in a way that was both insolent and arousing and made her suck in her breath.

"After Wednesday would be fine. How long would you like us to visit for?"

He propped one ankle on his knee and his smile widened. "Forever would be ideal, but why don't we start with a month."

"I'm afraid I can't take a month away from work." Or at least from looking for a job. Even if he was paying for everything in his country she needed something to come back to.

Vasco's expression softened. "I know you lost your job at the university."

"How do you know that?" Suspicion pricked her. Was he behind it somehow?

He shrugged. "I called them to see if you were affected by the cuts. I'm sorry."

Her face heated. "Me, too. I need to find more work right away. I can't have a big gap on my résumé." He wasn't behind it. Local finances were. All the stress was making her paranoid.

"No need for any gap at all." He leaned forward. "The palace library has over ten thousand books, some of them so old they were handwritten by monks. As far as I know they have seen no restoration efforts in generations, so you will be amply supplied with work if you'd be kind enough to turn your attentions to them."

Funny how his speech could get so formal and princely sometimes.

"That does sound interesting." She tried to contain her excitement. It sounded like every book restorer's fantasy. Old libraries could contain gems that no one even knew existed. Visions of medieval manuscripts and elegant editions of, say, Dante's *Commedia* danced in her mind.

"You'd be well paid. Since I'm not familiar with the field you can set your own rate. Any supplies and equipment you need will be furnished."

"I'll bring my own tools," she said quickly, then realized she sounded a little too keen. "A month should give me time to assess the condition of the collection and plan preliminary repairs to those volumes most in need."

"Excellent." His dimples deepened.

Today Vasco wore faded jeans and black boots with a suit jacket and casual white shirt. He could have stepped right out of the pages in *GQ*. Stella became conscious of her less than scintillating ensemble of black yoga pants and a striped T-shirt that might well be stained with baby food. She resisted the urge to look down.

Besides, one set of eyes on her body was quite enough. Vasco's gaze heated her skin. Was he flirting with her? She was so out of practice she couldn't even tell. Trevor had scoffed at romantic overtures and seductive gestures, and she'd grown to think of them as childish.

But the way Vasco was looking at her right now felt

anything but infantile. "Glass of water?" She didn't
know what else to say and the temperature in the room
was becoming dangerously uncomfortable.

"Why not?" He raised a brow.

She busied herself filling a glass and was relieved
to hear Nicky's voice rising in a plea for freedom from
upstairs. "He's up."

At least now she wouldn't be alone with Vasco, and
those penetrating gray eyes would have someone else
to look at. Vasco stood up to come with her.

"Why don't you wait here?" She didn't want him
upstairs in their personal space, knowing where Nicky's
crib was. She didn't much like leaving him alone in the
kitchen, either. Not because she had a bad feeling about
him—at least not that she could put her finger on—but
it was all way too much, too soon.

She'd committed to visiting his country for a month.
Which gave her a queasy feeling of being swept away
on a tide of destiny. For now, at least, she wanted to
keep her feet—and Nicky's—firmly planted in their
own little reality.

He was still standing as she left the room, possibly
ready to go snooping through the opened mail on the
sideboard or peering into her fridge and discovering
that she'd eaten three out of the six Boston cream donuts
inside it. She grabbed Nicky out of his crib and hurried
back down as fast as she could.

The expression on Vasco's face when he saw Nicky
almost melted her suspicious heart. Delight and wonder
softened his hard features. Part of her wanted to clutch
Nicky to her chest and protect him from this stranger
who hoped to love her son like she did, and part of
her wanted to put Nicky in Vasco's arms so he could

experience the happiness she'd known since he came into her life.

She lowered Nicky to the floor, where he took off at a high-speed crawl.

"I think he's been awake for a while. He seems full of beans."

"Maybe he was listening in on our conversation." Vasco's eyes didn't leave Nicky. Apparently she was way less fascinating now that he was in the room.

Stella's stomach tightened. She'd actually agreed to head off to Montmajor with Nicky. "Will we stay in a hotel while we're there?"

"The royal palace has more than ample room. You'll have your own suite—your own wing, if you like—and plenty of privacy."

A palace. Somehow she hadn't thought of that part. A royal palace where Nicky might be heir to the throne. The whole idea made her feel nauseous. And Nicky's diaper smelled. "He needs changing."

Karen's idea of asking Vasco to change him crossed her mind but she quickly dismissed it. Far too intimate. She didn't want Vasco assuming fatherly duties, at least not until after the DNA test proved he was Nicky's father.

And she suspected he'd be willing and able to rise to that and any other challenge she could throw at him.

Vasco followed her into the dining room, where she had a changing mat on the floor. "When do they stop wearing those things?"

"It depends. When we were kids our moms would be trying to take them off already. These days it's common for kids to wear them until three or four. Everyone has a theory on what's right."

Vasco seemed like the kind of guy who'd let his kid run around naked outdoors and discover things the old-fashioned way. She'd probably try that if she didn't live in the corner lot on a busy street in full view of half the neighborhood. She wasn't sure they'd appreciate the view.

This thought reminded her how little she knew about Vasco and what his life in Montmajor was like. She'd seen plenty of pictures of him with his arm around different women on the internet, but no hard information about his personal life. "Are you married?"

He laughed. "No."

"Why not?" The question was bold, but she couldn't resist asking. He was old enough, over thirty, certainly. Wealthy, gorgeous and royal, Vasco Montoya must have women trailing him like stray cats after a fish truck.

His throaty chuckle made her belly tighten. "Maybe I'm not the marrying kind. What about you? Why aren't you married?"

His question heated her face. "Maybe I'm not the marrying kind either." It was hard to sound cool and hard-boiled while wiping a rosy bottom.

"You do seem like the marrying kind." His voice was soft, suggestive, even.

"Maybe I would be if I ever met the right man. I was engaged for a long time, but eventually I decided I was better off on my own."

She'd probably still be engaged to Trevor, still childless and living alone, if she hadn't made a clean break. It was an easy relationship, if not an exciting one.

"You're independent. Don't need a man to take care of you. I like that."

Don't I? The sudden evaporation of her income and

career prospects had made her feel dangerously alone. It wasn't just herself she needed to support—Nicky was counting on her, too.

She fastened up his tiny dungarees and let him squirm off the mat and crawl away. She and Vasco both watched him scoot out of the dining room and back into the kitchen.

"Wassat?" A delighted cry accompanied by rustling alerted them that he'd discovered the wrapped gifts Vasco brought.

"Is he allowed to open them?"

"That's what they're for." They followed him into the kitchen where he'd already pulled the shiny silver paper off a large box containing a Thomas the Tank Engine starter set that must have cost almost as much as her book. Nicky put the corner of the box in his mouth.

Vasco laughed. "I bought the most delicious train I could find."

"He'll love it." She pulled the box out of Nicky's arms. "Let me open it up, sweetie."

Nicky reached for the next gift, a sparkly blue one.

Vasco shrugged. "I missed his first birthday." He watched with joy in his eyes as Nicky skinned the present, an elaborate construction set made from pieces of carved wood.

"You're good at picking age-appropriate stuff." She was relieved nothing so far looked like a choking hazard.

"I'm good at asking for and taking expert advice." His eyes met hers, and an annoying shiver sizzled down her spine. Again his voice had been almost suggestive.

Shame her body was so keen to pick up on the suggestion.

He'd removed his jacket, and she was chagrined to discover that his jeans hugged his well-formed backside in an appetizing way. Unfortunately, every time she looked at him something inside her lit up like Christmas tree lights, which was not at all appropriate to the situation.

Maybe Karen was right and she needed a little romance—or at least sex—in her life. Just to take the edge off, or something.

But not with Vasco. Since he was the father of her child, that would be way too heavy. And it was unlikely that a dashing royal bachelor would be interested in a short, frumpy book restorer. He probably looked at everyone like that.

The third gift, wrapped in green shimmery paper, proved to be a stuffed purple dinosaur. Not one with its own PBS show, happily, but rather an expensive, handmade-looking one with plush fur. "I don't know what kind of toys he likes, so I got a mix."

"Very sensible." She pulled apart the stiff plastic of the train packaging and set some cars down on the floor. Nicky spun them across the polished wood with a whoop of glee. "That one's a hit."

Vasco assembled the track, complete with bridges and a tunnel and two junctions, and helped Nicky get the train going around it.

Stella watched with a mix of quiet joy and stone-cold terror. Nicky was already getting attached to Vasco. She could see from the look of curiosity in his big, gray eyes that he liked the large new man in his kitchen. So far Vasco seemed to be thoughtful and kind. She'd worried about Nicky not having a father in his life, particularly if he needed male guidance as he got older.

Vasco's appearance seemed to offer a lot of exciting possibilities for him. And some rather worrying ones, too. Was Nicky expected to be king of Montmajor someday?

She'd better confirm that Vasco was Nicky's biological father before this situation went any further. "I need to take Nicky out and run some errands. How about we stop by the lab on the way and drop off the DNA samples."

Would he go there with her? That way she'd know he was serious, and wasn't going to pay someone off to produce the results he wanted.

He stood up and his dark brows lowered over narrowed eyes. For a moment she thought he'd say no or find an excuse. Doubts sprang to her mind—who was this man she'd allowed to play on the floor with her son, who she'd promised to move in with for a full month?

Then he nodded. "Sure. Let's go."

The DNA test results which arrived three days later confirmed what Vasco knew in his heart from the moment he saw Nicky—the boy was his flesh and blood.

He arrived on their doorstep that afternoon laden with more packages. Not the silly toys he'd brought last time, but luggage for their journey. He knew Stella was strapped for cash and it was easier to give her things than offer her money. She'd already turned that down when he'd offered at their last meeting.

He hadn't bothered to phone ahead, so she was surprised, and answered the door in a rather fetching pair of bike shorts and a tank top. She gasped when she saw him. "I was working out." She looked like she wanted to cover herself with her hands. "Pilates." She blushed.

"No wonder you look so good." Her body was delicious. Fit without being too slim, with high, plump breasts that beckoned his palms to cup them.

Lucky thing his palms were wrapped around suitcase handles. "I bought some bags for the trip and printed copies of your eTickets. I'll come by to pick you up when we leave for the airport."

Stella's pink mouth formed a round O.

"You did say you could leave anytime after Wednesday, so I booked us on a flight for Thursday. Plenty of time to pack."

"Did you book the return trip?" Her voice sounded a bit strained.

"Not yet, since we don't know how long you'll be staying." He smiled, in a way that he hoped was reassuring. He did not intend for them to come back, but it was far too early for her to know that. "Where shall I put these?"

Her eyes widened further at the sight of the luggage in his hands. "I didn't know Coach made suitcases."

"They're good quality." He decided to walk in and put them down. Maybe she was a little flustered by her Pilates workout. "Where's Nicky?"

"Napping."

"He naps a lot."

"They do at this age, which is a blessing since it's the only way I can do anything for myself. I can't take my eyes off him for an instant lately before he's climbing onto the back of the sofa or tugging on the lamp cords."

"In Montmajor you'll have plenty of time to yourself.

All the ladies in the palace are fighting with each other for the chance to take care of him."

"Ladies?" Her face paled.

"Older ladies with gray hair." He fought the urge to chuckle. Had she seen them as competition? "They won't try to take him away from you, just to squeeze his cheeks a lot and cluck over him."

She blew out a breath. "It's a lot to take in. Nicky has the advantage of being too young to worry about everything."

He wanted to take her in his arms and give her a reassuring hug, but right now he could see that would be anything but reassuring. Her whole body stiffened up whenever he came within about five feet of her.

There'd be plenty of time for caressing and soothing once they arrived in Montmajor. "Don't you worry about anything. I'll take great care of both of you."

Four

The journey to Montmajor was an adventure in itself. Naturally everyone assumed they were a family. Stella was called Mrs. Montoya twice at the airport, even though her ticket and passport were in her own name.

Vasco carried Nicky at every opportunity, and the little boy looked quite at home in his strong arms. Vasco himself beamed with paternal pride, and handled each situation from Stella's overweight luggage to Nicky running around the airport—he'd started walking that Monday, and quickly progressed to sprinting—with good humor and tireless charm.

And then there were the stares.

Every woman in the airport, from the headphone-wearing teenagers to the elderly bathroom attendants, stared at Vasco wherever he went. His easy swagger and piratical good looks drew female attention like a beacon. He wore a long, dark raincoat—it was pouring when they left—and army green pants with black boots, so no one would have guessed he was a king. His passport was black and larger than hers, bearing an elaborate seal, and she wondered if all his royal titles were listed inside.

He still had to go through security like everyone else, but he'd bought them some kind of VIP tickets that entitled them to fly past most of the lines and get right onto the plane with almost no waiting.

Stella tried to ignore the envious looks. She certainly didn't feel smug about strolling around with Vasco. Probably none of these people would covet the situation she was in, her future uncertain and her son's affections at stake.

The long plane ride passed quickly. Nicky sat between them in the wide first-class seats, and they were both so busy keeping him entertained, or being agonizingly quiet while he napped, that she didn't have to worry about keeping a conversation going.

A small private plane met them at Barcelona Airport for the rest of the journey to Montmajor, whose airport wasn't large enough for commercial jets.

Suddenly things felt different. Men in black jackets with walkie-talkies swept them onto the plane, bowing to Vasco and generally treating him like a monarch. The inside of the plane was arranged like a lounge, with plush purple leather seats and a well-stocked bar. Except for takeoff and landing, Nicky was allowed the run of the plane, and two stern male attendants indulged his every whim. Vasco smiled and watched.

Stella felt herself shrinking into the background. They were now in Vasco's world and she wasn't at all sure of her place there.

Once they'd landed, a black limo drove them from the airport through some hilly countryside, then up toward an imposing sandstone castle with a wide, arched entrance. Inside the arch, the castle spread out around them, long galleries of carved stone columns lining a paved courtyard.

People rushed out from all directions to greet them. Vasco put his arm around her and introduced her— in Catalan she presumed, since it sounded somewhere between Spanish and French—with a proprietary air that made her stomach flip.

Did he want people to think they were a couple? His arm around her shoulders set alarm bells ringing all over her body. She gripped Nicky's hand with force. She hadn't got used to him toddling beside her rather than traveling in her arms.

"Stella, this is my aunt Frida, my aunt Mari and my aunt Lilli." Three women, all dressed in black and too old to be literally his aunts, nodded and smiled and gazed longingly at Nicky. She'd presumed that his father was dead, or he wouldn't be king, but it hadn't occurred to her to ask about his mother or any siblings. How blindly she'd walked into this whole thing.

"Nice to meet you," she stammered. They didn't extend their hands to shake, which was lucky as she didn't want to let go of Nicky. He seemed the safest anchor in this strange, foreign world. Vasco's arm still rested on her neck, his fingers curling gently around her shoulder.

"I'll take Stella inside and show her around." He squeezed her shoulder with his fingers, which made her eyes widen, then ushered her up a wide flight of stairs and through a double door into a large foyer. A vast woven tapestry covered one stone wall—a hunting scene, lavishly decorated with foliage and flowers. Vasco walked toward a curving flight of stone stairs with a carved balustrade. "And on the way we'll pass by the library, which I suspect is far more interesting to you than your bedroom."

Another squeeze made her heart beat faster. He seemed to be giving the false impression that they were involved. Her face heated and she wondered how she could pull away without seeming rude. Anger rose inside her alongside the heat Vasco seemed to generate whenever he came near her. It wasn't fair of him to toy with her like this. She bent down, pretending to adjust Nicky's dungarees, and managed to slip from his grasp.

Vasco simply strode ahead, pointing out what lay behind each carved doorway. An attendant had taken his raincoat so she had an annoying view of his tight rear end as he marched along the hallway. She tugged her eyes to the timeworn stone carvings that lined the walls.

Nicky pulled his grip from hers and ran forward, toward Vasco. A shriek of glee bounced off the ancient stone and echoed around them. Vasco turned to her with a grin on his face. "Just what this old place needs—some youthful enthusiasm." She couldn't help smiling.

The library was every bit as awe-inspiring as she could have dreamed. Two stories of volumes lined its walls and the long oak table in the center of the room was scarred by centuries of scholars and their ink. Nicky ran up to an ancient chair and she dashed to scoop him up before he could pull it over on himself. She couldn't even begin to imagine what treasures must lurk on those high shelves, accessed by rolling ladders.

The one tall window was shaded, probably to protect the books from sun, so the room had a mystical gloom that fueled her excitement.

Nicky yawned and fidgeted, and for a second she felt guilty about wanting to be alone with all those magnificent books. "He needs a nap."

"Or a good run." Vasco took Nicky's other hand. "Come on, Nicky!" He took off toward the door, with Nicky running beside him. Stella stood staring after her son for a moment, then hurried after them, torn between her pleasure at watching Nicky so secure on his tiny feet, and fearing that the pace of everything, including her son's development, was happening way too fast for her to keep up.

With Nicky tucked up in bed, under the watchful eye of one of the "aunts," Stella joined Vasco in the grand dining room for supper. The majestic surroundings demanded elegant attire, and in anticipation she'd made sure to bring several dresses with her. Karen was a talented thrift shop hunter and had scored four lovely vintage dresses for her at her favorite shop in an expensive neighborhood, each from a different era. Tonight she wore a rather fitted 1950s dress in steel-gray silk. Its perfect condition suggested that it had never been worn, and the crisp fabric hugged her body like reassuring armor. Karen loved to choose matching accessories, so tiny clusters of 1950s paste diamonds ornamented her ears. She had one pair of shoes for all her ensembles, gunmetal silver with pointed toes and medium heels. She tucked her hair into a 1950s-style chignon and felt—if not as glamorous as the type of women Vasco was used to—pretty elegant and well put together.

Vasco rose from the table as she descended a small flight of stairs into the dining room. His gray eyes swept her from head to toe, and darkened with appreciation. He walked toward her, took her hand and kissed it.

"You look stunning." Throaty and sincere, his words made her blink.

Luckily the stiff peaks of silk hid the way her nipples tightened under his admiring gaze. "Thanks. Jeans and a T-shirt didn't feel right for dinner in such a dramatic environment."

Vasco himself wore tailored black pants and a fine-striped shirt, open at the collar. Considerably more formal than his clothes in the U.S. "I'm not sure it matters what you wear here. The palace drapes around one like a velvet robe." His white teeth flashed a grin. "But you make everything around you vanish."

Her hand tingled where his lips had touched it. Normally this kind of flattery would make her roll her eyes, but from Vasco's lips it sounded oddly sincere. He pulled out a carved chair and she sat in it. The table was elaborately set for the two of them. Glass goblets glittered with both red and white wine, and the silver cutlery shone from recent polishing. As soon as Vasco was seated, two waiters appeared carrying an array of dishes, which they offered to her one by one, spooning their contents onto her plate when she agreed.

She didn't understand the words they'd said but the aromas spoke for themselves. Crispy-skinned game hen, fragrant rice with snippets of fresh herbs and a rich ratatouille. Her mouth watered.

"It's good to be home." Vasco smiled at the feast. "I

miss the cooking almost more than anything when I'm gone."

"How long were you gone? When you were younger, I mean." She wanted to know more about his past, and the circumstances that had conspired to bring them together.

"Almost ten years." He took a swig of red wine. "I left when I was eighteen and I didn't plan to ever come back."

"Why not?" He seemed so deeply rooted in the place.

"There's only room for one male heir in Montmajor. He inherits the palace, the crown, the country and everything in it. Any other male heirs must set forth to seek their fortune elsewhere. It's a thousand-year-old tradition."

"But why?"

"To avoid conflict and struggles for the throne. One of my ancestors made it a law after he seized the throne from his own older brother. On his eighteenth birthday the younger son must leave the country with a thousand Quirils in his pocket. It's been enforced rigidly ever since."

"So they literally drove you out of the country on your eighteenth birthday."

"No one had to drive me. I knew to make myself scarce."

Stella tried not to shiver. She couldn't imagine what it would feel like growing up knowing you'd be banished one day. "And I bet one thousand Quirils doesn't go as far as it did a thousand years ago."

Vasco laughed. "Nope. Then it was the equivalent of a couple of million dollars. Now it's about seventy-five."

"What did your parents think of all this?"

He shrugged. "It's the law." The candlelight emphasized the strong planes of his face. "I suppose I thought they wouldn't enforce it. What boy thinks his own parents plan to send him away? But when the time drew near…and there was my brother." Vasco's brow lowered and his whole expression seemed to darken.

Stella gulped down a morsel of tender meat. She had the feeling she'd hit on a very sensitive topic. "I assume your brother is dead." She said it as quietly as possible. "Which is why you came home."

"Yes. He killed himself and both my parents in a car accident. Drunk at the time, as usual." He growled the words. "And it's over all of their dead bodies that I'm back here." His eyes flashed, and he took another swig of wine. "Lovely story, isn't it?"

She drew in a breath. "I'm so sorry."

"That was nine months ago, when my father's oldest friend called me up and told me to return." He raised a brow. "I flew back the following day for the first time in ten years."

Something in his expression touched her. He looked wistful. "You must have missed Montmajor while you were away."

"Like a missing part of me." His gray eyes were serious. "I didn't think I'd ever see it again."

"The laws demanded that you never even visit?"

He nodded. "In case I was tempted to lead a coup." His eyes sparkled with humor. "Paranoid country, huh?"

"Very." Stella swallowed some wine. Was Nicky heir to the throne here? The question seemed far too huge to just say out loud. "Do you plan to change the law, so that if you have several children the younger ones don't have to be turfed out at age 18?"

"Already did it." He grinned. "My first edict when I came back. People were really happy about it. That and I made it legal to have sex outside marriage."

Stella laughed. "I bet that law was broken a lot anyway."

"I know it. Sounded pretty funny when the official speaker pronounced it from the castle walls. Maybe that's why no one ever had the nerve to change it before."

"So I guess you're not under pressure to marry anyone in order to enjoy life."

"That's a fact." He smiled and lifted his glass. "Marriage and the Montoya men generally don't agree with each other."

Stella lifted her glass, but wondered what he meant. Did he not intend to marry? If Nicky was his heir he didn't need to. The next in line was already born and he hadn't had to break any ancient laws, either. "Maybe you just haven't met the right person yet."

Vasco's eyes darkened. "Or maybe I have?"

His suggestive tone sent a ripple of awareness to her core, and she shifted slightly in her fitted dress. "There must be a lot of women who'd be happy to be your queen."

"Oh yes. They've been coming out of the woodwork from all over." His dimples showed. "A crown has amazing aphrodisiac effects."

Not that he needed them. With those looks he wasn't in much danger of being lonely. But could he marry some glamorous woman and expect that she'd put up with his sperm bank son becoming king?

Frightening as it was, she needed a clearer picture of what he had in mind. "What are you hoping for, with Nicky? He's not really next in line to the throne, is he?" The whole thing sounded so ridiculous that she blushed when she said it. Maybe a lot of moms would love their child to carry a scepter, but she wasn't one of them.

"Right now he is. He's my only heir." Vasco frowned. "However, if I were to marry someone, the first son I had with her would become heir. Children born in marriage take precedence over illegitimate heirs."

"That doesn't seem fair." Indignation flared in her chest, which was insane, considering that she didn't want Nicky to be king. Still, it implied that somehow he was less important, and maybe that tugged at her sense of guilt over choosing to bring him into the world in a nontraditional family.

"You're right. It's not. I could change the law but it doesn't seem to be an urgent problem right now."

"Not like the need to have unmarried sex."

"Exactly." His eyes twinkled. "First things first."

Heat sizzled inside her and she wished his seductive gaze didn't have such a dramatic effect. She had no intention of having any kind of sex with him. She'd managed without sex for more than two years since she broke up with Trevor, and hadn't missed it at all. Of course being woken up several times a night by a baby could put a damper on anyone's libido. Maybe now that she was getting sleep again it had come back?

Not a very convenient time for lust to reappear in her life. She tugged her gaze to her plate and pushed some rice onto her fork.

"How did you get into restoring books?"

The innocuous question surprised her. What a change

of subject. "It happened by accident. My mom had an old edition of *Alice in Wonderland* that had belonged to her great-grandmother, and she gave it to me when I was in college. The spine was starting to come apart so I asked for advice at a local bookseller, who told me about a course in book restoring—and I got hooked. There's something addictive about restoring someone's treasure so it can be enjoyed by another generation of readers."

"An appreciation for the past is one thing that links us. My ancestors have lived here for more than a millennium and I grew up walking in their footsteps, using their furnishings and reading their books." He gestured at the long wood table, its surface polished to a sheen but scarred with tiny nicks by generations of diners.

"It must be nice to have such a sense of belonging."

"It is, until you're turned out of the place where you belong." He lifted a brow. "Then you search and search for somewhere else to belong."

"Did you find that place?"

He laughed. "Never. Not until I came home. Though I traveled far and wide looking for it." His expression turned serious. "I want Nicky to have that sense of belonging. To grow up breathing the air of his ancestral homeland, singing our songs and eating our food."

Stella swallowed. He was getting carried away and she'd better set some boundaries right now. "I can understand why you feel that way, but you didn't write any of that…" She leaned in and whispered. "In the sperm donor information." She put down her fork. "Because if you had I wouldn't have chosen you as the donor. You gave away the right to decide what happens to Nicky when you visited Westlake Cryobank."

His eyes narrowed. "I made a terrible mistake."

"We all have to live with our mistakes." She could say she'd made one in choosing Vasco as Nicky's father—except that now she had Nicky, the center of her world. "Don't think you can tell me and Nicky what to do." She tried to sound stern. "Just because you're a king and from a thousand-year-old dynasty..." she gestured around the elegant chamber "...doesn't mean that you're more important or special than me and Nicky or that your needs and desires come first. We were raised in American democracy where everyone is equal—at least in theory—and I intend to keep it that way."

Humor flashed in his eyes. "I like your fire. I'd never coerce you into staying. After a few days or weeks in Montmajor I doubt you'll be able to imagine living anywhere else."

"We'll see about that." Soft golden candlelight reflected in the polished glass of their goblets and illuminated the ancient sandstone walls around them. Already Montmajor was beginning its process of seduction.

And so was Vasco.

He tilted his head, smiling at her. "Let's take a walk before dessert." He rose and rounded the table, then extended his hand.

She cursed the way her fingers tingled as she slid them inside his. Still, she rose to her feet and followed him, heels clicking on the stone floor as she walked with him through a vast wooden double door into a tall gallery and out onto a veranda.

They stood high above the surrounding landscape.

The last sliver of sun was setting in the west—to their left—and the mountains fell away at their feet like crumpled tissue paper. As the peaks disappeared into the mist she almost thought she could make out the shimmering glass of the Mediterranean sea in the far distance.

Hardly any sign of human habitation was visible. Just the odd clay-tiled roof of a remote homestead, or the winding ribbon of a distant road. "Amazing," she managed when she caught her breath. "I bet it looked like this in medieval times."

"In medieval times there were more people." Vasco smiled, the sun highlighting his bronzed features and deepening the laugh lines around his eyes. "This area was a center for weaving and leatherwork. Our population is about half what it was in the tenth century. We're one of Europe's best kept secrets and I think most people here like it that way."

His thumb stroked the outside of her hand and sent heat slithering up it. Again her nipples tightened inside her gray silk dress and she sucked in a breath and pulled her hand back. "What about schools? How are the children educated?" Anything to get the conversation on some kind of prosaic track, so she wasn't falling prey to the seductive majesty of the landscape and its monarch.

"There's only one school, in the town. It's one of the finest educational institutions in Europe. Children here learn all the major European languages—now Chinese is popular, too—and go on to university at places like Harvard and Cambridge, the University of Barcelona. All over the world."

"Don't you lose a lot of well-educated people that way? When they go on to work in other countries."

"Sure, for a while. But they always come back." He gestured at the dramatic landscape around them. "Where else can you live once you've left your heart in Montmajor?"

Stella felt an odd flutter in her chest. The place was already taking hold of her. "I'd like to see the town." She glanced at him. "There is a town, isn't there?"

"We call it the city." His white teeth flashed in the setting sun. "And it would be my great pleasure to give you a tour tomorrow. Let's go finish dinner."

She stiffened as he slid his arm inside hers. Really, she should protest at all these intimate gestures, but somehow that felt petty, when he might just think he was being a gracious host. People were different in this part of the world, more demonstrative and touchy-feely, and she didn't want to come across like an uptight puritan when she'd chosen for her son to have Mediterranean heritage.

Her own elbow jostled against his soft shirt, and the hairs on her arm stood on end. In fact every inch of her body stood to attention as they strolled through a dimly illuminated forest of stone columns back to the candlelit dining room.

Their plates had been cleared and as soon as they sat—Vasco pulled out her chair, old-world style— servants appeared with gleaming platters of glazed pears and homemade ice cream.

Stella's eyes widened. "I'm not going to fit into any of my clothes after a week here."

"That would be a shame." Vasco glanced up, mischief dancing in his eyes. "That dress fits you so beautifully." His gaze flicked to her chest, which jumped in excitement.

She felt heat rising to her face. "I'll have to do some exercise."

"There's nowhere better. Tomorrow we can ride in the hills."

"On a horse? I've never ridden in my life."

"You could learn. Or we could walk."

"I like the second option. Nicky can't walk too far, though. He's only starting."

"Nicky can stay with his new aunts while you and I stride through the landscape."

She had to admit that sounded pretty good. "I used to walk in the hills all the time, but since I had Nicky it's been hard to find the time."

"Here we'll have all the time in the world." His smile broadened. "And we can do *anything* you like."

The emphasis sent a shiver down her spine. Already her body had a few suggestions, mostly involving peeling those well-cut clothes off Vasco's ripped and tanned physique.

What was it about this guy that set her on fire? Maybe his being Nicky's father had something to do with it. There was already a bond between them, forged in blood, a connection with him that went far beyond their brief acquaintance.

And maybe the strange and worrying situation had set her nerves on edge, which made her emotions and senses all the more likely to flare up in unexpected ways. She'd have to watch out for that.

"When you look out the window tomorrow and see the sunrise, you'll know you've come home." Vasco's voice startled her out of her thoughts. His eyes heavy-lidded, he looked at her over a sparkling glass of white wine.

"I'm not at all sure I'll be awake at sunrise."

"I could come rouse you." His eyes glittered.

"No, thanks!" She said it too fast, and a little too loud. She needed to keep this man out of her bedroom.

Which might be a very serious challenge.

Five

Stella had rather dreaded seeing Vasco's handsome countenance over the breakfast table the next morning, but found herself put out when he wasn't here. Apparently he'd gone off on royal business and wouldn't be back until late. So much for her tour of the town and walk in the hills.

Was she turning into a pouting, jealous girlfriend, when she wasn't even his girlfriend?

"Ma!" Nicky played with the omelet the kitchen staff had made for him. "Cheerios!"

"Hey, you can say real words when you truly need something." She wiped his chin. "But I'm not sure they have Cheerios here."

"Cheerios!" He banged his spoon on the gleaming wood surface of the table, which made Stella seize his wrist and glance over her shoulder to see if anyone else had witnessed the desecration.

"This table is very precious, sweetie. We have to be careful with it."

"Cheerios, peez." His big gray eyes now brimmed with tears. Why hadn't she thought to bring some with her? She'd had a ziplock bag of them for the plane, but she hadn't thought about people eating different foods here.

"I'll go ask the cook, okay? We'll find something."

She left him at the table and pushed open the door that the staff seemed to appear and disappear from. She was a little alarmed to find a young man hovering right behind it. "Do you have any breakfast cereal?" She spoke in Spanish. He nodded and summoned her into a tiled hallway that led to a series of pantries. One of them turned out to be lined floor to ceiling with boxes of pasta, crackers and cereals, all imported from the U.S.

"For little Nicky," he said with a smile. "His Majesty requested them."

Stella bit her lip. How thoughtful. She pointed at the giant box of Cheerios on a high shelf. "Could he have some of those in a bowl—no milk?"

"Of course, Madam."

She heaved a sigh of relief—or was it awe—and walked back to the table. Alarm filled her heart when she pushed through the door and saw Nicky's chair empty. He always sat in a high chair at home but they didn't seem to have one here.

"Nicky?" She glanced around the room. There was no sign of him. And so many doors he could have gone out through. Panic snapped through her. This palace was vast, and probably had plenty of high walls and ledges a child could fall off. It wasn't safe to leave him unattended for a single moment in such a labyrinthine and nonchildproof space, and she'd have to keep that in mind from now on. "Nicky?"

She hurried out into the main hallway, and waved to an older footman. "Excuse me, I… My son…"

He simply smiled and gestured for her to follow him. More doors and stone hallways—they all looked alike, even though they weren't—led to an interior courtyard with a large, round pool in the middle. A fountain bubbled water and her pulse began to return to normal when she saw Nicky floating a small wooden sailboat in the water under the watchful gaze of two of the "aunts."

She heaved a sigh. "Thank goodness you're here! Sweetie, please don't take off without telling me where you're going." As if he could have explained it. Still, she wanted the women to know, since they must have brought him here. "Mommy needs to know where you are at all times."

She gave the "aunts" a frosty smile. "This water looks rather deep." She spoke in Spanish. They gave no sign of having understood. The fountain was lovely, but the patterned tiles at the bottom of the pool shimmered beneath a good foot and a half of water. Quite enough for a toddler to drown in if someone's back was turned. She'd have to talk to Vasco about safety, so he could lay down some guidelines for the "aunts."

"I found you some Cheerios, Nicky. Come have some." She held out her hand. He glanced up at her, then turned his attention right back to the sailboat. It was quite an elaborate one with cotton rigging and a striped sail. "We'll come back to the boat after breakfast."

"No! Nicky sail boat."

Her eyes widened at the longest sentence he'd ever said. "Have some Cheerios first." Her eyes turned to the aunts in a silent plea.

"Don't worry, Ms. Greco. He just ate two cherry pastries." The smaller aunt—Mari—spoke in flawless, barely accented English. "And we'll take care of him while you eat your own breakfast and do anything else you like."

Cherry pastries? Not the most nutritious breakfast, but at least he'd eaten. And maybe she could go have hers quickly. "Are you sure?"

"I raised eight of my own children and there's nothing I'd like better than to spend time with little Nicky. Frida feels the same and when Lilli's back from her doctor's appointment, she'd agree, too." She beamed at Nicky. "He's such a dear child."

"Yes." Stella bit her lip. "You won't let him fall into the water." It was a statement not a question.

"Absolutely not." Frida's reply showed that she spoke perfect English, too. Stella felt embarrassed for thinking they wouldn't. Though Mari was already speaking softly to Nicky in Catalan, encouraging him to move one of the sails, from what she could gather. "Vasco tells us you restore antique books. We're so lucky to enjoy your expertise here. I used to be a professor of medieval literature at the University of Barcelona, and I know this palace is a treasure trove."

Stella swallowed. "Yes. I saw some of the library yesterday. Maybe I will go there now. We'll have to have a long chat later." She was far too flustered to talk now. These white-haired old grannies were more accomplished and educated than she'd ever be.

Never mind what they could teach her son—*she* could probably learn a lot from them. "I'll see you later."

She kissed Nicky on the forehead, trying to ignore her maternal misgivings at leaving him in such capable hands. No worse than leaving him at the local day care, which she'd used regularly for work.

She spent the day in the library fondling impressive volumes dating back to the time of Charlemagne. Vasco had arranged for a selection of the finest restoration tools, including a vast array of delicate leathers and sheets of gold leaf, to be used for repairing or replacing damaged covers.

Just touching the books was a sensual experience. Reading the words, stories, poems and dramatic tales from history brought her imagination to life. She knew French and Spanish, and quite a bit of Latin and Italian, so she could understand and enjoy much of what she read in the same way the lucky residents of this palace must have done for generations.

She made mental notes of different things she wanted to show Vasco, because she thought he'd enjoy them: tales from his own family history, intriguing Montmajor folktales, even a journal of sorts written by a young king in the 1470s.

But Vasco didn't show up that afternoon.

He was absent at dinnertime, which made her feel rather silly in the aqua vintage maxi dress Karen had chosen for her along with some pretty turquoise earrings. She ate alone in the grand dining room, wishing she'd shared Nicky's feast of scrambled eggs and toast. Nicky was now tucked up in bed under the watchful gaze of a local girl. It was awkward sitting there as waiters brought dishes to her and refilled her glass, and she stared at the empty chair on the other side of the table.

Where was Vasco? Of course it wasn't really her business. They weren't involved or anything. Even if he was out to dinner with another woman, that was absolutely fine.

She swallowed more wine. Maybe she wasn't so crazy about the idea of him carrying on with other women while she and Nicky were there. Couldn't he save that for after they'd gone? They were his guests, after all.

He was probably at a party, schmoozing with wealthy aristocrats, and had forgotten all about them. Or maybe he'd flown off somewhere in his purple-seated plane, to spend a few days on someone's yacht or attend a grand wedding.

Why did she care? She was busy and happy with the library and its amazing collection of books and manuscripts. So why did she glance up and catch her breath every time the door opened? And why did her heart sink each time she saw it was just the waiter again?

She only ate half of the pretty apricot tart in its lake of fresh cream. It seemed a shame to waste such carefully prepared and delicious food, but then it was also foolish to eat it if she wasn't hungry and no one was here to share the pleasure.

She'd removed her napkin from her lap and was about to head upstairs to her room, when the door opened again. This time her startled glance and increased pulse rate were rewarded by the appearance of the man whose presence seemed to hover everywhere in the palace.

Gray eyes flashing, and hair tousled by the wind,

Vasco swept into the room like a sirocco. "I'm so sorry I missed dinner."

He strode toward her, long legs clad in dusty black pants. A white T-shirt clung to his pecs and biceps, revealing a physique more developed and chiseled than her wildest imaginings.

She struggled to find a sensible thing to say, and failed. "Where have you been?"

He looked surprised, and she regretted her rude question. "I rode over to Monteleon, to visit an old friend. We got to talking and the hours slipped away."

So that was the "royal business" he'd been called away on? Again she felt slightly offended. She wondered if the old friend was male or female, but she didn't want to know that. "I found some interesting things in the library."

"Oh?" He'd rounded the table, where he picked up her wineglass and drank from it. Before she had time to blink, a rather flustered male waiter appeared with a filled glass for him. He thanked the waiter, but as soon as the man had disappeared he looked ruefully at his glass. "I'm sure this won't taste as good as one blessed by your lips."

Then he sipped and walked on around the table, leaving Stella staring after him. How did he get away with saying stuff like that? She glanced at her own glass back on the table, and it suddenly seemed unbearably sensual to drink from it again.

"I thought I should start the restoration project by focusing on books and papers that directly relate to the royal family. I've found quite a few interesting things buried amongst the other books, and I thought you might want to organize them into a separate archive of their own."

"Great idea." He was now at the far end of the table, where he put his glass down and stretched, which sent ripples traveling through the muscles of his broad back.

Was he trying to taunt her with his impressive physique? He should know by now that she was the bookish type and didn't notice such things. "Would you like me to show you the book I plan to work on first? After you have dinner, of course."

"I've had dinner." His eyes wandered to her cleavage, which swelled under his admiring gaze. "Though I wish I'd had it here instead. The view is much better." His gaze drifted lower, which made her belly tighten, then to her hips, which had to resist a powerful urge to sway under his intense stare.

"It was strange eating all alone in this big dining room."

"I apologize for making you do that. I'll make sure it never happens again."

She didn't quite believe him. He was a flatterer who knew the right thing to say at any moment. Like his promise of taking her for a walk today.

"Shall we head to the library now?"

"Sure." He walked back to her and slid his arm around her waist. Her eyes opened wide as a shiver of sheer arousal snapped through her. How many glasses of wine had she drunk? Surely it was only two, though it was hard to keep track when they kept refilling it for her.

"I am dusty. Maybe we should stop by my room on the way so I can change. No need to add any dust to the considerable amount that must be on the books already."

His smile made her knees weak. She cursed herself for it. "No need. Did you ride your horse there?"

"Many horses." He grinned. "My bike. It's a far better way to get around these mountains than a big royal sedan. The dirt is the only drawback. I should have showered before coming to find you, but I couldn't wait."

Her cheeks heated under his glance, and she sucked in a breath. Her pewter shoes made an impressive noise on the stone flags of the grand hallway. Vasco turned to the right, in a direction she'd never been before. The carvings on the walls grew more elaborate and the floor turned into an intricate mosaic, which led to a grand, arched doorway.

"The royal bedchamber?" She looked up at the embossed shield carved right into the stone above the door.

"Exactly." He made a courtly gesture with his hand. "Please come in."

She didn't have much choice with his arm still tucked around her waist. A vast bed rose almost to the twenty-foot high ceiling. Heavy curtains hung from a carved wood frame. Candles burned in elaborate candelabra on each side of the room, throwing off a surprising amount of light.

"They've invented something called electricity. Have you heard of it?" The host of candles made shapes and colors dance on the walls and ceiling.

"These newfangled inventions never last. Much better to stick with what's tried and true." She saw his dimples for a second before he peeled off his white T-shirt to reveal bronzed muscles that made her jaw drop.

When he unbuttoned his pants she turned away. "Maybe I should wait outside?"

"No need. I'll be ready in a moment."

He was doing this to torment her. And it was working. She couldn't resist sneaking a peak in the age-clouded mirror than hung on a nearby wall. His tight backside looked very fetching in classic white underwear. His thighs were powerful and dusted with dark hair, and she admired them for a split second before they disappeared into a crisply ironed pair of black pants that seemed to have appeared out of thin air.

He stretched again, causing her to close her eyes for a moment. No one needed that much overstimulation. When she opened them she was relieved to see his thick biceps hidden behind the creamy cotton of a collarless shirt.

"Now I'm ready. Take me to your library." He walked toward her, barefoot on the stone floor, a smile in his gray eyes.

Stella swallowed. Her library? Obviously he'd decided it was her domain for the duration of her stay, which gave her an interesting feeling of pleasure.

Vasco took her cold, rather nervous hand in his warm one, and they set off along the corridor. Even with her in heels and him barefoot she only came up to his cheekbone—and a dramatic, well-shaped cheekbone it was.

Anticipation tingled through her veins as she switched on the low hanging lights in the library, illuminating the magical kingdom of books. She led him to the table where she'd started to arrange the volumes most in need of repair. One heavy tome, its delicate leather cover almost in tatters, sat apart from the others.

Vasco ran his fingers over the rough surface, where the tooled gold had all but vanished under the wear of centuries of hands. "It's a history of Montmajor."

"Written in 1370." Stella laughed. "Rather amazing that they had so much to write already."

"We always have a lot to say about ourselves." That mischievous white grin flashed in his tanned face. "And apparently we love to read about ourselves, too."

He flipped open the book with a casual hand, which almost made Stella want to grab his wrist. This book was six hundred and fifty years old, after all. Vasco began to read, his deep, rich voice wrapping itself around the handwritten Catalan words that she could almost understand, but not quite. Something swelled inside her as Vasco spoke the ancient words aloud with obvious enjoyment.

He stopped and looked at her. "Do you know what it says?"

"I need to learn Catalan. I know French and Spanish and a little Italian and it sounds to me like it's a bit of all of them mixed together."

"It's so much more than that." His eyes narrowed into a smile. "I'll have to teach you."

"That's a big project."

"Then we'll tackle it one word at a time." He pressed a finger to his sensual mouth. "First things first. What's the most important thing in life?"

Stella frowned. "Good health?"

Vasco shook his head. "Passion. *La passio.*"

"La passio." She let the word roll off her tongue, and decided not to start a debate about how crucial passion was to people who were starving. Kings clearly lived in a rather more gilded and hedonistic reality.

"Ben fet."

"I'm guessing that means *well done,* since it sounds a bit like *bien fait* in French."

His grin widened. "You're catching on. Soon you'll be speaking it like a native."

She couldn't help a little flush of pride. "I'll do my best. I can't help but feel *la passio* for the work I'll be doing." She glanced down at the lovely book and managed to restrain herself from moving Vasco's large hand from the page. No need to bore him with her worries about natural oils seeping into ancient handmade paper and tiny microscopic creatures eating away at natural inks. "I plan to restore the cover first. I'll preserve the original then make a leather slipcover that mirrors how it would have looked when new. Then I'll go through page by page and stabilize the book. The inside is in surprisingly good shape."

"Which means it hasn't been read enough times, yet." He flipped a page and started to read again, letting his tongue wrap around the words, bringing them to life in the quiet library.

Stella watched, entranced. Even though the book was about history, it was written in some kind of verse, and Vasco's voice rode the cadence of the words in a sensual rhythm. She could figure out the meaning of enough words to recognize a description of a battle, lances flying and flags fluttering in the wind, horses galloping on an open plain. The vision of it all danced before her eyes, brought to life centuries after it was written so painstakingly in the book.

Her heart was beating fast by the time Vasco stopped, or pulled up, since it felt more as if she'd been riding along in the tale and they'd slid to a halt, dust flying and hooves clattering.

"Beautiful." Her voice was breathless, as if she'd been running alongside the riders.

"Bell." Vasco smiled. "And thank you for awakening me to it. I'd never have opened this book if you weren't here. I confess I'm not much of a reader, by nature."

"You're more action oriented." She noticed how Vasco always seemed to have the wind in his hair, even here in the quiet calm of the library. "And this book has a lot of action in it."

"It does. And plenty of *passio.*" He took her hand in his. Part of her was glad he'd removed it from the fragile old book, but the rest of her started to quiver in a mix of excitement and terror as desire rose inside her, hot and inevitable.

Was this just a friendly gesture for him? Everything about Vasco was sensual and dramatic, so maybe she read too much into his bold touches and looks. Her hand heated inside his and her fingers tingled with the desire to explore his warm skin. All the sexual feelings that had lain dormant in her for the last two years—or more if she was honest—rose up like a river after a rainstorm.

She tugged her hand back and stepped away. "Let me show you another book I plan to work on." She reached for a black leather volume, its pages coming loose from the worn binding. Her hands trembled as she heaved its weight toward Vasco, anxious to break the seductive spell he seemed to have cast over her.

She didn't dare look at him but she imagined his eyes laughing. He knew how much power he had over her and he found it amusing. Flirtation came naturally to him and he used it like a weapon. She'd better find some good armor, possibly the polished set of inlaid sixteenth century armor in the great hall. That looked about her size.

"What's so funny?" His voice tickled her ears.

"Just wondering how I'd look in a suit of armor."

"It's easy to find out. I used to try them on myself when I was a kid—even rode my horse in one, which wasn't too comfortable." He laughed. "But none of them fit me now. Our ancestors were smaller than we are." His daring eyes swept over her again. "Though you're about the right size for Francesca's. Come on."

He'd been leaning on the table with one hip, but he rose and headed for the door, beckoning her.

Stella swallowed. Did he really intend for her to try on some armor? She had to admit the idea had some appeal. How often did you have an opportunity to peek into the experiences of people in another era? Now she'd know how a nervous eighteen-year-old count might feel as he dressed for battle with a neighboring fiefdom.

Her pace quickened as she followed him. She wasn't exactly dressed for battle, medieval or otherwise. Her long dress swept around her legs as she hurried down the hallway. Would he expect her to take it off? Karen had convinced her to buy new lingerie for her trip on the pretext that if servants would be arranging her belongings, they should fit in with a royal household, not scream "bargain bin."

She wasn't sure how many royal guests wore skimpy pale silver satin and lace, but at least her underwear drawer did look smart and she felt glamorous when she put them on.

Vasco led her along a gloomy passageway, illuminated by a single lamp, and into a vast chamber with no lighting of any kind. He flicked a switch and spotlights in the ceiling splashed over a startling display of weaponry arranged on the walls in intricate patterns. Swords crisscrossed each other and muskets fanned out like lace petticoats. Armaments covered most of three walls, shining and polished as if ready for immediate use.

"My ancestors liked to keep their defenses at hand." Vasco grinned. "But they also liked things to be pretty."

"Does someone take these down to polish them?"

"Only once a year. They haven't been pressed into service for quite some time."

"That's a relief. Besides, it can't be easy to buy ammunition for a seventeenth century musket these days."

"You'd be surprised..." he winked "...at what you can find on eBay."

Spotlights also illuminated three suits of armor, each standing in a corner. Two were silver metal with tooled decoration, the other was black and bronze, very elaborate and slightly smaller than the others.

"It's so pretty." She walked toward the unusual one. "Is it Italian?"

"It is." He sounded surprised that she knew. "My ancestor Francesc Turmeda Montoya had it made in Genoa and brought here over the mountains. By the time it arrived he'd grown and it didn't fit."

"What a waste. So it was never worn?"

"Not by him. I'd imagine it was pressed into service over the years from time to time." His long, strong fingers caressed the tooled metal. "But it's possible that it's never experienced the pleasure of encasing a woman's body."

Stella felt every inch a woman as Vasco's gaze met hers. "It does look like it might fit."

He reached behind the torso and unbuckled something. The breastplate, arms still attached, loosened from the stand. "I think you'd better slip out of your dress."

Stella fought the urge to laugh. "What if someone comes?"

"They won't."

"What if war breaks out and all the staff comes running to find the weapons?"

"Then you'll be dressed for battle." His dimples deepened. "Let me help you." He pulled his hands away from the armor and stepped behind her. The sound of her zipper sliding down her back made tiny hairs stand on end all over her body. She shrugged out of the arms and let the dress slide to the floor.

"Lucky thing I'm not self-conscious," she said, wishing she really wasn't. At least the spotlights focused on the armaments, so she stood in relative shadow outside the pool of light on the armor.

She glanced at Vasco to find his eyes feasting unashamedly on her bare skin. Her nipples thickened inside her elegant bra and she felt an urgent need to hide behind the black and gold metal. "Hold it out for me."

He lifted the breastplate off the stand. The arms clanked against the torso with a sound that could wake the dead, and she glanced behind her before sliding her arms into the dark holes and letting Vasco step behind her to fasten the straps. His fingers brushed her back as he closed the armor and she tried not to shiver.

The legs fastened individually, strapping over her thighs and attaching to the main body, so Vasco's fingers had a lot of intimate contact with her skin. The mere touch of his hands made her breath catch at the bottom of her lungs. At last she was entirely encased in metal except her head. "Let's see if I can walk." She felt precarious. The armor was heavy and with her hands in metal gauntlets she wasn't sure she could catch herself if she fell.

"You look like a very elegant Joan of Arc."

She took a tentative step forward. Surprisingly, the armor moved with her like a second, if heavyweight, skin, though the shoe part was too large and clanked on the stone floor. "It's not easy to walk in these things."

"That's why you need a horse." Vasco smiled. "No one marched into battle in that getup. Want to try the helmet?" He lifted the tooled headpiece.

Stella nodded, and let Vasco lower it over her head. She'd worn her hair loose tonight, curling around her neck, and she tucked in the bottom ends so they wouldn't stick out. It was dark inside the helmet, and had an interesting smell, more like wood than metal. She wondered about the people who'd stood in here before. Were they preparing for battle and fighting their fears, or were they like her, just trying it on for fun?

She couldn't see Vasco at all. The eye slits weren't quite in the right place so she could only see the floor and up to his knees. They must work better up on a horse.

She pulled off the helmet, and even the spare illumination in the armaments chamber seemed blinding after the darkness inside. "Phew. It's nice to be able to breathe again. I can picture you riding around the countryside carrying a lance. Rescuing a fair maiden or two."

One dark brow lifted. "What makes you think I would be rescuing them?"

"Okay, endangering their virtue."

"Probably closer to the truth." Even the way the skin around his eyes crinkled only made him more handsome. "But I would mean well." His seductive smile and tilted head seemed to gently ask forgiveness.

"I'll bet." Even in the armor she didn't feel at all safe around Vasco. And it was getting uncomfortably hot in here. "I'd better get this off."

Vasco's slow smile crept across his mouth again. "Let me help you with that."

Six

Vasco had noticed that Stella's hair changed color depending on the light. Right now the spotlight that usually shone on the armor picked out bright gold and red strands from the silky bob.

Sweet and excited but slightly hesitant, her smile tormented him. Her pink lips were mobile, soft and tempting. He could almost imagine how it would feel to kiss her.

But not quite. There was only one way to find out what her mouth would feel like pressed against his.

His knuckles caressed her back as he unbuckled the armor. Soft and warm, her skin begged to be touched. The clasp on her bra beckoned him like the key to a hidden chamber, and with difficulty he managed to prevent himself from unlocking it.

Stella slid out of the armor and he lifted it back onto its armature, irked that he had to drag his eyes from the inviting vision of her body. Luckily the legs required some assistance to remove. The darkness hid his appreciative gaze as he released her deliciously athletic thighs from their metal casing, and pulled the heavy shoes from her delicate feet with their coral-tipped toes.

Her silky underwear didn't help matters. It took all his self-control not to cup the sweet roundness of her backside. Instead he held up her dress and helped her back into it. Her cheeks were pink, even in the dim light. He'd like to see them flushed deeper, with exertion and desire.

Good things come to those who wait.

"I enjoyed that." She fastened the matching belt back around her waist. "Although it's heavy, it's also surprisingly flexible. I'd never have imagined that."

"This armor was cutting-edge technology in its time. No expense would have been spared in kitting out the son and heir to defend the family lands and honor and live to tell the tale."

Stella's eyes looked golden in the half-light of the chamber. "Do you wish you'd lived back then?"

"What man wouldn't?"

"The ones who'd rather play battle games on a computer, I suppose."

"I don't have the patience for those. I'd rather feel the blood pulsing in my veins."

"Or pulsing right out of them if it was a real battle. I'm glad Nicky won't be expected to ride into battle on a galloping horse. That would scare the life out of me."

"I'd imagine mothers have felt the same throughout history." He picked up her hand, an instinctive gesture.

"However, they haven't often had the final say in such matters."

She raised a brow. "Luckily women do have an equal say now. At least in civilized countries." He saw the glint of a challenge in her eyes.

"I suppose it remains to be seen whether Montmajor is civilized in your eyes." He couldn't keep a smile from his lips. "Though it's a hard thing to quantify. We do bathe somewhat regularly and use utensils at the table."

"I'll make up my own mind." A smile tugged at her soft, pink mouth. "I certainly have my doubts about their king."

"I imagine a lot of people do." He loved that she wasn't intimidated by his titles and all the pomp and circumstance that came with them. "I do my best to convince them that under this rough exterior beats a heart of gold."

Her laugh bounced off the weapon-laden walls and filled the air with its soft music. "No one could accuse you of being modest."

"Modesty is not a quality people seek in their king." He let his hungry eyes feast for a moment on Stella's delicious body. Her dress wrapped snugly around her waist, then flared out, concealing the curve of her hips and those silky thighs. Lucky thing the memory of them—and her seductively elegant underwear— was imprinted on his brain like a freshly switched-off lightbulb.

"I suppose arrogance and a sense of entitlement are more appropriate to a monarch." She lifted her neat chin.

"But only in measured doses, otherwise people might

want to rise up and overthrow me." He grinned. "We don't want them storming the castle."

"No, it would take too long to get all these weapons down off the wall."

"Don't worry. The palace staff is trained in kung fu."

"Really?"

"No." He took her hand and kissed it. Couldn't help himself. He knew it would be soft and warm and feel sensational against his lips.

The color in her cheeks deepened. She was ready. He could tell she was interested. Hell, he'd seen the first sparks of it in her eyes during his first surprise visit, somewhere behind the alarm and fear. Now she'd had time to get to know him and his world a little, to relax and realize that he wanted the best for her and Nicky. Even if she was still wary, she was open-minded and prepared to like both him and his country.

Now he needed to apply a little glue.

He stepped toward her and her eyes widened. Before she had a chance to move, he cupped her head with his free hand and kissed her gently but firmly on the lips.

She tasted fresh, like summer wine. A jolt of arousal crashed through him, and his fingers sank into the softness of her hair. His tongue slid between her lips, prying them open, and he longed to press his body against hers.

But two small hands on his chest pushed him back.

He blinked, aching as the intoxicating kiss came to an abrupt end.

"I don't think we should do this." Stella sounded breathless. Her eyes sparkled with a mix of shock and arousal. "Things are so complicated already."

"Then let's make them simple." He stroked her cheek. The hot, flushed skin begged to be cooled by kisses.

"This doesn't make anything simple. We barely know each other."

"We share the strongest bond any man and woman can enjoy—a child."

"That's what worries me. We owe it to Nicky to keep things harmonious between us. Once…romance comes into the picture, that's when problems start."

"Has that been your experience?" He raised a brow. Maybe she was single with good reason.

"I was in a long relationship that I ultimately decided wasn't what I wanted."

"What made you decide that?"

She hesitated, blinked. "Partly, at least, because he didn't want children."

He smiled. "So, problem solved in this case." Her mouth looked so lush, and now that he'd tasted it he couldn't bear to simply look at it.

"But what if we decide we hate each other?"

"Impossible."

"So you think we'll just kiss and live happily ever after?"

"Why not?" Happily ever after was an awfully long time, but the sight of her tempting body a few hot inches away made him ready to promise almost anything. He liked Stella immensely. She'd gone to a lot of trouble to come here and adjust herself to Montmajor for Nicky's sake and his sake, and he could tell she was a woman with a big heart as well as a lovely face.

"Why not?" She blew out a sharp breath. "I'd love to live in a world of fairy tales but reality does keep poking its ugly head back up. What will the other people at the palace say?"

"Who cares? I'm the king. I don't trouble myself with the thoughts of other people." He grinned. He hadn't troubled himself all that much with them when he wasn't king, either, but no need to mention that.

He trailed his fingers down her neck and to her shoulder. Her collarbone disappeared into the pretty aqua dress and he followed it with his fingertips. Stella shivered slightly, and he watched her chest rise and fall.

She wanted him.

His own arousal strained uncomfortably against his pants. His need to seduce her into bed tonight was becoming urgent. He slid his arms around her waist. "Trust your instincts."

"My instincts are telling me to run a mile." The smile dancing around the corners of her mouth made him doubt her statement.

"No, that's some silly part of your brain that wants to prevent you from enjoying too much pleasure."

"Is it really?" Her eyes twinkled.

Almost there.

"Absolutely. You need to switch it off."

"How do I do that?" She raised a brow.

"Like this." He pulled her close and pressed his lips to hers again, this time deepening the kiss right away, enjoying the hot softness of her mouth with his tongue.

Her arms rose around his neck and he felt her sink into his embrace. A tiny sigh rose in her throat as their bodies bumped together, her nipples brushed against his chest through the fabric of their clothes. He let his hands roam lower, to enjoy the curve of her backside and thigh.

Stella writhed against him, pulling him closer, her hot cheek against his and her eyes closed tight. Desire built inside him almost to the boiling point as her lush body tempted him into a state of rock-hard arousal.

With great difficulty he pulled back an inch or two. It was time to transfer this scene to a room with a comfortable surface of some kind. Like a bed.

"Come with me." He was half-tempted to pick her up and carry her, to reduce the chance of her changing her mind, but he managed to resist. Holding her hand tightly, he led her out of the armaments chamber and up the flight of stairs into the east tower.

He'd ordered fresh sheets for the round bedroom in happy anticipation of this moment. With windows on all sides, but no one outside to see in, this room was the most private in the whole palace and had no doubt been used for royal trysts for hundreds of years.

He pushed open the door and was pleased to see a vase filled with fresh flowers glowing under an already lit lamp. The grand hangings on the bed shone, the embroidery shimmering with gold thread, and the covers were turned back to reveal soft, freshly laundered linen.

"What a lovely room." Stella hesitated in the doorway. "It's not your bedroom, is it?" She'd seen him change clothes in his own bedroom.

"It's *our* bedroom." He pulled her into his arms and shoved the door closed behind them with his foot, then drew her into a kiss that silenced all thought, let alone conversation.

Stella couldn't believe she was able to kiss Vasco and breathe at the same time, but it must be happening because the kiss went on and on, drawing her deeper into a sensual trance.

She'd never experienced anything like this kiss. Sensation cascaded through her, bringing every inch of her alive and making her aware of her body in an entirely new way. Colors danced behind her eyelids and her fingers and toes tingled with awareness as Vasco's tongue jousted with hers.

When he finally pulled back—she would have been totally unable to—she emerged blinking and breathless back into reality like a creature startled out of hibernation.

So *this* is what people made such a fuss about. She'd always wondered about the poems and songs and all the drama surrounding romance and sex. Her own love life had been prosaic enough that she thought they were all exaggerating for effect. Now she could see she'd been missing out on the more exciting aspects of the experience.

And they hadn't even had sex yet...

Vasco's eyes shone with passion that mirrored her own and electricity crackled in the air around them. This was the chemistry people talked about, she could feel it like an explosive reaction about to happen, heating her blood and stirring her senses into a witches' brew of excitement.

Vasco reached behind him and switched off the light. A fat pale-gold moon hung outside the windows, bathing them both in its soft glow, turning the dramatic round room into a magical space.

Her hands were buried in the soft cotton of Vasco's shirt, clutching at the muscle beneath. She longed to pull the fabric from his body, but some vestige of modesty prevented her. Vasco had no such scruples. He undid the tie that held the waist of her dress together and unwrapped her like a gift. For the second time that night her dress descended to the floor and she stood before him in her underwear. This time, however, she had no armor to hide in.

His eyes roamed over her body, heating her skin with their warm admiration. His fingers followed, stirring currents of sensation wherever they touched. She let herself move under his hands, enjoying their sensual touch as she ran her fingers over his shirt, feeling the muscle beneath.

Soon enough her fingers found themselves plucking the buttons from their holes and pushing the fabric back over his shoulders. She'd had a glimpse of Vasco's chest earlier—surely that was his real bedroom?—and it was even firmer and more enticing at close range. A shadow of dark hair disappeared into his belt buckle, and soon she found herself sliding the leather out of it and unzipping his black pants.

It was glaringly obvious that he was every bit as aroused as her. His erection jutted against his briefs. She let her knuckles graze against it as she pushed his pants down past his thighs, and the hardness of it made her shiver. Trevor had always needed a good deal of coaxing to get ready, by which point her interest had sometimes waned. Clearly Vasco did not need any encouragement.

She glanced up at his face, and his predatory gaze only deepened the intensity of her desire. His lips were parted and she could feel his breathing, watch his chest rise and fall as anticipation jumped between them like a spark. Her own heart thumped so loud she could almost hear it in the still nighttime silence. It grew louder and faster as Vasco reached around her back and unhooked her bra.

She could pretend it was the cool night air that tightened her nipples, but they both knew better. Vasco lowered his head and licked one, then looked up at her, eyes shining with desire. She pushed his underwear down and he kicked it away. Glazed with moonlight, his hard body looked like an ancient statue. She could hardly believe such a gorgeous vision was interested in her.

Vasco plucked at her scanty lace briefs, then slid them down her thighs, leaving them both naked. The moonlight felt like a warm robe around her, making her unselfconscious and hungry for the feel of his body against hers. She stepped forward, until the tips of her breasts brushed his chest. The tickling sensation almost made her laugh and step back, but Vasco's big hands caught her around the waist and pulled her closer.

Their bellies met, Vasco's fierce arousal trapped between them. He captured her mouth in a kiss that made her head spin and ran his fingers through her hair. Stella's hands wandered over his muscled back, enjoying the athletic perfection of his body as the pressure of their desire built between them like water held behind a dam.

Stella felt the soft edge of the mattress behind her thighs, and realized they'd been moving backward to the bed. Vasco's hands cupped her buttocks and lifted her onto the high surface, without breaking their kiss. The soft fabric felt cool beneath her hot skin, and she wriggled a little, enjoying the sensation. Vasco laid her backward, easing himself over her. He pulled back enough to look into her eyes. "You're a very sensual woman."

"Who knew?" She sounded as surprised as she felt. Her senses were alight with wonder and excitement she'd never imagined. She'd not given sex more than a passing thought in so long she almost wondered if she'd ever have it again. Or if she even cared.

Now she craved it like her next breath.

Vasco slid into her slowly and she arched her back to take him deep. A groan of sheer pleasure slid from her lips and flew into his mouth as it covered hers again. He moved with creativity and elegance, shifting his body over hers and drawing her closer into a tangle of delight.

As they writhed together on the bed, she felt like the partner of an expert dancer who knew how to bring out her own innate talent. She found herself guiding them, too, climbing on top to deepen the dramatic sensations coursing through her, then letting him tilt her body to daring angles and roll with her in perfectly executed moments that made her gasp for breath as passion crashed through her.

Vasco's warm skin against hers felt so right. His arms around her waist or her shoulders, his fingers in her hair or caressing the skin of her face, every touch was gloriously perfect. When her climax reached the point of no return she let herself disappear into the ecstatic madness of the moment, clinging to him while the real world fell away.

In his arms afterward, wrung out by the intensity of the experience, she could barely remember her name or even breathe. His mouth and hands and tongue had explored every inch of her, making her whole body quiver with desire and anticipation, then giving her satisfaction she'd never known before. Now she felt soft and pliable, relaxed and content. Happy.

Vasco whispered to her, sometimes in English, sometimes in Catalan, telling her how beautiful she was, what a sensual lover, what a fantastic mother and how pleased he was to have her here in Montmajor. And in his bed.

Everything he said seemed normal and natural and made her smile though she could rarely summon the energy to reply. That didn't seem to matter. She rested her head on the firm pillow of his chest and drifted off to sleep, lulled by the rhythm of his big heart.

Her dreams were surreal visions of their imagined life in the palace. Walking, laughing and talking together. The perfect happy family living a comfortable and enjoyable life amidst the sandstone walls of a thousand-year-old castle. Normal and natural and predictable as the sunrise—which poked its bright harsh fingers through all those windows around the room and jolted her from sleep with alarming suddenness.

Only then did she realize what she'd done.

Seven

Stella sat up in bed and raised a hand to keep the bright sun out of her eyes. A quick glance at the pillow next to hers confirmed that Vasco was gone. When had he left? Did he sleep with her all night or disappear the moment she fell asleep?

Had he used a condom? She hadn't spared a thought for contraception. Trevor had always been the one to worry about that, since he was so terrified of having children and the responsibility and expense it would entail. He'd always come armed with condoms despite the fact he'd convinced her to have an IUD fitted. She'd had the IUD removed to conceive Nicky, and hadn't bothered with birth control since because she hadn't been on a single date.

She swallowed. Her insides still pulsed with traces of the fierce contractions she'd enjoyed at the peak of their lovemaking. Vasco had turned her inside and out, guiding her to feats of sexual acrobatics that made her blink as she remembered them. Wow. Who knew there was a whole new world of sexual pleasure out there that she'd barely even dipped her toes in?

Now she'd dived in headfirst, with a man she barely knew, who just happened to be the father of her son.

She climbed out of bed, scanning the room for her clothes. Light blazed in through the windows, leaving her naked and exposed. She found her dress in a crumpled heap on the floor, and her skimpy lingerie under the bed, where it must have been kicked by eager feet. She fished them out and tugged them back on with shaky hands.

How easy it had been for Vasco to seduce her. Her face heated. She hadn't even been here a week. Or all of three days. She'd leaped into bed with him the first time he even kissed her.

Her dress was crumpled, but she pulled it on and fastened the tie at the waist. She'd wanted him to see her as attractive, desirable. She didn't want him to think that the woman who'd bought his sperm was someone who couldn't find a man the old-fashioned way. Had she bent over backwards to convince herself she could tempt Vasco?

She certainly had put effort into looking nice and attempting to be a charming guest. He must know she wanted him to like her, and now he'd obliged by taking her to bed.

The large four-poster bed with its long curtains loomed over her. Whose bed was this? Not Vasco's, for sure. Was this room reserved for sexual escapades with visiting women? There were no signs of habitation, no pictures or bits of clothing or toiletries. It looked like a museum recreation of an ancient castle bedroom. Except that it was the real thing.

The sun had just lifted over the horizon, so hopefully Nicky was still asleep, but what if he'd woken up in the night, wanting her? He could have been calling for her for hours and no one knew where she was.

Heartbeat quickening, she picked up her shoes from under a chair and hurried to the door. Hopefully most of the staff was still asleep and she could sneak back to her room without being seen.

She pulled open the tall, heavy wood door and peered outside. The lightless hallway looked like a black hole after the blinding light of dawn illuminating the bedroom. She hadn't paid close attention on the way here, so she wasn't even sure which part of the palace she was in.

The cold stone stung her feet as she tiptoed into a narrow corridor which led to a flight of spiral stone stairs heading up and down. She went down, and out through the next arched doorway into a small courtyard where dew clung to ornate iron railings. Had she come this way last night? She'd been so wrapped up in Vasco she hadn't noticed. No doubt she'd assumed he'd be escorting her back, as well.

She should have known better than to think Vasco so predictable.

The courtyard had two doors leading out the other side, and she picked the one on the right, only to find it locked. The door on the left was open, and she crept through it with relief, but didn't recognize the wide hall she found herself in. A large, rather faded tapestry covered one wall, and an ancient wooden chair stood in one corner. There were doors at both ends, but no clue which one led to the busier part of the castle.

Stella hurried to the nearest door and peeped through it. It scraped on the floor as she pushed it open a crack and her heart almost stopped when she found herself peering into what was obviously a chapel. Tall candles burned on a small altar and the smell of incense wafted from a censer above it. The morning sun lit up a series of jewellike stained-glass windows, strung amid carved columns like stones in a necklace.

Worse yet, three black-clothed bodies knelt at the altar—the "aunts"—deep in morning prayer. She shrank back from the door, but it was too late. One of them—Lilli—had already turned.

"Stella." Her voice rang through the sacred space, rooting Stella to the spot like one of the carved statues above the altar.

Shoes in hand, she felt her face flush purple as all three heads turned to stare at her.

"Come join us for Matins." For the first time she noticed the priest, a shadowy figure near the altar. Was this the right time to explain that she'd been raised Lutheran? She gulped and smiled. She was probably supposed to cross herself or curtsy or some of the things she'd seen in films, but right now she just wanted to die.

"Sorry, wrong room." She backed away, shame pulsing through her veins, hoping they hadn't seen too much of her crumpled dress. Maybe they wouldn't put two and two together. What kind of woman would they think her if they knew she'd slept with Vasco on her second night at the palace?

She ran a hand through her tangled hair and scurried in the opposite direction, where she found herself in the great armaments chamber, facing the suit of armor she'd so readily stripped to don last night. What happened to her when Vasco was around? Normally she was a modest and reasonably sensible person.

Footsteps on the stone outside the room made her sink into a corner. Luckily the spotlights were turned off and she pressed herself against the wall beside a polished silver suit of armor until the sound disappeared into the distance.

This time she put her shoes on before venturing out again. At least then she could pretend she was up and dressed—if inappropriately—for the day, rather than creeping about in last night's rumpled finery. She found her way back to the suite she shared with Nicky without too much trouble. The door to Nicky's adjoining room was open and the sitter—a girl who worked in events planning—was asleep in an armchair next to the bed. Stella cringed at the realization that at least this one person would know exactly what she'd been up to last night.

Nicky was still sweetly asleep in the bed they'd made up for him, clutching the dinosaur Vasco gave him.

I'm so sorry, Nicky. I don't know what I was thinking. What happened last night would certainly complicate things. Would it develop into some kind of romantic relationship? Or was it just a one night fling?

The latter would be awful. She'd rather not have known how astonishing and enjoyable good sex could be. And the thought of not being able to kiss Vasco again…

She shook her head, trying to clear it, as she walked back into her room. For now she had to keep going. She ruffled the bed, as if she'd just climbed out of it, then went into the adjoining bathroom for a shower. She almost laughed but the sight of her flushed face and wild hair in the mirror made it shrivel in her throat.

Everyone would know. And she couldn't help thinking that's exactly what Vasco intended. He'd been hugging her and fondling her and flirting with her since they got here, apparently keen for people to think they were an item. Maybe he didn't want anyone to find out that he donated the royal seed to a sperm bank. That wouldn't go over too well with his devout Catholic "aunties."

Stella climbed into the stream of steamy water and wished she could scrub away her guilt and embarrassment at being so quick to jump into bed with him. He started it!

This time she did laugh, and when she emerged from the shower, she felt much better. She was also relieved to see that the sitter had left, so who knew, maybe her rumpled sheet ruse could have worked, too?

She took Nicky down for breakfast, hoping to finish quickly and go hide among the books—even though that would mean facing the "aunts" again so she could place Nicky in their care—before Vasco came down. She gulped hard when she saw him sitting at the table, biting into a slice of melon.

He rose to his feet with a mischievous smile when she entered. He held her gaze just a little longer than appropriate, then glanced down at Nicky and said something in Catalan.

Nicky smiled. "*Hola,* Papa."

Stella stared at him. Now he was saying complete sentences in a foreign language? Not to mention calling this virtual stranger Dad. Vasco grinned, those inviting dimples puckering his tanned skin.

"Come join me." He gestured at the chair beside his for Stella. "I bet you're hungry." His eyes flashed in a way that made her belly quiver and her face heat. Was he trying to embarrass her? Probably not. He was just being Vasco.

She rounded the table, still holding Nicky's hand, and settled him into the chair next to Vasco. Better to have some distance between them. As soon as the child was seated, however, Vasco moved up to her and pressed his lips to hers. Too startled to protest, she found herself kissing him right over Nicky's head. Desire roared to life inside her, and she was blinking and breathless when she finally managed to pull back.

She couldn't help glancing nervously about to see if any of the staff were there.

"You look radiant."

Hopefully that's not because I'm pregnant. Now was not the time to ask if he'd used anything, though. She was furious with him for kissing her in front of Nicky—not that he'd noticed—and anyone else who might walk in.

"I'm not sure what got into me," she murmured, avoiding his gaze.

"I am." His secretive smile only stoked the infuriating fires burning inside her. He handed her a plate of fruit. "You need to rebuild your strength."

"My stamina is just fine, thank you." She took a seat on the far side of Nicky and primly spread her napkin on her lap.

"I'm tempted to make you prove it." He took another

bite of melon, sinking his teeth in with obvious gusto. The gesture made her hips wriggle.

How could he carry on like this in front of his own innocent son? Obviously the man had no scruples. She reached for a piece of toasted muffin from a plate in the center of the table and spread it with butter. Vasco chattered away to Nicky in Catalan as if they were having a conversation. Stella almost dropped her knife when Nicky replied, "*Sì*, Papa."

"Nicky, that's fantastic. You're learning to speak a new language."

"Of course he is." Vasco rubbed Nicky's blond hair, messing it up. "It's his native tongue."

"He does seem to be picking it up surprisingly fast. He barely said a word until this month."

"Because he was speaking the wrong language." He spoke to Nicky again in Catalan. Stella couldn't make out what he said, but Nicky laughed.

A knot formed in her stomach and she realized she felt left out. Which was ridiculous. She could learn Catalan, too, even if it wasn't intricately woven into her DNA.

"Today I'll take Nicky for a tour of the town while you work on your books." Vasco took another bite of melon. It was a declaration rather than a suggestion.

She tensed. "He might get anxious being away from me."

"Don't worry. If he fusses I'll bring him right back." He stroked Nicky's tiny chin with his thumb and spooned in a mouthful of Nicky's favorite oatmeal that one of the staff had magically appeared with. "And we'll come play with your books."

"Great. Bring some crayons. Nicky can decorate you with gold leaf."

"I like that idea. This shirt is a bit dull." He glanced down at his well-cut black shirt. "But we'll let you get some work done first."

Why did she trust him completely with Nicky? She wanted to be nervous, or suspicious, but it was hard. She knew that most of the reservations she had concerned herself, not Nicky.

And if this morning's kiss was anything to go by, last night was not a one-night stand.

A week later, little had changed. Nicky was now babbling complete nursery rhymes in Catalan. Stella had plenty of time to lose herself in the demanding but exhilarating world of the ancient library. And she'd slept with Vasco every night.

They always slept in the same room. She'd asked again whose room it was, and he always replied that it was "theirs." Vasco was never there when she awoke. Her feelings on this had developed from surprise into disappointment, but she didn't like to whine about it. They'd only been involved for one week, so she was hardly in a position to ask him to adjust his lifestyle to her needs. Or maybe she didn't want to make waves when she enjoyed their time together so much. Now at least she knew the way back to her room.

During the day Vasco was flirtatious and affectionate, treating her like his lover, regardless of who was around. They'd even strolled through the town with Nicky twice, as if they were a real family.

Stella's ears burned all the time. She could imagine the gossip that must result when the nation's dashing young king showed up with a woman and child and no wedding ring in sight. The "aunts" said nothing, just smiled sweetly and doted over Nicky. The staff members were polite and somewhat deferent, treating her as a guest rather than one of themselves, though theoretically at least she was there to do a job.

And there was no discussion about the future. Vasco seemed to operate under the assumption that she and Nicky were there for good, and since it was too early to decide whether they were or not, she didn't ask any pointed questions. Most of the time they were together they were either within earshot of the staff, at dinner for example, or in bed. Neither was the ideal place for a "state of the state" conversation.

The moment Vasco kissed her, all practical concerns melted away and she floated on a cloud of bliss that could be temporary or eternal, her mind and body didn't seem to care. The palace was like a little country in its own right and—busy with Nicky and Vasco and the library—she almost forgot about the rest of the world chugging along all around them.

So it was a rude awakening when a former work colleague in L.A. sent her an abrupt email with the heading "OMG Stella—this you?" and a link to *CelebCrush* magazine's website. Stella clicked the link wondering if she had a job lead. She and the sender had been out for lunch a few times and she knew Elaine, an archivist, had found a new position at the Getty Museum.

The link took her to a headline blaring "Royal Romance?" The tone of the article was breathless. "Dashing King of Montmajor Vasco Montoya has been spotted out on the town with a mysterious

American—and her young child. Rumors are buzzing that he's the dad. Royal mistress, or future wife?" Stella blinked. There was a large picture of her and Vasco, each of them holding one of Nicky's hands, as they walked past a fruit stall in the main square of the town. She was staring at Vasco with a goofy grin on her face, while he looked boldly ahead, all windswept good looks and photogenic charm.

There wasn't any more to the story. Apparently that's what passed for journalism at *CelebCrush* magazine. Not that there was much more to the story in real life.

Her heart pounded beneath her neat yellow blouse as she sat in the library in full view of the elderly caretaker who dusted the volumes daily. Who else might see this? She was tempted to email back, "Nope, not me!" but she couldn't.

Royal mistress or future wife? Cringeworthy. What if Vasco saw this? She clicked away from the page and back to her Yahoo! homepage. At least she'd never heard of this magazine. A little research told her it was based out of Luxembourg, and for all she knew had a circulation of about twenty-five. Still, the fact that Elaine had stumbled across the website out in California was a bit alarming, since she hadn't mentioned Vasco to anyone except her best friend, Karen. She'd told other friends and neighbors she was taking Nicky to Europe for a vacation.

She typed back the words "Out of office autoreply— Stella is busy sleeping with a European monarch, and will attend to your email as soon as possible. Until then, please mind your own business." She wanted to laugh hysterically. Or cry. Then she deleted it all except the first phrase, wrote a more prosaic version and sent it out right away. That at least would keep Elaine from asking for more details.

She slammed the laptop and hurried from the library, unable to sit still, let alone do delicate restoration work. Maybe it was time to ask Vasco where this whole thing was going. It might be nice to know the answer for when a reporter thrust a microphone in her face.

At least she wasn't likely to be pregnant. He'd used condoms on all the subsequent trysts so she probably just hadn't noticed him rolling it deftly on in the excitement of their first encounter.

"Stella." Vasco's voice behind her stopped her in her tracks. "Where are you rushing?" He walked up behind her and slid his arms around her waist. Her belly shuddered with awareness. "To find me, I hope." His deep voice curled into her ear. It was hard to think straight and be practical around Vasco.

"Can we talk about something?" She drew in a breath, trying to steady her nerves.

"We can talk about anything. Astrophysics, the Holy Grail, the works of J.D. Salinger, what to eat for lunch…" He pressed a kiss to the back of her neck and she felt her knees turn to jelly.

"Let's go somewhere private."

"An excellent idea. Let's go to our room."

"No, somewhere without a bed." She couldn't stop the smile that tugged at her mouth even as she spun around to extricate herself from his embrace.

"Tired of beds?" A piratical grin lit his features. "Then we'll head outside. Follow me." He hooked his arm through hers and marched her along the corridor. They exited the palace through a side door and headed down a long, curving flight of stairs onto the hillside below the castle walls.

Grassy hills dotted with sheep and cattle unfurled around them like a rumpled blanket. "Where are we going?" She was glad she wore ballet flats, not heels, as they set out on a narrow track.

"Nowhere." Vasco marched ahead, holding her hand. "Which is one of my favorite places."

"Oh." Now would be a good time for discussion. Nicky was with two of the "aunts" and almost due for his nap, so he wouldn't miss her if she was gone for a while. She cleared her throat. "I'm a little confused about my status here."

"Really? Right now I'd say you're walking." He flashed that pearly grin before turning around to stride ahead again.

"Very funny. I mean the status of me and you."

"Intimate, definitely." He squeezed her hand.

"I know that, but am I…" How did you put this stuff without sounding like a middle schooler? "…your girlfriend?"

"Most definitely."

"Oh." Relief filled her chest. So they were dating. That was something she could understand.

"And much more than that. You're the mother of my child. We're a family." His dark gaze was meaningful, serious.

The complicated part again. Vasco seemed to assume that Nicky tied them together permanently, no matter what else happened. Which he did, of course, but did that mean they were going to get married?

On less than a month's acquaintance she wasn't brave

enough to ask that. Did she even want to marry him and abandon her freewheeling single life?

Yes, of course she did. Her heart sank as she realized how much she'd fallen in love with him in such a short time. He'd swept her right off her sensible shoes and deposited her here in his fairy kingdom, where he spent hours seducing her to shocking new heights and depths of sensual pleasure. Montmajor was a peaceful and lovely place, with seemingly no poverty or social unrest, and was less than two hours by plane to nearly every capital in Europe. And then there was a lifetime of satisfying work—probably several lifetimes, in fact—restoring all those magnificent books.

But did Vasco intend to make her his queen, or was the "royal mistress" scenario more realistic?

In her heart, she knew the answer. "Why don't we sleep in my room or your room? Why the round chamber?"

"That's a special place just for us."

"But my bedroom is lovely, and I wouldn't need anyone to listen for Nicky overnight if we were right next door."

"You might get tired of finding me in your bed."

Or you might get tired of me. "Why do you always leave in the night?" She'd never dared to ask before.

Vasco squeezed her hand again, still walking. "I do business in Asia, and that's the best time to make phone calls. I wouldn't want to disturb you."

She frowned. It was a good reason, but not entirely convincing. "I can sleep through anything, you really don't need to leave."

"It's easier if I'm in my office." He picked up the

pace a bit as they climbed a small hill, and she had to struggle to keep up. "It's all quite tiresome."

"If it was tiresome, you wouldn't do it. I know you too well already."

He laughed. "Okay, I enjoy my businesses. I can't just sit around on the throne all day gassing with the citizens. I need new challenges."

That's what worries me.

The round room with all its windows was their room—which he could leave at any time to take up in a different room with someone else.

"Is the palace always this quiet? I mean, do you not have to entertain foreign dignitaries and that kind of thing?"

Vasco slowed. "I didn't want to scare you off by thrusting you into the middle of a social whirl, so I told my events planner to keep things light while you settled in. Are you ready for some more excitement?"

"Um, I don't know." She wasn't wild about the prospect of being surrounded by medal-laden dignitaries or glossy-haired princesses. What would they think of a simple girl from suburban L.A.?

She straightened her back. She didn't have anything to be embarrassed about. She was educated and intelligent and could hold a conversation. As an American, she wasn't intimidated by blue blood or piles of wealth. It would be interesting to meet different people. "Sure, why not?"

At a social event he'd have to introduce her as something. Then maybe she'd know where she stood. *My fiancée,* perhaps?

"Then we'll send out some invitations." Vasco

raised a brow. "Though I admit I'd rather keep you all to myself."

He pulled her gently along with him as they climbed another small slope, then they paused at the top. The view was incredible. Hills and mountains all around, including the castle-topped one behind them. There was no sign of civilization.

Stella stared around them. Not even a distant plane in the sky. "I feel like we're all alone in the world." The sun glazed peaks and valleys with pale gold light.

"We are, for now." Vasco's strong features glowed in the warm light.

For now. Those words rang a little ominous in her ears. She'd asked her question about her status and received an answer. She was his girlfriend as well as the mother of his child.

That would just have to do. For now.

She'd been here barely a week, so who was she to start making demands and asking pointed questions when she didn't even know what she wanted. She might tire of Vasco and Montmajor and decide to head home, so it didn't make sense to demand a commitment from him when she wasn't ready to offer one herself.

Why was it so hard to be patient and let events evolve naturally? They'd just started dating. Okay, so it was a little more intense than usual since they lived under the same roof—and had a son—but any relationship was a delicate thing that could suffocate and die under too much pressure. She needed to relax and go with the flow a bit, enjoy the moment, live in the present and let their relationship grow in its own way.

Eight

Nicky was safely tucked up in bed when the first guests arrived. Stella had spent hours getting ready, or at least it seemed like hours. She'd bought a new dress and shoes in the town, with a credit card Vasco gave her and told her to "enjoy." She felt appallingly self-conscious flicking through racks of dresses at the local boutique under the watchful eye of the proprietor, who must know exactly what she was doing with Vasco every night.

She'd said "No, thank you," to the more flirty dresses with low-cut cleavage and plunging backs, and picked a rather demure ice-blue satin dress that fell to her ankles. It draped flatteringly over her curves but didn't reveal too much. Why give them more to gossip about?

"You look beautiful." Vasco's warm breath on her neck made her jump. She stood at the top of the stairs looking down into the foyer, as a well-dressed crowd of visitors trickled in, removing velvet capes and even furs despite the warm fall temperatures. All of the women were stunning, including the older ones, and dressed with the elaborate elegance of people who took seeing and being seen seriously.

"I'm a little nervous." Her palms were sweating and she didn't dare wipe them on her delicate dress.

"Don't be. Everyone's thrilled to meet you."

"Do they know, about Nicky and you and..."

"Only that you're my guest of honor." He kissed her hand, which made the tiny hairs on her skin stand on end. If only this were all over and she could lie in his arms in "their" bed.

She wasn't sure whether to be relieved that the guests didn't know the truth or worried that this meant they could therefore guess and speculate in all directions.

Vasco slid his arm into hers and guided her down the stairs. His proprietary touch silently introduced her as his girlfriend. The bright, winning stares of richly dressed females raked her skin like sharp nails and their tinkling laughter hurt her ears. Still she made her best effort at conversation—people spoke in English most of the time, presumably for her benefit—and managed to keep a smile plastered on her face.

Vasco looked devastatingly handsome in black tie. Somehow he made even the formal dinner jacket look rakish and daring. He touched her whenever they were near, just a brush of his knuckles along her hip, or a dusting of fingers over her wrist. Each time it made her heart leap into her mouth and her skin tingle with awareness.

Hushed voices, especially in Spanish or Catalan, made Stella's face heat. She knew they were wondering and whispering. Did they think her too plain and ordinary for Vasco? Did they suspect a "compelling reason" of some sort to explain his interest in her?

"What brings you to Montmajor?" asked a woman about her age, with short dark hair swept into a glossy updo and a curious expression on her carefully made-up face.

"The library." Stella smiled as sweetly as possible. "I'm a book restorer and the chance to work with these ancient volumes is a dream come true." Ha. Didn't even have to fib.

The woman smoothed an imaginary wrinkle out of her black lace dress. "Are you enjoying our local hotel?"

Stella swallowed. "Actually it's easier for me to stay here at the palace. Closer to the library." She cleared her throat.

"Of course it is." A slim eyebrow arched upward. "Such a lovely building. With so many bedrooms." Her voice dropped slightly for the last phrase. "I've seen some of them myself." Her dark eyes sparkled a challenge.

"Really?" Stella tried to sound amused. "Are you one of Vasco's old girlfriends?"

A crease appeared between the carefully plucked eyebrows. "Vasco and I are very old friends, but he could never claim I was simply his girlfriend." She said the word as if it tasted nasty.

Stella felt herself shrink a couple of inches. She'd been so pleased and proud to have Vasco call her his girlfriend. "Oh, you were just lovers, then?" She couldn't believe how bold she was being.

And it backfired again.

"Yes." The woman glanced across the room, and

her eyes darkened. Stella ventured a guess that she was looking right at Vasco. "Lovers." A lascivious grin crept across her reddened lips. "That's exactly what we are."

The use of the present tense dried Stella's response on her tongue. She took a hasty swig of champagne.

"Have I embarrassed you?" The velvety voice seemed to mock her. "I am accused of being blunt sometimes. But nothing embarrasses Vasco, I assure you."

She turned and walked away, leaving Stella staring, openmouthed. This woman obviously considered herself to be Vasco's current lover. Or one of them, at least. Maybe she was housed in some other well-appointed room at the palace. A square turret, perhaps, or an octagon.

She glanced around, looking for Vasco, and spotted him laughing with a bubbly redhead, whose pale breasts practically poured out of her red bustier. Now, that was what a royal mistress should look like.

Stella glanced down at her frosty-colored ensemble. Maybe she would have been better off with more *va-va-voom* so these women might see her as competition. She hated the pointy little spears of jealousy that pricked her as he took the woman's hand and kissed it, just as he'd done with hers earlier that evening.

Vasco was a charmer. A ladies' man. He couldn't help flirting and teasing and seducing women. Which made him utterly unsuited to any kind of lasting relationship.

A rather chinless young man asked her to dance and she accepted, glad of the opportunity to keep busy. They chatted about books and the local language and culture in his halting English while he whirled her around the floor to a brisk waltz. Stella inadvertently looked at Vasco a couple of times, but was never gratified by him staring jealously back. He seemed to be enjoying himself and had probably forgotten she was there.

After midnight and the end of a multicourse buffet dinner she was tempted to sneak upstairs on the pretext of checking on Nicky and not come back. As she slipped out a side door of the ballroom into a quiet corridor, a hand on her arm made her jump.

"I've missed you tonight." Vasco's eyes glittered. "I prefer being alone with you."

"Me, too," she said honestly.

"Let's go to our room."

Her whole body said yes. In the privacy of the round chamber, Vasco peeled off her dress and devoured her with a ravenous gaze that made her feel like the most gorgeous woman on earth. He feasted on her with his tongue and she enjoyed caressing and tasting his whole body. A banquet much more tempting and satisfying than the one downstairs.

By the time they finally made love she was so aroused she thought she'd climax immediately, but Vasco made a meal of delaying and slowing his movements, taking her right to the brink, then pulling back, until she was almost hysterical with passion. They climaxed together then lay breathless and happy in each other's arms.

No one else mattered. How could they? When she was alone with Vasco everything was perfect.

But when she woke up later in the night he'd gone. Did he go back to join the party? Possibly even to share his advanced lovemaking skills with another woman? She'd left her son in the care of a sitter night after night for a man who claimed they were a family but offered no permanent commitment.

Sooner or later riding this emotional roller coaster was going to catch up with her.

Vasco returned to the party feeling a buzz that didn't come from the vintage Montmajor wines they enjoyed. Time with Stella always left him feeling refreshed and glowing with good cheer.

"Hey, Vasco." His old friend Tomy called to him from near the bar. "I thought we'd lost you for a while there."

"I had some urgent business." He took a glass of champagne from a waiter.

"I noticed. The American girl seems to have quite a hold on you." Tomy raised a blond brow.

"She does indeed." He sipped the bubbly liquid, which only echoed the fizzing of arousal that still pumped through his system. "She's the mother of my son."

Tomy's eyes widened. "So the rumors are true."

"Every word of them. Little Nicky has brought life to the palace and so much joy to all of us."

"Why didn't any of us know about him?"

"It's complicated. I didn't know about the boy until recently. I'm having to move carefully and take my time."

"You will marry her, won't you?" Tomy looked skeptical even as he asked the question.

Vasco's muscles tightened. "You know the Montoya men aren't cut out for marriage."

"That's never stopped them before. You know the people of Montmajor will expect it of you."

"I've spent my life defying expectations and I don't plan to stop now. I have no wish to marry anyone."

"What does the girl think about this?"

Vasco frowned. "We haven't discussed it. Like I said, it's early days, and she's a freethinking American who values her independence. She's not looking for a man to marry."

They hadn't discussed it, mostly because despite the intimate tie of Nicky, they were just getting to know each other. How many people started discussing marriage after a month? Usually people dated for years before committing these days. She probably didn't know what she wanted yet any better than he did.

Tomy's lips curved into a smile. "So you intend to keep her here as some kind of concubine?"

"No!" He took a swig of his champagne. "Of course not."

"A lover, then."

Vasco took in his friend's amused expression. "Yes, a lover. Why not?"

"Because women are never satisfied with simply being a lover. Maybe it won't happen this week, or this month, or even this year, but sooner or later she'll want some kind of commitment from you, in the form of a ring. Especially since there's a child involved."

"I'll keep her happy." He'd found that a kiss soon dissolved any tension or confusion that arose between him and Stella.

Tomy gave him a wry smile. "For a while you will, then she'll want to marry you."

"A fate to be avoided at all costs." Vasco glanced around at the crowded room. At five in the morning the party was still going strong. "Marriage ruins all good relationships. How many of the married couples in this room don't despise each other? They all go out to parties so they can dance and flirt with other people. The wedding day is when a relationship starts a perilous downhill journey to hatred and resentment."

"Your parents were married for more than forty years."

"And despised each other for every second of it. They only married because my dad was forced into it when she became pregnant with my brother. They may have even loved each other once but there was no evidence of that during my childhood."

"Your father did like to share his affections."

Vasco snorted. "With every woman in Montmajor. My mother only put up with it because she hated scandal and drama."

Tomy shrugged. "That's how it goes. You marry the pretty mother, then continue to enjoy extracurricular activities. No need for the fun to end because you find a queen. Have your cake and eat it too, as the Americans say."

Vasco shuddered. "No, thanks. Too much cake will rot your teeth and clog your arteries. There are some Montoya traditions I mean to break with."

"We noticed when we saw your proclamation making relations legal between unmarried couples." Tomy grinned. "Very romantic."

"There's no reason to make the mother of my child a criminal."

"You're such a sweet guy." Tomy shoved him playfully. "No wonder every woman in Western Europe has the hots for you. You do know all the other girls will take your unmarried status to be an open invitation."

"If I got married they'd just see it as an intriguing

challenge." Vasco raised a brow. "I think I'm safer single."

Tomy shook his head. "If only I was you."

The ball, with its large and gossipy guest list, set rumors buzzing round Europe. Stella found herself drawn to the websites of paparazzi rags which linked her name with Vasco's and speculated openly about Nicky.

It was humiliating to know that people all over the world could ooh and ahh and guess over their romance—and she didn't know any more about where it was headed than they did.

"You're taking it too seriously," protested Karen, when she phoned her late one night. She knew Vasco would be waiting for her in "their room" and she hated herself for being so eager to head there. "Let loose and enjoy yourself."

"Trust me, I have been. That's half the problem. If I had any discipline I'd confront him and ask him where this is going."

"Why don't you just let things take their own course?"

"I'm trying." She sighed. "But I have a feeling we'll carry on like this forever."

Karen laughed. "What's wrong with that? It sounds like you're having a fabulous time."

"I came here to Montmajor so Vasco could get to know his son. I've done everything his way and I've even discovered that I love it here. But I can't stay here, sleeping with him every night, as some kind of live-in girlfriend."

"Why not? Sounds perfect to me."

Stella stretched herself out on the bed in her own room. "I guess I'm not cut out for prolonged dating. I must be old-fashioned. Remember how I was always trying to get Trevor to go one step further?"

"That's because you wanted kids."

"Yes, but I also wanted to get engaged, and married. Does that make me strange?"

"No, it makes you boringly normal. Don't be boringly normal. Seize life by the horns and Vasco by the…well, whichever bit sticks out most."

"You're horrible. I don't know why I even called you." She couldn't help smiling as she let her head rest on the pillows. "And of course that's exactly what I'll go do the moment I hang up this phone."

"Thank goodness. I'd hate to think of him going to waste. I saw the pics of you on the *Hello* website and he's seriously droolworthy."

"You're looking at those websites, too?"

"Human interest. Those of us who don't have a life of our own live vicariously through the exploits of lucky ladies like you."

"All I wanted was to quietly raise my son and restore books."

"Now you're doing both of those and sleeping with the hottest guy in Europe. Oh, and he's a king. I'm crying into my coffee for you."

"Be serious. I have to decide whether to stay here with Nicky, or bring him back to the States. Vasco wants me to stay, but I've already decided that I can't live here as his lover indefinitely. It's not fair to me or to Nicky. We've been here a month and I'm sure it's starting to feel like home to Nicky. I need to know whether it will be our permanent home, or if I'm just another in a long line of girlfriends."

"A month isn't a very long time."

"It's been long enough for me…" *To fall in love.* She didn't want to say it out loud. Right now it was just her secret.

A month might not be much in a conventional relationship where you meet the person for a date once or twice a week, but they were living together and saw each other all day long, not to mention all night long. Well, except those lonely early mornings. It was a fast-forward kind of relationship, and in the public eye, too. If total strangers wondered and gossiped about where they were headed, she'd be foolish not to want some concrete answers, too.

"What, you're bored with him as a boy toy already?"

"I wish."

"Uh-oh. I think I get it now. You're getting in deeper than you imagined and you want to know whether to go all the way or pull back while you can still save yourself."

"You have amazing insight. I've never felt like this about anyone, including Trevor." Not even close. "And I know from my years of living on this planet that this kind of relationship ends in marriage or tears."

"Or both."

"Thanks for your support." Stella rolled over. Vasco would wonder where she was if she didn't leave soon. Maybe she should keep him guessing for a change, so he wouldn't take her for granted.

"Just ask him."

Stella laughed. "You make it sound so easy. Hey,

Vasco, will we be getting married or are you saving yourself for someone hotter?"

"Leave out the last part and you'll be fine. Or ask him to marry you."

Stella sucked in a breath. She could never do that. The prospect of rejection was far too agonizing. But there was another possibility. "Maybe I could ask him if he intends for Nicky to be his heir. If he doesn't marry me, then Nicky doesn't inherit. At least not if Vasco has another child."

"Go for it. That could be a good deciding factor on whether you stay. Does Nicky seem happy there?"

"Very. He's gone from being shy and almost nonverbal to the most babbling and outgoing little boy. I think he loves being doted on by caring relatives rather than competing with lots of little go-getters in day care. The slower pace of life here works nicely for him."

"And for you."

She hesitated. "I do love it here. It's a bit like living in a five-star hotel all the time. The people are so lovely and I have work most restorers could only dream of."

"And Vasco."

"For now."

"Go ask him." Karen sounded firm. "Just find out what's in his mind. And don't call me back until you do!"

The abrupt dial tone sent a frisson of anxiety through Stella. She peeled herself off the bed and slipped her feet into her shoes. Vasco would be waiting for her with that warm, seductive smile on his sensual mouth and a twinkle of mischief in his eyes. She had to get her question—whatever it might be—out before she fell under the spell of his touch and his kiss and all sensible thought retreated into oblivion.

She passed one of the porters in the hallway and nodded a greeting. She wasn't even too embarrassed anymore about running into people on her nightly perambulations. Surely everyone in the palace knew what went on between her and Vasco. No doubt they accepted it as a normal and natural part of life in a royal house.

With a royal mistress.

She didn't feel like a "girlfriend," whatever that was. She lived in his palace and ate his food and wore designer clothes he paid for. Girlfriends took care of their own rent and phone bills and went out for nights on the town with their other friends. She was a kept woman right now, even if she did have a job that paid far more than the going rate.

"El meu amor." Vasco's deep voice greeted her from the darkness of the round chamber. *My love.* Did he feel the same way she did?

She closed the door behind her and searched for Vasco's moonlit outline on the four-poster bed. Silver rays picked out his muscled torso and proud, handsome face. He lay naked on the covers, arms outstretched to welcome her. "Come here, I'll undress you."

She steeled herself against a desire to climb right into his embrace and surrender herself. "I've been here a month." Better spit it out before she succumbed. "I want to know where Nicky and I stand. Long-term, I mean."

"You live here and it's your home."

Her heart beat faster and her courage started to fail

her. Did she want to risk losing what they had? "I can't be your girlfriend forever."

"You're far more than that."

"I know, I'm the mother of your son, but what does that mean for us in the future?" She straightened her shoulders. "Will we marry? Will Nicky be king one day?"

He laughed. "Already looking ahead to when I'm dead and gone?"

"No." The word shot out. How rude she seemed with her demands. "No, not at all." The prospect of Vasco dying was unimaginable. A more vital and indestructible man would be hard to find. "It's just that…I want us to be a real family and…"

Her words trailed off. *I want us to live happily ever after.* Her face heated and she was grateful for the darkness. There, she'd said it. Put all her pathetic hopes and dreams out into the dark air, where they now hung in silence that stung her ears.

"Stella." He rose off the bed and moved toward her. "We are partners in every way."

She braced herself as he came close. The warm masculine scent of him drifted into her nostrils, taunting her. "I don't want to be a royal mistress. People are talking. All the papers are speculating. It's embarrassing."

"People always talk and write about members of the royal family. It's just part of life in the public eye. There's no need to read that stuff or trouble yourself with it. Our life is ours alone and no one else matters."

He slid a powerful arm around her waist and her belly shuddered in response. Why did he always sound so sensible and make her feel she was being silly?

She tried to picture the worst-case scenario. "Do you plan to marry someone else one day? Another aristocrat perhaps?"

Vasco's throaty laugh filled her ears. "Never. Never, never, never. Our son will be king and you will always be my queen." He pressed his lips to hers and a flash of desire scattered her thoughts. "Let's enjoy tonight."

His hand covered her breast through her thin blouse. Her nipple thickened under his palm and her head tilted back to meet his kiss. How did he always do this to her? Already her hands roamed over the warm, thick muscle of his chest. Again she was intoxicated by the sheer pleasure of the moment.

Maybe she wanted too much. Couldn't it be enough to enjoy life here in this lovely place with a man she was crazy about? Vasco undressed her slowly, working over her body with his tongue. She arched her back, letting herself slide into the ocean of pleasure he created around her. Most women would kill for a lover this sensitive and creative, let alone all the other things she enjoyed in the palace.

She ran her fingertips over the hard line of his jaw, enjoying the slight stubble that roughened his skin. Vasco's eyes gleamed with desire as he looked up at her while sliding her pants off. The chemistry between them was undeniable. She'd never felt anything like it. Would she seriously walk away from Vasco because he didn't plan to marry her?

Her whole body shouted "No!" Vasco took her in his arms and they rolled on the bed together, wrapped up in each other. Her body craved his and judging from his arousal and the soft words he breathed in her ear, the feeling was mutual.

She exhaled with relief as he entered her, and they moved together in a dance of erotic joy that swept them both up into their own world of bliss, where no one else existed. Afterward, she was too tired to think, let alone speak.

But she phoned Karen the next day, as promised.

"He said I'll always be his queen." It sounded pretty promising when you said it out loud like that.

"What more could you want?"

"A wedding date. You remember how Trevor always put me off with excuses and reasons for delay. All that *We're too young. We have our whole lives ahead of us. You can't rush these things.* Maybe he even meant it at first, but he got comfortable with the way things were and decided not the change them."

"Vasco's not Trevor, thank goodness."

"If there's one thing I've learned in the last decade, it's that a man who's determined to dig his feet in can stand like that forever. After we broke up, Trevor got more honest and admitted that he'd never have married me or had a child. He didn't want the responsibility."

"I always told you he was a creep."

"He's comfortable living in a pleasant limbo between carefree boyhood and the responsibilities of family life. He wanted the reassurance of knowing he had a date on Friday, but not the commitment of diapers to change or college fees to pay."

"Or a wife to still cherish and adore when she had silver hair and crow's-feet." Karen chimed in. "He's like my ex. They like to keep the escape clause open."

"I can't live like that. Not anymore. I decided that when I broke up with him and made the choice to start a family by myself. I chose a life on my own terms and embraced it, and I'm not going to turn around and live life on someone else's terms that I don't agree with, and that's what I'm doing right now."

"One month, Stella. It's not exactly the same as nine years."

"That nine years happened one month at a time, because I just kept waiting. Never again. It's worse now because people I don't even know are curious. You should see the headlines—'Royal wife or royal mistress?' It's totally humiliating."

Karen sighed. "I think I could get used to being a royal mistress, if there were enough diamonds involved."

"Oh, stop."

"But I have a crazy idea."

"Knowing you it really will be crazy."

"Listen, if you asked him whether you're getting married and he fobbed you off with some fluff about being his queen, then maybe you can call his bluff."

"How so?" Already a nasty sense of misgiving writhed in her gut.

"If you told one of those gossip rags that you and Vasco were getting married, would he deny it?"

Stella shrugged. "Probably not. He'd just nod and smile and say 'one day' or something like that."

"But what would he do if you told them you definitely weren't getting married?" Her voice had a calculating tone.

"You've lost me."

"He's used to running his life the way he wants it and having everyone follow along nicely. If you, the mother of his child and heir and the woman he sees as his queen, says she won't marry him, he's bound to protest, right? Men always want what they can't have. It's reverse psychology."

"Well…" Karen had a point. He probably would be upset by an outright refusal.

"And he'll want to prove you wrong."

"By proposing and making me his wife within the week?" She laughed, but the idea was oddly intriguing. "I don't know, Karen. It's not my style."

"You've tried your style and it's not working. If he won't discuss your future with you in private, flush him out in the open. At least then you'll get your answer one way or the other. If you really want it, that is."

Stella bit her lip. "You're right. If he's not going to marry me I'd rather know now, so I can move on with my life. Your idea is crazy, but it just might work."

Nine

Getting the information to the press was easy. Stella had figured out that the "mystery" gossip editor of the local paper was a rather glamorous older widow who lived on an estate near the town. Anything she printed had a way of getting out into the mainstream media, too. Probably because she couldn't resist telling everyone she knew when she found a piece of actual gossip.

Since this woman, Mimi Reyauld, was constantly fishing for new items, she would be easy to leak it to. After only three expeditions to the local town for magazines or a new toy for Nicky, Stella managed to "run into" her in the market square.

"Stella, my dear, don't you look lovely?" Mimi had a bouffant blond 'do that didn't move in the wind. "How is that gorgeous boy of yours?"

"Nicky's having his afternoon nap. It's a great time for me to come stretch my legs and do some shopping."

Mimi's gaze raked her hand. "He's such a dear. I'm sure he'll be the spitting image of his father one day."

Stella smiled. She hadn't openly acknowledged Nicky as Vasco's, but she knew people assumed he was. Clearly Mimi was fishing. "I'm sure he will. Are you coming to the masked ball on Friday?" Almost every adult in Montmajor was invited to the legendary annual festivities and the palace was abuzz with preparations.

"I wouldn't miss it for anything. Vasco throws such wonderful parties." She leaned in and her expensive scent stung Stella's nostrils. "When will we be celebrating your engagement?"

"Engagement?" Fear made her pulse skitter and she pushed back her hair with her ringless hand. "Vasco and I have no plans to be married." So far she'd said nothing but the honest and sad truth.

Mimi's eyes widened. "Come now, dear. Don't be modest. Everyone in Montmajor can see the two of you are madly in love."

Stella's tongue dried. They could? How embarrassing. She knew it was true for her, if not for Vasco. "I'm not sure where they're getting that idea. Vasco and I won't be getting married." It hurt to say it out loud, but if that was going to be the truth, better to find out now rather than months, or years, down the road when it would be harder to extricate herself from the awkward situation.

"Oh." Mimi's mouth formed a red circle of surprise. No doubt she'd been hoping to be the first with the engagement scoop because she looked disappointed.

"I imagine there will be a lot of other ladies who'll be happy to hear that." She hoisted her chic little bag higher on her shoulder. "And I look forward to seeing you at the ball, though I dare you to try to recognize me in my mask." Mimi air kissed and walked away, leaving Stella feeling a little stunned.

She'd done it. Other things she'd mentioned to Mimi even in passing had almost invariably shown up in print—there just wasn't that much good gossip in Montmajor—so it was inevitable this latest tidbit would, too. It seemed very European to have the local gossip columnist be an old friend of the family.

That night with Vasco she felt like a traitor. He hadn't sworn her to secrecy about their relationship but she'd been very discreet until now, not telling anyone except Karen what was—or wasn't—going on. Even his inviting embrace and his spine-tingling kisses didn't entirely banish the sense of guilt she felt for talking about their relationship in public.

The next morning, sure enough, the story had made it into the gossip column, and by the afternoon it had spread like wildfire through the European tabloids, culminating in headlines like "Dashing Vasco Montoya Still Europe's Most Eligible Bachelor."

It didn't take long until Vasco noticed.

"What's the meaning of this?" He brandished the local paper. "You told Mimi we're not getting married."

"Mimi?" She played innocent. "What does she have to do with the local paper?"

"She's Senyora Rivel, the gossip columnist. Everyone in Montmajor knows that."

"And you still invite her to the palace?"

"She's a sweet old lady who never writes anything harmful. But why did you say this?" His eyes flashed. She'd never seen him look so serious. Not exactly angry, but...annoyed.

Part of her was excited and grateful that he cared. "It's the truth. We're not getting married."

"Says who?" He strode toward her.

"We've made no plans. Every time I ask you about the future you start kissing me or change the subject." She couldn't believe how bold she was being. She'd never be capable of it if Nicky's future wasn't at stake, too. "Since apparently everyone else is talking about our marriage plans, I thought I'd better start setting them straight."

Confusion furrowed his noble brow. "I think our relationship should be between us, and not anyone else's business."

"I didn't make a proclamation, I just had a short chat with Mimi at the market. Since it's the truth, there's no harm done."

His eyes narrowed slightly. "Now everyone will want to know why we're not getting married."

Her heart contracted. He'd now confirmed what she said. Part of her wanted to die right now on the spot, or sink into the stone floor. She managed to keep a straight face. At least now she knew where she really stood.

"Then tell them the truth." She swallowed hard. "Tell them we're not in love." She held her breath, while her chest ached with hope and despair and she silently begged him to argue with her and say that he loved her with all his heart and soul.

But he didn't. He simply stared at her for one long, searing moment, then turned and sauntered away.

Crushed, Stella shrank against the nearest wall as she heard his footsteps recede into the distance. She'd hoped her little media revelation would be the catalyst that would draw them together. Instead it had just the opposite effect. At least she had an elaborate silver-sequined mask to hide her tears behind at the ball that night.

Vasco, masked like everyone else, stood amidst the flow of arriving guests. Anonymity added a certain feverish excitement to the occasion, and champagne flowed like a summer rainstorm. Anger still thudded through him like distant thunder. He'd been surprised by how much Stella's words wounded him.

He hadn't held up a magnifying glass to his feelings for Stella, but they were intricate and involving. She'd come here as the mother of his son but transformed into far more. Their nights together wove a web of passion that bound them tightly, even when Nicky was asleep on the other side of the castle. He loved her company and craved it when he was busy working or held up with other tasks.

Stella had quickly become the center of his existence and he shared his life with her in the most intimate way imaginable. Only to have her coldly deny their relationship in public.

There was no denying that he'd pushed back a little when she'd asked about the future. They'd known each other a short while and the future was a very long time. There'd be plenty of time to make decisions about that later. He'd been overwhelmed by the new emotions crowding him since he learned about Nicky, let alone his feelings for Stella. He needed time to adjust to the reality that his family had expanded and these new people were now closer to him than his own parents or siblings had been.

Then she came right out and said that they didn't love

each other? Something unfamiliar and painful gnawed at his gut.

He took a swig of his champagne and listened for the strains of music flowing over the crowds from the adjoining ballroom.

"Cavaller." A female masked in shimmering green sequins greeted him in the old style.

"At your service, madame." He kissed her hand, which was soft and scented, but not Stella's.

He knew exactly where Stella was right now. Standing on the far side of the room in a blue dress and matching mask. He'd determined to ignore her all night—shame he couldn't take his eyes off her.

The hurt and fury raging in his blood made him almost want her to flirt with another man so he could be angry and call her a tease and despise her for cheating on him. But so far she'd spoken only to women and men over the age of seventy.

"Your masked ball is a sensation, as always." The lady in green had a deep, seductive voice that he didn't quite recognize.

"You're too kind. Would you honor me with a dance?"

Her dark eyes glittered behind her mask. "I'd be delighted."

He slid his arm through hers and risked a glance at Stella to see if she'd noticed. Irritation rippled through him that she was deep in conversation with one of the town's elderly librarians and not paying any attention to him.

He tightened his arm around the waist of his companion's green silk dress and guided her to the dance floor. He gave the band's conductor the cue for a tango, and led her into the middle of the crowd as the first sultry strains swept through the room. He didn't need Stella. He'd always enjoyed a full and exciting life and there was nothing to stop him continuing that. Stella had as much as given him permission.

He twirled his partner and dipped her, and she flowed with the movements like hot butter, a smile curving on her red-painted mouth. Another lightning-fast glance at Stella revealed that she was watching him.

Ha. He pressed his partner against him and executed several quick steps and another turn that made her dress sweep around him. His muscles hummed with the sheer joy of movement. Another glance confirmed that Stella's eyes were still fixed on them, and he fought a triumphant smile. She might not love him, but she was certainly paying attention.

After the dance his green-masked partner gratefully accepted a glass of champagne and offered to remove her mask and reveal her face.

"Don't take off your mask," he murmured. "Tonight is for mysteries and magic."

"But I know who you are," she protested. "Doesn't it seem fair that you should know who I am?"

"Perhaps life isn't supposed to be fair."

"I suppose that's a good attitude for a king. Not everyone can inherit a nation." She hesitated and leaned closer. "Is it true that you've already sired an heir?"

"It is." He'd never deny Nicky.

"Then you've chosen your bride, as well." Her eyes shone with curiosity.

"Who knows what the future will bring." He picked up her hand and kissed it. His intention was to taunt Stella, though he managed to resist glancing at her to see if she was watching. He could feel her gaze on him like a touch.

Even if she didn't love him, Stella was deeply attracted to him and he'd be sure to stoke the fire of her passion when they were alone later tonight. In the meantime, apparently flirting and dancing with other women was an excellent aid to focusing her attention.

"Hello." A statuesque girl in silver with a long fall of blond hair and a pouting mouth touched his arm. "What a wonderful party."

He turned readily away from Ms. Green. "I'm pleased you're enjoying yourself."

"Very much so." Her eyes lit up inside her mask. "And I've always wanted to meet you. I'm—" She had a French accent.

He pressed a finger to her lips. "Don't spoil the enigma. Let's dance." He didn't want to know who she was. He took her hand and led her into the crowd of dancers, where he whirled around with her, losing himself in the pleasure of the dance. Stella was only one woman in a world of millions.

So why was she the only one he wanted?

Stella shrank further into the shadows each time she saw Vasco smile at another woman, or kiss her hand. At first she couldn't take her eyes off him when he danced. He moved with muscular grace and the skill of a professional dancer. Women seemed to melt into his embrace, and their besotted smiles dazzled her like car headlights when she made the mistake of looking at them.

Did she really think she could be his one and only? Even if she hadn't infuriated him with her little press leak, he'd still be dancing and flirting with other girls in his role as host. Women flocked to him like iron filings to a magnet. He wasn't just rich and royal, he was gorgeous and mischievous and charming and obviously enjoyed their company. No wonder he didn't want to marry her. Why would he give up all this to spend his life with her?

Far too much to hope for. She was an ordinary book restorer from an ordinary suburb who lived a quiet, humdrum and happy existence until Vasco swept into it like the Santa Ana winds and made her realize how much she'd been missing until now.

Thank goodness for the mask. It was hot and itchy but at least it hid her expression of despair. She'd been shamefully lax about looking for jobs—too busy enjoying her work here—and had barely kept in touch with anyone because she didn't want to reveal too much about her situation. Maybe she just couldn't bear to think about leaving.

And there was Nicky. Instead of being gone eight hours at a stretch with him in day care, she could spend time with him every hour or two when she took a break, and in the meantime he received individual attention from people who adored him. They'd even arranged for some staff to bring their young children to the palace so he had playmates to laugh and sail his boat with. His vocabulary had gone from less than five words to full sentences in both English and Catalan, and his joy in his daily existence was undeniable. No more tears as she left him at day care, or endless colds that he picked up from the other kids.

Could she pull him from this peaceful existence that

suited him perfectly and drop him back into their old hectic routine again? If she could cven find a job.

A waiter offered her champagne and she shook her head. She needed to keep it clear as both of their lives depended on the decisions she'd make now.

She didn't relish the idea of Nicky being king, but it didn't seem like such a hard life either, if things did work out that way. And if they didn't, because Vasco married another woman...

Fierce jealousy twisted her insides. It was physically painful to watch him laughing and talking with other girls, let alone marrying them and having children. At least if she went back to the States she wouldn't have to see him and be tormented by what she wanted but couldn't have. She knew Vasco had no legal rights to claim Nicky or even see him again. If she chose to, she could leave here tonight with her son and never look back.

The prospect made her cold. She knew in her heart she could never do that to Nicky, or to Vasco. Now that the father she hadn't intended for her son to have had manifested himself in their lives, she could see how much Nicky adored and looked up to him. Vasco himself had opened his home to them with such generosity and goodwill, and had thrown himself wholeheartedly into the role of father. In all honesty that was one of the reasons she'd fallen so hard in love with him, and she'd rather die than take his son away from him.

So she and Nicky had to stay.

A furtive glance across the crowded room found Vasco in the arms of yet another woman. Tall and wrapped in a slinky purple dress, her white mask flashing bright as her smile. Stella grimaced beneath her own festive disguise. She'd have to tell him that from now on they could no longer be intimate. She'd be an employee, like all the others, not his lover. She wasn't cut out to be a royal mistress and she should know by now that she'd never be anything else if she stayed here.

Clutching her sadness like a cloak about her, she slipped out of the room and into a quiet corridor. Vasco wouldn't even notice she was gone. He hadn't said a word to her since the party began. No doubt he wanted to put an end to any rumors about them being involved, let alone married.

She pulled off her mask, climbed up to her room and peered into Nicky's adjoining one where tonight's sitter, one of the palace cleaning staff, sat in a chair reading a thriller. "You can head off for the night. I'll be here." She managed a shaky smile.

"Are you sure? I don't mind staying until morning." The young girl looked a little bashful. Everyone in the palace knew that all-night sitters were the order of the day because Stella spent her nights in the round tower with Vasco.

But no more. "No thanks, I'll be here."

She washed her face and put on the cotton pajamas she hadn't worn in as long as she could remember. The bed felt cold as she climbed into it. She'd grown so used to having a warm body next to her that the sheets seemed empty and uninviting without one.

She'd get used to it. She hugged her arms around herself and tried not to picture Vasco downstairs dancing with beautiful masked women. Would he take another of them to the round tower tonight? Or would he expect her to meet him there regardless of their argument?

Rolling over, she pulled the covers over her head to block out the strains of music that crept into the room from the party. She'd managed just fine without Vasco for most of her life, and she'd be fine without him for the rest of it. Maybe she'd even find another man, a more sensible and reliable and ordinary guy with whom she could have a real relationship. Kings weren't really cut out for modern relationships. They too readily expected everyone to be at their beck and call, and she'd certainly obliged so far.

Though after Vasco it could prove very challenging to find anyone else appealing.

She tossed and turned, listening over the faint music for Nicky's sleeping sounds, but she couldn't hear anything. He'd been in bed for hours and was a solid sleeper, so she couldn't even distract herself by humming lullabies or stroking him to sleep. She needed someone to hum her lullabies, but clearly she'd have to make do without.

There was usually a half-finished novel next to her bed for her to dip into at moments like this, but she hadn't slept here for so long that she'd neglected to find one. She could sneak off to the library and bring back something to read—not all the books were ancient manuscripts—but then she'd run the risk of encountering party guests in her pajamas. Or worse, seeing Vasco creeping off to some turret with his mistress-of-the-minute.

No. She'd have to tough it out here in bed. She'd resolved to stare at the dark ceiling until she either fell asleep or passed out, when she heard the door open.

"Who's there?" She sat up in a panic. Hadn't she locked it?

"You didn't come to our room." Vasco's deep voice penetrated the darkness.

Her chest tightened. He'd really expected her to go there after they argued and stayed apart all evening? "I thought I'd better sleep here."

"You're angry with me."

Was that was he wanted? A jealous rage to gratify his male ego? "No, just sleepy." She didn't want him to know how upset she'd been by seeing him with those other women. She didn't even know why. He hadn't done anything but dance with them. She certainly didn't want to give him the satisfaction of letting him know she cared.

"Me too. It's been a tiring night."

The room was too dark for her to see more than his outline, but she heard the sliding sounds of clothing being removed. She held her breath. Did he intend to come climb into her bed without an invitation? Her skin tingled under her cotton pajamas.

She heard something hit the floor—his pants? Her heartbeat quickened and she scanned the darkness. His warm, masculine presence moved through the room toward her. She clutched the covers.

"You can't just come get in bed with me." Her voice sounded shrill, like she was trying to convince herself.

"Why not?"

"I came here to be alone."

"Every time I danced with someone, I was thinking about you." His soft voice crept through the darkness and caressed her. "I pretended I was holding you, moving with you. The masks made it a little easier, but nothing compares with the real thing."

She bit her lip in the dark. Already her muscles softened, forgiving him everything, wanting him close. When she felt his weight tip the mattress, she couldn't bring herself to push him away. Then the covers lifted and he slid underneath. His thighs were warm, rough with hair, and his arms wrapped around her before she could summon the energy to resist. How arrogant of him to assume he'd be welcome! Yet the scent of him disturbed her senses and sent lust sizzling through her.

"You need to take these off." His fingers plucked at the buttons of her PJs. What if she didn't want to take them off? Maybe she did want to sleep?

Her body said otherwise. Already her muscles relaxed and her nipples tightened into peaks. Vasco slid her top off and kissed her firmly on the mouth before licking each nipple with his tongue. Passion stirred deep inside her and she found her hands clutching at his muscle and drawing him closer. Hard and ready, his erection only intensified her arousal.

He'd danced with all those other women, but it was her he came looking for in the darkness, to spend the night with. Her heart sang at the truth of it, and their kisses filled her with feverish hope and joy.

I love you. She wanted to say it but common sense prevented her. Vasco feared commitment—that was obvious—so he might be scared off by declarations of undying love. Still, what wouldn't she give to hear it from him?

He entered her slowly, kissing her with measured passion. His movements were restrained, slow, his hips barely shifting and his hands holding her still, so that she could feel every beat of both their hearts and feel each breath that filled their lungs. They lay there, suspended in time, senses fully engaged and aroused, bodies moving as one. Her anger and hurt had evaporated, replaced by joy and excitement that stirred her body and mind.

Her demand for marriage felt foolish now. What did some official piece of paper matter when it was so obvious they were meant to be together? Vasco didn't have to tell her in mere words that he loved her. She could feel it in his touch, in a language much more subtle and ancient than any of the ones she'd learned to speak.

They started to move again, this time with a fevered energy that made her gasp and shiver with desire. They rolled together on the bed, taking turns driving each other to new heights of arousal and intense emotion. The music from downstairs now seemed an accompaniment to their erotic dance, a celebration of their private passion. None of those people downstairs mattered anymore, just the two of them, traveling further and further out onto a peninsula of bliss.

Her climax swept over her in a cool shiver of ecstasy, and she felt Vasco explode inside her, gripping her with force and murmuring her name over and over again.

I love you. Again the words hovered behind her lips, but she didn't need to say it. She'd told him with her body, as he'd told her. There was no mistaking the connection that joined them. They shared a child, but more they shared something less tangible but just as precious in its own way.

"I missed you tonight." His whispered confession made her smile.

"I missed you, too. I thought you were mad at me."

"I was. Mad at you, mad about you." He kissed her lips softly. "I wanted to make you jealous."

"It worked. I wanted to dance with you."

She gasped as Vasco's strong arms whipped her out of bed and onto her feet. The cool stone shocked her soles, but his arms wrapped around her like a blanket as he guided her into a dance in the dark bedroom. Music still swirled in through the doors and windows, caressing them with its delicate notes. A strong partner, Vasco pressed her against him as he moved across the floor of the large bedroom, whirling her round and round, so light on his feet they might be floating.

With her chest pressed against his, naked and still warm from lovemaking, she followed his motion effortlessly. Eyes closed, she imagined them gliding through the crowds, then through the clouds, a perfect partnership.

"Whatever you wish, my lady." He twirled her one last time, then pulled up her hand to kiss it.

"Except marriage." The words flew out before she could stop them. Immediately she wished she could inhale them back inside her.

Vasco stiffened, still holding her. She felt him draw away, even though he didn't move. She'd broken the spell that held them together with her petty worldly concerns. "You should be glad. You've made it clear that we won't be getting married." His voice was quiet.

She was tempted to say she'd only done it in the hopes that he'd change his mind, but that would just make her look pathetic. If Vasco wanted to marry her, it would just happen. He was like that, a thunderstorm in motion. She'd been swept along on its high winds and pierced by its lightning bolts enough to know that. How else had she ended up living here in a strange country within weeks—days, really—of meeting him?

Now he did pull back a little, putting a couple of inches of darkness between them. "I'd like to formalize my relationship with Nicky. I want to be his true father in the eyes of the law."

Her chest tightened. "I don't imagine that will be too hard since you can change the laws anytime you feel like it."

She could swear she saw his smile gleam, despite the lack of light. It must be quite something to have that much power. Tempting to abuse it. She knew Vasco wasn't a cruel man, but he could be arrogant and demanding. No doubt that came with the territory of being king.

"I think a simple declaration will suffice. And perhaps a law confirming that children born out of wedlock can inherit the throne." He sounded thoughtful.

"I suppose that's just keeping up with the times." He wouldn't even need her consent. The DNA tests had confirmed that he was Nicky's father. She wouldn't try to take Nicky away from him now. Her son adored his tireless and playful father.

"Indeed. And it ensures that one day Nicky will be king."

They weren't even touching now. Their bodies had slipped away from each other, and goose bumps rose on her skin in the night air coming in through the open window. Perhaps it was simply his love for Nicky that brought him to her? Maybe he wanted to make sure she'd stay and this was the only way he knew how. He paid for her loyalty—and for his son's presence in his life—with passion that fired her heart but left his cold.

An ache of despair and loneliness crept over her, extinguishing the joy she'd felt only moments earlier. She turned away from him and climbed back into the bed. "We'd both better get some sleep." He must be anxious to slip away, as he did every night, back to his own realm. Away from her.

She heard him don his clothes in the darkness, even his mask, because she saw the sequins that edged it shimmer in the pale moonbeams that crept around the curtains. "Good night, Stella. Sleep well."

His kiss made her lips hum, and she hated the way her heart squeezed at his touch.

Of course now she wouldn't be able to sleep at all. Not that she could earlier. Being around Vasco was driving her crazy. One minute she was drifting on a tide of joy, sure that she was the happiest woman alive. The next she was alone and filled with anguish, sure that he didn't love her and never would. She could make all the plans and conditions she liked when she was alone, but as soon as she was in Vasco's presence all common sense and resolve evaporated in the heat of passion.

There was no way she could stay here in the palace with him and remain sane.

Ten

The local librarian put her in touch with some owners of nearby private libraries who might want a restorer. She didn't mention that she was also looking to live in. She struck gold with a nearby family who spent most of the year in Paris but had a small estate in Montmajor only a ten-minute drive from the palace. After a phone call and a reference from her old boss in California, they hired her to restore some rare volumes over the next three months. Most importantly, she could live in their villa, which would buy her time to find somewhere permanent to move and give her space to think about her life.

She waited a few days until Vasco went out of town. She knew that if she tried to confront him he'd just wear her down, probably with nothing more than a meaningful look. She'd tried too many times to stand up to him and failed more miserably each time. She needed to make her break when he wasn't there to cajole her out of her decision.

While she waited for him to leave she slept in her own bedroom, alone, with the convenient excuse that it was "that time of the month." She'd felt a mix of relief and disappointment at the realization that she wasn't carrying another of Vasco's babies. And her monthly visitor was welcome protection. If she slept in Vasco's arms at night, she'd lose every last ounce of conviction.

With no possessions other than those in her suitcase, the move required no planning beyond packing some of Nicky's toys into a box and calling a taxi.

"What do you mean, you're leaving?" Aunt Lilli's eyes widened with alarm. Her arms reached for Nicky, who ran immediately into them.

"I'm only moving up the road, to Castell Blanc. I'll be working in their library and living in the house. If you agree, and if Vasco is okay with it, I'd like to bring Nicky here every day to spend time with you."

"Vasco's not going to like this." Aunt Frida pursed her lips and shook her head. "Not at all."

Stella swallowed. "I know, but's too difficult for me to live here. It complicates matters."

"How is it complicated? Vasco is crazy about you." Aunt Mari crossed her arms. "You must marry him."

Stella blinked. "He's made it clear that he won't marry me. Or anyone else, I think. He doesn't like the idea of marriage and said it ruins relationships."

"But you're the one who told Mimi you'd never marry him."

"Only because I knew his opinion already. To be honest I was hoping he'd see it differently, but he's as determined as ever to remain single and I can't live here as some kind of…" She glanced around, then lowered her voice. "Concubine."

Lilli sucked in a breath. "I've had words with him. I've tried to explain to him that you're a nice girl." She hesitated.

Stella pondered that if she was such a nice girl she wouldn't be in a position to be called his mistress.

"He's stubborn," Lilli continued. "Obstinate."

"A typical man," cut in Aunt Frida.

"Perhaps you moving out is for the best. He'll realize what he's missing."

Stella shrugged. She wasn't going to get carried away hoping things would change. People rarely changed. "I want Nicky to grow up with his family, including all of you. I intend for us to stay here in Montmajor, but I need to leave the palace right now, today."

Lilli nodded. "I understand." Still, she looked very sad as she stroked Nicky's cheek. "You'll bring him tomorrow?"

"Without fail. Unless Vasco barricades the castle against me."

"He's not that foolish." Aunt Mari looked down at Nicky. "I do hope he'll see sense before it's too late."

Her feet and her heart felt heavier than her suitcase as she walked through the grand archway out of the palace. Silly, as she hadn't come here to marry him. She also hadn't planned to fall madly in love with him. That was the real reason she had to go. It was just too painful to fall asleep in his arms dreaming of them as a real family, knowing all the while he saw her only as his girlfriend—enjoyable and potentially disposable— and that he had no plans to ever commit to a permanent relationship.

Heck, he wasn't even there when she woke up in the morning!

Maybe if she hadn't waited nine years for a commitment from Trevor—which never came—she'd feel differently, but her life had made her who she was, and she'd sworn she'd never let anyone do that to her again.

"What do you mean she's gone?" Vasco scanned the hallway behind Aunt Lilli. He'd returned from his short trip to Switzerland midday on Sunday, and the palace was eerily silent.

"She moved out four days ago." Lilli pursed her mouth in that disapproving way he remembered from his childhood. "She said it was a personal matter." She raised her brow on the word *personal*. No doubt she didn't want to reveal too many details in front of the staff.

"Come to my study." He strode past her. How could Stella do this? She was happy here in the palace, he knew it.

Though she had been avoiding him for the last week. Her excuse about having her period was convincing at the time but now he grew skeptical. She'd known all along that she was leaving and she wanted to keep her distance.

He flung open the door of his office and ushered Lilli in, then slammed it again. "Nicky, where is he?"

"He's with Stella, of course."

He blew out a curse. "She said she'd stay here. That she liked Montmajor and she knew it was a good place for Nicky to grow up."

"She hasn't left the country. She's living at Castell Blanc."

"Oscar Mayoral's old place? Why is she there?"

"She's working on books in the library. And living there."

"How does she even know Mayoral?"

Lilli shrugged.

At least the landowner was in his seventies. And married, with several children and grandchildren, so there was no immediate risk of losing Stella to him. "Doesn't he live abroad?"

"Yes."

He frowned. "So she's there alone?"

"There's a housekeeper, a handyman and a gardener."

He inhaled and tried to wrap his mind around Stella living anywhere other than right here in the palace. It felt wrong. "I must bring her back home."

"She no longer wishes to live here as your...lover." His elderly "aunt" narrowed her eyes slightly as she said the last word.

"She told you that?"

"In so many words. She knows you won't marry her and she's too principled a lady to live here in sin with you, especially with her son to consider."

Vasco snorted. "Live in sin? Not everyone has the same outdated moral code as my aunts."

Lilli lifted her pointed chin and crossed her arms. "No. They don't." Her gaze accused him. She clearly felt that he was at fault. "She wants to marry you."

"She told the press she'd never marry me."

His "aunt" clucked. "Nonsense. She told Mimi she knew *you'd* never marry her. That may not be how she phrased it but we all know it's the truth." She walked up to him and adjusted his collar, which made him feel like a naughty schoolboy again. "And she won't live here anymore unless you marry her."

Something deep in Vasco's gut recoiled from the implied ultimatum. "Marriage is not for me."

Lilli shook her head and clucked her tongue in that infuriating way of hers. "Then apparently Stella is not for you, either. Or Nicky."

Panic flashed through him for a second, then he calmed. "She agreed to let me become Nicky's legal parent. He'll officially be next in line to the throne."

His aunt snorted. "After you're dead? How consoling. Don't you want to enjoy him in your life right now?"

"Of course I do." Why did Stella have to mess things up when they were going so well? "Are you trying to say that Stella won't let me see Nicky unless I marry her?"

"Stella brings Nicky here in the mornings during the week to spend the day with us. She has no intention of keeping Nicky away. Just herself."

He frowned. "So she'll still be coming to the palace." He'd see her every day. He could tempt her. He'd already proved that.

"I know what you're thinking, young man. If you try to seduce her you'll only drive her further away. Stop thinking like a lover and start thinking like a father."

Vasco wheeled away. That's exactly what he didn't want to do. If he started planning his love life around domestic practicalities, it would end up as loveless and unromantic as his ancestors'. Passion and duty just didn't go together.

"Do you love her?" Lilli's quiet question penetrated

his thoughts and almost made a sweat break out on his brow.

"What kind of question is that to ask a king?"

"Don't make light of it. It's a question you need to ask yourself."

"I don't know what love is. I'm a Montoya man, remember?"

She snorted. "That's the trouble with you. Montoya men keep their brains in their breeches, that's why they've relied on women to keep this good country going all these years."

"I should have you thrown in the dungeons for such a treasonous statement."

She raised a stern penciled brow, but humor twinkled in her eyes. "I can see I'm making you think."

"Nonsense. You're making me annoyed. And hungry. Do they not serve lunch around here anymore?" He needed to end this conversation. "Please ask Joseph to serve it immediately." He turned away and pulled out his phone to signal that the conversation was over.

His aunt Lilli didn't budge. Barely more than five feet tall, she seemed to occupy the entire space of his office with her willful presence. "Bring her back home, Vasco. For all of us."

"Ms. Greco, there's someone very important here to see you." The elderly caretaker wiped her hands anxiously on her flowered housedress. Her wide eyes said it all.

"His majesty." Stella managed not to look up from the large letter *E* she was touching up on a seventeenth-century bible. It was Sunday and she was trying to squeeze some work in during Nicky's afternoon nap.

"Yes. He's at the door right now. Which room should I bring him into?"

Stella swallowed and put down her tiny paintbrush, sure she wouldn't be able to keep her hand steady enough not to destroy the precious book. She would have loved to say, "Send him away!" but that would have scandalized and horrified the housekeeper, and wasn't fair.

"I'll come to the door."

"I can't leave him standing there." Already the old lady was shocked.

"I'll go right now." She closed up her bottle of ink. The most important thing was not to weaken and fall into his arms. Not that he'd want her to. If he thought chatting with a gossip columnist about her lack of marriage prospects was a breach of trust, then moving out had probably set his hair on fire.

She hurried past the flushed housekeeper and headed for the front door. The housekeeper's gnarled husband, who was the live-in handyman, hovered hidden behind an archway.

"The king!" he sputtered, as she went by. Apparently they hadn't been reading the gossip columns or they might have expected his majesty to show up. Castell Blanc was a very quiet place. She'd been here four days—since Vasco left for his trip—and no one had visited at all, not even a Jehovah's Witness. Now suddenly the local monarch was cooling his heels on the doorstep.

She managed to prevent a hysterical giggle from rising to her throat. It was late afternoon and warm amber light brightened the foyer and poured through the half-open door. She could see Vasco silhouetted against it, standing just inside the doorway.

"What does this mean?" His deep voice greeted her before she could even see his face.

"Let's go outside."

"No, I'd like to come in."

"It's not my house so that's not appropriate." Her heart beat like a freight train. She didn't want the elderly couple to hear their conversation. He might be king but that didn't mean he could just march in anywhere like it was his own palace.

She walked past him, avoiding his glance, and out the front door. Unfortunately his spicy masculine scent tickled her nostrils as she passed, and sent darts of misgiving prickling through her.

He followed her down the wide steps. Castell Blanc was a large house, maybe three hundred years old, built of mellow golden stone. It had the air of a summer residence, not well updated or overly maintained, which suited its rustic charm. She hadn't even met the owner. He'd hired her over the phone on the strength of her Pacific College references and her acquaintance with a respected local librarian, who was too discreet to mention her circumstances. What would Senyor Mayoral think if he knew his new book restorer was angering royalty on his front doorstep?

A vast paved courtyard, surrounded by disused stable buildings, sprawled in front of the house.

"You're not going to let me in?" He looked both amused and astonished. Vasco had probably never been denied entry anywhere. She'd even let him into her L.A. house eventually.

"I can't."

"I'm sure Oscar wouldn't mind."

"I came here to get away from you." She felt indignant that he didn't even seem to be listening to her. "I need some space."

"There's plenty of space at the palace. You could have your own wing."

She felt the urge to growl. "And you'd be able to saunter into it whenever you pleased. That's what I'm trying to get away from."

Why did he have to be even more handsome and good-humored than she remembered? He looked striking and quite unroyal in jeans and a dark green shirt. The thin layer of dust suggested he'd arrived on his motorbike, which was just so…Vasco. It was hard to be mad at him in the flesh.

Which, of course, was the whole reason she needed distance between her flesh and his. "I don't want a relationship where I'm at your beck and call but there's no permanent commitment between us. You may find that bizarre, especially since we haven't been together very long, but that's just how I feel. I've been there already with my ex, and it's not for me. I'm sorry, but I can't do it again."

"Your ex and I are totally different people."

"On the surface, this is true. On the other hand, you're both men and neither of you wanted to commit, so maybe you have more in common than you think."

"This is all about marriage, for you?" He frowned.

She inhaled a breath. "That makes it sound like I'm making an ultimatum, but I guess it is about marriage, when you come right down to it. If I choose to be in a relationship, then it's because I am seeking the kind of lifetime partnership that I think all of us deserve.

I'm not a teenager looking to experiment, or a college student interested in playing the field. I'm a mature woman and the mother of a young child. At this point in my life I either want a committed relationship, or I'd rather be single."

She'd made that decision when she told Trevor she wouldn't be available on Friday nights anymore. No more dating "just for fun." Once she realized a relationship wasn't going anywhere, she wanted out. Which was probably why she hadn't taken a chance on one since. Was she a freak because she wanted a committed, loving relationship?

"We can be committed without being married." Vasco's gray gaze implored her. "Marriage doesn't work out well for the Montoyas."

Again desire warred with fierce irritation. Why did his eyes have such an infuriating sparkle to them? "You aren't your ancestors, you're you. We can't just live together in our situation. You're a king. We have a child. No one knows the true details but right now I have 'live-in royal mistress' stamped on my forehead like a supermarket chicken. Nell Gwynn may have been happy with that arrangement, as long as Charles II gave her enough money and houses, but I'm more old-fashioned and can't live like that."

She glanced around, suddenly worried the elderly caretakers might be listening. "I don't want people talking about me. About us."

"But they will anyway, because Nicky is our child."

"They don't know the truth about his conception." An idea made her stand up straight. "Maybe we should tell them? We're not lovers at all, simply strangers brought together by the freezers of a California sperm bank."

Vasco shivered. "No."

"Why not? It's the truth. You made the choice to leave your deposit there. It's not like you didn't know what you were doing."

"I wasn't the king then, and didn't think I ever would be."

"I don't see the difference." She tilted her head. "You made the generous act of donating your DNA—for a small fee—and I made the choice to buy it. Why does it matter if you're the king or just some bored teenager with a grudge against his family."

"Because as king my children inherit the throne of Montmajor."

"As you've pointed out, that can happen anyway. Wave your magic wand and change whatever laws you need to." Speaking to him like this was liberating. Now that they were out of the castle—his domain—she felt freer and able to be irreverent and argumentative in a way that she couldn't while she was his guest.

"If people knew they'd be shocked."

"So shock them." She smiled sweetly. "I never intended to conceal the truth when I made a choice to use a sperm bank. I don't think it's any different than adopting, you're just doing it at an earlier stage of life."

"You're saying I put my sperm up for adoption?" Vasco squinted in the sun.

"Exactly. Nothing embarrassing about it."

He snorted. "I'm ashamed of doing it. I was young and stupid."

"But if you hadn't done it, Nicky wouldn't exist."

"True, and I'll always be grateful for him, but..." He turned and stared into the distance for a moment.

"But you'd rather have people think he was conceived during a moment of breathless passion." She narrowed her eyes.

His dimples reappeared and that infuriating twinkle lit his eyes. "Exactly." He walked toward her, and she crossed her arms and braced herself against the appeal of his outstretched hands.

"How come there isn't a male word for *mistress?* It doesn't seem fair that I get to be the naughty one in everyone's eyes. I could tell the papers you're my royal boy toy."

He laughed. "Go right ahead. Happy to oblige. Now if you'll just invite me inside..." He stepped closer, until his warm, intoxicating scent crept into her nose.

"No, thanks. I have books to restore."

"Including the ones at my library. Surely you haven't abandoned your duties?"

"I'd be happy to continue my work once relations between us are settled." Ack. That sounded like another ultimatum. At least she knew he'd never agree to anything just to get his books restored. He wasn't that much of a bibliophile. Still this whole situation was mortifying.

"My aunts told me you'll bring Nicky to spend the day with them." His gaze softened. He looked almost apprehensive, if such a thing was possible.

"I will. I have. I don't want to take Nicky away from you. That's why I'm still in Montmajor. I can see that this is his home and he loves it here."

"And you?" Again, his eyes shone with something different from their usual mischievous sparkle.

"I love it here, too." Her heart ached.

I love you, too. But he knew that already. It didn't matter. He knew she'd drop everything and rush back to the palace to marry him if he offered. But he didn't want that.

"So you're staying." He shifted his weight, arms hanging by his sides, but with tension in them as if he wanted to reach out and hold her there.

"I'm staying, but on my own terms. If I'm going to live here I'll have to build a life that suits me. I've been a guest in your house for long enough. Lovely as it is, it's not my home."

"Nor is Castell Blanc." He gestured at the big house behind her.

"No, but it's a good place to stay while I figure out my long-term plan. I need to settle in and assess my employment prospects and what kind of house I can afford."

Vasco laughed. "You have the coffers of Montmajor at your disposal and you're worried about finding a job?"

She wrapped her arms around herself. "My independence is important to me. I don't want to be a kept woman."

He frowned. It was clear he had trouble understanding her point of view at all, which was exactly why she needed to keep distance between them. She suspected that under his thoughtful exterior he was just waiting for another opportunity to seduce her back to his lotus-eating isle of pleasure where she didn't care about the future but only the blissful present.

Which would undoubtedly happen if she let him get too close.

"Stella." He said her name softly. His gaze rested on hers for a long moment that made her breathing shallow. She had the feeling he was about to say something powerful and important. Maybe he would ask her to marry him? Her heart quickened and she felt blood rise to her face.

How quickly that would solve everything. She could accept his offer and return right home with him. Oscar Mayoral wouldn't mind very much if his books didn't get restored, at least not right away. They'd been in the same condition for at least two hundred years, so what was another year or two?

Vasco still hadn't said anything. Emotion passed over his face, deepening a tiny groove between his brows. His mouth twitched slightly, which reminded her of how it felt pressed to hers. Her palms heated, itching to reach out and hold him.

"Come home with me now." He stepped toward her until she could almost feel his body heat through her clothes. How easy it would have been to say yes.

But she stepped back. "Have you not been listening to me at all?" Tears hovered at the edges of her voice. "Next you'll come out and issue a law that I have to come live with you at the palace. You can't have things all your own way. I've been very obliging so far, in moving across the world with my son—who is probably standing in his crib wondering where I am right now— and settling into a brand-new country and culture. But I have my limits. You can't just seduce me into fitting into your life on your terms twenty-four hours a day. I'm staying here and that's final."

Why did he not look more shocked? He seemed almost amused, as if he was contemplating her idea of enacting a law to keep her at his side. Anger fired her mind and body. "If you try any sneaky moves I'll tell the press how Nicky was conceived."

She watched his Adam's apple move as he swallowed. "I'll respect your wishes." *For now.* The unspoken words hung between them. Vasco was not used to having his plans thwarted. She had a feeling he'd be back with some new scheme to wrap her up in his palace cocoon and keep her and Nicky there on his terms.

She'd have to be strong.

Which was so hard when she wanted nothing more than to run into Vasco's warm embrace.

"Please leave. I need to check on Nicky and you can't come in. I'll bring him to the palace on Monday as usual." She turned away, feeling rude and cruel even though she knew he deserved it.

She half expected to hear his footsteps behind her on the courtyard, but he didn't move. Suddenly chilly, she ran up the steps and in through the door. She didn't stop running until she got to Nicky's bright bedroom on the second floor, to see him still peacefully asleep in the antique crib.

"Oh, Nicky." Unable to resist, she picked him up and squeezed him. He snuffled and rubbed his eyes, not quite ready to wake up. "You're the only man in my life who matters." She held him close, his big head heavy on her shoulder, and his warm, sweet-smelling body filling her arms and soothing the tension in her limbs.

He was the reason she couldn't stay at the palace as Vasco's concubine. He was too young to understand now, but in only two or three years he'd know about moms and dads and marriages. She was well prepared to be a single mom. That she'd planned for and eagerly anticipated. But when her son asked why she and Daddy weren't married, she wanted to be able to answer truthfully, and say it simply wasn't meant to be, rather than still be sleeping in Vasco's bed and hoping and praying that one day he'd finally ask her to be his bride.

She was cured of that kind of false hope. If a man wanted to marry a woman he came out and asked her. If he didn't…well, then the woman moved on, no matter how hard it was to make that break.

Eleven

"So you admit I was right." Still astride his Yamaha, Tomy pulled off his helmet.

"About what?" Vasco removed his own helmet. Hot and sweaty, he didn't feel any more relaxed after burning fuel up and down the Pyrenees all day.

"That your lady would want a ring on her finger."

"You're supposed to be taking my mind off the situation." He shot his friend a scowl. The sun was high in the sky, scouring both them and the mountaintops with harsh light. Tomy's blond hair stuck up in spikes.

"How does that help? The situation is still there when you go home."

"I wish it was. I told you Stella moved out." Just saying it out loud made him feel hollow inside. The palace seemed like the loneliest place on earth since she'd been gone.

"Are you just going to give up on her?"

Every nerve in Vasco's body recoiled with a snap. "No way!"

Tomy laughed. "You are in love."

"I have no idea what love is." It couldn't be this painful ache that haunted him every time he thought of Stella.

"Sure you do. It's like the feeling you have for your Kawasaki." He gestured at Vasco's dark blue bike, which was covered in a thick layer of dust.

"I have three of these. And two Hondas and a Suzuki."

"Okay, then the feeling you have for Montmajor."

"That's pride, and passion. And a whole bunch of stuff that's probably twisted into my DNA. Not love."

"Hmm." Tomy's mouth twisted with amusement. "Methinks he doth protest too much."

"Lust, I know all about. That's a powerful emotion." It stirred inside him right now, as he let Stella's face drift into his imagination. He wanted nothing more than to hold her in his arms, kiss her...

"Lust is a sensation, not an emotion, so if you're feeling it in your heart, it's probably love."

His heart just plain hurt. And talking about it made it worse. Usually he could count on Tomy to distract him from serious matters. "Are we really having this conversation?" He wiped a grimy sleeve across his face to mop up the sweat. "Because if we are I think some alien has seized my friend's body and is holding him hostage somewhere."

"Entirely possible." Tomy glanced down at his big hand, sprinkled with pale hairs. "I hope the alien chicks are having fun with me."

Vasco snorted. "See? What do you know about love? You're with a different girl every time I see you."

"And I love each and every one of them." Tomy smiled and stared at the horizon. "Especially Felicia. I'm seeing her tonight."

"You're a bad influence."

"I know. You shouldn't associate with me." Tomy drew a heart in the dust on his engine casing. "Something's different since you met Stella."

"Since I learned about Nicky, you mean." Was that when everything changed? His life hadn't been the same since he laid eyes on his son.

"That too. Stella and Nicky come as a package, but I can tell it's not just the kid you're crazy about."

Vasco inhaled a long, deep draught of mountain air. Shame the air was hot, and somewhat smoky from a nearby fire. "Stella's an amazing woman. She's bright and funny and gorgeous. I love that she restores books and that she was prepared to do anything to fulfill her dream of having a child."

"So marry her."

"Marriage is the death of fun. Suddenly we'll be bickering about palace protocol or what to have for dinner and everything will seem like a chore."

"Says who? I can't see you arguing with anyone about palace protocol."

"This is an observation. Not just of my parents but other married couples both of their generation and ours. Once you marry, the relationship becomes a job."

"They're not you, Vasco. Even your job is play. Look at you, for crying out loud." He gestured at Vasco seated on his bike high on a sunny hilltop. "You're not only king of a small nation but you have a large stone mining company with offices on several continents. You manage to turn any work into play."

"Or maybe I've figured out how to keep work where it belongs and play where it belongs." That's what he'd always told himself. Why didn't it seem a satisfying answer anymore?

"Is that why you don't ever have women in your bedroom?"

"I told you that?"

Tomy nodded. "You want to be able to skip off at a moment's notice."

"Exactly. See? Stella is better off without me." Why hadn't he invited her into his own room when he had the chance? Now his attempt to keep his life ordered and compartmentalized seemed petty and foolish.

"You might find you like waking up with her."

Vasco shoved a hand through his damp hair. It certainly was hell spending all night alone and waking up without her. "I might." Right now nothing seemed more appealing than the prospect of waking to Stella's sweet face.

"So marry her."

"But I know marriage will ruin everything."

Tomy laughed, then shook his head. "Vasco, my friend, you've already ruined everything. She's moved out and taken your son with her. How much worse can it get?"

"Good point."

"Besides, you're a king. If it doesn't work out you can always lock her up in a tower and have some fresh maidens delivered." Tomy's eyes twinkled.

Vasco's muscles tightened. This was no laughing matter. "If I wasn't sitting on a bike I'd…"

"What?" Tomy climbed back astride his own bike. "How about you race me down to the river instead."

Adrenaline surged through his veins. "You're on."

Vasco had paced the halls all night trying to decide if he should marry Stella. Whenever he decided "yes," it felt strange and frightening—not feelings he had much acquaintance with.

Whenever he decided "no," it felt wrong. The prospect of spending the next few decades without Stella in his bed, or at his dining room table, or by his side made his soul rattle.

Which meant he should do it.

But would she even say yes? He was pretty sure she had wanted to marry him. She'd even said as much. She was attracted to him, she seemed to like him a lot, and he was Nicky's father.

On the other hand, he'd done enough wrong to drive her out of the palace and he'd come right out and said that he didn't believe in marriage. Not very confidence-inspiring words for a potential fiancé.

The prospect of her rejection made him realize how much he desperately wanted her to say yes. Just think, she could be back in the palace by tomorrow night, with his ring on her finger and a smile on her lovely face as she climbed into his bed.

In his bedroom.

He marched through the palace, heels thundering over the stone. Dawn was just beginning to throw daggers of light onto the vast array of weapons in the armaments hall when he came up with his plan. He paused in front of the ornate armor that had recently encased Stella's lovely body. Stella loved pageantry, all the old medieval stories of knights and maidens. He'd get dressed up as a knight and ride over to Castell Blanc, where he'd serenade her and ask for her hand.

How could she resist that?

There was no sign of Vasco that morning when Stella dropped Nicky off at the palace. Her son looked so happy to be back in the loving arms of his aunts, who had planned a picnic for him and a playdate with two children from the village. Still, she felt a little empty leaving the palace without even seeing him.

He must be angry that she wouldn't come back and slot into the routine he'd planned, especially after her threat that she'd reveal the truth about how Nicky was conceived.

It was the truth, after all.

She left the palace feeling a little downcast, but determined to throw herself into her work and enjoy the sunny day. The car she drove belonged to Castell Blanc, and the owner had agreed to let her share it with the caretakers. It had turned out that neither of them could or would drive—they cycled into town for what minor supplies were needed—so it was hers alone. Everything was working out almost too well to be believed. She had a lovely, if temporary, home for her and Nicky, a job doing what she loved, and she could bring Nicky to see Vasco and his other relatives every day.

Yes, she felt a little empty inside, but that was just the wrench of leaving the only romantic relationship she'd ever really enjoyed, and because she didn't have any other friends here. She'd been so wrapped up in Vasco she hadn't bothered to make any. Now that she'd found her backbone and taken her life back, she resolved to join an evening class at the local school—there was one about Catalan poetry, and a series on sushi preparation—and get more settled into the local community. Sure, they might look at her strangely at first, but as long as she didn't confirm or deny anything they'd soon realize she was a person, not a tabloid headline.

She bought a baguette in the bakery and some of the local cheese, along with some olives and salami, and made herself a pleasant brunch on the terrace outside Castell Blanc. After a cup of coffee she settled into the enjoyable work of restitching the worn binding of an eighteenth-century book about the Roman conquest of Europe.

It had not been easy for Vasco to squeeze himself into the largest suit of armor in the palace. People were a lot smaller back then. There was no way the leg pieces would fit, but he managed to buckle the breast piece and arms on loosely and jam his feet into the crazy metal shoes. The big problems started when the horse saw him.

"Tinto, it's just me." He clanked over the cobbles toward the terrified beast. "Your ancestors would think nothing of this getup."

The pretty gray mare snorted and jerked her head up, eyes staring. The groom held tight to her bridle, but couldn't keep her feet still. Vasco propped up the visor, and looked at her. "I need you to work with me, Tinto. I have a maiden to woo."

The groom tried to disguise a grin.

"Once I get on her she'll be fine." He tried to reassure himself as much as the horse and her handler. Tinto herself was wearing fancy ceremonial tack, including an embroidered saddlecloth and tasseled reins. They'd make quite the romantic picture together—if he could just mount up.

He clanked a few steps closer, but the horse only skittered farther away across the stone courtyard. The groom tried to reason with her but she looked like she was about to turn and bolt for her field. Riding her would be interesting, under the circumstances. Still, he knew Stella would love it, and surely the armor functioned much like safety gear, right?

"Lead her to me while I stand still. Maybe that will work." He smiled reassuringly at the mare, who responded by snorting and pawing at the ground. Jaume, the groom, tried to lead her closer, but she planted her feet and peered suspiciously at him down the length of her proud nose. "Maybe give me some treats. Some of those mints she likes."

Jaume called out to Luis, who came running over with a fistful of candies and placed them awkwardly in Vasco's armored hand. Lucky the metal cased gloves were leather underneath and surprisingly flexible. He managed to get the wrapper off and place one on his other palm, then reach out his hand. "Here, Tinto. It's your favorite."

Tinto looked interested, but wary. She tossed her head and sent her white mane flying. After about a minute she took a hesitant step toward him, then another, and took the treat. "See, I knew you'd figure out it's me. You're part of a very important plan." He spoke softly to the mare. "Now we just have to figure out how to get me up on your back." He looked from his metal clad foot to the wide, ceremonial stirrup. This armor must weigh a good seventy-five pounds. It wouldn't be easy to get airborne. "Luis, could you give me a hand?"

Luis, who was neither young nor tall, shuffled over and wove his fingers together into a kind of human stirrup. Vasco knew he'd probably cripple the man if he stepped on his hand. "How about Luis holds Tinto and Jaume gives me a leg up." Jaume was young and strapping. A relieved Luis took hold of the reins and Jaume strode boldly over, in turn looking relieved not to be holding one thousand pounds of potentially explosive horse.

"One, two..." Tinto neatly sidestepped out of the way before Jaume could give him a leg up. "Oh, come on. No more mints until I'm up." He frowned meaningfully at the horse. "It's barely a fifteen-minute ride. You'll be home eating hay before you know it."

Luis maneuvered Tinto back into position. Lightning-fast, Jaume helped heave Vasco up into the saddle and he slung his leg over and came down as lightly as possible on Tinto's back. Tinto immediately wrenched free of Luis's grasp and took off bucking across the courtyard. "Easy!" Vasco grabbed the reins and tried to bend her neck to get control. He clanked and rattled like a bag of bolts as she skated over the cobblestones. "All right, we're off." He had the ring in his pocket. As long as that didn't fall out he was good.

He managed to steer her toward the gate that led from the stable yard out to the fields beyond, and all went surprisingly well until they got through the gate. Once they were outside the palace, Tinto threw in one more almighty buck, which pitched Vasco over her head. He landed on the ground with a loud series of clanks— and some very nasty sensations in his muscles—and managed to get his visor up in time to see her galloping off over the crest of the nearest hill.

He cursed. Luis and Jaume came running and helped him to his feet. The breast plate was dented and he felt pretty dinged, as well.

"You okay?"

"Still alive in here, I think. We need to catch her before she trips on the reins." He peeled off the armor and they spend most of the next hour following Tinto's trail until they caught up with her grazing quietly under an oak in a disused sheep pen. She had a small cut to one of her legs, so they led her back quietly and bandaged her up.

"Guess I'd better ride one of my other faithful steeds." He had enough bruises for one day. He changed into different clothes, this time a Chevalier costume he wore for parties sometimes. With the ring safely in the new pocket, he went and mounted his trusty Kawasaki. Not quite as romantic as a horse, but much more predictable. Within minutes he rode up to the entrance of Castell Blanc, propped his bike, and launched into song.

The roar of an engine made Stella look up from her sewing. It sounded like a motorcycle engine. Her heart started to rev and she put down her needle and moved to the window. The first strains of a male voice— singing—stopped her in her tracks.

Powerful and haunting, the raw music stole in through the open window and rooted her to the spot. Was it Vasco?

She stepped forward and peered gingerly outside. Her eyes widened as she looked down on Vasco dressed in embroidered silk breeches like a character from a

Cervantes story. Windswept and rugged as usual, and with his dark motorcycle only a few feet away, he looked impossibly masculine in the ornate costume.

But his voice… Deep and rich, it wrapped around the unfamiliar Catalan words and filled the air. Sound reverberated off the stone facade of the house and bounced back to the surrounding hills, growing and swelling around them.

"Oh, Vasco." She said it quietly, to herself. Just when she thought he couldn't be any more outrageous or adorable, he pulled some new stunt like this. Her heart squeezed and she wanted nothing more than to run into his arms.

Resisting that impulse, she had a sudden urge to show Nicky the fantastical vision of his father singing like an ancient troubador, then she remembered he was still at the palace with his aunts. Vasco was singing for her alone.

As she listened, she could make out a few of the words. Impassioned and heartfelt, the song seemed to tell of a heartbroken man who'd lost his true love and would never see her again. Tears almost rose in her eyes, not because of the lyrics, but because of the raw emotion in Vasco's melodious voice. Could he do everything? It didn't seem fair. How was anyone supposed to stand a chance around him?

He'd spotted her at the window, and even from the second floor she could see his eyes light up as he launched into another verse. Her own heart beat faster and excitement swelled in her chest. She soon found herself leaning out the casement window to fully enjoy the rapturous sound. Even a cappella, Vasco gave off more energy and intent than an entire orchestra of professional musicians.

And he was doing it all for her.

As a way to get into a woman's underwear, she had to recommend it. Right now she had chills and hot flashes going on at the same time. Still, she had to remain strong. This was about the rest of her life here, not some steamy afternoon scandalizing the housekeeper and her husband while their boss was away.

Tempting as that seemed.

Vasco reached the end of the song and made a dramatic bow and flourish. Stella clapped and couldn't help smiling. "Beautiful," she murmured, not even loud enough for him to hear.

"Would you do me the honor of coming to the door?" His courtly attitude amused and pleased her. Normally he'd just storm through the door without asking.

She nodded, and hurried away, pulse pounding. She dashed down the steps, telling herself over and over again to be strong. *Don't fall into his arms. Just say hello and tell him he's a good singer.*

"Hi," was the best she could manage, with a goofy grin, when she pulled open the front door to greet her dashing cavalier.

Vasco immediately got down on one knee and bowed his head. Stella froze. He reached into his pocket and fumbled for a moment, then pulled out a ring.

She almost fell down the steps. Surely he wasn't…?

He raised his head, and his gray eyes met hers with intensity that felt like a punch to the stomach. "Stella, I love you. I've thought about nothing but you since the moment I heard you were gone. I'm miserable without you and I know with agonizing certainty that I want to spend the rest of my life with you. Will you marry me?"

She stood rooted to the spot. Was she dreaming? She wanted to pinch herself but couldn't seem to move.

Vasco's gaze searched hers. She could swear she even saw a trace of anxiety cross his handsome face. He held out the ring a little farther. "Please Stella, be my wife."

"Yes." The word fled her lips without any permission from her brain. Why had she said that? His sudden change of heart was shocking and not entirely convincing. Still…

Vasco rose and slid the ring on her finger. The metal felt cool and sensual on her skin. He kissed her hand with deliberate passion, eyes closed. Then, face taut with emotion, he took her in his arms and pressed his lips to hers.

Her body went limp under the force of his kiss. If he weren't holding her close she'd have fallen to the ground. The whole situation was too amazing to be real.

When they finally pulled apart she looked down at his elaborate and historically accurate costume. Her doubts crowded back over her. "Is this a scene from a play that you're acting?"

"No, the words and emotions are entirely my own."

She frowned. "But yesterday you said…"

"Yesterday was an age ago. I had all night to contemplate the prospect of living without you and to realize how miserable I'd be if I lost you." His eyes shone with conviction that echoed deep inside her. "I've behaved like a spoiled child who wants to have everything his way, and ignore the feelings of others. Nicky needs a father who's a family man." He lifted his chin proudly.

Stella hesitated for a moment. "You're marrying me so that Nicky can have a proper family." An official marriage, without emotion. Something that looked good on paper, like all the Montmajor marriages before it. Her stomach tightened.

He took her hand, the one with the ring. "I said I love you and I mean it. You should know me well enough to understand that I'd never marry simply out of duty. I made it clear from the beginning that was out of the question." He paused and looked down for a moment, before his eyes fixed on hers with a penetrating stare. "It took some soul-searching to realize that what I feel for you has nothing to do with duty, or responsibilities, or anything else other than the joy I feel when I'm with you."

A strange warm sensation rose inside her. "I love you, too." It was a sweet release to let the truth out. "I think I've loved you almost from the start, when you showed up on my doorstep demanding a place in your son's life and unwilling to take no for an answer."

"Guess I'm lucky you didn't boot me out on my ear." He grinned.

"Well, I did try, but you're not easy to get rid of." She smiled, too. "And I'm glad of that, now." She glanced down at the ring. It was unusual, with an ornate tooled gold setting, and the stone was a bright blue sapphire rather than the more conventional diamond. "Is this an old ring from your family?"

Vasco faked a shudder. "No way. I don't want us following down their dreary path in marriage. I had it flown in from Barcelona overnight. Given your love of history I thought you might like something dramatic and historical looking, rather than an ordinary diamond solitaire like everyone else."

"You're so right. I adore it." The clear blue stone reflected the bright sky above.

"The stone was mined by my company in Madagascar, and I had it tooled by my favorite jeweler. I bet if you look closely enough you can see the whole universe in there."

She lifted the ring. It sparkled with astonishing brilliance and drew her eye to its depths. "I've never seen anything like it. I keep forgetting that you have a whole company out there in addition to being king."

"Comes in useful at times like this."

"And you're the type of person who needs to keep busy."

"Like yourself. I don't see you wanting to sit around all day staring out the window. Still, I do think you should be restoring the royal collection rather than a few tatty old novels here at Castell Blanc." His dimples showed as he made a dismissive gesture at the house behind her.

"Mr. Mayoral has a wonderful collection. Not as large as yours, of course, but every bit as distinguished in its own way." She smiled. "Still, I admit that I miss the lovely palace library. There isn't enough room for me to set up my tools in the library here so I have to bring the books into a spare bedroom."

Vasco looked pleased. "Perhaps you can bring his books to the palace to work on, if you still want to restore them."

"Maybe I will." Her muscles tingled with excitement at the thought of moving back to the beautiful palace with Nicky. It must be almost time to go pick him up.

Except that she didn't have to pick him up. The thought struck her hard and she glanced at her ring just to check again that she wasn't dreaming. "Are we really getting married?"

"You still don't believe me?" He stroked her chin, humor in his eyes.

"I want to, it's just a bit much for me."

"We're one hundred percent absolutely definitely getting married. As soon as possible. Today would be fine, in fact."

"Today?" She glanced down at her jeans and plain blue shirt.

"Or tomorrow. Or the next day. Or next month. I'll leave it entirely up to you. It depends on what kind of wedding you'd like to have. I vote for big and fancy with everyone we've ever met in attendance." His teeth gleamed as he smiled. "Just so they know we really mean it."

She laughed. "You know, you might have a point there. A big, fancy, over-the-top royal wedding with all the trimmings would give the paparazzi what they're looking for, and then maybe they'll leave us in peace."

"Never happen." He grinned.

"Oh, well. Maybe we should seize some peace right now." She glanced back at the house. A week and a half of abstinence from Vasco's lovemaking was catching up with her. His intoxicating male presence, especially in the dashing musketeer outfit, made her want to rip his clothes off right there. "Would you care to come inside?"

Her courtly invitation made him laugh. "I certainly would. I'm so glad I'm now permitted entry."

"We'd better not tell Mr. Mayoral about what we're about to do."

He raised a brow. "My lips are sealed. And I can't wait to find out what we are about to do."

Twelve

The carriage wheels rattled over the ancient cobbled streets as crowds cheered the wedding procession. Stella didn't need to worry about smiling for all the people watching. She'd had a grin plastered to her face all morning.

"I'm amazed the horses aren't spooked by all the helicopters." A fleet of them had hovered overhead since dawn, filming the wedding party as they emerged from the cathedral, and the long, colorful procession as it wound through the streets of Montmajor.

"They're used to them." Vasco beamed, as well. "Much less scary than a man in a suit of armor."

"Suits of armor seem to be a theme in our relationship." She murmured the words in his ear.

"So true. We'll have to get the horses acclimatized to them so we can try jousting." His arm rested around her waist and he pulled her closer. Arousal sizzled through her. How long would it be until they were alone again? The aunts had hovered over them all morning, and hairdressers and dressmakers had fussed and prodded and poked her until she was ready to scream. Now it was torture being right next to Vasco—in full view of the entire world.

Nicky sat opposite them in the carriage, with aunt Lilli holding tightly to the sash of his waistcoat to prevent him from jumping out into the throng. He even waved along with the grownups, and people called out "*Hola,* Nicky!" as he passed, much to his delight.

At last the carriage pulled up at the palace, where preparations were underway for the biggest party in Europe. Friends and family and thousands of diplomats and dignitaries had flown in from all over the world. Every room in the palace had been pressed into service as accommodation, and guests were billeted throughout the town.

A red carpet of rose petals covered the ground between where the carriage stopped and their entrance to the palace, and their sweet scent filled the air. A hundred white doves flapped and pecked around the petals and gravel and glided silently overhead. "Why don't they just fly away?" Stella whispered, as she alighted from the carriage and looked around her in awe.

"They prefer caviar on toast to grubbing for insects." Vasco grinned and waved to the assembled palace staff, who launched into some ancient Montmajorian greeting, half spoken, half sung. Vasco led her into the castle. Her lush ivory dress had a train nearly fifty feet long, and the six little train-bearers—boys of only seven or eight—rushed forward to gather and lift it behind her.

"I really do feel like a queen in this getup." She smiled at their serious expressions.

"You look like one." Vasco kissed her hand. "A coronet suits you." The tiny crown, tipped with rubies, was pinned to her elaborate hairstyle. If anyone had ever told her she'd wear an outfit this outrageous to any occasion, she'd have laughed, but the palace staff and wedding planners had snuck each detail in gradually until it was far too late to protest. Vasco simply laughed and said that if people enjoyed a bit of pomp and ceremony, why not give it to them?

Vasco himself was in a rather dashing getup that made him look like a nineteenth-century cavalryman. It even had tall shiny boots and acres of gold braid. His hair, of course, still looked windblown and wild, which only made him even more gorgeous. She could imagine women all over the world sighing and smiling as they looked at the pictures, and wishing they were her.

And who wouldn't?

Vasco lifted Nicky into his arms, and she squinted against the glare of flashbulbs. There seemed to be an insatiable appetite for pictures of Europe's most eligible bachelor as a family man. She hadn't told anyone that Nicky was conceived in a lab. It didn't seem relevant now they'd long since made up for the lack of sex during his conception.

Her skin tingled as Vasco took her hand and led her into the grand ballroom. A large glass fountain in the middle of the room bubbled with champagne. A waiter scooped two slender glasses of it for her and Vasco, and they turned to face the crowds—and yet more media—to raise a toast to their marriage.

"I'm the luckiest man in the world." Vasco lifted

his glass. "I live in the best country, I'm married to the kindest, loveliest woman and I have a wonderful son. Who could ask for more?"

Stella wanted to laugh. Even if they did ask for more, Vasco had that, too, starting with the fountain of champagne. The crowd cheered and the guests flocked around them with congratulations. Champagne poured late into the night and the guests enjoyed a feast of Montmajor specialties and hours of rousing traditional dances. By the time the guests finally trickled away to their beds, Stella was exhausted.

"I think you might have to carry me upstairs."

Vasco seemed tireless, as usual. "I'd be delighted."

"I may even have to actually sleep tonight." She raised a brow.

"Sleep?" Vasco whisked her off her feet. The train had been removed from her dress shortly after the toast, but she still wore about an acre of frothy taffeta that threatened to swallow him. "Sleep can be such a waste of time."

He lowered his lips to hers, and stirred a sudden rush of energy with his kiss. "Okay, maybe you have a point there," she gasped, when he finally pulled his mouth away. "I feel strangely invigorated." A funny thought occurred to her. "Wouldn't it be something if our second child was conceived on our wedding night?"

Vasco's eyes met hers, wide with surprise. "A second child?"

"Why not? Nicky would enjoy having a playmate." A tiny flame of fear licked inside her. Did he not want more children? They hadn't discussed it at all, and of course Vasco had never intended to have Nicky. Still, he seemed to enjoy fatherhood.

His expression turned thoughtful. Still holding her in his arms he strode for the stairs. He carried her into his old bedroom, which now truly was their room, and closed the door. They'd slept here since the night he proposed and brought her back to the castle. Her clothes had been moved into the large wardrobes that day, Nicky's things and child-safe bed were moved into one of the adjoining chambers, and there was no more talk of trysts in the round tower.

He laid her gently on the grand four-poster bed and tugged at the fastenings on her elegant dress. "You're so right. Tonight would be the perfect time to make Nicky's little brother or sister." A warm twinkle in his eyes warred with his serious expression. She wriggled slightly as he eased the bodice of her dress down past her waist.

She tugged at his cravat, then realized she needed to take out the gold pin that held it in place. It was hard removing all this crisp formal clothing when you were addled by lust and exhaustion. Probably in the old days they had servants standing around the bed to help.

"What are you laughing at?" Vasco's eyes crinkled into a smile.

"Just wondering if we'll get all these clothes off before dawn."

He pretended to tear at her fancy bra with his teeth. "We can always resort to scissors."

When she finally got his buttons undone she sighed at the sight of his hard, bronzed torso. Vasco really was hers, to have and to hold. Since she'd come back to the palace with the ring on her finger, their lovemaking had a whole new dimension. Gone were the nagging worries that she was making a huge mistake sleeping with her son's father.

And now they truly were married. She pressed her cheek to his chest, enjoying the strong beat of his heart. For a long time she thought she'd never know the joy of joining her life with another person. She'd achieved it in part when she had Nicky, but marrying Vasco made her life complete. They were a real family now, an inseparable unit. For the first time she could remember, she felt safe and protected, able to relax and enjoy the present without harboring doubts and fears about an uncertain future.

She gasped as Vasco pushed his fingers inside her delicate panties. Hot and wet, she shuddered against his touch. She'd never known her body could enjoy so many different sensations. There seemed to be no limit to the new feelings and emotions that crowded her mind since they became engaged. She could love Vasco, adore and enjoy him, without wondering what tomorrow would bring.

She wriggled under his sensual touch, suddenly aching to feel him inside her, to move with him and lose herself in the fevered intensity of the moment.

She reached for his erection and guided him in, and he let out a shuddering groan as he sank deep inside her. A wave of relief swept over her as it had every time since she'd come back. For those few brief but agonizing days at Castell Blanc she thought she'd never know this sensation again. She knew it would never be the same with anyone else after Vasco. He was a tornado that tore into her life and left it changed forever. Without him the aftermath would have been drab and lonely, but with him...

She arched her back and took him deeper still, then climbed over him and guided him into a fast rhythm. She felt no sense of self-consciousness making love with Vasco, just pure pleasure. He rose and fell with her, holding her close and kissing her face when she leaned forward, then flipping her under him and pinning her to the bed while he tormented her with his tongue and hands.

"Which would you prefer, a boy or a girl?" He whispered, at one intensely pleasurable moment.

Stella hugged him tight. "I don't care at all. I never did."

"I never even knew I wanted children." Vasco kissed her, holding her tight. "I didn't even think I wanted a wife. Thank heaven I found you."

They played in bed for hours, bringing each other to climax, pulling back, then starting over, in a rapturous exploration of their bodies and free-spirited baring of their souls. Somehow knowing that they could do this every night for the rest of their lives didn't diminish their hunger to enjoy each moment.

By the time dawn peeked in around the curtains they lay snoozing in each other's arms. "How long until we know if Nicky will have a new sibling soon?" Vasco's deep voice tickled her ear.

"About a month. It was an agonizing wait to find out if I was pregnant with him the first time. And the conception wasn't nearly as enjoyable."

"I'm not even going to ask how that happened, since I know I wasn't there in person." He stroked her cheek. "I should have been."

"We would never have met if it hadn't been for Westlake Cryobank." Stella grew thoughtful. "Instead of suing them for giving out my information I should send them flowers."

"Thank heavens for corruptible employees." Vasco grinned.

"You did pay someone off, didn't you?" They hadn't talked about it once. Somehow it was off-limits, too sensitive. Now that they were married, however, no topic seemed too touchy.

"Of course. Wouldn't you?"

She laughed. "No, probably not. But then I'm not a European monarch."

"Yes, you are." His steady gray gaze sparkled with humor.

Stella blinked. "You're right. How extremely weird."

"Queen Stella." He kissed her on the mouth. "Of Montmajor."

She shivered slightly. How strange. That's who she really was now. And her son—their son—was Prince Nicholas of Montmajor. It seemed a very dramatic title for a little boy who still loved to mash Cheerios with his fingers. "I suppose I'll get used to it eventually." She ran her fingers into his hair, then along his stubble-roughened cheekbone. "You've been married a whole day, almost. Is it as dreadful as you thought?"

His dimples appeared and he squeezed her with his strong, warm arms. "So far, so good. I think that since we broke with royal tradition by conceiving a child together before we even met, it's safe to say everything else will be different, and wonderful."

"I agree. And we'd better try to get a few minutes of sleep before our son wakes up."

Epilogue

One year and eight months later

"Blow, sweetie, blow!" Aunt Lilli held little Francesca up in front of her cake.

Stella laughed. "She doesn't understand. I bet she can extinguish the candles with her drool, though." She leaned forward to help blow out the single candle flickering amidst the shiny frosted decorations. They all sat around a big wooden table in the palace gardens, afternoon sun warming their glasses of fruit punch and sparkling over the silver cutlery.

Stella and Vasco had been thrilled to find out that they were indeed pregnant within the first month of their marriage. When little Francesca emerged a month before they expected, they realized that in fact she might have been conceived even before the wedding, though no one could be sure as Francesca was quite petite and it wasn't so unusual for a baby to be born a month early. Unlike Nicky she had silky dark hair, but she did have those big, gray eyes that marked her unmistakably as a Montoya.

She waved her chubby arms and her plump fingers danced dangerously near the elaborate icing. "I think she wants a slice." Vasco picked up the knife and handed it to Nicky. Now almost three, he took great pride in being an older brother and helping his baby sister.

"I'll cut her a big one, since it's her birthday." Guided by Vasco, Nicky plunged the knife into the rose-covered frosting with gusto. "And then I'll cut myself an even bigger one, because I'm older." He looked up with a toothy grin.

"What about us? We're even older." Vasco ruffled Nicky's blond hair.

"I think that means you have to save the biggest pieces of all for your aunties." Aunt Mari clapped her hands. "We're so old we don't even remember how many birthdays we've had."

Stella found it hard to remember how she'd coped without a large extended family to help. She still spent time every day working with the books in the library, and she and Mari had started to catalog the books, making several intriguing discoveries along the way. Her duties as queen were pretty light. Being a monarch in Montmajor mostly consisted of holding large parties and inviting everyone for miles around. Nice work if you could get it.

Vasco passed out the slices of cake, then lifted his glass. "A toast to our little princess." Francesca waved her sippy cup around with flair, giggling and slapping her other palm on the table. "Who will never have to leave Montmajor unless she wants to."

His words surprised Stella for a moment, then she remembered the strange ancient law that had driven Vasco from his homeland when he was still a boy.

"It's good to travel and see the world." Aunt Frida waved a forkful of cake in the air. "I spent three years touring Africa when I was in my twenties. And I ran a catering company in Paris for a while, too." The aunts—who did seem to have lived for several centuries—were constantly surprising her with their life stories. "But you always want to come back home to Montmajor."

"There's nowhere as peaceful," agreed Aunt Lilli.

"Or as beautiful," sighed Aunt Mari.

"Or with such good food," exclaimed Nicky, through a mouthful of cake.

"I have to agree." Stella smiled. "Though I think it's the people that make it so special. I don't know of anywhere on earth that's so quick to welcome strangers and make them feel like they've always lived here."

Vasco slid his arm around her waist. "Every now and then we have to venture into the outside world and find some more special people to come live here." He pressed a soft kiss to her cheek—which still tingled with excitement like it was the first time.

She sighed and smiled at her husband, and their growing extended family. "I'm glad you found us."

* * * * *

MILLS & BOON®
By Request

RELIVE THE ROMANCE WITH THE BEST OF THE BEST

A sneak peek at next month's titles...

In stores from 18th December 2015:

- **One Night With Her Ex** – Kelly Hunter, Susan Stephens & Kate Hardy

- **At the Playboy's Command** – Robyn Grady, Brenda Jackson & Kathie DeNosky

In stores from 1st January 2016:

- **Secrets in Sydney** – Fiona Lowe, Melanie Milburne & Emily Forbes

- **A Second Chance for the Millionaire** – Lucy Gordon, Nicola Marsh & Barbara Wallace

---

MILLS & BOON®
The Billionaires Collection!

This fabulous 6 book collection features stories from some of our talented writers. Feel the temperature rise with our ultra-sexy and powerful billionaires. Don't miss this great offer – buy the collection today to get two books free!

2 FREE BOOKS!

Order yours at
**www.millsandboon.co.uk
/billionaires**

1215_MB16

MILLS & BOON®

Why shop at millsandboon.co.uk?

Each year, thousands of romance readers find their perfect read at millsandboon.co.uk. That's because we're passionate about bringing you the very best romantic fiction. Here are some of the advantages of shopping at www.millsandboon.co.uk:

* **Get new books first**—you'll be able to buy your favourite books one month before they hit the shops

* **Get exclusive discounts**—you'll also be able to buy our specially created monthly collections, with up to 50% off the RRP

* **Find your favourite authors**—latest news, interviews and new releases for all your favourite authors and series on our website, plus ideas for what to try next

* **Join in**—once you've bought your favourite books, don't forget to register with us to rate, review and join in the discussions

Visit **www.millsandboon.co.uk**
for all this and more today!